Praise for *A Bitter Remedy*

'A dead student at Oxford University in the 1880s is the starting point for this deftly-drawn historical mystery. This is a book that fearlessly tackles taboo attitudes of the era, taking aim at misogyny, homophobia, and sexual politics. An excellent addition to the historical mystery canon. Marvellous!'

Vaseem Khan, *Sunday Times* bestselling author

'A compelling mystery, and a deep dive into a very real Victorian Britain. Exquisitely written, ultra-dark and very, very clever'

Paul Finch, *Sunday Times* bestselling author

'The most sublime historical crime fiction is that which is able to combine a thoughtful, complex and engrossing murder mystery with a doorway into a time or place that is perhaps largely unknown or unfamiliar to the reader and that opens up whole new worlds of interest. In *A Bitter Remedy*, Alis Hawkins achieves just that, and so much more'

Chris Lloyd, author of *The Unwanted Dead*

'*A Bitter Remedy* is a perfect tonic for our times. Alis Hawkins has given us a host of fresh and engaging characters in a story that zips along like a determined young Welshwoman flying through Victorian Oxford on her tandem'

S.G. MacLean, author of *The Seeker*

'I absolutely loved it. Brilliantly researched, rich in atmosphere and with two likeable and intriguing protagonists at the centre. The start of a series that deserves to run and run'

Philip Gwynne Jones, *Sunday Times* bestselling author

'An evocative sense of time and place, a strong yet flawed protagonist, and a mystifying plotline make *A Bitter Remedy* most palatable indeed'

Douglas Skelton, author of *An Honourable Thief*

'It's dripping with historical detail and I loved Non's passion. The tragic death of Parker was handled sensitively and really drew me in, it's so well written and the dialogue is edgy and pithy. A superb atmospheric mystery to the last page'

Rachel Lynch, author of *Dark Game*

'*A Bitter Remedy* is a beautifully written, atmospheric murder story set in 1881 Oxford. An ingenious, complex plot grips the reader from the outset'

Mark Ellis, author of *Prince's Gate*

'An elixir of intrigue [and] a sparkling historical gem'

Nick Louth, author of *The Body in the Marsh*

'An immersive dose of top-class mystery, *A Bitter Remedy* is a witty and gritty delight that will keep you guessing … Any fan of historical fiction will want to devour this intricately plotted delight that wears its considerable historical pedigree lightly and with humour'

B. E. Jones, author of *Where She Went*

'Both a neatly constructed novel and a hugely impressive piece of historical research. It shines a fascinating light on the experience of both Welsh students and women in late 19th Century Oxford, and students of the period will appreciate the level of historical detail that lurks within its pages'

Martin Davies, author of *Mrs Hudson and the Malabar Rose*

'An absolute delight. Non is a marvellous creation, and her relationship with Basil Rice is beautifully handled. They are a charismatic and unique pair of amateur detectives. The mystery is twisty until the very end, with revelation after revelation. *A Bitter Remedy* deserves to be a great hit'

David Penny, author of *The Red Hill*

A Bitter Remedy

Alis Hawkins writes Victorian crime fiction – but not *that* kind. It's set in west Wales and Oxford rather than London. There are no serial killers because Alis is keen on representing some kind of real life and most murders are committed by ordinary people. And policemen are mostly nowhere to be seen: if they are in evidence, they're usually getting in the way.

Her plots are driven by her characters who take any idea Alis might have about the murder at the beginning of the book, and go off with it in whatever direction appeals to them, leaving her to follow, writing furiously. Her readers, who are gratifyingly fascinated by the little-known aspects of Victorian life that her characters investigate their way through, tell her that's a good thing. Evidently the Crime Writers' Association agrees because two of her four Teifi Valley Coroner novels have been shortlisted for the CWA's prestigious Historical Dagger award.

A former speech and language therapist and current freelance writer and editor, Alis is a founder member of Welsh crime writers' collective, Crime Cymru, chair of Wales's only crime fiction festival, Gŵyl CRIME CYMRU Festival, and a member of the Society of Authors and the Crime Writers' Association. She lives on the Welsh/English border in the Forest of Dean with her partner, and makes regular forays to west Wales and Oxford.

Also by Alis Hawkins

The Teifi Valley Coroner Series

None So Blind
In Two Minds
Those Who Know
Not One Of Us

The Oxford Mysteries

A Bitter Remedy

A BITTER REMEDY

ALIS HAWKINS

CANELOCRIME

First published in the United Kingdom in 2023 by

Canelo
Unit 9, 5th Floor
Cargo Works, 1-2 Hatfields
London SE1 9PG
United Kingdom

A CIP catalogue record for this book is available from the British Library.

Print ISBN 978 1 80032 857 0
Ebook ISBN 978 1 80032 856 3

Image in Chapter 15 from the Internet Archive

Cover design by Sarah Whittaker

Cover images © A South Prospect of the City of Oxford – Veuë de la Ville d'Oxford du Côtè du Midi' by John Boydell. Via The British Library on Flickr

Look for more great books at www.canelo.co

Printed and bound in Great Britain by Clays Ltd, Elcograf S.p.A.

1

For Edwina,

who makes me, me.

Our advice, always, to everyone, is and will be, if you feel sure you can do something well, offer to do it; if you are prevented, no doubt you will feel guidance within as to how to act.

Ein cyngor ni bob amser i bob un, ydyw ac a fydd, os y teimlwch yn sicr y medrwch wneyd rhywbeth yn dda, cynygiwch ei wneyd; os y gwaheddir chwi, ond odid na theimlwch ynoch gyfarwyddyd pa fodd i weithredu.

—Cranogwen (Sarah Jane Rees), *Y Frythones*

Chapter 1

Tuesday 18th January 1881

Non

You can tell a lot from the way an undergraduate walks into a lecture hall. Especially if he's in company.

If he stumbles in, looking over his shoulder, he's probably been pushed in first because he's easy to bully.

The one who's jostling with another student or two is one of the lads, he won't have much to say.

A young man who comes in quietly – not first, not last – watchful, aware: he's one you might think about paying a bit more attention to. One who observes, waits, then acts.

But the one you really need to watch out for – the one who's going to cause you trouble – is the Popinjay. He's the one who struts in, academic gown worn so far back on his shoulders that he's barely wearing it at all, displaying his finery while his followers tag along behind him.

And make no mistake: they are his followers. Where he goes, they trot along beside him; and where their feet lead, their mouths follow. They go along with him in every way.

A Popinjay is trouble; and I watched as one stalked into the Jesus College hall.

His eyes fastened on me. And before Lily, my chaperone, could stop me, I was on my feet, all the speeches I'd listened to about *appropriate conduct* pushed to one side. Because, sometimes, you just have to rise to the challenge.

'Ladies!' our Popinjay squawked. 'I do believe you've wandered into the wrong building.'

I very much wanted to put him in his place – him and his guffawing buffoons – tell him I'd never *wandered* anywhere in my life, thank you very much. But a speech from Miss Shaw LeFevre, the Principal of Somerville Hall, stuck in my mind.

'When you go into the colleges,' she'd told us at the beginning of the academic year, when we were gathered in a little, rented lecture room that resembled this panelled and galleried hall about as much as a coracle resembles a frigate, 'you do not simply represent *yourselves*, you represent *us all*. Every frustrated sister who watches her less intelligent brother go off to university while she is obliged to sit at home. Every nurse who knows she has the capacity to be a doctor. You represent those of us in the AEW who work now, and *have* worked for the last decade, for women to be allowed full access to an Oxford University education. *Do not* make things more difficult for your sisters. *Do not* antagonise the men you will encounter.'

Unfortunately, what Miss Shaw LeFevre's speech hadn't told us was what to do when *they* antagonised *us*.

The Popinjay put one foot on the dais where I stood and leaned forward, hands in his pockets. I expect he thought it made him look commanding. In fact, it made him look like a cocky deckhand with his foot up on the capstan.

'So.' He stared at me. 'Perhaps you'd better scurry off to wherever it is you're expected for tea and gossip.'

I stared right back at him. His over-full lips were pulled back into what passed for a smile but there was nothing friendly in his cold little eyes. I could've just stood there and stared him down. I'd faced off with far more intimidating men than him.

But, at my side, Lily spoke one word. My name.

'Non.'

It was her 'don't you dare' voice.

I opened the notebook on the table in front of me and picked up the note I'd tucked inside.

'*Miss Vaughan*,' I read, then glanced back up to the Popinjay. 'That's me, in case you were wondering. *Many thanks for your note. I can confirm that, in accordance with the agreement between the University and the AEW, you and a chaperone would be most welcome to attend the lectures I give at Jesus College.*

Yours most sincerely,

Basil Rice, Fellow.'

I took my time re-folding the letter and putting it back inside the notebook. It would take the Popinjay's tiny brain a little while to realise that a) he hadn't won and b) he couldn't intimidate me.

'Vaughan,' he said, his eyes narrow. 'Are you related to that Welshie who came top in the local board exam, then never showed his face for the exhibition Merton had offered?'

That Welshie? Had he forgotten which college this lecture was being held in? Jesus College took all its students and at least half of its fellows from Wales, but this self-important squawker still thought he could stand here and talk about *Welshies*!

I leaned towards him, hands flat on the table. 'No. I'm not *related* to that Welshie. I *am* that Welshie. R. A. Vaughan. Rhiannon. Angharad. Vaughan. I beat all the men in the exam, but I didn't *not show my face*, I wasn't *allowed* to take up the place I'd earned.'

He recovered quickly, I'll say that for him. 'So, which of the *houses for ladies* has offered you shelter, then?' he sneered.

Halls, I wanted to correct him. Somerville *Hall* and Lady Margaret *Hall*. Like St Edmund *Hall*.

Except that they weren't, were they? St Edmund Hall's students were members of the University; young women at Somerville and Lady Margaret Hall weren't. Not by a long chalk.

'Neither,' I told him. 'I attend lectures as a resident of Oxford.'

'Oho! One of the *unattached*!' He swung around to his smirking cronies. 'And, no doubt, she'll remain unattached for the rest of her life, eh gentlemen?'

'You can call non-collegiate members of the University "unattached" if you like,' I said, raising my voice over the honking and braying. 'But the title doesn't apply to female students. We're here under the auspices of the Association for Promoting the Education of Women in Oxford.' We might call it the AEW, but I was going to make him swallow the whole title.

He turned back to me as the jeering subsided. 'So, if you're not unattached, what *are* you, pray?'

What he meant was *Why are you here? Why are you spoiling our boys' club?*

I looked him up and down. It was a trick I'd learned on my father's ship: when somebody's trying to put you in your place, take a long hard look at them from crown to sole. Very few men can withstand that without being terrified that you'll see all their inadequacies.

'I'm a student,' I said. 'I'm here to study. Can you say the same?'

He smirked. 'I'm not here to become an academic drudge. I'm here to take my place in society. As a leader. That's what Oxford's for. Which is why it's pointless you being here. You'll never be able to *do* anything.' He curled one of his fat lips. 'Nothing of importance, anyway.'

I could hear the blood rushing in my ears and my hands shook with the need to hit him. *You'll never be able to do anything*. But this buffoon might end up as prime minister, God help us.

I stepped out from behind the table and walked towards him. I couldn't actually punch him, or all hell would break loose, so I asked him a question instead. 'Right then Mr Future Leader of our Country, which of the comedies do you most admire?'

Behind me, I heard Lily take out her knitting and start clicking away. She'd warned me, but if I was going to get into an argument, she was washing her hands of me.

The Popinjay gave me a blank look.

'We're here for a lecture on Greek drama,' I reminded him as if he was slow. 'You have *read* some?'

As a matter of fact, I thought he probably hadn't. You could tell he wasn't any kind of scholar – he'd walked into the hall carrying nothing. Not a bound edition of a play, not a notebook, not so much as a pencil as far as I could see.

'This is an introductory lecture,' he blustered. 'We'll study the texts Mr Rice recommends.'

Pah. Typical trick of his kind. Hide behind a sham deference to authority. If he did get to be prime minister he'd hide behind his party. And *tradition*.

'Personally, I think the most interesting is *Lysistrata*,' I said. 'Perhaps Mr Rice will mention it today.' Actually, I knew he wouldn't dare. Far too dangerous to mention in mixed company. 'It's very amusing. Though perhaps more so for the women in the audience than the men. You know the premise, obviously?'

Of course he didn't. He tried to turn away and say something to his cronies, but he found them all looking at me. *Doing something*, now, wasn't I?

'The city states,' I went on, 'you remember – Athens, Sparta, Corinth? – are at war with each other. It's been going on some time and the Greek women have had enough. It's disrupting their lives. So, they decide to *do something*. To put a stop to all the fighting.' I paused to give him a chance to ask the obvious question, but of course, the Popinjay wouldn't ask me the time of day if his life depended on knowing it. 'They gather together and swear an oath that they'll withhold any kind of physical intimacy from their husbands and lovers until they agree to bring an end to the war.' I was careful to sound about as interested in the women's sex strike as I would've been in Greek verb declensions. 'Of course, the men are furious but it's not long before they come to heel,' I said, lightly. 'The so-called leaders of the country soon realised the women had them beaten.'

The Popinjay finally found his voice. 'That's ridiculous,' he said.

Not that I'd ever have admitted it, but I agreed with him. *Lysistrata* was a comedy, so of course the women got their way in the end, and the men were made to look weak and foolish. But we all knew what would really have happened in those circumstances. Those warriors would have turned to violence to get what they wanted without a second thought.

'Of course it's ridiculous, Mr Peacock,' another voice said. Basil Rice was striding up the hall, his MA gown billowing around him. 'Aristophanes was writing a comedy. A social satire. The juxtaposition of the women's actions and the progress of the Peloponnesian War is meant to illustrate, by analogy, how *irrational* the men's continual warmongering was.'

As he reached the end of the hall where we all stood, I grinned at him. Partly, I must admit, because I found it ridiculously apt that the Popinjay was actually called Peacock, but also because Basil had come in on my side of the argument. The letter I'd read out to Peacock was meant to give the impression that I'd applied to Mr Rice as an unknown academic for permission to attend his lectures, but the truth was, Basil Rice and I had known each other for some time.

Chapter 2

Basil

Her tone told me all I needed to know; as I had feared, Rhiannon Vaughan – Non, as she preferred to be called – had not been able to restrain her robustly confrontational instincts.

Knowing that Non would be at my lecture this morning, I had tried my best to be in hall when the undergraduates started arriving, to avoid any unpleasantness. After breakfasting in North Oxford, I had hurried back to college, but a message waiting for me at the lodge had led to my wasting time in answering an urgent summons from the Principal. Having failed to find Dr Harper in his lodgings, I had decided that, rather than make myself more difficult to locate by presenting a constantly moving target, the best thing I could do was place myself exactly where I was meant to be, so I'd left my own message with the porters and made my way to the hall.

Finding the argument in progress, my best course seemed to be to quell it instantly. I knew Mr Peacock of old – he tended to come to my lectures as they were conveniently close to his own college, Exeter – and I knew he needed a firm hand.

As soon as I'd spoken, however, I realised my error. Commenting implicitly legitimised both the argument and Non's stance; and planting any kind of flag in the small and contested plot of women's place at the University could only aggravate an undergraduate like Peacock. Young men of his ilk saw the University as their exclusive preserve. They didn't wish to share it, even to the very hesitant extent currently on offer.

Silently, I cursed the Principal. Had it not been for the fact that my mind was on Dr Harper and his sudden wish to see me, I might have acted more prudently and simply allowed my presence to silence the debate.

Setting out my books, I watched as the young men arranged themselves as far away as possible from Non and Mrs Lily Maddox. It was a transparent attempt to make me deliver my lecture with my back to the ladies.

Had it been Non and Lily's choice of seating that had sparked Peacock's antagonism? Now that ladies of the AEW had begun to be admitted, on a very limited basis, to college lectures, they were generally invited to sit at high table where they would remain unmolested by hot undergraduate eyes; but finding Non and her chaperone ensconced there might well have lit a fuse in an undergraduate predisposed to take offence at women's presence in the colleges.

Had I not been held up by my search for the Principal, Peacock would have been denied the opportunity to air his prejudices and I wondered, once more, why Dr Harper wished to see me so urgently. The wording of his note had been unusually imperative.

Those young men who had come equipped with notebooks now opened them and looked expectantly at me. To my right, her back to the bay window that overlooked Second Quad, Non's pencil would already be hovering. Sadly, I was unlikely to say anything this morning that would justify her writing it down.

Knowing she would be here, I'd been obliged to modify my introductory thoughts on Aristophanes which I usually illustrated with reference to *The Wasps*, *The Clouds* and *Lysistrata*. Discussing *Lysistrata* with ladies present was out of the question. The Principal had allowed me to admit women to my lectures, but the content of those lectures must, he had impressed upon me, always be *suitable for feminine ears*.

I was, therefore, making some anodyne introductory remarks when the door opened at the other end of the hall and the Principal himself entered.

All the undergraduates stood as Dr Harper strode past them and, out of the corner of my eye, I saw Non make to rise. Swiftly, I indicated that she should remain seated. Current policy dictated that, while on college premises, young women should in no way ape the behaviour of the undergraduates.

The Principal drew me to the end of high table opposite Lily Maddox and Non, where we stood beneath a periwigged eighteenth century head of house. I was acutely aware both that we were within easy eavesdropping distance and that it was not in Non's nature to close her ears to what did not concern her.

'A most unfortunate event has occurred,' Dr Harper said. 'One of the undergraduates has been found dead in his room.'

'Dead?' Harper glared but my exclamation had been quite involuntary. I kept my eyes firmly on the Principal and away from Non as I asked, more moderately, 'How did he die?'

'That is, as yet, unclear.'

Why had the Principal come to me? I had no more responsibility for the undergraduates than any other college fellow. 'Who is it?' I asked.

'Parker.'

I felt a tremor that was part shock, part sadness. Sidney Parker: pinched, not entirely healthy-looking, with a brow too lined for his years. He had been struggling, academically, and, when his performance had been discussed at the fellows' meeting, I had been assigned to give him extra tuition. I found it expedient to nurture the good opinion Dr Harper had of me, and he often exploited that.

'I'd like you to come and see the body with me.'

'*Now?*'

'There is a degree of urgency, here, Rice. The coroner will have to be summoned and we don't want to seem to be dragging our feet.'

I stared at him. Why didn't he just summon the coroner immediately? Why involve me? 'You're surely not saying—'

'No! There's no reason to suspect… anything. But given the circumstances… with his living out and so on…'

In other words, who knew what went on in private lodgings? There might be embarrassments the coroner – and the college – could be spared.

'Very well. Just one moment, if you please.' I stepped down from the dais. 'Ladies and gentlemen. I'm afraid circumstances oblige me to postpone this lecture. We shall reconvene next week at the same time.'

Dr Harper would have quit the hall immediately, but I indicated that we should wait until the undergraduates had left. I did not want to leave the ladies alone with them.

The young men traipsed out, casting curious glances as they went, and I turned to Non and Mrs Maddox, indicating that we would escort them out. However, instead of moving silently ahead of us down the hall, Non stopped in front of the Principal.

'Dr Harper, I couldn't help overhearing the unfortunate news,' she said. 'I believe I may be able to help.'

Harper stared at her. 'Help? I fail to see how, Miss…?'

I stepped forward. 'Miss Vaughan—'

Non ignored me and kept her eyes on the Principal. 'If there's any doubt as to how this poor young man came by his death, I am acquainted with an excellent forensic medical practitioner. He could be here tomorrow if I send a telegram now. But first, I'd need to see the body.'

'Out of the question.'

Before he could say any more, I fixed Non with a glare. 'Miss Vaughan.'

I might as well not have been there. Her attention was pinned to the Principal. 'Dr Reckitt trusts my judgement. And he's accustomed to working closely with the coroner in—'

'He may be accustomed to working with a coroner in the fastnesses of Wales, Miss Vaughan,' Dr Harper's normally pale face had become flushed, 'but this is Oxford. We have our own doctors here. Doctors who are second to none. As are the University coroners.'

I saw Non draw breath. 'Thank you, Miss Vaughan,' I said, oppressively. 'Your offer of help is most kind but, as the Principal says, I believe we are more than adequately provided for.' I willed her to keep silent as Dr Harper gave a nod and turned towards the door.

'Later,' I hissed, when she tried to speak. 'Go home. Now.'

Lily Maddox took Non by the arm and led her firmly down the hall in Harper's wake, leaving me to follow.

In the bright January sunshine outside, I started to escort the two women across the quad, but Lily turned to me. 'We'll be fine, Mr Rice. You get off and do what needs to be done.'

Non looked mutinous but Lily Maddox drew her firmly away. 'We'll be fine,' she repeated, looking back at me. And, though she said nothing more, I knew what her parting look meant. *Come and see her later or you know there'll be trouble.*

Chapter 3

Non

'For somebody who's supposed to be so clever you can be very stupid,' Lily said as she marched me through the Jesus College gates and on to Turl Street. 'Did your fool of a father teach you nothing about men at all?'

I was furious. With the Principal. With Peacock the Popinjay. With every man that made Oxford what it was. But not with my father. Never with him. 'Don't talk about my father like that.'

'He was my cousin. I'll talk about him however I like.' Lily waited for a trolley coming out of Market Street to go over to Brasenose Lane before marching on. 'He was a fool when he was a boy and he never improved if you're anything to go by. He should've got you married off, like a normal person, instead of encouraging you to come here with your foolish ideas.'

Peacock the Popinjay brayed inside my head. *It's pointless you being here. You'll never be able to do anything.*

'Why are you giving me houseroom if you think studying's foolish?'

Two ladies in frills, with bustles so big they looked as if they were sitting on teapots, turned their heads to stare at me as they came out of a haberdashery shop. I didn't care. They could stare all they liked. And I could shout all I liked.

'I never said *studying* was foolish.' Lily was trying to keep her voice down. Why she was bothering was anybody's guess. Even this near Jesus College the likelihood of anybody understanding Welsh was small to none. 'It's your *ideas* that are foolish. Thinking you can be as good as the men. Better than them, even.'

This time it was two young men coming out of a barber's shop in a rush of warm, steamy air who stared at us.

'But I *am* as good as them!' I said, glaring at the two youths until they turned away. 'I'm *better* than most of them.' If Lily didn't understand that after a year of having me as her lodger, there was no hope of me persuading anybody else.

'I'm not saying you're not *cleverer* than them. But you'll never be as *good* as them. Not in the eyes of the world. And if you haven't worked that out yet then you're a fool. This is a man's world, Non. You can't go head-to-head with them like rams in a field.'

I glanced sideways at her. Back as stiff as a poker. Sober dark blue dress just right for a chaperone. Cheeks pink with embarrassment. Mouth in a thin line. And a small, feather-trimmed hat that sat low over her brow as if she was using it to keep a lid on her exasperation. As a rule, Lily – who was actually my father's *second* cousin – was a sunny person. She smiled a lot, sang while she worked and wasn't one to take offence easily. But once her dander was up, it was hard to bring it down again.

'You think, now that you've got the AEW, and the ladies' halls, and permission from a few dons to go to lectures, that it's all going to be easy, don't you? You think it's only a matter of time before they let you in to the University, give you your own colleges, let you wear the cap and gown. But you want to remember, my girl, anything that's given can be taken away. Just like that.' She tried to snap her fingers, but she'd forgotten she was wearing gloves. 'If you go around showing off, they'll take back your permission to go to lectures as quick as look at you.'

I ground my teeth. 'Why is it *showing off* when I use what I know in an argument and *commendable scholarship* when they do?'

She stopped dead, taking no notice of the barrow boy who swore as he swerved around us. 'Stop behaving like a child, Rhiannon. You know perfectly well why. Men don't like to be shown up. They won't stand for it.'

'Basil doesn't mind when I win an argument.'

'And now you're arguing against yourself. Proves you're just in a contrary mood.' She set off again. 'Anyway, Basil's not like the rest of them.'

'And Professor Rhys *wants* me to argue.' The University's Jesus Professor of Celtic appeared in my mind's eye, all impish grin and springy hair. '*Evidence, Non,*' he'd say in our tutorials. '*If you're going to argue that I'm wrong, give me evidence that you're right.*'

Lily made an impatient noise. 'Professor Rhys is one of *us*, isn't he? From Cardiganshire. And his wife's a sensible woman, even if she is from North Wales.'

We were almost at our destination – the shop where Lily's friend, Mrs Long, offered a private ladies' hairdressing room three days a week. 'But there aren't enough men like Basil and Professor Rhys, are there? It's all going to take *time*, Non. And you're not going to make it come any sooner if you behave like that. Offering to drag in that doctor.'

'But if there's any doubt about how this young man died—'

'No!' Lily stopped and grabbed me by the arm. 'Stop this now. It's none of your business. Nor your doctor friend's.'

'Yes, it is.' If I'd been a different sort of woman, I'd have stamped a little foot. As it was, I just glared at her. 'When somebody dies suddenly like that, it's everybody's business. That's why inquests are *public*.'

Lily let go of my arm and looked around to see if anybody was watching. But the street was suddenly quiet. 'Don't be clever with me, my girl,' she hissed. 'You know what I mean. There are plenty of people who'll be looking into this young man's death.'

'But they'll just call the University coroner in, and unless the dead boy's got a bullet hole in his head or a knife sticking out of him, the coroner'll just rule "natural causes" to stop any scandal, won't he?'

Lily took my arm again and propelled me forward. 'You've got no reason to think he died of anything *other* than natural causes.'

Nothing apart from a long acquaintance with Dr Benton Reckitt. Dr Reckitt believed very strongly that unless every single death was investigated by autopsy examination, murders would go undetected and fatal conditions would go undescribed, depriving doctors of the chance to treat them in future. I'd known him since I was a child and he'd given me good reason to agree with him.

'Your mother warned me,' Lily said, marching me on.

I didn't ask what she meant. I knew my mother's list of my failings off by heart and in alphabetical order.

'Your father indulged you too much. Let you go about looking at dead bodies with a doctor who should've known better than to encourage a young woman – a *girl* – to do such a thing. Well, your father's gone now, and I agree with your mother. It's not right. Dr Harper obviously thinks so too. And you know who else would agree with me? Miss Rees. Don't make me write and tell her that you're trying to bring Dr Reckitt here so you can watch him cutting dead bodies open again.'

I wrenched my elbow out of her grasp just as we got to Mrs Long's door. 'You should. Go on, write to her. She'll be on *my* side.'

Miss Sarah Jane Rees, my benefactor, wouldn't agree with Lily and my mother. I was certain of that. But I also knew that her support wouldn't be of much practical use to me. Not here.

When Miss Rees had first offered to find me lodgings in Oxford so that I could attend the AEW's 'lectures for ladies', I'd imagined that her name would open doors for me. I'd been wrong.

Sarah Jane Rees might be famous at home, but Oxford had never heard of her. It wasn't interested in her, and it wasn't interested in me. It especially wasn't interested in my ambitions. Most of the young women who came here to study just wanted a bit more education than they'd had so far, usually so that they could be better teachers. So they were *thrilled* with what was on offer. Not me. I wanted to sit at the table, not take charitable crumbs from the back door.

'Don't expect too much of the other girls,' Miss Rees had written when I'd complained, in my weekly letter, that I hadn't found a single other female student who was interested in real scholarship. 'Most of them will be lucky if they've had *any* decent schooling, never mind the standard you've reached. It's going to take our sisters a while to be ready for the kind of thinking a university encourages.'

The lack of a university education hadn't stopped Miss Rees thinking independently. Or acting independently, either. She'd been a sailor in her youth, and a teacher of navigation. Now, she was a poet, public speaker, writer and editor. And it was her writing that had made her name known throughout Wales. Even though I'd been brought up to call her Miss Rees, respectfully, like all the other children, I always thought of her as Cranogwen, because that was the bardic name she'd used when she'd beaten our country's most famous male poets at the national eisteddfod.

It had been a big disappointment when I'd realised that there wasn't anybody like Cranogwen – or like me – at Oxford. Most of the young women I'd met here were desperate to please and so overwhelmed at the notion of being allowed into lectures, and the Bodleian Library, that they could barely keep their feet on the ground. I'd only found one who didn't set my teeth on edge and make me want to push her into the Cherwell, and that was Annie Rogers. Annie was the nearest we had to a female don, and she was famous for having beaten all the male candidates in the local examinations six years ago. It was her example that'd given me the idea to sit the men's papers and submit them under my initials.

But what was the point of all the exams and lectures if we weren't going to be allowed to *use* what we knew?

It's pointless you being here. You'll never be able to do anything.

I should have listened to Dr Reckitt. He'd been against me coming to Oxford. He'd wanted me to go to London where he had friends and colleagues who could have helped me.

Dr Reckitt was a recognised expert in his field, but the Jesus College Principal had dismissed him just because I'd suggested him. The thought made me rage.

Lily pushed me out of the way, opened the door to number three and bundled me into the passage. She stuck her head through the doorway into the parlour and nodded at Mrs Long, who was busy showing a lady pictures of different hairstyles in one of the illustrated magazines. Mrs Long nodded back, and Lily shut the door again. 'Right then, let's get this contraption out and get home.'

Lily always spoke about my tandem as if it was a huge inconvenience to her. But the walk to her house from Jesus College was almost a quarter of an hour; on the tricycle it took barely five minutes. If she'd been prepared to ride about on her own, like me, she'd have saved herself hours every week. But no. She'd only ride 'the contraption' when I was there to do the steering. To be honest, I don't think she'd really forgiven me for bringing the tricycle home.

Or perhaps she just hadn't forgiven me for the way I'd come by it.

I'd won it in a bet.

Chapter 4

Basil

Halfway through his third term at Jesus, the dead man, Sidney Parker, had asked permission to move out of his college rooms and into lodgings, claiming that, after years of living in boarding institutions he yearned for a semblance of family life. These protestations notwithstanding, it was clear to me that his real need was to remove himself from the orbit of some of the other young men in college. I'd seen Parker being ragged on and knew that he lacked the quickness of wit to defend himself. Though he'd come to Jesus on a scholarship, he'd never seemed at ease in college; undergraduates flexing their muscles in the relative freedom of Oxford could be unforgiving of those who didn't readily rise to the challenge of independence.

Parker's highly unusual request would not normally have been granted – the expectation that undergraduates would live in college generally went unquestioned – but sympathising with his distress, and feeling a certain degree of responsibility towards him as his tutor, I had petitioned the fellowship to allow him two terms' non-residence while continuing to pursue his studies.

'Presumably, Mr Trent brought the news this morning?' I asked, as Dr Harper and I made our way up the Turl to the Broad to find a hackney cab. Trent had been Parker's bedmaker in college, and the conditions under which the boy had been allowed to go out of residence had been that he should live in the lodging house that Trent and his wife ran, and that he should continue to attend college chapel every morning.

'No. His death hadn't been discovered by the time Trent left the house. His wife sent their son down.' Disconcertingly, the Principal didn't look at me as he spoke, his eyes fixed on the taxi rank outside Trinity. I wouldn't have minded walking to the Kingston Road, it was a dry, mild day, and the walk wouldn't have taken more than twenty minutes, but Dr Harper obviously felt it would be beneath his dignity to arrive on foot.

Abruptly, he turned to face me. 'Where were you this morning?'

Resentment stirred at his assumption that he had the right to enquire about my whereabouts as if I were an undergraduate. 'As it happens, I was breakfasting with Professor Rhys and his family.'

Out of the corner of my eye, I watched Harper's nostrils flare. As far as I knew, he had nothing against Rhys personally, but disliked the fact that the University Chair of Celtic had been attached to Jesus College via its associated fellowship. Anything that linked the college with Wales was a hindrance to Dr Harper's campaign to loosen the college's historic – and exclusive – ties to the Principality.

'Your absence from college was inconvenient. It would have been far better if we'd been able to ascertain the details of Parker's death immediately rather than wasting half the morning.'

I quelled a rising indignation. Allowing the Principal to see my feelings would only make things worse. Harper would become defensive and that would make him even more antagonistic. I'd seen it often enough at college meetings.

'Had the boy said anything to you recently?' he asked.

'Said anything, Principal? In what sense?'

'Did he confide in you about any troubles?'

A sudden fear that Dr Harper might see me as a man inclined to encourage the sharing of certain specific confidences crept, like a cold draught, up my spine. I was suddenly aware of my pulse in a way I hadn't been five seconds before.

'No,' I said. 'We confined ourselves entirely to getting him through his Moderations and back into residence.'

'Was he up to it?' Harper asked. 'Is there any chance he feared he would fail?'

'It took him two attempts to pass Responsions,' I admitted. 'He'd been here almost a year before he managed it.' The examination, designed to ensure that all new undergraduates had a basic foundation in Greek, Latin and mathematics, was referred to derisively by the young men as the Little-Go, but for all their mockery, it wasn't a hurdle that was always easily overcome. Parker's Greek had been his downfall then, as now. Abruptly, the implication behind Harper's question dawned on me. 'You surely don't think he—'

Harper held up a quelling hand. 'I prefer not to think about it at all. But every time there's a University death, the coroners go out of their way to emphasise that it was the purest accident. And every time, that very assertion makes people wonder whether perhaps it wasn't.'

Harper had been appointed Principal four years ago, with the express aim of improving Jesus College's academic reputation and, thus, the number and calibre of the undergraduates who chose to study here. Some of the more patriotic Welsh fellows opposed his plans to accept students from England as well as Wales, and they would seize on anything that reflected badly on him and weakened his position. The last thing the Principal needed were rumours of the less than entirely natural death of a failing student.

'When did you last see him?' Harper asked as we got into a cab.

'Last Friday.'

'Was he in good spirits?'

'As good as he ever was, I think. He was never full of what you'd call *joie de vivre*. He seemed…' I hesitated as I sat down. 'Burdened, I suppose would be the best word.'

'Burdened? He was twenty years old, what did he have to be burdened by?'

Dr Harper had been a headmaster for thirty years before coming to Jesus College and he firmly believed that a boy's schooldays – and, by extension, his undergraduate days – were the happiest of his life. Parker, I very much suspected, would not have agreed. No more, for that matter, did I.

'He was an orphan,' I said, trying to get comfortable on the narrow cab seat. 'When he left Oxford, he would have to have made his own way in the world, with no parents to turn to. That weighed on him, I think.'

'He had a guardian though?'

'Yes. But I had the impression that they weren't close.' I searched my mind for everything I knew about Parker's circumstances. 'There was the expectation of an inheritance, I believe, but not enough to live on.'

'Did he have a profession in mind?'

'When he first came up, he told me that he intended to sit the civil service exam once he'd graduated,' I said. In the end, it had been Parker's need to seek gainful employment on graduation that had persuaded me to support his request to go out of residence. Unlike his better-off peers, if he was to have a decent chance in life, Parker had no choice but to leave Oxford with a degree, and I had felt there was a good chance of his failing to progress beyond his Honour Moderations if he remained in college.

Poor chap. He would no longer be troubled by exams of any kind, nor fears for his future. Sidney Parker had not inspired a great deal of affection, but I had felt a certain admiration for the way he battled his own lack of ability with hard work and grim determination.

-

The cab took us to one of the tall, bay-windowed villas on Kingston Road that had been under construction when I was an undergraduate. St John's College, which owned much of the land west of the city centre, had opened up land for house building in the Jericho area in the mid '60s, when the Great Western Railway had proposed building a huge new carriage works in Oxford, creating a demand for artisan housing. The plan had come to nothing – partly due to University opposition to a scheme that would, inevitably, have changed the character of Oxford – and the houses were now occupied by the city's aspirant middle class. Including college servants.

As we opened the gate to the small front garden, Dr Harper glanced at me. 'I do hope your keenness that Parker be allowed to take up residence here hasn't contributed to his death, Rice.'

I stared at him. Still somewhat unnerved by his earlier intimation that Parker might have taken his own life, this unexpected apportioning of blame almost knocked me off my feet. 'But we all agreed,' I protested, finding my voice after several seconds during which words refused to emerge. 'His being allowed to lodge with the Trents was a decision agreed on by the whole governing body.'

'But, as his tutor, it was your duty to keep a weather eye on his health as well as his academic performance,' Dr Harper said, effectively ending the conversation with a decisive application of the door knocker.

My heart was still pounding at the enormity of the Principal's words when a middle-aged person whom I took to be Mrs Trent opened the door. She was wearing a dark grey dress which, unless she generally favoured funereal colours, showed a commendably respectful response to her lodger's demise.

'Come in Dr Harper,' she invited, flicking her eyes to me as I followed him.

'Basil Rice,' I introduced myself. 'I was Mr Parker's tutor.' Had she called him Sidney, this homely-looking woman? Some lodging houses for non-collegiate undergraduates were run like family homes whereas others were strictly business.

As she led us up the stairs, Mrs Trent explained that she had come to wake Sidney when he'd failed to appear for breakfast that morning. 'Sometimes he oversleeps because he's been working so late,' she said. I liked her for trying to show Parker in the best light but, surely, when a student lodger overslept it was much more likely that he'd over-indulged himself the night before?

'Such a nice-mannered young man,' she said as if she could hear my thoughts. 'And no trouble. A teetotaller. And devoted to Barney's.' She glanced back down the stars at us. 'The church – St Barnabas.'

As we turned onto the first-floor landing with its linoleum runner, and started up the second flight of stairs, I felt ashamed. This woman knew Parker in a way I never had, despite the hours I had spent with him. I had asked after his family and background – especially when he had told me, at the end of his first term, that he wouldn't be going home for Christmas – but I had had no idea of how he spent his time when he wasn't studying.

Mrs Trent opened a door off the small second-floor landing. 'He's in here, gentlemen. I'm sorry about the smell but… well… you know.'

We entered the room, Mrs Trent nervously waiting in the doorway. 'Shall I open the curtains?'

Harper was staring at the bed. Somebody had pulled a sheet over Sidney Parker's body. 'Is this how you found him? Lying like this, in bed?'

Mrs Trent hesitated. 'Well… no. He was on the floor. I got my boy, Fred, to lift him with me.'

She glanced down and I followed her gaze to the threadbare rug in the middle of the room. The edge nearest the bed was damp. 'You've been cleaning, Mrs Trent,' I suggested.

'He was lying there in such a state, Mr Rice. He'd knocked the pot over and...' She didn't know how to tell us that Sidney Parker had been lying in his own excrement.

'Have you washed the body, too?' Dr Harper's voice was sharp, as if he suspected her of covering something up.

'No, sir. Fred said not to. Said the coroner'd want to see him as he was.'

'But he's not as he was, is he, Mrs Trent?'

'Principal,' I intervened. 'I'm sure Mrs Trent was only trying to spare us as much unpleasantness as possible. Her thoughtfulness means that we can see the body without having to stand in...'

Harper nodded curtly. 'Yes. Quite. I beg your pardon, Mrs Trent. This is all most upsetting for us all.'

I gazed at the form under the sheet. Parker was on his side, knees drawn up towards his chest.

I walked around the bed and pulled the thin curtains open, less from a need for light and more to put off the moment when I would have to draw back the sheet and look at the reality of Parker's corpse.

Turning around, it occurred to me that, as a place to spend one's final moments, Parker's room could have been a great deal worse.

The rug provided some comfort, and relief from draughts between the floorboards, and the place was decently furnished. An old dining chair was tucked beneath the table which did duty as a desk, and another, rather more comfortable, chair stood in front of the small grate. In the corner nearest the fire was a washstand with a towel rack to one side, the towel carefully draped over it to dry. And, while I found that small gesture towards personal care almost unbearably poignant in the circumstances, more prosaically it argued against self-destruction. Why bother drying your towel for a morning you weren't going to see?

The books Parker had been working on for his most recent essay were stacked, neatly on the table, and a tidy pile of foolscap lay to one side, held in place by a worn wooden box that looked as if it might hold a razor. I raised the lid. Pens and nibs.

Had Parker's late father given him the box to use, having been made a present of a better case for his razor? Or was the boy's death making me see everything in his life as pitiable?

Finally, I stepped up to the bed. The stench of faeces was stronger on this side of the room, less masked by the lingering smell of carbolic soap on the damp rug. Carefully, I drew the sheet back, forcing myself to look at the body. Parker's right arm was flung up, above his head, his left jammed into his side, hand clutching at his nightshirt which had been pulled up, revealing his drawers. Both garments were stained with liquid faeces.

'We couldn't lie him down flat,' Mrs Trent said, apologetically. 'He was already stiff.'

Harper spoke, making me jump slightly. 'When did you last speak to him, Mrs Trent?'

'Yesterday evening. About seven. I brought him some supper up because he'd been a bit under the weather with his digestion, but he said he'd never keep it down.'

'Did you give him anything else?'

'Some water and a drop of Godfrey's to help him sleep.'

The familiar name seemed out of place in such a scene. Godfrey's Cordial was what every mother used for her children when they were fretful or unwell, and the memory of my mother giving it to me was enough to summon its bitter-syrup taste to my mouth.

Swallowing a sudden lump in my throat, I forced myself to look at Parker's face. In the dim light, his drawn features were a bluish grey. For a second, I thought how unhealthy he looked, then I remembered that he was dead. I pulled the sheet back over his stiff form and somewhat self-consciously made the sign of the cross. I was not a high churchman, but something seemed necessary.

'I assume Dr Fielding's been asked to attend?' I asked.

Fielding was the physician who generally dealt with our ailing undergraduates. He was not attached to Jesus College in any formal way, but there was an association that went back at least to my own undergraduate days, more than a decade ago.

'Actually,' Harper said, 'I wanted to speak to you before sending for Fielding. If there's a physician who was better acquainted with the boy, he should be asked to come and give an opinion. Do you know of Parker consulting a doctor for any reason?'

'I don't, no.'

'Mrs Trent?'

'No, sir. He never had a doctor here to him. Do you think I should have?'

'No, no. Please don't upset yourself,' Harper said. 'You weren't to know.'

'We thought it was just his usual bowel complaint. He did suffer dreadfully now and again, but he always got over it, you see.'

'We quite understand, Mrs Trent,' I said. 'The doctor might want to speak to you about Sidney's health if he was prone to bouts like this.' I turned to the Principal. 'I think we'd be as well to ask Fielding as anybody.'

'He was a fighter, Sidney,' Mrs Trent volunteered. 'Told me once he'd rather be dead than be an invalid. I found something he'd written. It was on the floor with him.'

She crossed to the nightstand next to the bed and took a single sheet of paper from beneath the Bible which lay there. I took it from her.

DO NOT BE FAINT HEARTED.

I showed it to the Principal who asked, 'Is it Parker's handwriting?'

Familiar as I was with Parker's crabbed script, this was in capitals. 'Possibly. I can't say definitively, I'm afraid.' I turned back to Mrs Trent. 'Did he often write himself notes like this?'

'Never saw any but that one.'

I looked at the nightstand. Apart from a candlestick and the Bible, its surface was bare but, above the door which concealed the chamber pot was a drawer. Pulling it out carefully, I heard the unmistakeable clink of glass. The drawer was full of small medicine bottles.

I picked a couple up and read the labels. *Chlorodyne. Paregoric.* Remedies that had been advertised so relentlessly over the years that the names had ceased to catch one's eye; until, that is, they had begun to appear in coroners' inquest reports, along with warnings that the public should use such remedies only as prescribed on the bottle. Both were empty. The drawer held many more with the same labels, also empty.

As the Principal watched, I picked up two more bottles. One was labelled *Opium Tincture (Laudanum)* and was half-full while the other – a square-sided brown bottle labelled *Dr Aurum's Tonic* – was empty. There were several more Dr Aurum bottles, all empty. And, at the very front of the drawer, I found one, solitary, blue bottle. It bore neither label nor raised letters and it was quite empty. For reasons I couldn't have articulated, I unstoppered it and sniffed. A faint smell that was two parts bitterness to one part alcohol lingered.

Looking into the drawer I wondered whether all these empty bottles contained the cure for the burdens Parker laboured under, or the burden itself. Over-consumption of remedies like these could become a habit that was hard to break.

A small bottle of laudanum would not represent much of an outlay, even for somebody of limited means like Parker, and neither would Chlorodyne or paregoric, both of which were advertised to everybody from the mothers of croupy children to elderly rheumatism sufferers. But in these quantities, a habit might become expensive. And the unfamiliar Dr Aurum's Tonic might be considerably more expensive.

How many weeks' worth of self-dosing did the bottles in the drawer represent?

I turned to the landlady. 'These bottles, Mrs Trent, have you seen them before?'

'No, sir. I don't look in the young men's drawers and cupboards. I only dust the surfaces.'

'So he hadn't asked you to get anything like this for him from the pharmacist?'

'No.'

'And you hadn't disposed of any bottles like this for him?'

'No, sir.'

Harper had watched the exchange without comment. 'Dr Fielding might be able to cast some light on all this,' I said, indicating the drawer. 'Parker didn't mention having been unwell to me, but he may have consulted the doctor. Allen in the lodge would have pointed him in the right direction if he'd asked.'

'Quite so. When we get back to college, send the messenger to Fielding's house, and ask him to meet us here this afternoon to certify death. Meanwhile, I must see the bursar about an address for the boy's guardian.'

I bent to replace the bottles in the drawer and, as I did so, I saw that there was a spoon lying on the floor between the nightstand and the bed. Had Parker dosed himself before lying down to sleep? And, if so, had whatever he'd taken contributed to his death?

I kept the question to myself. Best to see what Fielding had to say first.

The Principal moved towards the door and, as I followed him, I looked behind me, suddenly struck by something.

'One moment, Principal.'

Where had Parker kept all his personal items – letters, keepsakes? Even loose change, which I might have expected to find on his desk or in the drawer of his nightstand, was absent.

I stepped over to the narrow wardrobe in the corner. Only two jackets hung inside: one that Parker had worn to every tutorial he'd attended with me, and a slightly better-quality one that I hadn't seen before. Two pairs of trousers and a few shirts were folded neatly on shelves beneath, as was a pitifully small collection of underlinen and socks. Nothing else.

Opening the trunk that sat at the foot of his bed, I found a pair of elderly boots, two folded jerseys, a pair of rowing tights, two pairs of gloves and a somewhat elderly silk hat. Nothing that might contain money or letters, nor invitations, calling cards, timetables of events or any of the pocket-sized paraphernalia of daily life.

Where were Sidney Parker's most personal belongings?

Chapter 5

Non

Before we rode home, I made Lily stop at Jesus College so that I could leave Basil a message at the porters' lodge. I didn't want the porters reading it, so I wrote it in Welsh. I suppose Latin or Greek would've done just as well, but the reason Basil and I knew each other was because I was teaching him to speak Welsh. He was from a Monmouthshire family and, like all the upper-class families in that area, they'd abandoned the language generations ago. Basil had a good grasp of Old Welsh – which he was teaching me in return – but he wanted to learn to speak the language I spoke. What you'd call modern Welsh, I suppose. So, Professor Rhys had introduced us.

I'm sorry if my behaviour was inappropriate, I wrote on a page torn out of my notebook. *Please forgive me and come and have supper with us this evening.*

Your obedient servant,

Non Vaughan.

The obedient servant bit was tongue-in-cheek, but Basil knew I always signed myself Non when I was being contrite. I used Rhiannon when I was feeling haughty and Rhiannon Angharad when he'd annoyed me.

To be honest, he didn't annoy me very often, and I was afraid the boot was on the other foot today. How could I make amends? I could lend him my copy of *Lectures On Welsh Philology* but, seeing as he visited Professor Rhys's house as often as he visited ours, lending him the professor's book might be coals to Newcastle. Still, Basil knew it was my most prized possession, so perhaps it would do.

Lily tutted and complained about having to stand about in the cold, waiting for me, but she didn't object to me inviting Basil. She was very fond of him. According to Lily, Basil was the only man I ever listened to. And perhaps she was right. Apart from Professor Rhys there was no other man I'd respected enough to listen to since my father had died.

I steered the tandem past the rows of patient, head-down cab horses on Broad Street – or 'the Broad' as University types called it, like 'the Turl' and 'the High' – down George Street, past the empty cattle market pens at Gloucester Green, then followed a stinking trail left by pigs going to the slaughterhouse in Jericho. When I'd first arrived in Oxford, I'd been astonished at the number of animals in the city. But then, it had been foolish to think of the place just consisting of colleges. How would people get about without horses, and how, except by having a market and a slaughterhouse, would the butchers in the covered market get their meat?

Oxford had been surprising in many ways.

-

'I'm going for a walk,' I told Lily when we got home.

She frowned. 'Where? Nowhere near the college and that poor dead boy?'

'No. Just over to the meadows.'

'They're still flooded.'

'There's enough dry land to walk on.' As long as dry meant not actually underwater. 'I won't get wet,' I promised. 'Not in my walking dress.'

Compressed lips joined the frown. Lily didn't approve of my walking dress. According to her, it wasn't respectable.

The clothes – specifically, the layers of petticoats – that I was expected to wear as a 'respectable' young woman in Oxford had come as a shock. They were heavy, they dragged in the mud, and they didn't let your legs work as nature intended. So, instead of trussing myself up like the young ladies of Somerville and Lady Margaret Hall, who looked as if they were trying to hide the scandalous existence of female legs, I dressed pretty much as I had done at home. I confined myself to one flannel petticoat and absolutely refused to strap a bustle around my waist. If people thought that that made me look *unshapely*, then that was their lookout.

Actually, they probably thought it made me look *common*. Most working women couldn't afford to wear all those layers – you try cleaning a house or going to the market and coming back with heavy bags if you're already wearing a stone's worth of underwear.

I'd devised my walking dress so that I could walk in the meadows without getting filthy. It looked like a normal dress, but I'd stitched three ribbons to the bottom third of the skirt in contrasting hoops of colour at vertical intervals of three inches. Each concealed a row of hooks, with the corresponding eyelets attached to the bottom hem of my grey flannel petticoat. When I wanted to stride out, I hooked the petticoat up over the bottom of the dress so that both were gathered up, leaving a variable gap (to allow for different terrain and wetness) of between four and ten inches between the ground and the new, raised hem of my dress.

Lily wasn't impressed. But she'd had to give in when I pointed out that a modified dress was preferable to trousers.

'You'd never dare!' she'd said.

'I wore them when I was working on my father's ship.'

What Lily didn't know was that I also wore trousers – in fact, a whole suit of boy's clothes – whenever I needed to go out onto Port Meadow at night. Sometimes, Oxford and all its restrictions just got too much for me and, on a windy night, I'd change out of my dress and go out into the emptiness of the meadow. I'd just stand and let the wind buffet and pull at me as if I was on board ship and the wind had blown all the way across the Atlantic from America. Then I'd run all the way home. Boys' clothes gave me the freedom to move without feminine restrictions.

Despite Lily's fears, Jericho people didn't bat an eyelid at my walking dress. Well, not any more, anyway. I'd had to put up with a few comments the first few times I went out in it, but people soon lost interest when they realised that they couldn't embarrass me. So, now I was free to walk about with my ankles on show for all to see.

-

I splashed along the rough, unmacademised road which took me over the canal and the railway, and into the vast flatness of Port Meadow. Last summer I'd come here with Lily and the rest of the family to watch the Oxford Races. It had been my first experience of horse races and I'd been amazed at how different the horses were from the ones at home, even the gentry's hunters. These animals were much taller and finer and looked as if they'd bolt as soon as look at you – and snap their legs into the bargain. Not a practical animal at all. There were seemingly dozens of different races, and the meeting went on for two days. What with all the stalls and stands selling everything from toffee apples to china, and the colourful merriment (and drunkenness), it had reminded me of nothing so much as the fairs back home, only on a much grander scale.

Then, before Christmas there'd been snow and a big freeze and we'd come skating here on the flooded meadows.

By now it had all thawed, and the floods had spread the river over acres and acres on either side of its banks. It was odd to watch the sails of boats and barges moving along in a neat ribbon in the middle of it all, as their pilots kept them safely on the invisible course of the river.

Seeing the boats opened a hollow feeling in me where the sea had always been. Here in landlocked Oxford, I missed the sea in a way I hadn't had the wit to imagine. All my life, it had just been *there*, literally within sight of our house, and I'd taken it for granted. Two tides a day, come rain or shine, midsummer or Christmas. The sound of waves in the little cove beneath our house was as regular as a heartbeat and varied in its intensity in response to wind and sun, just like the beat of a responsive heart to sadness or joy.

I missed the sea as much as I missed hearing my own language on the streets, as much as I missed being greeted everywhere I went. Almost as much as I missed my father and the feeling that I'd always be safe because he was in the world.

But I didn't want to think about Dada. His death was still too recent.

Daw popeth mas yn iawn, 'merch i. That had always been my father's response to my rages. Everything'll turn out right.

And, with him at our hearth, it always had. He'd made sure of that. But now, I was fighting alone.

My blood, whipped into a race around my veins by my confrontation with Dr Harper and my argument with Lily, was still pumping at a faster rate than a walk called for. It was always like this. Arguments stayed with me for hours, going round and round in my head, making my body itch to run or hit somebody.

It's pointless you being here. You'll never be able to do anything!

The Popinjay was wrong. I'd show him he was wrong. I didn't need anybody's permission to write to Dr Reckitt and tell him about the boy's death, did I?

I came to a halt at the edge of the floodwater. In summer, I'd just strike straight across the meadow, through the grazing cattle, to the river, but the floods had brought the river to me, so my options were limited.

'*You know why you want Dr Reckitt here, don't you?*'

My twin sister. I should have known she'd have something to say.

She'd died when we were six, but that had never stopped me talking to her, or her to me. At that age, you don't really understand death. You know somebody's gone, but you can't really get hold of the idea that they've gone *for ever*. Children are used to people coming and going without explanation and the two of us – children of a ship's captain – were more used to absences than most. So, when Hara died (she was Angharad Rhiannon to my Rhiannon Angharad because my father said we were mirror images of each other) even though I'd watched her coffin lid being nailed down and the coffin lowered into the earth, I'd kept on asking Dada when she was coming back.

'*You'll see her again one day*,' he'd promised, sure of a faith he never questioned. '*But for now, you can talk to her if you like, tell her things. That'll stop you missing her so much.*'

To start with, I'd spoken to Hara in the sign language the pair of us had invented for ourselves because she was deaf. But, as I got older, the limited vocabulary we'd needed as small children had become inadequate, so I'd switched to Welsh.

And, mostly, she'd answer. Don't ask me how, because, of all the things in the world that I didn't know, that was the most perplexing. That and her voice. I'd never heard Hara speak, of course, so I didn't know what her voice would've sounded like, but her voice in my head sounded just like mine.

She was unpredictable, Hara. Some days, she just didn't seem to be there, and occasionally, like now, she'd speak when she wasn't spoken to. Mostly when she thought I needed putting right about something.

'*You offered Dr Reckitt's help because you want to prove to him that you're still interested in medicine, in the work we did together.*'

'*Of course I'm still interested!*' How could I not be interested in all the things Dr Reckitt had taught me? The human body and the forensic examination of it were some of the most fascinating things in the world to me. Second only to languages.

'*Yes, but you want him to* know *that. You still haven't got over him saying he was disappointed in you when you decided not to study medicine.*'

There had been a period, when I was seventeen or eighteen, when I'd been determined to follow in Dr Elizabeth Garrett-Anderson's footsteps and become a female doctor. I'd even written to Dr Garrett-Anderson, and she'd been kind enough to write back.

But my ambitions to be a doctor had faded when I'd been given Professor Rhys's book not long after receiving her letter. *Lectures in Welsh Philology* had changed my view of the world and my place in it.

'*Dr Reckitt understands why I decided not to be a doctor.*'

'*I know. But you still worry that he thinks you let him down.*'

'*Shut up, Angharad.*'

'*Angharad is it? You* must *be feeling guilty.*'

I sighed. '*Hara, I don't want to fight.*' My twin was the one person I never wanted to fight with. Part of me was worried that she'd stop talking to me if I argued with her too much. Everybody else did.

'*You're still thinking of writing to him though, aren't you?*'

'*Why not?*'

Benton Reckitt had spent thirty years working with the coroner in Cardiganshire and, even before that, he'd probably been the most skilled forensic doctor and anatomist in Wales. If Basil couldn't tell me, when he came to supper, that the boy had died a natural death, then why shouldn't I write to Dr Reckitt? He might like a trip to Oxford.

I thought of the occasional letters we'd exchanged in the year since I'd left home. I don't suppose Benton Reckitt gave me a second thought from one month's end to the next, but then he'd come across something in a post-mortem examination or in one of the journals he read, and he'd write to me.

'*Are you sure he'd be interested?*' Hara asked.

'*It's a suspicious death. Of course he'd be interested.*'

'*How do you know it's suspicious?*'

'*All right, it's a sudden,* unexpected *death. There'll be an inquest. If we were at home, he'd be involved, wouldn't he?*'

I picked my way along, avoiding the pools of standing water left by the floods and breathing in the smells of wet earth, muddy water and rushing wind. The clean air of the meadow was a welcome change from the sootiness at the back of your throat that followed you everywhere in town.

'Just wait and see what Basil says before you go writing to Dr Reckitt,' Hara said. *'No point getting him up here without good reason. And anyway, you shouldn't really be interfering. What would the ladies of the AEW have to say?'*

'They won't know, will they?'

Well, even I couldn't always be right.

Chapter 6

Basil

At Lily Maddox's dining table that evening, I realised that this was what I envied most in my married colleagues; a life away from college, a kinder, more domestic sphere where one need not be on one's guard or mettle the whole time.

Many of the current generation of fellows who had come up to Oxford with me in the late '60s were now married and had decamped to the villas of North Oxford, leaving colleges full of older, less vibrant, more conservative men. Sitting in the midst of such domestic felicity in Shene Road, the prospect of becoming one of those fossilised celibates was quite terrifying.

I had just finished satisfying Non's clamorous curiosity as to what had taken place after the lecture had been postponed, and Lily was obviously keen to put an end to that particular conversation. 'I'm glad Dr Fielding thinks that the poor boy's death was from natural causes,' she said, casting a cautionary glance at Non, who was sitting at my side.

But Non was not to be quelled. 'Yes, but that's only Dr Fielding's *preliminary* opinion,' she said. 'We should wait until he's done a *proper* examination before we can say anything more definite.' She looked from Lily to me. 'I hope the doctor hasn't put natural causes on the death certificate because he'll look a fool if he discovers something suspicious tomorrow.'

Unwisely, I had admitted that, after conducting an initial view of Sidney Parker's body, Dr Fielding had proposed a more thorough examination the following day, once the effects of *rigor mortis* had abated.

'I don't believe the death certificate has yet been completed,' I said, mildly.

'Where's the post-mortem examination going to be done?' Non asked.

I put my knife and fork down and gave her my whole attention. 'There's not necessarily going to be one. My impression was that Dr Fielding simply wants to conduct a proper surface examination.' With Parker's body stiffly contorted and entangled in his nightwear, it had been impossible to make an adequate assessment.

'So, the body's still at his lodgings?'

'Yes.'

'Him dying in the Trents' house'll have 'em all gossiping. You wait and see if it doesn't.' I looked across the table at the speaker. Lily's son-in-law, Billy Nicholson, sat between his mother-in-law and his wife, Ivy.

'Billy!' Ivy remonstrated. 'I hope you don't mean the Trents? They're a college family. They know better than that.'

'Joking, aren't you? Gordon Trent's a bedmaker. They're the biggest gossips out.' Billy looked to me. 'That's right, isn't it, Mr Rice?'

'Well...' Much though I would have liked to defend the college servants who, on the whole, were tremendously loyal to their 'young gentlemen', bedmakers' capacity for scurrilous gossip was legendary.

For some reason, though Non and Lily had long called me Basil when we were away from disapproving ears, both Billy and Ivy insisted on calling me Mr Rice. Ivy's brother, Albert – Albie as he was known in the family – seemed caught between the two factions and followed the habit of whoever had spoken last.

'The question,' Non took up the conversational reins once more, 'is whether this Dr Fielding is the right man to be conducting an examination of the body. What was his name, by the way, the dead undergraduate? We can't keep on talking about him as "that poor young man".'

'Parker. Sidney Parker.'

At the head of the table, Lily's hand flew to her mouth. 'Oh no. I know him!'

Every eye in the place turned to her.

'He helps the vicar with the young people at St Barnabas's.' Though we had been discussing the poor man's death for the last five minutes, now that he had a name and a face, Lily couldn't imagine him in the past tense.

'I'm sorry, Lily,' I said. 'I wouldn't have discussed all this so freely if I'd realised you knew Mr Parker.'

'We all did.' She looked around the table. 'You remember – I asked him for supper once, when he first joined the church.'

'What, that wet week of a boy who shaved once a month if he was lucky?' Billy scoffed. 'All he could talk about was Father Noel and the church.'

Lily ignored his scorn. 'Father Noel thought he needed company,' she told me, provoking renewed feelings of guilt at Jesus college's failure to embrace the boy. 'He always speaks – spoke – very highly of Mr Parker. It's not many undergraduates that want to help in the parish.'

That was true enough. Various University members, both junior and senior, had been drawn to St Barnabas by its charismatic vicar, Montague Noel, and its High-Church ritualism, but few of them were to be seen there outside Sunday services.

The fact that Parker might have been lonely and in need of company was an indictment of life at Jesus, and it made me acutely uncomfortable to think that Lily Maddox and her family had tried to offer him a companionship he hadn't found in college.

'I didn't realise he lodged with Betty,' Lily said. 'Whatever you think, Billy, Betty Trent is always very discreet. She never so much as mentions the names of their lodgers to anybody else. I must go and see if she needs any help.'

'Do you know Mrs Trent well?' I asked.

'We're not big pals, but I've known her a long time. From church.'

'Would you—' I broke off, unsure how best to voice my request. 'It's just that I noticed something when I was in Mr Parker's room. Or rather,' I floundered, 'I noticed something that wasn't there.'

All eyes around the table were on me now, eating suspended.

'I couldn't find any of Mr Parker's most personal possessions,' I stammered. 'Apart from his Bible which was on his nightstand. No letters, no mementoes, no loose change, the sort of thing a man takes out of his pockets before going to bed every night.'

'And you'd like me to ask Betty where it's all gone?'

'No. Well, not exactly.' That made it sound as if I suspected the Trents of theft. 'I just wondered, that is to say, perhaps she moved his things. For safekeeping. It just seemed wrong,' I floundered again, 'him lying there dead with no personal items at all around him.'

Non rescued me from drowning in my own embarrassment. 'I'd have thought Mrs Trent would've told you if she'd moved any of his things.' She turned to Lily. 'Don't you think?' Then, without waiting for an answer, she addressed herself to me once more. 'Something's not quite right there, is it? And I know Dr Harper wasn't interested in an expert coming to give advice—' she ignored my attempt to respond to such a blatant dig, 'but is this Dr Fielding really the right person to be examining the body? A doctor who knows the deceased is supposed to sign the death certificate. Did Dr Fielding know him? Because, if not, surely nobody'd be offended if somebody more qualified was asked to come and give an opinion.'

I swallowed my last mouthful of curried mutton. 'As it happens, Dr Fielding *had* examined Parker relatively recently. He'd had some kind of accident at McLaren's gymnasium and required medical attention. Apparently, he went to the gym regularly.'

Non put her cutlery down. 'And that qualifies Dr Fielding to give an opinion on how he died, does it? A quick once-over when he'd strained a muscle?'

'I daresay he made a thorough assessment of the young man while he was about it,' Lily said, glancing at me. 'Gave him his money's worth.'

The company's attention was suddenly diverted by the sound of a baby crying elsewhere in the house. Ivy rose. 'He'll be hungry,' she said. 'I'll bid you good night, Dr Rice.'

I stood as she slid out from her place at the table and went to her son. 'Is he thriving?' I asked Billy, glad of the distraction and wishing to acknowledge that the baby was a person, not simply the reason for his wife's leaving the table.

'Growing like a weed,' the proud father beamed. 'He'll be on his feet and walking before we know where we are.'

'Steady on, Billy,' Lily remonstrated, 'he's not even sitting up by himself yet. He'll be a while finding his feet.'

'Nah, you'll see. He'll be toddling up the road after me before we know where we are, wanting to come to work with his dad.'

Billy, like Lily's late husband, was a printer at the University Press, though he lacked his father-in-law's entrepreneurial spirit. Sam Maddox had, by all accounts, been a canny businessman and his shrewd investments meant that Lily need never worry about how to pay the rent on the family's solid, four-storey house. She had taken Non as a lodger not from financial necessity but as a favour to Non's benefactor and sponsor, Miss Sarah Jane Rees.

'Little Tom going to be a printer then is he, Billy?' I asked. 'Like his dad and his grandad?'

'Don't see why not. It's good work for decent pay, isn't it? He could do a lot worse.'

'Don't decide the poor child's fate before he's even weaned.' Non protested. 'It'll be a different world in ten, fifteen years. He might surprise you. Maybe he'll go to the University to study.'

'What? No son of mine'll get in amongst that uppish lot so he can look down on his own family.'

'What do you mean by that?' Non flared.

'You know exactly what I mean by it. When did you last go home to see your old mum, eh? You've not been back since you've been here.'

'Because my mother's better off coming here. She has the chance to see Lily then, too.'

'That's an excuse. You just think you're too good for your own people, now.'

'Don't talk nonsense, Billy Nicholson. It's not easy to just go back. I've got a lot of work to do here.'

'Work?' he jeered. 'Call what you're doing work? You want to give Lil here a bit more of a hand, my girl, then she wouldn't have to keep young Edie on.'

Lily, however, didn't appreciate being implicated in his criticism of Non. 'That's enough. You two make me tired with your endless squabbling. If you can't say anything nice to each other,' she said, collecting our dirty plates, 'you'd best not say anything at all.'

Seeing the need for a change of topic, I turned to Albie who was an apprentice draughtsman at William Lucy's Eagle Ironworks. 'How are things progressing at Lucy's, Albie?'

'Very well, thanks. The technical drawing was a bit of a poser to begin with, but I'm getting the hang of it, now. Non's been a big help.' He glanced at his brother-in-law, torn between instinctive male solidarity and – I suspected – a certain dislike of Billy. 'She's been going over all the technicalities with me.'

'Geometry and algebra,' Non supplied. 'Albie's quick – doesn't need to be shown something more than once.'

I knew that Non was repaying him for sticking up for her but, from the way Albie beamed, it was clear that she didn't offer praise very often.

'Speaking of geometry,' I said, in an attempt to steer us on to a different topic before Billy could take up the cudgels again, 'or rather, a teacher of geometry, has the Cipher Club started meeting this term yet?'

Non rose to open the door so that Lily could take the plates to the scullery and bring back the pudding. 'Terms don't come into it,' she said. 'It's not a University club. Rev Dodgson just calls a meeting when the fancy takes him. But, as a matter of fact,' she reached into her pocket and withdrew a folded note, 'we're due to meet tomorrow.'

She put the note on the table in front of me. The script was loopy but highly legible.

> *Dear Miss Vaughan,*
>
> *I would be most gratified by your attendance at the next meeting of The Cipher Club, 4pm this coming Wednesday at our usual haunt.*
>
> *Sincerely yours,*
>
> *CLD.*

Though Charles Dodgson might sign himself with his true initials, he might just as well have used 'LC' because this note – and indeed the Cipher Club itself – was much more in keeping with the whimsicality of Lewis Carroll than the gravitas of Christ Church's lecturer in mathematics.

I hoped the meeting would divert Non from her fixation with Parker's death.

I should have known better.

DR. J. COLLIS BROWNE'S CHLORODYNE

THE ORIGINAL AND ONLY GENUINE

CHLORODYNE is admitted by the Profession to be the most wonderful and valuable remedy ever discovered.

CHLORODYNE is the best remedy known for Coughs, Consumption, Bronchitis, Asthma.

CHLORODYNE checks & arrests those too often fatal diseases—Diphtheria, Fever, Croup, Ague.

CHLORODYNE acts like a charm in Diarrhoea, and is the only specific in Cholera & Dysentery.

CHLORODYNE effectually cuts short all attacks of Epilepsy, Hysteria, Palpitations & Spasms.

CHLORODYNE is the only palliative in Neuralgia, Rheumatism, Gout, Cancer, Toothache, Meningitis, &c

From Dr. B. J. BOULTON & CO, Horncastle.

"Earl Russell communicated to the College of Physicians that he received a dispatch from Her Majesty's Consul at Manilla, to the effect that Cholera has been raging fearfully, and that the ONLY remedy of any service was CHLORODYNE." – See *Lancet*, 1st December 1864.

CAUTION. – BEWARE OF PIRACY and IMITATIONS

Sold in Bottles at 1s 11/2d, 2s 9d and 4s 6d each. None is genuine without the words "DR. J. COLLIS BROWNE'S CHLORODYNE" on the Government Stamp. Overwhelming Medical Testimony accompanies each bottle.

SOLE MANUFACTURER: – J. T. DAVENPORT, 33 Great Russell Street, Bloomsbury, London.

(Contemporary Newspaper advertisement.)

Chapter 7

Non

The following morning, we'd only just cleared breakfast away when there was a knock at the door.

Edie, our maid of all work, came back from answering it with an envelope in her hand. 'Letter for you. Hand delivered.'

I was still holding the tablecloth which I'd taken to the back door to shake out, so I put it back on the table and made a show of arranging it just so before I took the letter from her. As a rule, I took no notice of anything Billy Nicholson said – as far as I could see, he was an unintelligent man who'd married Ivy so he could live in a big house where he thought he'd be master – but his nasty comment about me doing more around the house had made me uncomfortable.

I didn't recognise the handwriting on the envelope, but it was sealed with a blue and gold wafer which it almost seemed a shame to break. Somebody who did a lot of writing then.

The firm, upright hand got straight to the point.

> *Dear Miss Vaughan*
>
> *I would be most grateful if you would come and see me at the AEW rooms this morning at 9.30 to discuss a matter which has been brought to my attention.*
>
> *Sincerely,*
>
> *T. H. Green (Mrs)*

There was nothing more likely to convince me that being married was not for me than this business of women calling themselves by their husband's name. Mrs Green's name was Charlotte but here she was, signing herself 'T. H.' because those were her husband's initials. As if she was just a female reflection of him.

'I'm summoned to see the secretary of the AEW,' I told Lily, who'd just shooed Edie back to her work. Strictly speaking, Mrs Green was the honorary 'lady secretary'; some man whose name I'd forgotten was the official secretary. The University's Hebdomadal Council would never have agreed to negotiate with an organisation run entirely by women, even if they were the wives, sisters and daughters of fellows and heads of houses.

'In trouble, are you?' Lily asked.

'Why should I be?'

'Because you thought it was a good idea to suggest to the Principal of Jesus College that you should keep him company while he went to look at a dead body. And then you started boasting about knowing famous doctors who'd come at the click of your fingers.' She sucked her teeth. 'I don't suppose the door to his lodgings had shut behind him before he was writing to the AEW committee.'

Cold prickles ran up the back of my neck to my scalp and I suddenly felt sick. Was that what Mrs Green's letter was about? As far as I knew, she hadn't known I existed until today.

'I'll go and change,' Lily said.

It was on the tip of my tongue to tell her I didn't need a chaperone, but I managed to keep my mouth shut. If I was in trouble, it might be better to present myself looking demure and following the rules. Strictly speaking, chaperones were only required on University premises, but the girls at Somerville and Lady Margaret Hall were barely allowed out unaccompanied, even when two or three of them were together. It was one of the reasons I'd decided to stay at Lily's and not apply for residence at one of the halls.

I followed Lily upstairs. Probably just as well to make an effort with my dress, too. It was the kind of thing the likes of Mrs Green thought was important.

-

Looking up at the building where the AEW rented rooms, I hoped to goodness that no undergraduate ever came near the place. A nondescript building on a little backstreet behind St Giles didn't create quite the same impression as imposing buildings and semi-fortified quadrangles.

'Do bring your machine inside,' Mrs Green said when she came to let us in. 'There's no telling what might happen to it if you leave it on the street.'

'This is Mrs Maddox, my landlady.' I introduced Lily once we'd manoeuvred the tandem inside. 'She very kindly acts as my chaperone.' As a matter of fact, kindness didn't come into it: Cranogwen paid Lily for the time she spent traipsing about after me. But mentioning money would be vulgar.

Upstairs, Mrs Green opened the door to a room that wouldn't have been out of place in any don's house in Park Town. It was the smaller of the two rooms that the ladies' committee rented here, mostly used for tutorials.

'Would you care to sit here, Mrs Maddox, while Rhiannon and I have a chat?'

Lily nodded and went through into the drawing room, but not before she'd given me a look which told me to mind my p's and q's. Mrs Green ushered me into the bigger room on the other side of the corridor, the one we used for lectures. This room was furnished in domestic fashion too.

Like Somerville and Lady Margaret Hall, our rooms here were meant to remind the girls of home: safe, domestic spaces where parents who were anxious about the damage an education might do to their daughters' brains and chances of marriage could be sure their little chicks would be safe. It was all so cautious and conventional it made me want to scream. But then, if those same parents knew that their daughters were mixing with the likes of me, a young woman with no middle-class credentials who'd worked as a sailor on the coastal runs, they'd have done more than scream.

'Do sit down, Miss Vaughan. You know Miss Rogers, of course?'

Annie Rogers, who'd caused such embarrassment for the men in the local examinations eight years before, smiled at me. But it wasn't her usual mischievous smile; she was on duty as a member of the AEW board.

Annie's main job was to give lectures to the female students, but she also did her fair share of chaperoning, so we'd fallen into conversation fairly often. She was an Oxford girl through and through. Her father was an MP now, but while she was growing up, he'd held an Oxford professorship.

We sat in front of the fireplace, as if this was some kind of tea party instead of a disciplinary meeting. Behind us was the long dining table where girls took notes while Annie or, more usually, one of the University's fellows, delivered lectures. At first, I'd attended a few lectures here but, generally, they were at a level that was uninteresting to me.

Mrs Green got straight to the point. 'Miss Vaughan, you have the dubious privilege of being the first female student about whom the AEW has received a complaint. And you have compounded that distinction by being the subject of not one complaint but two on the very same day.'

'*Two?*'

The lady secretary of the AEW stared straight at me, her face revealing as little about what she was thinking as her plain dress and single row of pearls revealed about her station in life. You'd never have guessed she was the wife of a professor at Balliol.

'Your question implies that you'd already anticipated at least one objection to your conduct, Miss Vaughan?'

I tried to look contrite, but Mrs Green's pursed lips told me I hadn't been very convincing. Probably because I hadn't had a lot of practice.

'The first, and more serious, complaint came from the Principal of Jesus College, Dr Harper. I assume you know what he found to complain of?'

'A woman daring to offer him advice?'

Mrs Green drew in a breath but said nothing. She was only in her early thirties, but she'd have learned the middle-class woman's habit of keeping her thoughts to herself at her mother's knee.

'I warned you,' Annie Rogers grinned. 'She's quite untamed.'

Mrs Green ignored her. 'You inserted yourself into what was quite clearly a private and highly sensitive conversation between Dr Harper and Mr Rice. Not only that but you proposed to go with them to view the body of a dead undergraduate. Can you not see how shocking such a suggestion was?'

I knew the right answer – 'Yes, Mrs Green, sorry Mrs Green,' – I just couldn't bring myself to say it.

'What did you hope to gain by your intervention, Miss Vaughan?'

'I didn't hope to gain anything. I was just trying to help. Dr Harper was obviously worried about the death, and my medical acquaintance, Dr Reckitt, is second to none—'

'Dr Reckitt?' Mrs Green interrupted. 'Not Dr *Benton* Reckitt?'

'Yes. Do you know him?'

'Not personally, but his name is very familiar. I recall my father quoting extensively from Dr Reckitt's various contributions to *The Lancet*.'

I grinned. Dr Reckitt was a great one for writing letters and articles, particularly for the medical journal.

'My father lectured in forensic medicine as a young man,' Mrs Green went on, 'and he retained an interest in the subject all his life. Dr Reckitt's articles were a source of constant interest to him. In fact, they corresponded occasionally.'

'I wish Dr Harper could hear you say that. He seems to think no doctor practising in Wales could possibly be worthy of consideration in Oxford.'

Mrs Green sighed. 'Dr Reckitt's reputation is, however, not the point at issue, Miss Vaughan.' Her eyes rested on me slightly more kindly now that she'd found a personal connection between us. 'Perhaps,' she said, 'I might constructively have begun this conversation at a less contentious point.' She clasped her hands in her lap. 'Miss Vaughan, may I ask why your benefactress suggested that you come to Oxford to pursue your studies? After all, Cambridge is already somewhat further advanced on the path of female education, and London already offers women degrees.'

I was surprised – not by the question so much as the fact that Mrs Green knew that Cranogwen was paying my way here – and I didn't know what to say. I had very little experience of women like Charlotte Green and, if I'm honest, I was a bit intimidated by her practised restraint. But our chapel minister at home had given me a very useful piece of advice before I'd left for Oxford. It was probably the only useful thing he'd ever said to me.

Just remember, Non, people are the same wherever you find them. If they seem strange and different, just imagine them in situations you're familiar with. That'll help you see them as they really are.

I took his advice and imagined Mrs Green standing behind the counter in one of the higher-class shops in Cardigan. That made it easier to just be honest with her.

'Miss Rees agreed with you that I'd be better off in London,' I admitted. 'But I'm here because of Professor Rhys. His book, *Lectures in Welsh Philology*, changed the way I thought about my country, my language and my history.' As the wife of a don, hopefully she'd appreciate the effect a scholarly work could have on a person.

'Professor Rhys? Ah, yes, of course. Celtic at Jesus. He's sympathetic to our cause, I believe?'

'Very. And his wife, too.'

'Perhaps Professor and Mrs Rhys's enthusiasm has prevented you from understanding just how tenuous our position here is, Miss Vaughan. Believe it or not, Dr Harper is actually an ally. We have had many a meeting at the Jesus lodgings, but he understands that female conduct while on college premises is of paramount importance if other colleges are to extend the same invitation to us that Jesus and a handful of others already have.'

She paused to let me adjust my opinion of Dr Harper. But I hadn't forgiven his dismissal of Dr Reckitt, so I left my opinion where it was.

It was as if Mrs Green had read my mind. 'In fact, it wasn't your attempt to involve Dr Reckitt that primarily concerned Dr Harper, but your unseemly spat with an undergraduate.'

How did Dr Harper know about my little chat with the Popinjay, Peacock?

'He feels that, if we don't make it clear that we take your conduct very seriously, it will have a detrimental effect on our progress.' She fixed me with her calm stare. 'For years, we've worked to make the education of women palatable to the men of Oxford, Miss Vaughan. What you must understand is that Oxford is not like London. We don't train doctors and engineers and scientists. We train clergymen and politicians. And those men are, on the whole, conservative – cautious about changing the place of women in the world. Even those who broadly support our aims.'

'But there are plenty of men on the AEW board,' I protested. 'And they're Oxford men!'

'But they're far from representative of the University as a whole, and Dr Harper is well aware of that.'

'The thing is, Non,' Annie butted in, 'we have to take care not to alienate men who *are* on our side. We can't afford to play into the hands of the men who maintain that too much education will make us unfit to be wives and mothers.'

'What about those of us who have no ambition to be a wife or mother?' I asked.

'If we don't promote education for *all* women, we promote it for *none*,' Mrs Green said, firmly, stepping out from behind my Cardigan shop counter and insisting on being an Oxford don's wife. 'The AEW cannot allow you to destroy everything we have worked for simply because you do not aspire to what most members of womankind see as their natural place.'

A woman's natural place. Hearth and home. The domestic sphere. The female realm. Phrases that confined us to a tiny, circumscribed life with the children begotten on us by the husbands our fathers had handed us over to at the altar.

I'd learned from Cranogwen to find that situation intolerable, and the thought of her and her determination not to follow a woman's prescribed way of life stiffened my backbone now.

'Was Mr Peacock the other person who complained?' I asked.

'I beg your pardon?'

'You said I had the distinction of having two complaints made against me on the same day.' The Popinjay must have gone whining to Dr Harper, mustn't he? How else would the Jesus College Principal know about our argument? 'Was Mr Peacock the other?'

'He was.'

'And what exactly did he complain of?'

Mrs Green glared at me, her back very straight.

'You'll have to tell her, Charlotte,' Annie said. 'Even in a court of law a woman has a right to know what she's accused of.'

Only Charlotte Green's eyes moved, the rest of her was as stiff as a board. 'Very well. His letter – copied to Dr Harper – accuses you of lewdness.'

'*Lewdness?*'

'Apparently,' Annie drawled, 'you lectured him on aspects of *Lysistrata* that he thought you should have found chastely baffling.' She grinned, and this time it was her proper, amused grin. 'Mr Peacock didn't appreciate that at all.'

No. What he hadn't appreciated was me getting the better of him. 'Am I not allowed to discuss Aristophanes in a lecture specifically about Greek drama?' I asked.

'Don't be disingenuous, Miss Vaughan.' Mrs Green was losing patience. 'You know perfectly well that you were goading this young man.'

I couldn't deny that. The trouble was, if a Cardigan shopkeeper's wife had seen me goading a pompous young man like Peacock, she'd probably have joined in. But Oxford wasn't like home.

'Miss Vaughan. Rhiannon. Mr Peacock has made it very clear that if we do not sanction you, he will take his complaint to the Hebdomadal Council. The AEW cannot allow that to happen.'

'So, you'll sacrifice me on the altar of his hurt pride?'

'We're not sacrificing anybody. The conditions under which you were allowed to attend lectures in college were made very clear and you have flagrantly ignored them.'

Yes, because the conditions were intolerable. 'What is it then, this *sanction*?'

Mrs Green took a forbearing breath, eyes on me as if she'd much rather have given me a slap. 'We've decided that you will not attend lectures – here or in any college – for the rest of this term.'

Could they do that? The AEW had no jurisdiction over who attended lectures in colleges: that was down to the handful that had begun to allow it. Still, it wouldn't be a good idea to fall out with Mrs Green and the rest of them.

'Very well,' I said. Then, because it seemed like a good idea to show a bit of contrition, I added. 'And I'm sorry to have caused the AEW embarrassment.'

'I trust you will restrain your impulses in future, Miss Vaughan. We're playing the long game here. And we will win, in the end.'

'Meanwhile, you'll need to write a letter of apology to Dr Harper,' Annie said.

It went totally against the grain, but I wanted to be allowed back into lectures next term. 'If that's what's necessary, yes.'

'It's not simply what's *necessary*, Miss Vaughan,' Mrs Green said. 'It's what's *appropriate*.'

'But I won't write to Peacock.'

'Indeed you will not. I shall write to him myself to tell him that suitable measures have been taken.' She rose to her feet. 'Now, let's invite Mrs Maddox in for tea and you can tell me all about Dr Benton Reckitt.'

Chapter 8

Basil

'You do understand, Dr Harper, that I'm very unlikely to be able to tell you, definitively, what killed this young man?' Dr Fielding said as Sidney Parker's erstwhile bedmaker, Gordon Trent, and his son, Fred, lifted Parker's body. Some degree of *rigor mortis* remained but Parker's limbs were now sufficiently mobile to strip him of his nightclothes. 'From what Mrs Trent has already told us it's likely that he had an infection which led to a sudden fever. But, not having seen him yesterday, it's very difficult to be sure.'

Prior to this examination, Fielding had insisted on speaking to Parker's landlady about the boy's demeanour in the days before his death. The information she'd given had added nothing to the snippets she'd let slip to the Principal and me: Parker had 'suffered dreadfully with his bowels as a general rule' and he'd been 'a bit under the weather' the previous day.

Dr Harper stood with Fielding in the doorway, while I hovered uncertainly at the bedside in case I could be of help to the Trents. And also, I must confess, from some sense of responsibility towards Parker during these most intimate rites.

While his father held Parker's body clear of the bed, Fred Trent raised the dead youth's arms sufficiently to remove his nightshirt, leaving him in his drawers.

Fielding motioned towards the almost naked body. 'I think we'd better have those off as well, please.'

I caught the look Trent shared with his son. And, to a certain extent, I agreed; I would have spared Parker that final indignity. But the boy was dead and beyond caring, and a thorough examination was necessary.

Fred lifted Parker's legs, raising his slim hips off the bed and, as Trent removed his stained drawers, manfully trying to include expelled faecal matter within them, I averted my eyes, focusing instead on Parker's torso.

The boy's ribs were clearly visible beneath his pale skin and his stomach was concave, but I found myself staring at the pronounced pads of fat beneath his nipples which looked almost like tiny breasts. The growths would not have been noticeable on a well-fleshed youth but on Parker's unhealthily thin frame they were rather prominent.

Abruptly, my attention was snatched away by an exclamation from Gordon Trent.

'What the shitten' hell is that?' Trent glanced up at me and started to apologise but I shook my head, my eyes on the object that had caused his outburst.

Around the boy's flaccid penis, just below the point at which it disappeared into his pubic hair, was a steel ring, its inner aspect armed with wickedly serrated teeth.

Chapter 9

Non

When we left the AEW offices, Lily and I cycled up St Giles to make our way to Professor Rhys's house on the Banbury Road.

Lily'd questioned whether I should be going to see the professor, now that I was temporarily off the AEW approved list. But, as I pointed out, this wasn't any of the AEW's business. I wasn't going to a lecture, nor setting foot on University property. My sessions with Professor Rhys were strictly between the two of us.

Strictly speaking, University fellows didn't *tutor* women because we weren't members of the University; no, what we were offered was *coaching*, usually given by undergraduates or would-be dons hanging around Oxford in the hopes of being elected to a fellowship. Not the likes of Professor Rhys.

But then, as I'd told Mrs Green, Professor Rhys was the reason I was here. I'd written to him after reading his book on the development of the Welsh language, and it was he who'd suggested that I should think of coming to Oxford.

But then my father's ship had gone down with all hands in an Irish Sea gale, and my mother and I had been thrown back on our own resources. That would've put an end to my ambitions if it hadn't been for our neighbour, Cranogwen, who'd known my family since before I was born.

We'd not gone far up St Giles when Lily turned in the saddle to look at me, as if she could feel my mood. Or, more likely, because she was worried I'd been quiet for too long.

'I'd say you were lucky there – with Mrs Green knowing of your Dr Reckitt.'

It was true. Mrs Green had been quite cordial over tea with Lily.

She wouldn't have been so friendly if she'd known I was thinking of writing to Dr Reckitt about Sidney Parker's sudden death.

I was troubled by thoughts of Mr Parker. When Lily'd told Basil about him coming for supper, I'd recalled him quite clearly. And what I'd thought of him at the time. Insipid. No conversation. And, compared to Billy and Albie, who played football every weekend, a poor physical specimen.

Lily'd been sharp with me after his visit, said I should've tried harder with him.

'*And so you should.*'

Hara. She'd been on Lily's side at the time, too.

'*I didn't want him to think I was leading him on.*'

'*Liar. You just didn't like him. You thought he was unintelligent.*'

'*He was.*'

'*That shouldn't have stopped you talking to him while he was sitting at your table. You've shown more interest in the poor man since he died than you did while he was alive.*'

'*Is it wrong to take an interest in seeing that his death is properly looked into? From what Basil's said, all this Dr Fielding's going to do is look at the body and say, "Oh look, he's dead".*'

'*It's nothing to do with you. That's not what you're here for.*'

Another voice wormed its way into my head then. Peacock the Popinjay: *It's pointless you being here. You'll never be able to do anything.*

Wrong. I was very *able*. I just wasn't *allowed*. I knew a lot about finding out how people had died from watching dissections with Dr Reckitt and listening to him talk to relatives. I was perfectly able to offer help. They just weren't going to let me.

'*Non, stop it.*'

'*Why? You think this is just vanity, don't you? Well, I'm thinking of Sidney Parker's family, too. I know what it's like not to know why somebody's died, don't I?*'

That shut her up. It was the one subject Hara would never speak about. Her own death.

I waited. But she'd gone. Fine. She could go if she liked. But she wasn't going to stop me doing whatever I could to find out more about why Sidney Parker had died. Somebody had to and it didn't look as if it was going to be this Dr Fielding. I knew Basil wanted to avoid a scandal but that wasn't the same as wanting to know how and why the boy had died, was it?

I waited for Hara to pipe up again but bringing up the subject of her death had chased her away.

Even when it was my fault, I always felt an aching emptiness when Hara disappeared, and I'd learned that the best thing to do was to stop listening for her and pay attention to what was around me.

I turned my head to one side and my eye was caught by the ridiculous, stripy brick of Keble College, a hundred yards or so away. Keble was Oxford's newest college and it divided opinion: half the population thought it was the ugliest building in the city and the other half thought it was a work of modern genius. To me it was just another college devoted to the education of sometimes quite stupid men, in this case men who were going into the Anglican ministry.

But Keble wasn't the only new building in this part of Oxford. The city was growing northwards at a tremendous rate, with grand new houses and residential streets going up all the time between the Banbury and Woodstock roads. University folk liked to say that all this building was happening for the benefit of the dons who'd moved out of the colleges when they'd finally been allowed to marry a handful of years ago, but according to Lily, the new streets had been going up long before that. There were plenty of prosperous Oxford tradesmen who were doing well out of all the railway traffic to Oxford and wanted nicer houses.

As we cycled on through a ragged patchwork of fields and market gardens, spanking new houses and building work, I wondered what changes the new horse tram would bring when it ran up here.

The first stage, from the station to the middle of town, and out to the working men's suburb on the Cowley Road, was set to open later in the year, and I knew there were plans to run the second stage up this road as soon as possible. The reason was easy to see. It was a long way into town for the servants of well-off people who lived in the grand new houses. Summertown, a village about a mile and a half out of Oxford also had shops but, whether you walked there or into the city, it was a fair step with shopping to carry. The whiskery old dons who barely stirred from their college rooms except to go to dinner with each other in their panelled halls would say it was the beginning of the end of Oxford, but for everybody else the tram would be a boon.

–

Mrs Rhys always insisted that we should stay for tea after my coaching sessions with the professor. Partly to sympathise with my arguments with Professor Rhys (today's was the relationship between Celtic folklore and the history of our people: he thought fairies represented our ancestors, I thought we'd just made them up) and partly because she wanted to know how women were being received at lectures. She was very interested to hear about my run-in with the AEW.

'Barred from lectures for a term,' I complained, '*and* I've got to write Dr Harper a grovelling letter of apology.'

Mrs Rhys put her teacup back onto its saucer with a very definite clink. 'Don't grovel, Rhiannon. It's not necessary. Just tell him that your natural reticence and sense of propriety was overcome by your wish to protect the reputation of the college.'

'You think Dr Harper will be more likely to forgive me if I show concern for the college?' Was that the way to get him to think about consulting Dr Reckitt?

Elspeth Rhys looked at me as if I was slow on the uptake. 'No, Rhiannon. I think he'll get the message you're sending and back down. By saying that you want to *protect the college's reputation*, you're implicitly telling him that if he carries on making trouble for you, you can spread a lot of gossip about what's happened. And he won't want that. Not at all.'

Mrs Rhys wasn't Dr Harper's biggest admirer, mainly because of his proposal to open Jesus College to English boys. I wondered whether she knew the part he'd played in opening college lectures to women. Probably not. Elspeth Rhys was a fair-minded woman and if she'd known, I think her attitude would've been different. But the Rhyses had only recently taken this house in Oxford. They were still spending a lot of their time in North Wales.

'Subtlety's never been Non's strong point,' Lily said, giving me a sly smile. 'She generally prefers the bull-at-a-gate approach.'

Lily might think that was funny but, where I'd grown up, *implying* things didn't get you very far. You had to make threats outright, in so many words, and be prepared to back them up, or you'd go under.

Elspeth Rhys smiled. 'Right, ladies, I must leave you. The girls and I have lessons at the gymnasium.'

'Mr McLaren's gymnasium?' I glanced at Lily. Basil had mentioned Sidney Parker being a regular at the gym, would she remember? Apparently not. If she had, I would've spotted the 'poor Mr Parker' look that came over her whenever his death was mentioned.

'Yes,' Elspeth said. 'Oxford has no other gym, as far as I'm aware.'

Keeping my eyes well away from Lily, I asked, 'Would you mind if I came with you?'

Whatever Basil thought, I was convinced that there would have to be a post-mortem examination. And, in my experience, the doctor carrying it out would appreciate any information I – via Basil, obviously – could give them about Mr Parker's habits and general fitness.

And who better to give me that information than his exercise instructor?

Chapter 10

Basil

'Well, well, well,' Dr Fielding said, approaching Parker's corpse, 'a spermatorrhoea ring. One has heard of them, of course, but I've never actually seen one deployed.'

The Principal's attention, however, was on Trent and his son who were staring at the toothed ring on Parker's penis. 'That will be all, gentlemen,' he said, apparently oblivious to the fact that he had no authority to dismiss Gordon Trent in his own house. 'And not a word to anybody about anything you have seen here, please.'

Mr Trent stood his ground. 'When are you having him moved, Dr Harper?'

'Moved?'

'To wherever he's going to be laid out. He can't stay here. It's not right. We're not family. He's not our responsibility.' I wondered whether Mrs Trent would agree but, as head of the family, the decision was Trent's to make. 'He can go to the Infirmary, can't he?'

All eyes turned to Dr Harper. Parker had been a member of Jesus College and, while his body remained in Oxford, Dr Harper and the fellows of Jesus were *in loco parentis*.

Fielding looked up from the body. 'If I may, I would advise against. The dead house at the Infirmary is not appropriate for viewings by next of kin. The place stinks with putrefaction,' he added, apparently assuming that Dr Harper's silence meant that he was yet to be persuaded. 'Bodies are literally left there to rot. Those that the medical students aren't given to mutilate, that is. Not only is it distasteful, it's insanitary. Porters who have to go to and from the place fall sick at the drop of a hat.'

The Principal frowned. 'Can you suggest anywhere more appropriate?'

'Far be it from me to teach you your job, Dr Harper,' the physician said, turning his attention back to Parker's corpse, 'but I would have thought that taking him back to college would be the most suitable course of action.'

The Principal blinked rapidly, clearly unable to come to a satisfactory decision. Gordon Trent and his son watched impassively, and I could see that, if we weren't careful, father and son would dine out on the fact that Jesus College's Principal had been flummoxed by the question of what to do with a dead body.

'A word in private, Principal?' Without waiting for his response, I ushered him out onto the small landing.

'We cannot afford to give Mr Parker's next of kin any cause for complaint,' I said, keeping my voice low. 'And, while we're waiting for them to visit, his body needs to lie somewhere cold. The old coach house might be suitable, as long as it's possible to clear a decent space.'

Harper weighed what I'd said. 'Very well. See to it when we get back.' And, having re-established his primacy by foisting the responsibility on to me, he strode back into Parker's room.

'If you want him laid out, properly, I can see to that, if you like,' Trent said, generous with his assistance now that his right to decide what bodies he did and did not accommodate had been established. 'My Betty knows a woman.'

'Yes. Please ask her to have that done.' Harper said.

'Thank you, Mr Trent,' I added, 'that would be most helpful.'

'Going rate?'

The question was directed at me, but Harper answered. 'Whatever we pay the laundry women.'

Though I found the equating of washing dirty linen and laying out the dead for burial faintly repugnant, Trent seemed to find Dr Harper's terms satisfactory, and he and Fred made to leave the room.

'Just one last thing, Mr Trent,' I said. 'The ring must be left where it is for the coroner's view.'

The bedmaker stared at me, his face expressionless. I could not tell whether he was surprised that I would allow such evidence of Parker's infirmity to be made public, or resentful at the possible implication that he might remove the spermatorrhoea ring for his own gain. Once more, I wondered where Parker's personal belongings were. Had Trent or his wife already removed anything of value from the room? Surely they would not be so blatant? I hoped Lily would feel able to raise the subject with Mrs Trent.

'And, by the same token, don't let the women dress him,' Dr Fielding said. 'The inquest jury will need to see the body naked.'

'Just as you like.' Trent motioned to his son, and they left.

Once they were gone, Harper crossed the small room to stand at Dr Fielding's side. They were an ill-matched pair: Harper tall and well-made, his grey hair swept back from a strong, somewhat immobile face; Fielding smaller and slighter, lacking the academic gown which provided the Principal with gravitas, his sober dark suit making him look more like a professional mourner than a doctor. Only his spectacles rescued him from insignificance, drawing attention to the shrewdness of his gaze.

'Kindly explain this object,' Dr Harper said, motioning to the spermatorrhoea ring.

'It's designed to prevent nocturnal emissions,' the doctor replied, his eyes on the offending article. 'When the penis becomes engorged in erection, the inner ring expands, allowing the teeth inside the outer ring to impinge on the penis, waking the sufferer.'

'Sufferer' seemed exactly the right word; the device sounded positively torturous.

'Had this young man complained to you of nocturnal emissions?' Harper asked.

'As I explained yesterday, he had consulted me only once, after a fall at the gymnasium. Besides, he may not have worn the ring only at night. Spermatorrhoea leads to involuntary emissions and loss of semen at any time of the day.'

Harper turned to me. 'Despite your instructions to Trent, don't you think it would be best if his guardian were spared the sight of such a thing?'

'Has he said he's coming to see the body?'

'I sent a telegram yesterday and received a reply from Mr Reardon this morning. He'll be in Oxford this afternoon.'

Fielding looked up. 'I agree with Mr Rice. The ring should remain *in situ* until the coroner and his jury have seen the body.'

Harper's look stopped just short of a glare. 'Did it contribute in any way to the boy's death?'

'No, but that is hardly—'

'If it did not contribute, then it is not relevant.'

Fielding's chin rose a fraction. 'That's not for us to decide.'

'What possible relevance *can* it have?'

'At the very least, it suggests a particular state of mind. This young man was concerned enough about involuntary emissions that he was prepared to endure pain, and possibly injury, to prevent them. Does that not suggest a certain desperation to you?'

'If you're suggesting that such desperation might have led to his taking his own life, doctor, I can only suggest that, had that been his intention, he would hardly have allowed himself to be found wearing that thing.'

What Dr Harper lacked in tact, he more than made up for in logical analysis and Fielding couldn't help but agree. 'Nevertheless,' he insisted, 'resorting to such a remedy speaks to his state of mind, and I think that should be recorded by the coroner.'

'To what end?'

'I'm not the coroner!' Fielding was losing patience. 'But I know that Dr Hussey doesn't appreciate the corpses for which he becomes responsible being tampered with.'

'Then it's fortunate that Dr Hussey will not preside.' Harper's tone was acerbic. 'Parker's inquest will be the responsibility of a University coroner.'

Fielding's mistake was quite understandable. As a medical practitioner, he would be very familiar with the borough coroner – whose inquests were reported weekly in the local press – while possibly having very little to do with either of the University's coroners, who were unlucky if they were called on to preside at more than a couple of inquests in a year. But the doctor was not to be cowed. 'I'm sure that the University coroners would adhere to standards equally as high as Dr Hussey's,' he said before turning his attention to Parker's body.

With the fire unlit, the room was cold, but I thought I detected a faint sheen of moisture on the corpse's exposed skin which made me glad that it was not I who would have to touch its clamminess.

Fielding, however, placed his hands fearlessly on Parker's head and turned it this way and that, feeling its rotation on the spine and running his fingers through the boy's disordered hair as he searched – I assumed – for wounds that might not have been visible.

'No contusions. No obvious disruption or disarticulation of the cervical vertebrae.' He bent to examine the boy's throat. 'No bruising to the neck.' Fielding put out a hand and pulled up one of Parker's eyelids. 'No petechial haemorrhaging.' He ran his hands down the boy's very visible ribs. 'No palpable evidence of fracture and no visible evidence of trauma or violence.' He pressed firmly several times on different parts of the boy's abdomen and, apart from an audible fart from the corpse which startled me into a snort of embarrassment, there was apparently nothing to report.

Turning Parker's body to look at the boy's back, Fielding reported nothing but what he would expect – evidence that the body had lain on its right side for some time after death, causing blood to pool in the tissues nearest the bed, marking them with what looked like livid bruises.

'I can find no evidence of violence,' the doctor told Harper, 'but that doesn't mean that this was a natural death. To be definitive, the possibility that he'd ingested some kind of poison must be ruled out. Besides,' he looked up at the Principal, 'there are these pectoral growths to be explained.' He pointed at the lumps of fat beneath Parker's nipples. 'Gynaecomastia.'

'Womanly breasts?' Harper might have taken his degree in mathematics but there was nothing wrong with his Latin. 'They're not breasts, surely? For one thing they're not big enough—'

'And for another, he's a man?' Fielding asked sardonically. 'I'm aware of that. The lower appendage gives it away, somewhat. But large enough to warrant the name or not, that's what this condition is called.'

'What causes it?'

'It's seen in newborn boys and youths at puberty,' Fielding said, doing what doctors always do when they lack a proper explanation and falling back on observation. 'And in men who drink a great deal of beer. But, as the torsos of habitual beer drinkers also often display a great deal of excess fat, gynaecomastia in those individuals may have a different aetiology.' He looked from Harper to me. 'Was this young man a habitual toper?'

'On the contrary,' I said, recalling what Mrs Trent had said, 'I believe he was a total abstainer.'

'How old was he?'

'Twenty.'

'Any evidence of late puberty – voice still in the process of breaking, for instance?'

'No. Nothing like that.'

Dr Harper was becoming impatient with what he clearly saw as an irrelevant, if not esoteric, discussion. 'You mentioned poisoning – surely there would be some visible indications of that?'

'There are sometimes physical signs after death,' Fielding said, 'but not always. It depends on the poison.' He stared at the Principal, his spectacles catching the weak light from the window. 'I would recommend a post-mortem dissection, but perhaps you'd prefer to let the coroner decide? I'll report this death when I get back into town. Mr Morrell's office is on my way.'

Chapter 11

Non

The Oxford gymnasium was a modern, two-storey building, and unlike most of the new buildings around the centre of town, it wasn't designed to look as if it had been there for hundreds of years. Instead of fake medieval turrets and pointed windows, it had large, round-headed windows that looked quite Roman. You almost expected to be able to peer through and see gladiators practising inside.

'The children's gym is here,' Elspeth said, as we got out of the cab in front of a single storey building which was attached to the larger gymnasium. I followed her in, curious to see what kind of exercises were offered to children as young as her two little daughters, and found myself in a large, airy room full of wooden equipment: leather-bodied items on four legs, four-inch beams set up between sets of steps, ropes dangling from the ceiling, a wooden frame fixed to one wall which was obviously for climbing and a net slung from another which reminded me of rigging. There were no floorboards. Instead, I had the strange sensation of my feet sinking into some soft, elastic material. I suppose it was meant to stop the little ones hurting themselves if they fell.

There were a few children already in the big room, and Olwen and Myfanwy ran over to them immediately. Elspeth smiled at the other mothers and guided me towards an athletic-looking young man in tights and a jersey. I'd told her what I wanted to do, and she'd agreed to help.

'Mr Thatcher, may I introduce Miss Rhiannon Vaughan,' she said. Lily wasn't there to introduce. She'd decided to push the tandem home alone, rather than accompany us into town. She claimed she had too much work to do but I think she just didn't want to get caught up in whatever I was up to. I suspected that she'd remembered where she'd heard about McLaren's gymnasium recently. But she couldn't very well warn me off getting involved in front of Elspeth Rhys.

Mr Thatcher and I exchanged the usual platitudes and Elspeth went off to join the other mothers. I watched her go, then turned again to face Mr Thatcher, and caught him smoothing his hair back. Did he blush? I didn't care either way but being embarrassed might make him a bit keener to oblige.

'Mr Thatcher, I wonder if you could help me?' I'd learned that from Lily. Don't come straight out and tell a man what you want, ask if he can help you, then he's already said yes before he knows what he's letting himself in for.

Mr Thatcher smiled. 'If I can, of course.'

'A young man of my acquaintance has just died very suddenly,' I said, trying to sound appropriately sombre. Just as well I'd worn quite a dark dress today: it would pass for mourning for a friend. 'And I know he used to come to the gymnasium often. I was hoping to speak to his instructor to break the news of his death. And to tell him how much Sidney benefited from his physical training here.'

Mr Thatcher glanced around at the mothers and children gathering for his class. 'Well, I—'

'I don't want to take up too much of your time, but if you *could* just take me next door and introduce me to somebody who might be able to help, I'd be *so* grateful.'

Lily would have called me a minx and wanted to know why I couldn't keep such a civil tongue in my head when I was telling the truth. Which wasn't a question I had an answer for.

'It wouldn't take more than a minute,' I begged, 'and I'm sure the ladies wouldn't mind if they knew you were helping me. I'll go and tell my friend, Professor Rhys's wife, shall I?' It never hurts to drop a professor's name into a conversation when you want something.

'No, I'll tell the ladies. You just wait there, Miss Vaughan, and I'll be with you in two ticks.'

-

The main gymnasium was impressive. Once you'd made your way in via a narrow passage and a porter's desk, the whole of the ground floor was one huge space. Everywhere I looked, there were bigger versions of the gymnastic equipment I'd seen in the children's wing, as well as rows of weights and dumbbells. What looked like a ship's mast rose up through a central atrium lit by a huge lantern window in the roof.

Mr Thatcher went over and spoke to a dark-haired young man dressed – just like Thatcher himself – in buff tights and a navy-blue sweater, then came back to me.

'Apparently, your friend was due at a class with our fencing master this morning and he was concerned when he didn't turn up.'

'Oh dear,' I said, 'Sidney wouldn't have wanted to inconvenience anybody. Would it be possible for me to have a few words with the fencing master do you think, Mr Thatcher?'

And soft boy that he was, Mr Thatcher nodded and led me upstairs.

Light from both the lantern in the roof and the large windows made the upper floor feel almost as if it was in the open air. One half of the room had the same kind of soft floor that I'd seen in the children's gym and the other half was boarded. 'That's Mr Henry over there,' Mr Thatcher said, nodding in the direction of a man in white tights and a padded jacket.

I thanked him and walked over to the sandy-haired, whip-thin fencing master. 'Mr Henry?' I put my hand out. 'Rhiannon Vaughan. I'm a friend of Sidney Parker's.'

He took my hand but, instead of shaking it, just pressed it limply. 'Ah, the absent Mr Parker. Has he sent you to apologise on his behalf?'

Interesting question. Had Sidney Parker been the kind of person who preferred not to do his own dirty work?

'No, I'm afraid I'm here with sad news.' I lowered my eyes. 'Sidney died, very suddenly, yesterday.'

His attitude turned on a sixpence. 'Oh, I'm so sorry. Did he have an accident?'

'No.' I kept my eyes down, as if I might be fighting back tears. 'He died in his sleep.'

'But he was just a young man!'

'Yes,' I gave him a quick glance. 'And he loved coming here. Said he felt so much better for it.' It seemed like a safe thing to say. If Sidney Parker hadn't felt better for it, why would he have kept paying to come? 'And I just wondered, did he seem different in any way, these last few weeks? I hadn't seen him since Christmas,' I said, making up the details of my supposed acquaintance with Mr Parker on the fly. 'Do you think his health was failing in any way? I'd hate to think we could have saved him if we'd known.'

Dr Reckitt was always very insistent on a 'case history' being taken when somebody died. How had they seemed in the weeks leading up to their death? Had they complained of pain, weakness or feeling ill? Had they been irritable or anxious? Had they changed their habits at all? I would like to have asked Mr Henry all those questions, but I didn't want to arouse his suspicions too much. Of course, he wouldn't have turned a hair if a man had asked.

Archie Peacock's sneering face appeared in my mind's eye, but I wasn't going to listen to him telling me I couldn't do anything. I was too busy doing something.

'Failing in what way, exactly?'

'I don't know.' I wrung my hands a bit. I'd never had much use for expressions of helpless dejection, but I did my best. 'His death was just such a shock... I wondered if you'd noticed anything. You being an expert in physical fitness, I mean. Was his fencing improving as he'd hoped?' Again, I felt that I was on safe ground; anybody taking lessons must be wanting to improve, and I hoped the question would make the fencing master believe that Sidney Parker had shared his innermost desires and ambitions with me.

'Well, he wasn't my *best* pupil,' Mr Henry said, cautiously. 'But he worked hard.'

In other words, he'd been talentless and hadn't known when to give up.

'Had he not made as much progress as his friends in the class?'

Mr Henry looked away. 'The other young men... They'd nearly all learned fencing at school...'

The other young men. I'd referred to Sidney's *friends*, but Mr Henry's response suggested that the other fencers in Sidney's class hadn't had much time for him. Like the other undergraduates at Jesus if his moving out of college was anything to go by. I'd never heard of a student doing that unless he'd been 'rusticated'.

'Please tell me they didn't laugh at him!'

'No, of course not. I wouldn't let that happen in my class. We're all swordsmen here. Equals.'

But he couldn't look me in the eye. Maybe he'd like to believe that he treated everybody equally, but when the majority have money and the one being looked down on doesn't, it takes a man of very firm character to be even-handed. And Mr Henry didn't strike me as that man.

A shout came from the other, padded-floor side of the gym where two men were wrestling. One had just been thrown onto his back and his opponent held out a hand to pull him up, grinning. As I watched them laughing, I thought of the fights I'd seen on Cardigan docks. The sudden, animal violence of a real fight was about as much like this playfighting as a marlinspike was like a butterknife. Oxford undergraduates played at things which men in the real world did in earnest: swordsmanship, fighting, climbing. The gownsmen at the gym were here to work muscles made flabby by intellectual work, something most of them also played at. It was hard not to despise them and their padded floors.

I carried on staring past Mr Henry as if I couldn't bear to meet his eye. 'Perhaps they despised his piety,' I said. Lily'd talked about his parish work, maybe that had made him unpopular with his more worldly peers?

'Oh no, I don't think it was that,' the fencing master said. Then he looked uncomfortable when he realised that he'd as good as admitted that they despised him for something.

'Did he seem happy, these last weeks?' That was the kind of question somebody who might be – or might have wanted to be – Sidney's sweetheart would ask, wasn't it?

Mr Henry gave an awkward half-shrug. 'To be honest, Miss Vaughan, he just seemed much as he always had.'

'He wasn't happy, then?'

'But he wasn't sad either. You knew Sidney. He wasn't the hail-fellow-well-met type, was he? He was a grafter. He just set himself a challenge and bashed away at it.'

His words brought a Welsh proverb to mind. *Dyfal donc a dyr y garreg.* Many blows will break the rock. Which was fine for a mason but didn't suggest the sharpness that Oxford preferred in its young men.

'He had exams coming up,' I said. 'Perhaps he was worried about those?'

'Yes, perhaps,' the fencing master nodded. But he couldn't meet my eye.

'Sidney's wasn't an easy life,' I confided without actually giving anything away. 'But you don't think he was unwell at all?'

It was on the tip of my tongue to ask whether Mr Henry had ever heard Sidney talking about taking medicine. Basil had mentioned to me, out of earshot of the rest of the family, that he'd found proprietary medicine bottles in Sidney Parker's nightstand, including one that was unlabelled. His Dr Fielding hadn't known anything about Sidney Parker taking quack remedies, but I knew Basil was worried that the boy might have dosed himself too liberally with something he didn't understand. But as the words 'I know he was taking some tonics' lined themselves up on my tongue, I realised that mentioning Mr Parker's little bottles to Mr Henry might give rise to rumours that I wouldn't want traced back to me.

The fencing master looked quizzically at me. Perhaps I was asking too many questions.

'It's just that he boarded with us before going to college,' I improvised. What could be more likely than the daughter of the house becoming attached to a prospective undergraduate, even if he hadn't been very impressive, poor dab? 'And I begged him to come back and stay with us over Christmas – he seemed so thin. I'd feel awful if I thought he'd still be alive if I'd convinced him to come back to us.'

'He was a slim young man, it's true. But that wasn't new. I never knew him to have much flesh on his bones.'

I nodded, slowly, my eyes on the floor. Casting my mind back to his one visit to Lily's house, Sidney Parker hadn't just been thin, he'd been weak-looking, not an ounce of muscle on him. 'I'm glad you don't think there was anything we could have done.'

'Sometimes, it is just a person's time. Ours not to reason why, and all that.'

That line of Tennyson's was always getting misquoted, and I wondered how he'd feel about a boy's sad and unexplained death in University-approved lodgings being put on a par with the senseless slaughter at the battle of Balaclava.

But misquoting poetry was one thing, not looking hard enough into a sudden death was another. As far as I was concerned, it was very much our responsibility to reason why. The dead deserved justice, for their death not just to be tidied away neatly and never spoken about.

I might not have been the friend Sidney Parker needed while he was alive, but it seemed to me that I might be exactly the friend he needed now he was dead.

Chapter 12

Basil

'Parker's guardian is due at four o'clock,' Dr Harper said as we parted ways on our return from Kingston Road. 'Be so good as to meet him in the lodge, will you, and show him up to the lodgings.'

Much though I resented being treated like a glorified servant, having the Principal in my debt, even if only morally, might yet prove to be prudent, so I resigned myself to being party to an uncomfortable encounter.

-

I knew very little about George Reardon beyond the fact that, as a distant cousin of Parker's father, he was the young man's legal guardian until he came of age.

'Does Mr Reardon also live in South Wales?' I had asked Parker when the subject had been raised, knowing that the boy had been a boarder at Cowbridge Grammar School.

'No. He lives in Berkshire. Reading. At any rate, that's where his letters come from.'

'You've never been there?' I was surprised; the college's communications with Cowbridge had indicated that Parker had been this man's ward for several years before coming up to Oxford.

'No.'

I recalled, now, that Parker had been disinclined to meet my eye while we were discussing his guardian, staring, instead, at my bookcases where classical texts jostled with journals of Celtic studies, collections of medieval Welsh poetry and theological tomes. (My father had encouraged me to think of a career in the church and remained baffled by my decision to study what he referred to as 'an assortment of moribund languages'.)

'George Reardon's never shown the remotest interest in me,' Parker had said. 'He always made sure that I stayed at school during the holidays. While I was at Cowbridge, I saw him precisely once, when he came to tell me my mother was dead and that he'd be looking after my interests from then on.'

'And has he?' I asked, slightly unnerved by the latent hostility in Parker's tone. 'Has he looked after your interests?'

'I suppose somebody got me my place here.'

I found it sad that Parker did not know the fond esteem in which he had been held at Cowbridge Grammar School, an esteem that had secured him a scholarship at Jesus. Cowbridge school had been linked with the college since its foundation. In fact, Dr Harper had been headmaster there as a young man. The current headmaster had written to Harper asking whether some assistance might be offered to a promising young student who did not have the means to take up the place at Oxford that he merited.

Unfortunately, fondness seemed to have blunted the headmaster's critical faculties. When Parker arrived, it became clear that the lily of his academic prowess had been gilded rather liberally. However, not wishing to sour relations with a school that was in a position to furnish Jesus with exactly the kind of bright young Welshman the college had been founded to educate, Dr Harper had chosen not to complain of the headmaster's unmerited recommendation. I wondered, now, whether Parker had felt embarrassed by the way in which his poor academic performance might reflect on his *alma mater*.

As I waited at the lodge for Mr Reardon, later that afternoon, I contemplated Harper's likely approach to the man. The Principal would, I suspected, re-write Parker's career at Jesus for his guardian's benefit, partly to conceal the fact that the college had been sold a pup, but mainly to persuade Mr Reardon not to enquire too deeply into Parker's mood in recent months. On our way back to college from the boy's Kingston Road lodgings, I had been forced to confess that Parker had been a little... disheartened of late.

I was aware that there were many outside the University sphere who denigrated intellectual work as not fit to be compared with more practical learning – how to make furniture or balance accounts for instance. But struggling academically is hard work. And if the struggler knows, in his heart of hearts, that he's not up to the task, it's harder still. I had hesitated to say as much to Dr Harper, but it would have been a miracle if Parker had scraped through his mods. Instead of coming back into residence, I had feared that, when the boy quit the Trents' house, it would be to leave Oxford altogether.

Only now did it occur to me to wonder why Parker's guardian had not queried his removal to Kingston Road. It would, after all, have involved him in rental expense that Parker's scholarship-funded rooms in college had not. Perhaps, unfamiliar with university life, Mr Reardon had simply not realised that Parker's removal was unusual.

'I'd have brought your visitor up to the Principal's lodgings, Mr Rice,' the college porter said, slightly affronted by the sight of me hovering outside the lodge.

'I know you would, Frank. But this isn't an ordinary kind of visit, is it?' I dipped my head and motioned to the black ribbons attached to the top of my academic cap.

Dr Harper wanted to give George Reardon as little reason as possible to consider himself or his late ward slighted. With Jesus attracting only half the number of undergraduates that flocked to colleges like Balliol or Brasenose each year, reputation mattered; especially as the Principal was committed to recruiting the brightest and best from England, in future, as well as Wales.

'Ah, o'course. Right you are, Mr Rice.' Allen nodded and winked.

The weak January sun had already disappeared from First Quad, and I drew my gown closer about me in the thin little wind that blew through the wicket gate. I turned my back on its chill and looked into the gravelled expanse of the quadrangle. Jesus College had been my home all my adult life and it was hard not to feel defensive on its behalf as I waited for Sidney Parker's guardian.

'Mr Rice?'

I turned at Frank's interrogative tone to see a man stepping over the threshold into college.

I approached him. 'Mr Reardon?'

'Yes.'

I introduced myself and we shook hands. 'The Principal has asked me to show you to his lodgings.'

Reardon nodded and fell into step with me. His coat was well-cut and might have passed for mourning black in the growing dusk. He also sported a black ribbon on his narrow-brimmed silk hat. I noticed that he didn't look about him, just kept his eyes forward and his shoulders back.

'I was Mr Parker's tutor,' I said, hoping to put him at ease, 'we met weekly, so I knew him reasonably well.'

He glanced at me. 'Shame you didn't look after him better then.'

His words were so unexpected that I felt as if I'd been struck, and could think of no suitable reply. Reardon, however, didn't wait for a response. 'I've not come here to listen to excuses, Mr Rice. I'll see my ward's body and then we'll discuss what's to be done.'

–

Dr Harper was waiting for us in the first-floor drawing room. The room looked very splendid and appropriately Jacobean in the lamplit dusk with its oak panelling and plasterwork ceiling, and Dr Harper had donned full academic dress, the scarlet facings of his gown glowing in the lamplight. In contrast, Reardon's coat – now clearly a dark bottle-green rather than black – seemed down-at-heel.

At first, I thought Reardon might refuse to shake the Principal's proffered hand but, after a second's hesitation, he put out his own.

'May I offer my deepest condolences, Mr Reardon,' the Principal began.

'It's a shame you didn't offer them in your telegram,' Reardon spat. '*Regret to inform you of sudden death of your ward* is a shocking message to receive with no warning.'

Had Dr Harper really been so parsimonious in his telegram as to deliver the news in such stark terms? Reardon's combative manner suddenly seemed more understandable.

'Mr Reardon, please do take a seat—'

'I'd prefer to stand, thank you. I'm not here for a convivial drink, I'm here to see poor Sidney's body. But first, I'd like you to tell me how my cousin has come to die so suddenly. When I went to his digs – that's another thing, you could've mentioned that his body was here, I went all the way up to the Kingston Road – his landlady said he hadn't had a doctor to him. Do you call that appropriate care for your students?'

Dr Harper's chin went up. 'I beg your pardon?'

Fearing that any discussion of Sidney's time in the house on Kingston Road could only end badly, I stepped in. 'If I may, Principal?' I asked. Harper glared at me, then flicked a hand, granting me permission to speak.

It seemed to me that perhaps Reardon was one of those people who, when intimidated, go on the attack. And an Oxford college is nothing if not intimidating to the uninitiated, especially in the presence of a head of house who has chosen to greet you in all his pomp. Added to which, Reardon had been presented with news of his ward's death in the starkest terms and provided with no information about where the body lay. He might well have persuaded himself that both he and Sidney were being treated with little respect.

'As far as we knew, Mr Reardon,' I said, 'there was nothing wrong with Sidney. I met with him weekly, and he'd never complained of ill health. If he had, we would have insisted that he see Dr Fielding who has looked after our undergraduates for many years. I assure you we take our duties to our students very seriously.'

'Then how has he ended up dead?'

It occurred to me that Reardon's belligerence might result from a feeling of guilt that he himself had not done more for Sidney while he was alive.

'I'm afraid we don't know,' I admitted, hoping that a little humility might mollify him. 'But a seizure of the heart or some kind of stroke to the brain seems the most likely.'

'*Seems the most likely?* Are you trying to tell me that he hasn't been seen by anybody qualified to say?'

'Of course he has!' Dr Harper flared. 'Mrs Trent must have informed you that Dr Fielding could find no evidence of anything but a natural death.'

'And that's it, is it?' Reardon demanded. 'Nothing more to be done? A young chap dies with absolutely no warning, and you all throw up your hands and declare it a sad tragedy that couldn't have been avoided?'

Dr Harper stood his ground. 'There was nothing to suggest otherwise.'

'Which is very convenient for you, isn't it? You didn't even have him here, where you could see if he was unwell.' Reardon's head was thrust forward, his slight frame tense. Still in the overcoat which he had refused to relinquish, he cut a slightly sad figure in the drawing room, and pity for him urged me to intervene. I had been on the receiving end of Dr Harper's intransigence and, Reardon's own hostility notwithstanding, I felt I should prevent the coals of antagonism being heaped on the ashes of bereavement if I could.

'Perhaps,' I said, 'this might be the moment to take Mr Reardon to see his cousin's body, Principal?'

'Yes. By all means.'

As Dr Harper saw us out of the drawing room, it became apparent that he didn't intend to come with us. 'I trust you'll take some refreshment with me once you have paid your respects, Mr Reardon?'

Reardon looked at him with hard eyes but did not reply. Instead, he turned to me. 'Let's go.'

As I led him downstairs, he said, 'I hear Oxford has no decent mortuary.'

Yet again we were found wanting, even if only by association on this occasion. 'I'm afraid not. It's a situation the borough coroner is keen to remedy.' The Oxford papers had been gleefully publishing Dr Hussey's letters to that effect ever since he came into office. 'But, at present, the dead house at the Infirmary is used as a dissection room for students, so we didn't feel it would be appropriate to have your cousin's body left there.'

'It's a charnel house, according to Mrs Trent.'

I winced at the thought of Gordon Trent relaying all Dr Fielding's comments on the Infirmary's dead house to his wife, ready to be passed on to Reardon.

'So where is he, then?' Reardon demanded.

I found myself unable to articulate the sentence 'he's in our old coach house,' so I simply said, 'Come this way, please.'

Dr Harper's butler, Potter, led us out through the back of the Principal's lodgings to the coach yard. Once upon a time, Jesus College's head of house had kept a carriage and pair, but these days hackney cabs and railway trains met any needs Dr Harper might have, and neither the coach house nor the adjoining stables had been in use as long as I had been a fellow.

In preparation for the arrival of Parker's body, I'd given instructions that the coach house should be thoroughly swept and sluiced out. To my relief, I saw that whoever had carried out my instructions had also hung clean sheeting from the beams to hide whatever was stored in the dusty gloom beyond. The drapery gave the place a welcome air of sanctuary and, in a well-judged gesture, candles had been brought from the chapel and were burning quietly at Parker's head and feet on the linen-draped trestle table.

I watched Reardon take in his surroundings. 'Please excuse our rather rudimentary attempt at a mortuary chapel, but we thought it was important to bring Sidney home from his lodgings to college. Of course, if you'd prefer to have his body removed to Reading, we could notify the coroner…'

'No need for that. I can see you've done your best to be respectful.' Reardon didn't go so far as to smile but he became somewhat less hostile.

'Sidney was an active member of his parish church,' I said, as if I knew this from conversations with Parker himself, rather than from Lily Maddox. 'I'm sure the vicar there would be honoured to conduct his funeral.'

Reardon seized on this suggestion with an alacrity which made me suspect that he'd been unsure how Oxford would expect Sidney's obsequies to be managed. 'Yes. I'm sure that's what he would've wanted. If you could point me in the right direction, I'll visit the vicar this evening and put things in motion. I have pressing business in London, and I must be away from Oxford first thing in the morning.'

I nodded, and Reardon stepped up to the body. There was no suggestion of tenderness or grief as he gazed at his dead ward's exposed face, he simply looked at the boy in the manner of a man gazing at a statue which he has been told is very fine but which he finds he cannot admire.

'He was coming into business with me, after he'd got his degree,' he said, abruptly. 'He was looking forward to it, getting out into the real world.'

Given how much Mr Parker had struggled with his studies, I did not doubt the latter statement, but I doubted very much that he had been looking forward to working with his guardian. Nothing in the exchanges we had had about Mr Reardon had suggested that Sidney had planned a future at his side.

'What line of business are you in, Mr Reardon?'

Reardon did not take his eyes off the linen-draped corpse. 'I own an advertising agency.'

Then, without warning, he grabbed the sheet that covered Parker's body and yanked it back so violently that it billowed up and fell in a disorderly heap at the foot of the makeshift bier.

'You didn't see fit to dress him decently?' Reardon's outrage reasserted itself at the sight of the boy's nakedness.

'The coroner and jury will need to see him, so we thought it best…'

Reardon turned back to the body. 'He's skin and bone! Don't you feed your students? And what in God's name is that?' he asked, pointing to the spermatorrhoea ring.

I explained, using Dr Fielding's clinical phraseology.

'Spermatorrhoea? That's the disease advertisements in the paper are always going on about. *Are you listless, lacking in vital energy, are your eyes dull and your chest sunken?* All that?'

'Indeed.'

'That about describes him, wouldn't you say?' Reardon waved a finger along the length of Sidney Parker's stick-thin torso. 'Except…' He stepped forward to peer at the corpse's chest, and the candle standing at Parker's head flickered with his sudden movement. 'Why has he grown tits?'

I was taken aback by the crudeness of the word. Reardon didn't strike me as uneducated.

'He has a condition called gynaecomastia,' I said.

'And what's that?'

'It's a condition in which men develop breast tissue.'

'Obviously. But *why*? How did he get it?'

I tried to recall what Dr Fielding had said but, as far as I could remember, he had provided no explanation. 'I'm afraid I don't know.'

'Is that what killed him?'

'I don't believe so, no.'

Reardon turned to stare once more at his ward's chest. 'This… condition, does it mean he was one of those inverts?'

One of those inverts. I swallowed. 'Not as far as I'm aware.'

'Good, because I don't want anybody saying anything like that about him now he's dead. Sidney was a normal boy.'

'Nobody has claimed otherwise, Mr Reardon,' I said, though his vehemence made me wonder whether, in fact, somebody had called

Parker's sexual habits into question. I felt a sudden panic that Harper might have thought that was why I had agreed to coach the boy, and why I had fought his case to be allowed to live in lodgings.

'Right. Now I've seen him, I've got something to clear up with Principal Harper,' Reardon said. 'I'll make my own way back and you can make him decent again. I want to speak to Harper alone.'

Chapter 13

Non

I was glad I didn't have far to walk to the Cipher Club because the dusk was getting damp and foggy. The shop windows along Walton Street were lit up like little theatre stages and the fog made the streetlights look as if they had halos around them. But it wasn't the weather I was thinking about as I walked. No, my mind was on Mr Sidney Parker and the little bottles in his nightstand. Something I'd seen outside the Oxford gymnasium earlier had made me think that Basil was right: those little bottles needed more looking into.

As I'd come out of the main gym to go back into the children's wing to speak to Elspeth Rhys, I'd passed a man leaning against the wall on the other side of the narrow lane. His eyes were closed as if he was lounging in the heat of the summer sun, which struck me as an odd thing to do in the dankness of a January day. He was quite well-dressed, almost dandified, but there was something about his face that made me think he hadn't grown up in finery. Even with his eyes closed, his face was hard, as if he could never relax. And then there was his bowler hat. Not what your nobs wear.

I heard the gym door swing shut and glanced over my shoulder. A young man in cap and gown was hurrying up to Bowler Hat whose eyes were open now. Neither of them took any notice of me.

They obviously knew one another because they exchanged that wordless greeting men give each other. You know, the small upward tilt of the head and a bit of eyebrow movement? It looked as if their meeting had been pre-arranged because the youth took something out of his pocket, gave it to Bowler Hat and received something in return. Something small enough to be slipped from Bowler Hat's jacket pocket into the youth's hand without me seeing more than a glimpse. And that was it. The whole transaction.

As I opened the door to the children's wing, the youth hurried past me in the direction of Oriel Square without so much as a glance. It was as if he thought I wouldn't notice him if he didn't make eye contact. But I had very much noticed him and his little exchange and, all the way home, I'd tried to decide whether what I'd seen him take from Bowler Hat might have been a small brown bottle like the ones Basil had described in Sidney Parker's nightstand. The ones labelled Dr Aurum's Tonic.

-

The Cipher Club had come into being years ago, when I had written to Mr Lewis Carroll after reading an article in a bundle of old children's magazines my father had bought for tuppence.

The article had described something called the Alphabet Cipher. I'd never come across the notion of ciphers before but, after playing with the Alphabet Cipher until I understood exactly how it worked, I'd tried to find a way to break it, without any success. So, I'd written to the author, care of the magazine's publishers.

Now, knowing how important and busy Rev Dodgson was, I was amazed that he'd taken the time to write back to a twelve-year-old girl but, at the time, I didn't know how important he was, so I'd carried on writing to him. And he'd carried on replying.

Is there a way of breaking the code? I'd asked in my first letter.

When I wrote that article, two or three years ago, he'd replied, *I thought not. But I have since learned that a Prussian army officer, Friedrich Kasiski, has written a book proposing a very clever way of going about finding a solution to such a cipher.*

Where might I obtain a copy of Herr Kasiski's book? I'd asked in my next letter. *I have started learning German and find it quite fascinating.*

All right, I was showing off. But I wanted him to know that I was quite capable of learning a language well enough to read a book about ciphers.

I'd received an answer a fortnight later in the form of the book itself. Inside, Mr Carroll, as I still thought of him then, had written: *You're a better scholar than me, Miss Vaughan! Good luck with your German.*

It had taken me almost as long to master Kasiski's method as it had to learn enough German to read it and I had to run the method many times before I finally felt I understood it.

Meanwhile, I realised that Lewis Carroll wasn't Rev Dodgson's real name when he sent me his first published book on geometry after I'd told him that I was studying navigation under Miss Sarah Jane Rees, while she trained my mother as an assistant instructor.

I'm finding it easier than any of the boys, I told him, *because I've already studied algebra and geometry.*

A Syllabus of Plane Geometry arrived in the post with his next letter. *This*, Rev Dodgson told me, *is what I teach my mathematics students, here at Christ Church.*

When I'd finished that, he followed it with *The Fifth Book of Euclid Treated Algebraically* and, later, *Euclid and His Modern Rivals* which wasn't a maths book but a kind of Greek drama where Euclid disputed with modern mathematicians.

And, meanwhile, we continued to correspond on the subject of ciphers. He sent me his Telegram Cipher, which he'd proposed to the government to make the sending of telegrams safer, and challenged me to make up my own.

We have formed our own little club, you and I, he said in a letter a couple of years after we'd first started corresponding. *The Cipher Club.*

When I'd written to tell him that I was coming up to Oxford with the intention of attending the Lectures for Ladies, he'd invited Lily and me to tea in his palatial suite of rooms at Christ Church College.

Once he'd sat down (which took about twenty minutes because he strode about the room while he was making the tea, waving the pot about as he talked) and the pair of us got going, Lily'd been so bored by all our talk of mathematics and ciphers that she refused ever to come again. Instead, Rev Dodgson had suggested that we form a proper club with meetings that we could invite others to.

And so, the Oxford Cipher Club was established at Jericho House – which most locals just called The Jericho – a public house less than five minutes' walk from where we lived in Shene Road. Rev Dodgson had decided that we should meet there so that I wouldn't be put to any inconvenience, but also to make it clear to anybody who heard of our meetings that the Cipher Club wasn't officially connected to the University.

'They'd have a fit if they thought a University club was meeting in a public house,' he said, with the wicked glint in his eye that, by now, I'd come to know very well.

That afternoon, I walked into The Jericho, nodded to John Higgins behind the bar, and pointed upwards to the room where our little club met. He nodded back and smiled. It wasn't often that he had a celebrity on the premises and letting it be known that Lewis Carroll was a regular visitor did his business no harm at all.

I was looking forward to the first Cipher Club meeting of the year. Who would Rev Dodgson have invited along this time? Besides the two of us, there was only one other consistent member of the club, a bespectacled, sandy-haired young man called Wilton who was one of Rev Dodgson's tutees. Others had come and gone, but so far there hadn't been anybody else who really shared our enthusiasm for inventing and solving ciphers.

I found Rev Dodgson and Mr Wilton in the small, private room that Dodgson had taken to calling our 'club room'. The fire had been going for some time from the thick warmth that greeted me as I walked in, and our coffee was already on the table, the tall drip-pots wrapped in towels to keep them hot. I smiled at Rev Dodgson and Mr Wilton, before taking my coat off and hanging it behind the door with theirs.

'I like the way you've had your hair cut,' a voice said, from the corner.

I touched my cropped curls and smiled at thirteen-year-old Eva Simkins, who was sitting, lamp at her side, reading a book. John Higgins and Rev Dodgson had agreed that it would never do for me to be the only female in the room, so John asked Eva, his neighbour's daughter, to sit in with us at our meetings. With two hours uninterrupted reading time, the Cipher Club was the highlight of any given week for Eva, and Rev Dodgson had started bringing books for her. Last term she'd got through Anthony Trollope's latest, *Cousin Henry*.

'As it's a new term,' Rev Dodgson said as I sat myself down at the table, 'I've invited a couple of new members to try out. It'll be interesting to see whether their facility for logic extends to an enthusiasm for ciphers.'

'They're mathematicians, then?' Mr Wilton asked.

'I don't necessarily say they're mathematicians as you and I are, Mr Wilton. They are yet to take their mods and decide on a final honours school, but they show some promise.'

Rev Dodgson was just enquiring about my Christmas – which my mother had spent with us at Lily's house – when we heard voices on the stairs. As their owners came along the corridor to the club room, their words carried through the not-very-well-fitting panel door.

'I'm telling you, I was there when the Principal came for Rice. All very cloak and dagger. And that was it. Lecture cancelled.'

'You're not saying Rice had something to do with the death?'

'No, you heard the bedmaker... natural death.'

'So why the cloak and dagger?'

The voices were outside the door now and I could almost see them collecting themselves and sobering up their facial expressions before coming in. Wouldn't do for the famous Rev Dodgson to hear them gossiping.

But what they didn't know about Charles Dodgson was that, though he was discretion itself when it came to anything to do with his own college, he loved to know what was going on in the rest of the University.

The door opened behind me, and Dodgson smiled. 'Do come in, gentlemen. Welcome to the Cipher Club.'

I didn't turn to see them, just waited for them to hang their coats up and join us at the table. And, when they did, I got a nasty surprise.

Peacock the Popinjay had just walked in.

Chapter 14

Basil

Once I'd escorted Reardon back to the Principal's lodgings, I returned to my rooms and waited to be summoned. Though he would have denied it, there was clearly a part of Dr Harper that believed that, as Parker's tutor, I should have foreseen his impending death and taken steps to prevent it; I had no doubt that he would want to make me listen to details of his conversation with Reardon.

I tried, unsuccessfully, to settle to something productive but found myself springing up from my desk every few minutes to light a lamp or close the shutters or tend to the perfectly established fire. Eventually, Carvel, a servant at the lodgings knocked. 'Principal would be very grateful if you'd step over to see him, Mr Rice.'

Darkness had fallen now and, in the thickening fog, lamplight from the occasional unshuttered window was almost as bright as the lamp Carvel held.

I didn't ask what kind of mood the Principal had been in when he summoned me. It would have made Carvel feel awkward, and besides, I didn't really want to know. I preferred to nurture the illusion that I might be wrong, that Dr Harper's conversation with Reardon might have been conciliatory after his unpromising start with the gentleman.

But just as I'd feared, that illusion evaporated as soon as I entered the drawing room.

'Blackmail!' Harper cried, when I asked what Reardon had wanted to 'clear up' with him. 'The fellow is trying to blackmail the college.'

I wasn't quite sure how to respond. I'd expected to hear of discourtesy and bluster from Reardon – possibly an insistence on the college footing the funeral bill – but blackmail? Was it possible that Dr Harper was over-reacting?

'He claims that we failed in our duty towards Parker – that we should never have allowed him to move out of college – and that he died as a result.' The Principal seemed hurt as well as shocked, and well he might. He had been a headmaster for thirty years before taking up his current position at Jesus, and his attitude towards his charges, here as at his schools, encompassed solicitude as well as paternalism. When one of our freshmen had contracted diphtheria the previous year, the lad had been taken into the Principal's lodgings and nursed by Mrs Harper, under her husband's constant supervision.

I recalled, now, Harper's opposition to Parker's being allowed to move out of college. Indeed, he had only acquiesced to the will of the governing body when I had insisted that, in my opinion as the boy's tutor, two terms' non-residence was essential both to his studies and his wellbeing.

Had Dr Harper been right in suggesting that my decision might, in some way, have contributed to the boy's demise?

'He further claims,' the Principal went on, 'that he invested significant sums in the boy's education, to fit him to be a partner in his business. To – as he so pungently put it – "shoulder some of the load". Now that the load will no longer be shared, he feels that the college should compensate him.'

Unreasonable, yes, opportunistic, certainly. But did Reardon's demand really amount to blackmail?

'And, if the college declines?' I asked, making the decision a collective one. In this room, which had seen three centuries of college politics, such an implication of communal responsibility seemed reasonable, though I was sure that news of Reardon's ultimatum would not be shared beyond the lodgings, that the decision would be taken by Harper alone. The Principal could not allow any suggestions of weakness in his position as his opponents on the governing body would seize any excuse to frustrate his plans for the college. Which raised a pressing question: why was he telling me?

'If we don't furnish him with the outrageous sum which he claims to have laid out in school fees, recent board and lodging and general upkeep of his ward, he has threatened to write a letter to the Oxford papers and the Hebdomadal Council, accusing the college of negligence and blaming us for the boy's death. Not only that but he will stand up at the inquest and let his feelings be known which – as we both know – would be quoted verbatim by the press.'

My earlier sympathy for Reardon, my willingness to see him as a man intimidated by the grandeur of the college and upset at his ward's death, now seemed naïve. Foolish even.

Humiliated, I concentrated my thoughts on Harper's fury. I knew perfectly well why he was so agitated. Charges of negligence would help neither his own plans, nor the reputation of the college.

He'd been appointed principal because of his extraordinary capacity to change the fortunes of failing academic institutions. He'd done so at Cowbridge Grammar School where, in just three years, he had increased the roll from twelve to eighty pupils, thirty of whom he had taken to his next post at Sherborne School. During his twenty-seven years there, he had overseen the transformation of the place, hugely expanding the school's premises and increasing the student roll seven-fold. Jesus College, dogged by an increasingly ill-deserved, early-century reputation for poor academic performance, had appointed him to change its fortunes.

What the fellowship had not anticipated, however, was that Harper would bring his expansionist zeal to bear by enacting one of the recommendations of a much-contested Royal Commission into the work of the University and attempting to remove Jesus's historic identity as 'the Welsh college'.

Accusations of negligence on the part of the college would give those opposed to Harper's reforms a stick to beat him with, and recent events in Oxford wouldn't help. The previous winter, two undergraduates had died in separate incidents while skating on frozen lakes. The authorities in both cases – the University Parks, and Blenheim Palace in Woodstock – had been much criticised, both at the inquests into the young men's deaths, and subsequently in the press. A cavalier attitude to public safety had been identified and condemned as unworthy of such august institutions.

Dr Harper would wish, at all costs, to avoid similar criticisms being levelled at Jesus College. And, implicitly, at him.

'What answer did you give him?' I asked.

'That I would consider the matter.'

'To which he responded…?'

'That he would expect a telegram from me no later than tomorrow evening.'

'Just in time to denounce us at the inquest if we don't comply, I suppose?'

Fielding had put the wheels in motion earlier in the day by informing the coroner of Parker's death, and inquests were generally conducted with as little delay as possible.

'Actually,' Harper drew a fortifying breath, 'Reardon intends to see Morrell this evening and ask him to postpone the inquest until next week. Apparently, he has to return to London first thing in the morning to attend to urgent business.'

The Principal's eyes glittered with suppressed rage in the candlelight. 'This man cannot be allowed to call into question the good name of the college, or our care for our undergraduates. The matter of Parker's death must be clarified beyond all doubt, and any vestige of blame removed from Jesus.'

He levelled his gaze at me. 'If he is called upon as medical witness, Dr Fielding would give it as his opinion that the boy died of natural causes. Whereupon, no doubt, Reardon would claim this as a biased opinion from a doctor long associated with the college. We *must* be in a position to state categorically what did, and did not, cause Mr Parker's death. This delay gives us the chance to present the inquest with a more informed and expert opinion. Only that will silence Reardon.'

I hesitated, unsure what the Principal expected of me. 'You'll ask the coroner to order a post-mortem examination, then?'

'Yes. But it must be carefully handled. This is a University inquest. The animosity between some of the medical men at the Infirmary and the University can't be ignored.'

As the Radcliffe Infirmary's treasurer, Dr Harper would be aware of just how infuriating the University's persistent refusal to establish a proper medical school was to some of the senior medical staff. An Infirmary doctor conducting a post-mortem on Mr Parker would be unlikely to feel the need to spare the college's blushes when it came to outlining details of Parker's breast tissue and spermatorrhoea ring.

But perhaps there was an alternative. Non's forensic specialist sprang to mind. However, I needed to be careful not to refer to him in any way that would remind Dr Harper of his encounter with her.

'Perhaps,' I suggested, 'we could find a specialist in post-mortem examinations who might be sympathetic to our cause? A well-respected physician with Welsh connections…'

Harper actually recoiled; the reaction was only slight, he wasn't a man given to extravagant gestures, but the feelings generated by my tentative suggestion were obvious. 'You can't possibly mean the doctor Miss Vaughan tried to foist on us? What are you thinking of, Rice? If you're going to have your head turned by a pretty face, perhaps I should reconsider my decision to admit women to your lectures.'

I stared at him, two opposing reactions fighting for dominance. On the one hand, resentment at his absolute control over who was admitted to hear me speak; on the other, relief that he believed me capable of having my head turned by a young woman's prettiness.

'No,' Harper ploughed on. 'The doctor to whom we must appeal is obvious. You must use your influence with Edmund Pritchard.'

Teddy! He'd laugh like a fool at the thought of Harper dragging him into this conundrum. Teddy loved to bait the Principal and see how long it was before Dr Harper realised that he was being deliberately provoked. But Harper's reference to my 'influence' worried me. Just what had he observed when he saw Teddy and me together?

'He's a Jesus man,' Harper went on, 'and he sits down at dinner in hall more often than some of the college fellows. He wouldn't allow our reputation to suffer.' He paused for a moment. 'Nor would he, I'm sure, wish to see you pilloried for your support of the boy's move to the lodgings where he died.'

I felt a growing alarm. The Principal's implication was obvious: if I valued my good name and my career, I would recruit Teddy Pritchard to the college's cause.

'But there's the matter of his suitability, Principal,' I protested. 'If Dr Pritchard carries out the examination, Reardon could accuse him of bias. Dr Hussey has a nominated surgeon who performs any dissections necessary for inquests. Surely he's the obvious candidate?'

'This is a University inquest, Rice. It's only fitting that we should have one of our own conducting the medical investigations.'

I swallowed a rising apprehension. The truth was, I was no longer sure of my influence with Teddy. He seemed to have withdrawn from me in the past few weeks and, unusually, I hadn't seen him for more than ten days.

'I see your point, of course, Principal. But Mr Morrell might feel the need to instruct somebody with more expertise.'

'Pritchard's eminence is beyond doubt. Besides, given his forthcoming move, recruiting him would mean that there wouldn't be the usual issue of loyalty towards colleagues to contend with.'

Forthcoming move? 'I'm sorry, Principal, I don't—'

'Well, I suppose there might be a little awkwardness as Dr Pritchard is still currently working at the Infirmary, but the doctors there can have no particular sway over him now he's heading for London.'

I felt as if I'd been punched in the solar plexus. I seemed to have lost the ability to breathe. Evidently, my reaction was obvious to Harper.

'Ah, I do beg your pardon, Rice. I assumed you would have been the first to know.'

Even the implications of that sentence could not disturb me more than the thought that Teddy had decided to leave Oxford without even raising it as a possibility with me.

'Well,' the Principal said, visibly hiding his embarrassment, 'you must go and see Morrell, Rice. Arrange things with him. We *must* avoid any kind of scandal.'

I was relieved of the need to respond by a knock at the door. Potter entered with a small tray. 'Telegram for you, Dr Harper.'

'A little late in the day, isn't it?'

As Harper picked up the telegram, Potter shot a glance at me. Did he blame me for the Principal's irritability or was he simply seeking a friendly face? I gave him a weak smile; it would do duty for either eventuality. Besides, it was all I could manage.

Having moved closer to one of the wall sconces to read the telegram, Dr Harper looked up. 'No answer at this time, Potter.'

The butler inclined his head and departed.

'It's from Cowbridge School,' Harper said when the door had closed. 'Given his enthusiastic recommendation of Parker for a scholarship I thought the headmaster would want to know of his death.'

I cleared my constricted throat. 'What does it say?'

Harper held the paper out to me. 'You may read it for yourself.'

I took the telegram and moved towards the lamp on the mantlepiece.

> WILL ARRIVE TOMORROW WITH INFORMATION, MEANWHILE BEWARE PARKER'S GUARDIAN.

The headmaster, Morris Price Williams, had simply signed himself MPW.

Beware Parker's guardian.

Reardon appeared in my mind's eye. This telegram, along with his attempt at blackmail, made the man's pugilistic attitude seem less like self-defence and more like a genuine threat.

What kind of information had Morris Williams felt unable to commit to a letter?

Chapter 15

Non

'You!' Peacock looked about as pleased to see me as I was to see him.

Rev Dodgson beamed. 'Yes, I believe you're already acquainted.'

I turned to ask what he meant, then realised that it was obvious. Peacock must have had a tutorial or a lecture with Rev Dodgson after our encounter at Jesus College and complained about me. Complaining seemed to be a hobby for him.

'However, I don't think you saw each other to best advantage when you met,' Rev Dodgson went on. 'And it seemed to me we might usefully remedy that.'

I glared at him. As far as I was concerned, I knew everything about the Popinjay Peacock that I'd ever want to know.

'But first,' he said, 'I gather from your conversation on the other side of the door, Mr Peacock, Mr Askew, that you have information about the death of the poor young chap from Jesus?'

Peacock and his companion – a marginally less vapid-looking specimen – sat down and Peacock ran his fingers through his blond hair where it'd been flattened by the rim of his hat. Like Rev Dodgson and Mr Wilton, neither Peacock nor his friend were wearing academic dress. We were in a public house, after all, where undergraduates weren't technically supposed to go. Except that they all did, of course.

'It's the talk of the saloon bar,' Peacock said, not at all embarrassed that we'd been able to hear his braying. 'Apparently the dead chap used to lodge nearby. Seems his landlord's a bedmaker at Jesus. Name of Trent.'

'Indeed?'

'Cove downstairs introduced him to us,' he said, as Rev Dodgson poured coffee and Mr Wilton slipped from the table to put more coal on the fire.

The Popinjay sounded different when he was speaking to Rev Dodgson. No drawling sneer, now.

'*So don't provoke him, then maybe he won't sneer at you either.*'

'*Don't be stupid, Hara, of course he will. He thinks I've got no right to be here.*'

'*Think of what Mrs Green would say.*'

I knew exactly what Mrs Green would say. But I wasn't Mrs Green.

'And what did you learn from Mr Trent, pray?' Rev Dodgson asked.

'Delegation came up from Jesus today with a medical chap in tow. The Jesus men wanted the doctor to say it was natural causes, but he wasn't having it, apparently.'

Wasn't having it? Why did the upper classes think it was amusing to copy the way working people spoke? It just made them sound ridiculous.

'*It doesn't hurt anybody.*'

'*Well, Hara, it offends me.*'

'*Everything he does offends you.*'

'Does the doctor suspect foul play?'

'Foul play might be a bit strong but, according to Mr Trent, the doctor was keen on the body going back to Jesus so the coroner could examine it there, but the Jesus men just wanted him taken off to the dead house with no questions asked.'

I was outraged on Basil's behalf. He would never try to hide something suspicious. I drew breath to say as much.

'*Don't. This one loves to flap his lips and if he thinks you and Basil are better acquainted than lecturer and student, he'll make something out of it.*'

'And what, pray, made the good doctor suspicious?' Dodgson wanted to know.

'In present company,' Peacock said, not even bothering to look at me, 'shall we just say that there were anomalies which the doctor thought the coroner should see.'

I knew all about those *anomalies*. When Lily'd gone to Betty Trent to offer help, she'd arrived just as the body was being washed and laid out. When he died, Sidney Parker'd been wearing a spiked ring around his pizzle and, according to Lily, had the breast buds of a twelve-year-old girl. But I didn't say anything. Wouldn't want to set the Popinjay off with his complaints again.

'Mr Trent implied that Jesus might try to hush things up,' Peacock's companion, Askew, finally joined the conversation. 'But I expect that was probably just an attempt to spice things up in the bar.'

'Whatever Trent thinks,' Peacock said, 'there'll be no chance of hushing things up at the inquest. The fact that Parker wasn't entirely normal will soon be common knowledge.' He glanced at me with a sly half-grin. 'Very embarrassing for Jesus College.'

Not entirely normal. That accusation had been flung at me so often I'd come to hate the word.

It's not normal, a girl on board ship.

A girl wearing trousers – that's not right, not normal.

You're not normal, Non Vaughan, with all your big words and big ideas.

What normal girl wants to study at university?

'*Non.*' Hara was trying to be stern. '*Don't.*'

But I couldn't let Peacock go unchallenged.

'Not entirely *normal*?' I asked. 'Isn't that just what people who have no imagination say about people who think differently from them?'

Peacock glanced at me then away. 'This is nothing to do with *thinking*, Miss—'

'Vaughan.' The primped fathead couldn't even retain a simple name. 'No,' I said. 'It's to do with something male and embarrassing, isn't it? Just as embarrassing as you found my talking about *Lysistrata*, yesterday.'

His chin went up at that. Under his brocaded waistcoat and paisley silk tie, he was no different from the lads on my father's ship; just another youth who didn't like being put in his place by a girl. 'That wasn't simply *embarrassing*, Miss Vaughan. I found your parading of certain knowledge shocking.'

'Yes, so shocking that you went straight back to your rooms and wrote a letter of complaint about me!' I turned to Rev Dodgson, furious that he'd engineered this meeting. 'Did you know that Mr Peacock had written to the AEW complaining that I had the audacity to discuss Aristophanes with him in a lecture about Greek drama? A lecture series I had decided to go to, I might add, in order to discuss the dramatic form of *Euclid and His Modern Rivals* with *you*.'

Caught between the Scylla of me discussing the Athenian women's withdrawal of sexual favours and the Charybdis of my interest in his work, Charles Dodgson had no idea which way to steer.

'I didn't know that… no,' he said. The hesitancy which always slowed his speech when he was uncomfortable told me how much he regretted inviting Peacock here. I decided to spill some wind from my sails.

'As it happens, no irreparable harm has been done.' I hoped that was true, at any rate. 'But the resulting conversation with Mrs Green was not the most pleasant half an hour I've ever spent.'

Dodgson turned to the Popinjay. 'Why did you feel it necessary to complain of Miss Vaughan's conduct, Mr Peacock?'

Peacock hesitated.

'*Non…*' Hara knew I was thinking about repeating the question.

'It's one thing to have ladies at lectures,' Peacock whined. 'But it's another thing entirely when they attack a man as soon as he walks through the door and demand to know whether he's read such and such a play or not.'

I wasn't going to put up with that, whatever Hara thought. 'As I recall, it was *you* who addressed *me* first. Me *and* my chaperone, Mrs Maddox. If I remember correctly,' – and I definitely did – 'you suggested that we'd "wandered into the wrong building" and that we should "scurry off to wherever we were expected for tea and gossip".'

'That was very uncivil of you, Mr Peacock,' Rev Dodgson said.

'Surely, sir, you don't support this ludicrous notion of ladies being allowed to attend lectures in college?'

'Steady on, Peacock!' Mr Askew intervened. 'You may not appreciate ladies in lectures but to call it a ludicrous notion is insulting.'

I saw him glance at me, but my attention was on Eva Simkins. She'd abandoned *Cousin Henry*'s successor and was enjoying the argument. It wasn't often that she got to see the quality bickering amongst themselves.

'Whether I support it or not,' Rev Dodgson said, 'I hope I wouldn't stoop to incivility. When one is in a superior social position, Mr Peacock, it behoves one to behave with impeccable manners to those who do not enjoy one's privileges.'

'But what's the *point* of their being here?' Peacock persisted. 'They have no place in the professions, or parliament. What's the use of a university education to them? What will they do with the knowledge they've gained?'

'We will *use* it, Mr Peacock,' I said, cutting across Mr Askew, who was looking at Peacock as if he'd turned into a toad.

Peacock turned to me. '*Use* it? How? To what ends? To make your husbands feel inferior?'

Hah! Yes. That was men's *real* objection to us being here, wasn't it? That we might turn out to be better at it than them.

'Perhaps,' Rev Dodgson suggested, 'we might move on to see what use Miss Vaughan can make of her very acute intelligence in the solution of ciphers?'

But he was much too late. He should have poured that particular oil on the troubled waters between Peacock and me five minutes ago. 'I'm sorry, Rev Dodgson, but I believe Mr Peacock and I are too much at odds to be discussing something as esoteric as ciphers.'

Mr Wilton suddenly found his voice. He'd been watching our argument with the kind of worried expression that suggested he'd been brought up in a home where nobody ever raised their voice above a whisper. 'But ciphers *aren't* esoteric. The Crimean War might have gone very differently if Charles Babbage hadn't found a way of deciphering Russian communiqués. What could be more practical than that?'

I sighed. Charles Babbage. Yet another man. What about Ada Lovelace, who'd collaborated with him?

'The Crimean War notwithstanding,' Peacock said, 'on this solitary occasion, I find myself in agreement with Miss Vaughan. We are too much at odds to be diverted by each other's company. Will you forgive me, sir, if I take my leave? I feel it would be best.'

Askew stood, too. 'Rev Dodson,' he tilted his head in a respectful half-bow. 'Mr Wilton.' He bowed slightly lower. 'Miss Vaughan.'

As they left, Charles Dodgson looked as crestfallen as I'd ever seen him. Perhaps he could see, now, how foolish it'd been to think that he could make friends of Peacock and me just by getting us to pit our wits against each other.

I pushed my chair back, ready to leave, but Rev Dodgson tried to persuade me to stay. 'Perhaps we might discuss *Euclid and His Modern Rivals* instead?'

I shook my head. 'Not tonight, if you don't mind.'

He sighed. 'Very well. But will you come and take luncheon with me on Saturday? You and Mrs Maddox?'

'I'd be delighted and I'm sure Mrs Maddox would, too.' I had to resist the urge to cross my fingers behind my back at telling such a blatant lie on Lily's behalf.

'Excellent,' Rev Dodgson brightened. 'Shall we say midday?'

I smiled and agreed to the time but, as soon as I was out of the door, the smile dropped off my face and I caught myself grinding my teeth.

I'd show Peacock – and the rest of them – what *use* a woman could put her intelligence to.

Illustration of a spermatorrhoea ring, 1915 surgical catalogue.

Chapter 16

Basil

On Thursday morning, I was woken from a fitful sleep by the quiet arrival of Hollins, the bedmaker who served my staircase, with coal and hot water. From my bed, I listened to him moving around my sitting room while rowers raced across the quad, calling to each other as they hared down to the river for an early morning outing, and a door thudded as somebody rose to take breakfast in hall.

I could never face the kind of desultory, half-resentful conversations that tended to take place at this hour so, once I heard my outer door close, I retrieved the jug of hot water Hollins had left outside my bedroom door and glanced over at the fire he'd lit. In twenty minutes or so it would be hot enough to boil a kettle for coffee.

Putting the steaming water jug on my washstand, I opened the shutters. The sun had not yet risen, and everything was cold and grey. That suited my mood, perfectly.

Having made use of the chamber pot, instead of putting on my dressing gown and setting about shaving, I got back into bed, pulled up the still-warm bedclothes and curled on my side. For the hundredth, lacerating time, the previous evening's conversation with Teddy played itself out in my mind.

Despite my reservations, he'd been enthusiastic about conducting a post-mortem examination on Parker's body.

'What larks!' He'd grinned. 'A post-mortem in the college coach house. Much nicer than the cutting room at the Infirmary.'

I'd gazed at him, baffled as always by his enthusiasm for dissecting his fellow human beings. After fifteen years, I was none the wiser as to the origin of my feelings for this man: he was as different from me as it was possible for two men from a similar background to be. Teddy had no interest in art or literature or the finer things of life. He was almost entirely occupied with physicality: sport, surgery, sex.

'You *will* bear in mind that this is a delicate case.'

'Yes, yes, understood.' He looked up at my pained silence. 'I heard you, Bas. The college mustn't be embarrassed.'

'But obviously, we want the truth...'

'And if the truth is embarrassing?' Teddy shared Non Vaughan's discomfiting tendency to ask awkward questions.

'Then we must try and make sure it's known only to those who need to know. Legally I mean.'

'Are you telling me not to gossip, Mr Rice?' He grinned.

Teddy was far more gregarious than I and, sometimes, in his cups he was less than discreet which could, frankly, be terrifying. He always dismissed my pleas for discretion with the confidence that all would be forgiven a young man racketing about town. But, at thirty-three, we were no longer young, and any licence granted to youthful high spirits had expired long ago. These days, we were held to a more sober standard, and should some of the things we got up to in London be generally known, both my place as an academic and Teddy's as a surgeon would be lost in an instant. We'd be lucky to stay out of gaol.

However, I knew there was no point arguing with him. He would swear black was white rather than admit he might be wrong; and he'd get most of the people listening to agree with him.

'Can you come to college and do it tomorrow?' I asked. I was very aware that Parker had now been dead two days and had no idea how much his body might deteriorate if the post-mortem examination was left any longer.

Teddy reached for his wine glass. 'You'll have to clear it with the coroner. Normally it's he who commissions post-mortems.'

'Of course.' I had already planned to visit Morrell.

'But I can't do it tomorrow, no. Or Friday. My time's already spoken for. Can't cry off or I'll be in bad odour.' He took a mouthful of wine, looking over the rim of his glass at me. 'Not that I particularly need to be in good odour at the moment.' He looked away. Was he, finally, going to tell me his plans?

'Why?'

He drained his glass. 'Because my references are in. Done. No need to be a good boy any more.'

My heart began to beat painfully fast. 'You're taking up a new position? Where?' I wasn't going to let him off the hook by telling him I already knew.

Finally, he looked me in the eye. 'King's. London.'

Had I been hoping that Harper was wrong, that he'd got hold of the wrong end of the stick? Apparently, I had, because as soon as Teddy said the words, a cold pain gripped at my stomach.

'Has to be done, Bas,' he said, matter-of-factly. 'I've waited long enough. Longer than I should, actually. It's clear they've no intention of setting up a proper medical school, here. Even for the purely academic stuff, the University's in the Dark Ages. Without even so much as separate departments for anatomy and physiology we're never going to attract the most talented men.'

'I thought you were happy here. At the Infirmary.'

His eyes moved away again. 'Up to a point. I enjoy surgery and the other doctors are decent chaps. Most of them. But it's not *going* anywhere, Bas. It's eighteen eighty-one. I'll still have years of life and work in me when the *twentieth century* dawns. I want to be part of modern medicine, not stuck here where everything's calcified.'

I stared at him, sprawled on my sofa. Teddy was like a lion; if he wasn't in motion, he lazed as if resting his muscles thoroughly for the next bout of activity.

'I'll never get a better offer than the one Lister's made me,' he said. 'You know how much I admire him.'

Am I not a better offer? Asking that question was inconceivable. As far as Teddy was concerned, we were fast friends and no more. But his having gone so far as to negotiate a position with Joseph Lister without having once mentioned his plans cut me to the quick.

As if he'd read my mind, he sighed. 'I didn't want to tell you until it was definite. But we always knew this day was coming, Bas. I was never going to make old bones in Oxford, and it's time to admit that I can't be a young rogue about town for ever. Time to become respectable. Find a wife.'

I hadn't been able to look at him, then. That acceptance was the sticking point: I'd long since resigned myself to being *one of nature's bachelors* but Teddy had always been clear that, one day, he would want a family.

Pushing him from my mind, I flung the bedclothes aside and swung myself out of bed, the floorboards' coldness beneath my bare feet a welcome distraction. Pouring the still-warm water into my bowl, I plunged my face into it as if, in submerging myself up to my ears, I could unhear the things we'd said and wash last night away; wash away the years Teddy and I had spent together. Years that had meant entirely different things to the two of us.

My mind filled with memories, images, sensations, until I felt a terrible urge to open my mouth under the water and breathe. I jerked my face from the bowl, water cascading down my neck and chest.

I sucked in air, shocked at the impulse that had gripped me. In my heart of hearts, I'd always known the truth, and Teddy's move to London proved it. He would never feel as I did. I had been deluding myself, allowing hope to overrule reason.

But if hope was gone, I must preserve what remained. Without Teddy, my position at Jesus was all I had, and in the anguished and wakeful watches of the night, I had decided that I must do anything I could to prevent the college's name becoming a byword either for neglect or deviance. Teddy's testimony would not be enough. An inquest verdict that Parker had died of natural causes would not stop the gossips if Reardon carried out his threat and accused us of negligence. That kind of accusation was liable to be picked up by the national press and the public – which included prospective undergraduates and their parents – might well decide that Jesus College was not a reputable institution. It would be the ruin of us. And, as Parker's tutor, the end of my career.

I'd already lost Teddy. I couldn't lose Oxford as well.

It seemed to me that it shouldn't be too difficult to show that our duty of care had not been neglected, Parker's living with the Trents notwithstanding. I had noticed no change in him at my weekly meetings with him, and Mrs Trent had already told Dr Fielding that she hadn't thought him anything more than a little under the weather with his usual bowel complaint. There must be others, who knew him well, who could tell the inquest that his health had given no real cause for concern. It might not be proof against gossip about spermatorrhoea rings and breast buds, but a consensus as to Sidney Parker's health might clear Jesus – and me – of the charge of neglecting our undergraduates' health.

The obvious person to speak to was his parish priest at St Barnabas. According to Lily Maddox, Parker had been a devoted member of the congregation; the vicar would know him if anybody did.

But, first, I had to persuade the University Coroner to order a post-mortem examination.

Chapter 17

Non

On the morning after the Cipher Club meeting, a very unexpected letter arrived just as I was making plans to set out for the Bodleian Library. (I might have been excluded from lectures, but nobody'd said anything about access to the University's library being rescinded. And I wasn't going to ask.)

When I picked the letter up from the doormat, I could see from the address – a simple 'Miss Vaughan' – that it had been hand delivered. My pulse started racing. Had this come, via the Jesus College messenger, from Dr Harper? Or the AEW? Had somebody seen me at the gym with Mr Henry and raised an objection? Or could Peacock have complained about me again after the meeting last night?

I stood in the narrow hallway, my hands shaking as I opened the envelope.

I unfolded the letter and, before reading a word, my eyes went straight to the signature at the bottom.

The breath that'd been stopped up in my nervous chest came out in a rush. Not Dr D. H. Harper. Nor any of the AEW women. But, with my heart racing, I couldn't place the name: Tarley Askew?

The letter was headed simply *Corpus Christi College, Wednesday 19th Jan.*

> *Dear Miss Vaughan*
>
> *You may not recognise the name at the foot of this letter, but we met this evening at the Cipher Club.*

Ah. The Popinjay's slightly less annoying companion.

I would like to say two things, and I hope my arriving at the Jericho at the same time as Archie Peacock will not deter you from reading on.

Firstly, I would like to say that I was mortified to hear that Peacock had been such a pompous idiot as to complain about you to the Lectures for Ladies committee. Though I wasn't at the lecture in question, I very much suspect – as you probably do, too – that it wasn't the subject matter of your comments that Peacock objected to but the fact that you knew more than he did.

Please, do not judge all of us undergraduates by his measure. Some of us are delighted to see ladies being admitted to lectures.

Secondly, I hope you won't be offended if I tell you how much I admired the way in which you dealt with both Peacock and Rev Dodgson. Your courage, resolve and plain speaking made me want to cheer! I hope it's not uncomplimentary to say that you remind me very much of my mother who is the woman I admire most in the world.

Miss Vaughan, should you ever stand in need of a friend, I would consider it the greatest honour if you would call on me. I can be contacted at my college on any day during term time and, should you request it, I would be honoured to provide my home address.

Your friend, if you will allow it,
Tarley Askew.

PS: Lest you worry that I have followed you to your home, I have left this with Mr Higgins at Jericho House. He has promised to see it delivered.

To say I was surprised by Mr Askew's letter would be like saying that the Virgin Mary must have been a bit taken aback by the Annunciation.

Men occasionally made unsolicited comments about the acceptability of my physical appearance – though not, I'd noticed, since I'd had my hair cut – but none had ever complimented me on my courage, resolve or plain speaking. And certainly, never by letter.

I have to admit, it was slightly gratifying.

My first thought was to write back, thanking Mr Askew for his compliments but saying that I was already well provided for in the friend department. I wasn't looking for a follower, so I shouldn't encourage him.

'*Don't be stupid, Non! And don't push away the first man to offer you any support. He'll think the nay-sayers are right and female students are all man-haters.*'

Hara had a point.

'*And anyway, you're not "well provided for" where friends are concerned, are you?*'

'*All right, have it your way. I'll write back and say I'll be his little friend.*'

It was hard to imagine what Hara would look like if she rolled her eyes. She'd look just like me, of course, but try as I might with a mirror, I couldn't see what I looked like when I rolled my eyes. It just wasn't physically possible.

So, I ignored her and asked myself what kind of gesture I could make to show Tarley Askew that I accepted his invitation at face value, but wasn't encouraging him to look for anything more intimate?

The Rev Dodgson had mentioned that the two new candidates for the Cipher Club had shown promise in logic. Perhaps that was the line to take.

As I put my coat and scarf on, I composed a letter in my head to see how the idea sounded.

> *Dear Mr Askew*
>
> *How kind of you to write.*
>
> *I find that a person can never have too many friends of honourable intent and I'm gratified that you should offer yourself in that capacity.*
>
> *Following Peacock's complaint, I am unable to attend Rev Dodgson's lectures on symbolic logic this term which I had very much been looking forward to. Always assuming that you plan to attend those lectures yourself, I wonder if you'd be kind enough to share your notes with me?*
>
> *Yours sincerely,*
>
> *Rhiannon Vaughan.*

Yes, that would do.

Just then, Lily came downstairs with a tray full of lamp glasses. She didn't trust Edie to wash them.

'Where are you off to?'

'To the library. But if you want me for something?' I needed to get back in Lily's good books because she was cross with me for accepting Rev Dodgson's invitation to lunch on Saturday. Mind, I wasn't sure how she thought I could've refused without being rude.

'Will you come with me to talk to the girl Sidney Parker was walking out with?'

'He had a sweetheart?' I remembered the way I'd allowed Mr Henry at the gymnasium to think I might be Sidney Parker's girl and felt guilty. I wouldn't have done that if I'd known.

'Yes, Betty Trent told me. A girl from church. Florence Spellman.' Lily rested the bottom of the tray on top of the newel post. 'I asked Betty if she was going to go and see her, tell her about Sidney, but she said she didn't have time, and Florrie'd have to wait till Sunday. But that doesn't seem fair, does it, hearing the news with everybody else when he was special to her? And, goodness knows, I don't want her to hear of it in gossip on the street.'

Considering the kind of gossip it was likely to be after what Peacock and Tarley Askew had heard in The Jericho, I agreed with her. 'When were you thinking of going?'

'After I've done the lamps.'

'All right then – I've got a letter to write so I'll do that now. Let me know when you're ready and I'll come with you.'

'Thank you, Non. It's just, if Florence has questions, you'll be able to answer them better than me.'

I didn't know about that. But, after pretending to be Sidney's girl, I owed it to Florence Spellman to do what I could for her, didn't I? Besides, if the Jesus College men weren't going to ask for proper forensic help, then somebody had to make sure that the right witnesses were called at the inquest. And if anybody'd have information on Sidney Parker's state of mind – and body – in the days before he died, it'd be his sweetheart.

Chapter 18

Basil

After shaving, I couldn't wait for the fire to boil my kettle for coffee. If I wasn't in motion, thoughts of the previous evening's conversation with Teddy filled my mind. *We always knew this day was coming, Bas.* He had always accepted this day's inevitability; I had stubbornly refused. If the world now felt out of kilter, it was no one's fault but my own, and that knowledge heightened the intense loneliness created by even the briefest contemplation of the future.

The coffee cart on Ship Street provided breakfast en-route to the coroner. I stood amongst the porters and traders of the covered market, drinking coffee laced with chicory, eating slices of 'thin' – bread and butter – and trying to ignore the fact that my academic gown had begun to attract curious glances. It was still very little after eight and townspeople weren't used to seeing dons abroad at such an hour, still less at a coffee cart.

Feeling somewhat exposed, it occurred to me that perhaps I might pay my visit to Mr Morrell sooner rather than later. In fact, it might be less inconvenient for him if I called to see him at home rather than disturb him at work.

Not much more than five minutes' brisk walk later, I presented myself at Morrell's residence, Black Hall, on the northern end of St Giles Street. I asked his butler to apologise on my behalf for appearing so early in the day and begged a few moments of his time.

Left in the hall while the man went on his errand, I looked about. The house was old but impressive and, as its name suggested, had once been a residential hall for scholars. The small, mullioned windows and unfashionably low ceilings were from another era, but it had been decorated and furnished with great care.

Frederick Morrell was making his mark in Oxford. He had succeeded his father as steward of St John's and, as well as being University Coroner, was Solicitor to the University, Registrar to the Vice-chancellor's court, and clerk to the local and school boards.

Very soon after the butler's disappearance, Morrell himself trotted down the staircase into the hall, hand extended. 'Mr Rice, good morning. I assume, since you're here to speak to me in my official capacity, that our subject is the unfortunate Mr Parker?'

'Indeed.'

'Do come into my study. We'll be more comfortable there.'

Morrell's study was decorated in a style not unlike that of the Harpers' drawing room, with carved panelling and a moulded ceiling. But there the resemblance ended. Whereas Dr and Mrs Harper's taste tended to the traditional, Morrell clearly favoured modern furniture and his study was arranged so that he could sit in well-lit splendour at the large desk that looked out on the garden.

'Please,' he said, indicating one of the wing-backed chesterfields that stood on either side of the fireplace, 'do sit. May I offer you a drink? Tea, coffee?'

'Thank you, no. I really won't keep you long, Mr Morrell. I'm simply here on behalf of Jesus College to consult with you about the inquest.'

The coroner sat opposite me. Behind him, framed by the study window, trees thrust their branches up into the morning fog, searching for the sun that would fatten buds and defy the damp dreariness of January.

'Yes,' Morrell said, 'in the normal run of things I would have had it all done and dusted by the end of today, but I assume you know that Mr Reardon has asked me to delay proceedings?'

I nodded. 'Do you know why he made such a request?'

'I understand he had urgent business which made it impossible for him to be in Oxford again until next week. But as he felt very strongly that it was his duty to be present at the inquest, I agreed to the hearing next Wednesday.'

Which gave us five days' grace. For the first time since I had gazed down at poor Parker's body on Tuesday morning, I felt that perhaps Jesus College was not simply being dragged along in the wake of events.

'Mr Morrell,' I began, 'as Dr Fielding didn't feel able to say, definitively, that Mr Parker died from natural causes, Dr Harper has asked me to consult with you about the possibility of a full post-mortem examination being carried out. Or perhaps,' I added, suddenly realising that my errand might be construed as telling the coroner his own job, 'you have already commissioned one?'

Morrell frowned. 'As a matter of fact, I've been very much in two minds on that subject. Whilst a post-mortem examination *might* clarify the cause of death, Mr Reardon was very loath to think of his ward's body being dissected.'

I hesitated. How honest should I be with him? 'Can we speak confidentially, Mr Morrell?'

The coroner smiled. 'I assumed we were.'

I returned his smile, but I fear it was a poor effort. The responsibility which Dr Harper had somehow foisted upon me to organise the inquest to Jesus's advantage weighed very heavily.

'Dr Harper believes – and I concur – that Mr Reardon would prefer that a post-mortem was not conducted so that he can later claim that the University presided over a slipshod inquest, and that this is all of a piece with the negligence of which he will accuse Jesus College.' There was no reaction from Morrell, so I ploughed on. 'In fact, he has threatened that, unless the college pays him a not inconsiderable sum of money, he will write to the papers, and the Hebdomadal Council, accusing us of neglecting Sidney's health and of failing to act sufficiently assiduously *in loco parentis*.'

As I said the words, my gut contracted fearfully: Reardon had required a response to his ultimatum by this evening and the Principal, I knew, was not going to oblige him. Dr Harper had concluded that the best way to handle Reardon's threat was to decline to communicate in any way. 'I shall,' he had said, 'leave the ball untouched in his court, so to speak, and see what he does with it.'

'I'm aware,' I continued, 'that, as borough coroner, Dr Hussey has a nominated surgeon whom he can call upon if a post-mortem examination is required, but given the animus that exists between some of the Infirmary's doctors and the University with regard to medical training, Dr Harper wouldn't wish to cause you any embarrassment. We wondered, therefore, whether you might allow us to suggest a Jesus man to conduct the examination? Always assuming that you felt that a post-mortem was justified.'

I watched Morrell take in my words. He was not, I thought, a great deal older than me, still at the stage of his career where he would wish to avoid any missteps.

'This doctor, who is he?'

'Dr Edmund Pritchard.' I managed to pronounce Teddy's given name steadily enough. 'He's a surgeon at the Infirmary and is well-regarded. In fact, he's lately been offered a position at King's College in London by Dr Joseph Lister – you may have heard of him?'

Morrell hadn't reacted to Lister's name, but nevertheless, he nodded.

'You'll know, then, that Dr Lister is a pioneer in the medical sciences. His offering a position is an indication of Dr Pritchard's competence. Added to which,' I said, recalling the Principal's comment, 'as Dr Pritchard is leaving Oxford to take up his new position, there would be no awkwardness with his colleagues if he were to carry out the dissection.'

Morrell gave me a searching look. 'Very well. In the circumstances, I'm minded to agree. But I should like Fielding to be present.'

'Of course.'

'However, if foul play is discovered – or even suspected – there will be press interest. Has the Principal considered the fact that a post-mortem examination might actually give rise to such a suspicion?'

He made a valid point, but Dr Fielding's inability to state, categorically, that Parker had died a natural death left open the possibility that the jury might bring in an open verdict. If that happened, rumour and speculation would be rife, strengthening Reardon's hand.

'We only want, if possible, to understand the reasons for Mr Parker's untimely death,' I said.

'In that case,' Morrell said, rising to his feet, 'I shall send a message to Dr Pritchard at the Infirmary and ask him to carry out the examination as soon as possible. Meanwhile, I'll empanel a jury so that they can view the body before it's dissected.'

As he shook my hand, I imagined the jury's reaction to Parker's body – breast tissue, spermatorrhoea ring and all. I hoped, fervently, that Teddy would find an incontrovertible, and entirely unavoidable, cause of death. Because, if he couldn't determine how Mr Parker had died, then the only thing people would have to talk about after the inquest was the decidedly sad figure Sidney Parker had cut in death.

Chapter 19

Non

Sidney Parker's sweetheart, Florence Spellman, was the daughter of a soot merchant, a trade I'd never heard of before I came to Oxford. At home, we put two things on our land: slaked lime to make the soil less acid, and manure to enrich it. It would never have occurred to us to spread what came out of the chimney on our fields. But apparently, Oxfordshire farmers couldn't get enough of the stuff. Florence booked two deliveries while we waited to speak to her.

'I do the books for my father and keep order in the yard,' she told us. 'Else people'd be coming and going and nobody'd know what was what.'

The Spellmans' house stood on a corner, so the yard Florence was talking about was bigger than you'd get behind most houses, with an approach at the side so that carts could come in and out. The place was stacked with rows of blackened sacks. I wanted to lift one of them to see how heavy it was, how much the soot'd been packed down. I remembered the first time I'd lifted a bag of charcoal: I'd been astonished at how light it was. Used to having to shift sacks of coal on my father's ship, I'd been expecting charcoal to be much the same, but it had been less than half the weight.

Florence Spellman was the only thing in the yard not covered in soot. I don't know how she stayed so clean, because the stuff covered every surface, but instead of dressing herself in a nice, concealing dark grey, Miss Spellman was in red and blue stripes. It mightn't show the dirt like white would, but it was still pretty bold. I wondered how many times a day she had to sponge smudges off.

Lily told Florence that we had something to talk to her about that would be better done inside. Because Florence already knew Lily and wasn't putting on airs, we trooped through the scullery into the Spellmans' kitchen so as not to dirty the oilcloth in the front of the house with the soot on our shoes.

It was a relief to get away from the smell. The soot hadn't seemed too bad at first but, in the end, it'd got into my nostrils and dried them out till I couldn't smell anything else.

We sat at the well-scrubbed table and talked about the weather, and about how Albie was getting on at Lucy's Foundry, while Florence made tea. Then, when she sat down, Lily broke the news of Sidney Parker's death.

Florence took it pretty well, all things considered.

'I knew he wasn't well,' she said, wiping the tears from her face with her fingertips. 'He wasn't himself at church on Sunday. But I thought it was just his usual thing – he had bouts with his stomach.' She bit her lip, but it didn't stop the next words coming out in a kind of anguished wail. 'Oh, God. He was always saying his condition'd be the death of him, but I never believed him.' A sob escaped then, and she put her face in her hands.

I wanted to ask what condition Sidney Parker'd been suffering from. Did she mean spermatorrhoea? Would he really have discussed that with her? But now didn't seem like the right moment to ask that kind of question.

'How did it happen?' Florence asked when she'd got hold of herself again.

I opened my mouth to reply, but Lily got there first. 'Died in his sleep, love. Quiet, no pain.'

I stared at her. We didn't know that. A post-mortem examination might tell a very different story. But a stern glance from Lily told me I'd better not contradict her.

Florence gulped a mouthful of tea and blinked back more tears. I felt uncomfortable watching her cry, so I looked around the kitchen instead. The place was just like its mistress: neat and orderly. The insides of the saucepans hanging from hooks over the range weren't just clean they were scoured, and the solitary copper one gleamed. Like every house I'd seen in Oxford, there was a range – blackleaded to a shine – so, with no cooking over the fire, the pans were even clean on the outside. I'd got used to English kitchens not having dressers, but it still seemed odd to me to see plates stacked flat on shelves instead of stood up on their sides. Mind you, the Spellmans' plates were mismatched, so they wouldn't have made much of a display anyway.

I wondered if Florence was the sort of young woman who had no time for domestic vanities like good willow plates. She was only keeping house for her father because, to use Lily's turn of phrase, her mother had 'slung her hook with a travelling salesman'.

I could understand Mrs Spellman wanting to leave; a woman can only take just so much mopping and wiping and sponging and rinsing. A travelling salesman must've seemed temptingly clean.

I suppose Sidney Parker had been tempting, too. He mightn't have been much to look at – Florence was pretty enough to have been looking for a far handsomer young man – but, as an undergraduate, he'd had *prospects*.

'Who'll be organising the funeral?' Florence asked, using the edge of a snowy-white tea towel (boiled no doubt) to dab her eyes.

Lily looked at me and I shrugged. When Basil had come to see us the night before last, he'd been far more concerned with how Sidney Parker had come to be dead than what would happen to his body.

'I expect the vicar'll know,' Lily said. 'But it won't be for a few days, I wouldn't think.'

'There'll have to be an inquest,' I said.

'Inquest?' Florence looked horrified at the thought. 'I thought you said he died in his sleep?'

'He did. But it was a sudden, unexpected death. The coroner has to make sure that it was from natural causes.' I wasn't going to mention the bottles Basil had found; there might be other explanations for those. 'He might have had an accident,' I said, 'and got an injury that nobody'd been able to see. Like a bump on the head or something.'

Florence frowned. Did she not understand the concept of a bump on the head?

'*Stop being so mean, the poor girl's had a shock.*'

Hara, always the kind one. I sometimes wondered if she'd have stayed like that if she'd lived.

'Sidney died on Monday night or early Tuesday morning,' I said. 'Do you know of anything that he might've been doing on Sunday or Monday to hurt himself?'

'No. He came here for his dinner, as usual, after church on Sunday and then he said he had work to do. I don't know what he did on

Monday.' She put her hands over her face and the sobs started again. She pulled herself together more quickly this time and wiped her eyes. 'No, I do remember one thing he was going to do on Monday. He was going to the Proctors' Office.'

The proctors were the University's disciplinary officers. 'What had he done?' I asked.

'Nothing! It was what they'd done. Me and Sidney were walking back from the theatre on Saturday evening – been to see Miss Rose Leclerq's London Comedy Company, we had.' She smiled at the memory, then remembered that Sidney would never take her to the theatre again and bit her lip. 'On the way home, one of the proctors' bulldogs stopped us. I don't know why they thought they had the right, because Sid wasn't wearing his academicals, but stop us they did. And very rude too! Wanted to know all about me and who I was. As if I was no better than I ought to be. Sid was furious. Said I was as respectable as any of the matrons in North Oxford and that we'd been walking out for some time. Well, they could tell he wasn't drunk so they couldn't complain of that. But one of them followed us all the way home, until Sid left me at the door.'

Florence was furious. And who wouldn't be, being accused of immoral intentions? 'Anyway, Sidney said he'd go and see them on Monday and make sure they didn't start spying on me. Because they do that. I know a girl on Albert Street that was followed for days as she went about her work. They even peered in at the windows to see what she was doing.'

I could well believe it. There was regular correspondence in the Oxford press from townsfolk complaining about the proctors and their assistants – the 'bulldogs' – overreaching their authority and harassing young women.

But the question was: if Sidney Parker hadn't been wearing his cap and gown, how had the bulldogs known that he was a member of the University? There was only one answer that I could see. He must've been in trouble with them before. That might be useful information for Basil.

'*He probably already knows.*'

'*Yes, Angharad, but he might not. Best to tell him, don't you think?*'

'*I'd leave it if I were you. He won't want you interfering.*'

'I'm not interfering. I'm doing what he should be doing. Talking to people who knew Sidney. Finding out how he'd been in the days before he died.'

'What'll happen to all his things?' Florence asked suddenly. 'Sidney's, I mean? All the things from his room at the Trents'?'

'They'll go to his next of kin, I expect,' I said.

She hesitated, dabbed her eyes again. 'What? That cousin of his? Reardon?'

I shrugged. Basil hadn't mentioned Sidney's next of kin. But evidently, he was an orphan. Poor dab.

'He'll be at the funeral, I suppose,' Florence said. 'Pretending to care.'

Lily opened her mouth to say something, but I put a hand on hers under the table. I wanted to hear what Florence had to say about this guardian. She obviously didn't like him much.

'Good thing he won't be doing the sermon,' Florence said. 'At least Father Noel will have nice things to say about Sidney.' Her eyes were glittering again but, this time, there was anger there as well as tears.

'You don't think this Mr Reardon would have anything nice to say about him?' I asked.

'He didn't care a fig about Sid. All he cared about was Sid going into his business when he came of age. He wasn't even going to let Sid finish his degree – said he was taking too long to pass the exams. But that wasn't Sid's fault. He only wanted to learn mathematics, but they were making him do all that stupid Greek and Latin first. What's the use of that?'

'Why was his guardian waiting for Sidney to come of age?' I asked. 'Why didn't he just bring him into the business as soon as he left school?'

'Because of Sid's money. He had money coming to him when he turned twenty-one. It was *that* his cousin wanted in the business, not Sid. Not really. He'd told him he'd pay for him to be at the University until he came into his money, then he'd make him a partner and they'd work together. Said it's what Sid's dad would have wanted. They grew up together, Sid's dad and Reardon. More like brothers than cousins if you believe him. But Sid barely knew his dad. He died when Sid was five. And after his mum died, Sid was under Reardon's thumb. But Sid wasn't going to work for him, I can tell you that. And he definitely wasn't going to put his money into the business.'

'Had plans of his own, did he, love?' Lily asked.

Florence pressed her lips together to stop them wobbling and blinked hard. 'He was going to go in with Dad. Branch out, away from chimneys and soot. And we were going to get married. As soon as he came of age and didn't need anybody's permission.'

She put her hands over her face and wept.

We waited while she cried herself out. I could hear a horse clopping by on the road outside and hoped it wouldn't stop at the soot yard. Florence had more to tell us yet, I was sure of it. I listened and breathed out as the slow hooves faded away down the street. Probably a dray going to the pub on the corner.

Florence sniffed and dabbed her eyes with the tea towel. 'We had it all planned. The Sunday after he turned twenty-one, Father Noel was going to start calling the banns. I can't believe we'll be burying Sid instead.'

I waited for more floods of tears, but she swallowed hard and they didn't come.

'When would Sidney have been twenty-one?' I asked. If his birthday and their wedding had been a long way off, would that make it easier to bear? I didn't know.

'The week after next,' Florence said. 'The fifth of February.' She looked from me to Lily. 'This is going to knock Dad sideways. He's been planning the new business with Sid for months and winding the soot down. He's not going to know what to do now.'

Florence dabbed at her eyes again. 'Can I get my letters back?' she asked. 'The ones I sent to Sid, I mean. Will his cousin have to give them to me if I ask?'

I looked sideways at Lily. She was the one who'd asked Basil's uncomfortable question for him – the one about things going missing – while she was helping Betty Trent pack Sidney's belongings to send down to Jesus College. If there'd been any letters she'd know.

'There were no letters, sweetheart. We didn't find anything like that in his room.'

'But he kept them all! I know he did. He used to read them when he couldn't sleep.'

Lily had ears. She'd hear the note of hysteria in Florence's voice at the thought of Reardon having possession of her love letters as well as I did. 'I'm sure they'll turn up, lovvie,' she said, soothingly. 'He'd probably put them somewhere safe, and we didn't see them.'

I knew Lily was just being kind, but Florence's face lit up. 'He did! He had a safe place under his bed.'

'But we looked—'

'No, not just under the *bed*. Under the *floorboards*.'

Chapter 20

Basil

Sidney Parker's parish church, St Barnabas in Jericho, wasn't one that I was particularly familiar with, save for its reputation as one of the foremost of the Oxford Movement churches.

The building itself had still been under construction when I had first come up to Oxford. With the population of Jericho growing rapidly due to the increasing numbers employed at the University Press and Lucy's ironworks, St Paul's church on Walton Street had no longer been adequate. Besides, the founders of St Barnabas – one of whom was a senior man at the Press – had seen that the area needed the kind of church that would pay more than lip service to the physical and spiritual wellbeing of its parishioners. An 'Oxford' church, with the movement's laudable commitment to the poor, was ideal.

Of course, Jericho had changed in fifteen years. It was no longer the kind of place where undergraduates were advised not to venture lest they be pelted with oyster shells and rats' tails, and some roads, like the one where Lily Maddox and her family lived, were very respectable, almost genteel in a quietly lower middle-class way. The church of St Barnabas had played a part in that increasing gentility with its significant influx of University folk every Sunday – undergraduates as well as a few dons and their families – all drawn by the choir, incense and sense of liturgical theatre.

But perhaps Sidney Parker had been drawn by something else? Lily Maddox had said he'd helped the vicar with parish work, which was unusual amongst undergraduates in my experience.

I made my way towards the church through still, foggy air, tainted with a sulphurous miasma from the iron works and the rancid fat stench of the nearby tallow factory. It seemed a world away from central

Oxford, though I was no more than half a mile from Jesus as the crow flies.

Passing the name plate for Cardigan Street, fixed high up on the house on the corner with Hart Street, I smiled at the thought of Non living so close to a street which bore the name of her native county. Perhaps she had always been fated to come to Oxford and live here, though she would never concede such a thing herself. Non declined to believe in anything as random as fate and kept her own counsel on God. She'd only commit herself to agreeing with Milton's Samson that it was foolish to deny the existence of God: *You can't prove non-existence, can you?* But it seemed to me that, on the other hand, perhaps she did not find God's existence adequately proven, either.

I felt a fresh wave of savage loss as my mind lurched back to Teddy, an arch materialist. What would my life be like once he'd left Oxford? I found I couldn't imagine living here with no prospect of seeing him at college dinners or going down to London with him.

I was so immersed in preoccupation that the appearance of St Barnabas almost took me by surprise. The church loomed up out of the murk, its structure very solid in the midst of the vaporous fog. I'd always found it rather un-English-looking. Round-headed windows and a rendered exterior were more reminiscent of French basilicas, while the separate bell tower looked as if it had come straight from Italy. I stared at the tower. It was over-tall and looked out of place in its surroundings. Had Sidney Parker liked the fact that it looked so very different from the city's colleges? Had it been an escape for him from a world he felt he didn't belong to?

There was no answer to my knock at the vicarage, so I turned back to a house I'd seen, opposite the church. Its front door had a brass plaque declaring its occupant to be:

John Foster
Sacristan and Coal Merchant

The middle-aged woman who came to the door informed me that Mr Foster was at his business on the wharf. 'The reverend's at the school,' she told me when I explained my real errand. 'The boys' school. Don't suppose he'll be long.'

As I stood, waiting, outside the church, I hoped she was right. My cap and gown were attracting a good deal of frank scrutiny from folk going about their business. Added to which, there were some rather alarming sounds coming from a street nearby which seemed to herald pigs on the move. I did not relish the thought of them running amok in the street where I stood.

Fortunately, before a squealing herd could appear, a man in early middle age, wearing a cassock and a black biretta, appeared out of the thinning fog.

'Father Noel?' I asked.

He smiled. 'The very same.'

I introduced myself and explained that I'd come to speak to him about Sidney Parker.

'Ah, yes.' He crossed himself. 'Gordon Trent came to see me yesterday with the shocking news. Poor young man. To have his life cut short so suddenly.'

I nodded gravely. 'I've been asked to write an obituary to share with the college community.' It was the pretext I'd decided on as I walked up to Jericho. I couldn't very well tell the priest that I was hoping to find evidence of a general obliviousness to any deterioration in Parker's health.

'Well, do come into the vicarage, Mr Rice. It's not a day to be standing on the street.'

-

'Sidney was a young man in search of a vocation,' Father Noel told me over a cup of coffee far superior to the stewed liquid I'd drunk at the Ship Street breakfast cart. 'He wanted something he could commit himself to, heart and soul.'

His words made me feel inadequate. I hadn't looked further than Parker's bland assertion that he was considering a career in the civil service. It had seemed so eminently suitable for somebody like him.

'He was thinking and praying about whether he might be called to the priesthood,' Father Noel added. 'But I wonder whether he simply needed somewhere to belong.' He gazed at his coffee, perhaps wondering how much he could tell me without breaking confidences.

'His was not a happy history,' he said. 'As I'm sure you know, he was an orphan.' He looked up at me, questioningly.

'Quite so. And he was none too enamoured of his guardian, was he?' I said. 'Sidney told me he'd felt abandoned at school.' That wasn't quite true but a lad who had never visited his guardian's home must, surely, have felt something of the sort?

The priest nodded. 'He felt rather badly let down there, did he not?'

Badly let down at school, or simply by Reardon's neglect of him? 'I assume you've met Mr Reardon by now?' I said. 'I know he intended to come and speak to you yesterday evening, about Sidney's funeral.'

'Yes, he's been to see me.'

I gave him the opportunity to say more about Reardon's visit, but a vicar's calling requires habitual discretion.

Glancing around the room, I wondered which had come first, a love of colour and ornament or the priest's Romish faith. The place was crowded with objects – books, paintings, occasional tables holding empty vases, a mantelpiece busy with candlesticks and all manner of knick-knacks. I wondered what his housekeeper made of it all. Perhaps she shared his penchant for clutter.

'As his tutor,' I said, putting my cup down next to a plaster angel, 'I only really knew the academic Sidney. Perhaps you could give me an idea of the young man you knew?'

Father Noel refilled his coffee cup and proffered the pot, but I declined. 'Did he start attending St Barnabas as soon as he came up?'

'No,' Noel said, carefully. 'I believe he'd been in Oxford a couple of terms before he made his way to us.'

Which meant that Parker had joined the congregation at St Barnabas at about the same time as he'd moved out of college. Of course, that was not particularly remarkable as St Barnabas was the church closest to Parker's lodgings in Kingston Road. Still, I made a mental note of the coincidence.

'He was a young man trying to find his way,' Father Noel continued. 'When I welcomed him on his first morning, he gave me the impression that he'd been on the wrong path, that he wanted to start again with a clean slate.'

That sounded surprisingly like low-church evangelical rhetoric – the language of being born again, one's sins washed away. 'Did he speak of religious conversion?' I asked.

'He never used that term, no. But I believe he'd had some kind of experience that changed his heart and mind.'

I wondered what that experience had been and what Parker's heart and mind might have been changed *from*.

'I believe he helped you with your work with the young people of the parish?'

Father Noel sipped his coffee and smiled. 'He did. I'm afraid he had no great gift for the work, but he was very willing. Though, I must confess, I'm glad he's been spared the need to seem interested in our proposed parish football team. He once told me that he loathed team sports.'

'And yet he was a sportsman, still,' I said. 'I believe he regularly attended the gymnasium for instruction.'

'Fencing, yes. Sidney might not have enjoyed his time at school but something of the *mens sana in corpore sano* ethos remained.'

Remained, or had been rekindled? The so-called Muscular Christians drew a direct line between manly athleticism and godly purity. Although the churchmanship at St Barnabas had little in common with their cold baths and rugby football ethos, Parker might still have come under their 'healthy mind, healthy body' influence.

'What other parish activities did he involve himself with, Father?' I asked, opening my notebook to take down his response.

'He was a marvel in helping design and run the spelling bees that we held last year. There was a lot of competition between the boys' and girls' schools. But if he had a particular gift, it was for working with the elderly members of our congregation. We have one poor chap in the parish who was blinded in the Crimea. Sidney used to take endless pains with him, listening to his stories, helping him at parish teas... He even went to his house to read to him every week.'

'That was kind.' I had not suspected Parker of such an altruistic streak and, once again I could not help feeling that I had failed him in some fundamental way. Even so, I was not here to listen to the boy's virtues being extolled. Somehow, I had to find out whether Father Noel knew anything about the physical ailments that had apparently sent Sidney back, again and again, to the druggist for Chlorodyne, paregoric and laudanum. Not to mention Doctor Aurum's Tonic and whatever the anonymous blue bottle might have contained.

'I don't know if you're aware,' I began, carefully, 'but, as a scholar, Sidney struggled a little. However, it was never clear to me whether the work was simply too challenging or whether there was something else. His death has made me ask myself whether he might have been suffering from some kind of illness we weren't aware of...'

Montague Noel met my eye with an entirely unreadable expression.

'I did try and draw him out,' I stumbled on, 'tried to encourage him to confide in me about any concerns he had.' Did my clumsy attempts really deserve to be dignified as encouragement? 'But to no avail. Now, I find myself wondering whether I should have done more.'

'What could you have done if you didn't know there was anything amiss?' Though Father Noel's words were sympathetic, his tone suggested that he thought I was seeking absolution when I should have been doing penance. Had George Reardon suggested to him that I had been dilatory in my care of his cousin?

He's skin and bone!

Sweat prickled in my armpits.

'Do you know if there was anything that might have been worrying him?' As I asked the question, I heard an uncomfortable echo of the one Dr Harper had asked me: *Had the boy said anything to you recently?*

'In my experience,' the vicar said, after swallowing the remains of his coffee, 'undergraduates would rather lose a limb than admit to being worried about anything. But you and I both know the things that prey on the minds of gownsmen, Mr Rice. Work, social standing, money...'

To my chagrin, it hadn't occurred to me that Parker might have had money troubles, but it was entirely plausible. He had been a young man of limited means in a city where virtually every tradesman was prepared to offer almost unlimited credit to undergraduates and where some of his friends would have been considerably better off than he. Now I considered it, it would have been surprising if Sidney Parker *hadn't* had money worries. I recalled, again, the lack of so much as a sixpence in his room. Even those who were in debt had small change. What had happened to Parker's?

The question reminded me of what *had* been found in the boy's room.

'Does the phrase "do not be faint hearted" have any significance to you, Father?'

Noel frowned slightly. 'There's something very like it in Deuteronomy. "Hear, O Israel, ye approach this day unto battle against your enemies: let not your hearts faint, fear not, and do not tremble, neither be ye terrified because of them."'

'There was a note with the words on, next to Parker's bed. Was he going into battle with enemies of any kind?'

'The spiritual life is a continual battle against the world, the flesh and the devil, Mr Rice.'

I felt chastened. 'Yes, quite so. But I wonder if Mr Parker might have had more specific enemies in mind?'

'Not that I know of.'

I took a deep breath. 'Strictly between the two of us, Father, various proprietary medications were discovered in Sidney's room… Did he ever give you any indication that he felt he was battling ill health?' The priest did not respond immediately so I added, 'Might you have had any reason to suspect that he was unwell?'

'He was a little pale, of course. And very slight. But some people are, and I didn't think anything of it. He never seemed—' He stopped and stared off over my shoulder, obviously recalling something. 'No, I suppose he did seem more than usually fatigued occasionally. I put it down to burning the candle at both ends, but perhaps not?'

When I did not reply immediately, the priest said, 'Mr Rice, if you don't mind my making an observation, these are odd questions for somebody who's writing an obituary.'

'I apologise. It's just that his death has come as a considerable shock to me and I'm trying to understand it.'

Father Noel rose to his feet. 'Perhaps, you might glean more material for your obituary from a recipient of Sidney's kindness. I can introduce you to Corporal Hanes, the old soldier I mentioned whom Sidney used to read to? I'm sure he would be delighted to give you a testimonial.'

'That would be helpful, thank you.'

Speaking to Corporal Hanes would be my penance for not being entirely honest with the priest.

Chapter 21

Non

I sat at my desk with the contents of Sidney Parker's hidey-hole spread out in front of me. We'd found his most personal belongings hidden beneath a loose floorboard under his bed, just like Florence had said.

It was ironic. The Principal of Jesus College had gone marching up to the Kingston Road house to look at the body and search his room, but Sidney Parker's things had only come to light because of Lily's kindness. If we hadn't gone to break the news of his death to Florence Spellman, nobody would have been any the wiser about what he'd kept hidden away. With her Christian instincts, Cranogwen would've seen a lesson of some sort, there.

Basil had suspected the Trents of helping themselves to Sidney's possessions; he could protest all he liked, but I knew that that's what he'd thought. Perhaps he'd never had anything he needed to hide, or maybe he'd just always had a cupboard or a box that he could lock, but anybody who hasn't had the luxury of a lock and key knows the need for a loose floorboard or the space at the bottom of a chest of drawers.

I'd never had much to hide, but there had been a book now and again that I hadn't wanted my mother or father to know about. A book that might provide the kind of education my parents didn't think it was suitable for me to have.

There'd been a book under Sidney Parker's floorboard that he obviously hadn't wanted people to see. Its strident title – *MANHOOD* – was explained by the subtitle which cascaded down the title page inside:

THE
CAUSES OF ITS PREMATURE DECLINE
WITH DIRECTIONS
FOR ITS

PERFECT RESTORATION
ADDRESSED
TO THOSE SUFFERING THE DESTRUCTIVE
EFFECTS OF EXCESSIVE INDULGENCE,
SOLITARY HABITS, &C, &C, &C

It claimed to have been written by L. Deslandes: 'a member of the Royal Academy of Medicine at Paris and other learned societies', and to have been translated 'with many additions' by 'an American physician'. Well, if that was the case, why hadn't this American put his name to it? Sounded to me as if he wanted any comeback to fall on Monsieur Deslandes.

A quick flick through the book showed me exactly what 'sufferers' were 'excessively indulging' in, which confirmed my suspicion about what 'solitary habits' might mean. Let's just say those habits didn't include long rambles in nature or curling up with a good book.

I put *MANHOOD* to one side and started sifting through the rest of the things Sidney Parker had seen fit to hide.

Florrie's bundle of letters, all addressed to 'S. Parker Esq' in the same girlish handwriting, tied with a ribbon. A small money bag containing an everyday amount of cash. A pile of newspaper clippings, pamphlets and the sort of handbills that Billy Nicholson in his printers' slang called 'leaflets'. And a cashbox. It was locked but wherever the key was, it wasn't with the rest of Sidney Parker's things.

I picked up the last and most interesting thing: a stiff-covered notebook. But just as I was about to look inside, a knock on the door pulled me to my feet and I went to let Basil in. I'd sent a boy down to Jesus College with a note as soon as we'd left Betty Trent's house telling him that we'd found Sidney's personal effects and inviting him for supper. Evidently, he hadn't been able to wait.

But it wasn't Basil, it was Florence. 'Did you find them? Did you find my letters?'

'We did,' I said, 'but—'

'Can I have them, then?'

'That's what I was about to say. I'm not sure you can. The coroner will probably want to see them.'

'*No!* He can't! They're private.'

I held the door open for her and, once she was inside, Florence grabbed me by the arm. 'You don't need to tell the coroner that the letters were there. What he doesn't know won't hurt him, will it?'

It was gloomy in the hallway, so I took her into the sitting room.

'Sit down,' I said. 'I'll just see about some tea.'

Edie was by herself in the kitchen. Lily was out with Ivy and the baby, thank goodness, otherwise she'd have interfered. 'Pot of tea, please, Edie... and is there any of that cake left?'

'As long as it's for you and not for Billy, there is.' Edie liked me because, even though I was what she called a 'lady scholar', I always spoke to her 'as if you're asking me a favour instead of giving me an order'. I'd grown up amongst people who were more likely to *be* housemaids than to employ them, so it wouldn't have occurred to me to speak to her in any other way. Edie and I were also allies in our dislike of Billy Nicholson. She'd told me that he was always sucking up to her, trying to get her to tell him the family secrets. 'Always wants one over on everybody, Billy does,' she'd said. 'Likes to think he's got the whip hand.'

'Was that Florrie Spellman I heard come in?' she asked.

Florence's voice would never have carried to the back of the house and down to the basement, so I knew Edie must've skulked in the hallway when she heard me coming down to open the door, instead of going back to the scullery. 'Yes, it was.'

'In a state, is she?'

Edie was fifteen or sixteen and had lived in Jericho all her life. I wasn't what you might call a regular attender at St Barnabas – I only went when Lily insisted – but Edie went every Sunday, along with the rest of the family. She was sharp, and she'd have watched the relationship between Florence and Sidney develop from noticing, to flirting and eventually to walking out. I was willing to bet that there'd been a lot of gossip about a soot merchant's daughter setting her cap at an undergraduate. Edie'd be the centre of attention at church on Sunday if she could say that Florence had been here, all upset, after Lily and I had been to see her. Edie missed nothing. The police could've employed her to watch people; she'd have been brilliant.

'Wouldn't you be in a state if you'd just heard that your sweetheart was dead?'

'Depends if I'd already tried it on with half the student boys in the congregation, I suppose.'

Sour grapes or genuine information? It might be worth finding out. 'A bit of a flirt, is she?'

Edie looked at me sideways as she put cups and saucers and a couple of plates on a tray. 'Had enough of living in Soot Hall, hasn't she?'

I snorted. Soot Hall! What a slap-down. 'You think Florrie was pulling the wool over Mr Parker's eyes?'

After setting the teapot to warm on the edge of the range, Edie turned to me. 'Well, he was nothing to look at, was he? And I could've beaten him in an arm-wrestling contest. 'Spect he had money, though. They mostly do.'

I suppose, in comparison with Edie's family, most of the undergraduates who worshipped at St Barnabas did have money, however poor they thought they were.

'I couldn't tell you, Edie. All I know is, Florence is upset, so I'd better get back to her.'

'Right you are.' Edie tipped tea from the caddy into the pot with a practised eye and poured the boiling water over it. 'Let me just go out the back for the milk then you can take the tray with you.'

When I got back to the sitting room, Florrie was sitting on the very edge of the chintz armchair by the fire, like a bird ready to take flight. Or, possibly, as if she was used to not making too much contact with the furniture in case she made it sooty. The room was chilly, so I put a match to the twists of newspaper under the kindling.

'Please don't tell the coroner about the letters, Miss Vaughan. Just let me take them away. I mean they're mine, really, aren't they? My paper, my ink.'

'I don't think it works like that,' I said. She'd called me Miss Vaughan, but I couldn't quite bring myself to 'Miss Spellman' her lest she thought I was being patronising. But calling her Florence would make it sound as if I thought I was better than her. Lily'd got away with it, but Lily was old enough to be her mother.

'How *does* it work then?' She'd taken her gloves off and was twisting them around and around in her lap. There was obviously money in soot; they looked like kid to me.

I sat down opposite her in a matching armchair. I'd never liked the fabric – huge tea-roses that looked like pink cabbages – but the chairs were very comfortable. 'Anything belonging to Sidney is of interest to the coroner,' I said. 'Unless there's a very good reason for him not to, he'd need to see anything that Sidney kept hidden.'

'But Sid only kept them hidden because he didn't have anywhere safe.'

Hidden, safe: it was the same thing, wasn't it?

'Please!' she begged when I didn't reply. 'There are things in those letters that were private to me and Sidney.'

The coroner – and any examining doctor worth his salt – would be grateful for information about Sidney Parker and his habits. But if I was going to get Florence to tell me the truth, I needed to stop her Miss Vaughan-ing me.

'Listen, Florrie,' I said, 'we're both women of the world, so let's lay our cards on the table. Are you in the family way?'

It was a phrase we never used at home, but I'd heard it more often than 'pregnant' here.

'No!'

'It's all right. You can tell me.'

'No, I'm not,' she said. 'It was only—'

I was pretty sure she'd been going to say 'only once', but she must have heard too many girls saying the same thing. We both knew that once was all it took.

'Look, Miss Vaughan.'

'Non.'

'What?'

'My name. Non. Short for Rhiannon.' Most English people found it easier, and besides, St Non had been St David's mother, which was a good pedigree for a name.

'Right. Well, look, Non, the thing is, it wasn't just that. In the letters, I mean. There were things… Sidney, he hadn't been well and…' She couldn't go on. Or look me in the eye.

'Florrie?' I looked at her steadily. 'Just spit it out.'

I got the whole story, then. Or, at least, enough of it to read between the lines and make an educated guess. What seemed to have happened was that Florence had noticed a certain, shall we say, *lack of response* when they were on their own together and had teased him about it. Sidney Parker obviously wasn't cut from the same cloth as Peacock the

Popinjay, or he'd have been scandalised at her knowing what should be going on in his trousers.

'Thing is,' she said, 'I know a girl who's on the game, and she told me what to do. How to help,' she explained, looking at me anxiously, wondering whether she'd spat out more than I'd bargained for. Which, to be honest, she had. Well, more than I'd expected, at any rate.

To cut a long story short, she'd tried some tricks on Sidney and they'd worked. At least once.

'And all that's in the letters?' I asked.

'Well, no, not all of it.'

'But enough?'

She nodded. I thought she was telling me the truth, but I couldn't be sure. And I didn't want to tamper with evidence if there was going to be an inquest.

'I'll let you have them,' I said.

'Oh, thank you, Non—'

'On one condition,' I interrupted. 'That you let me read them first, just to make sure there's nothing the coroner needs to know.'

And with that, she would have to be satisfied.

Chapter 22

Basil

Mr Hanes, as the old soldier asked me to call him once Montague Noel had left – 'Dunno why he always wants to give me my old rank, I bin a civilian for twenty-five years!' – might have been left blind by his time in the Crimea, but he proved to be a keen observer, nevertheless. Perhaps not being able to see the people around him made him more attentive to what they said, because he seemed to have gained considerable insight into Sidney Parker from their conversations.

'Neither one of us was much for talkin' about hisself,' he told me. 'The past's done an' gone, so what's the point maunderin' on about it? We mostly talked about things going on in town. Y'know, the tramway, and whether the electric lights are comin', and why the University's puttin' up a whole buildin' just for the students to sit their exams in. I mean, are there that number of exams happenin' all the time that they need somewhere special to do 'em?'

The truth was that there *were* quite a number of exams, but the University Examination Schools currently under construction on the High Street were really a symbol rather than a practical necessity, a symbol of how seriously the University took its examinations and the degrees it conferred. Now that we were competing not only with Cambridge but with London and Manchester, an Oxford degree needed to be given all the weight it could carry. In future, the fact that our undergraduates would sit their exams in a centrally managed venue would make it clear that degrees were examined and awarded by an impartial university, not the colleges that had nurtured the examinees and who might possibly be inclined towards generosity. Not that I felt the need to tell Mr Hanes that.

'What did he read to you?' I asked.

'Jackson's, mostly,' Mr Hanes said, referring to *Jackson's Oxford Journal*. 'Or sometimes the *Chronicle*, but I prefers Jackson's. He'd read the advertisements to me as well as the articles. "They're more entertainin'", he used to say.'

As Mr Hanes spoke, I looked around at the little room. I'd been surprised to find the fire lit so early in the day, but this had been explained when Hanes told me that his daughter took in washing. 'The minute you're gone, she'll be in here hangin' washin' off all the horses in the house. Can't dry so much as a threadbare clout outside in this weather.'

There was certainly room for clothes' horses. What little furniture there was occupied the edges of the room, though Hanes had pulled his own chair up to the fire and invited me to do the same. I noticed a jar full of rolled-up newspaper spills on the hearth and wondered whether he was responsible for making them. It was the kind of thing that could be done by touch alone and he struck me as a man who would want to be useful.

'We used to laugh at the way some of those advertisements went all around the houses,' he grinned. 'All "Mr John Smith begs to inform his valued customers this that and the other." Load of stuck-up nonsense, I'd say but Sidney'd say, "they're only trying to impress their customers, Mr Hanes, make themselves sound more high-class than they are, so people with money'll think they're worth patronising." He was clever like that, Sidney. He could always see what the advertisements were up to.'

I reflected, slightly sadly, that Sidney Parker had found it hard to apply such an apparently astute critical faculty to his studies. Perhaps he had been intending to join Reardon in his advertising business, after all.

''E used to ask me, sometimes, did they have advertisements like this in your day, Mr Hanes? 'E always wanted to know about the pills and remedies, 'specially. "They promise so much, don't they," he'd say to me, "but d'you think they do any good?" And I'd tell him they were a mug's game. Save your money, son, I'd tell 'im. 'E reckoned he never parted with money for nothin' like that but, truth be told, I di'n't believe 'im. Asked too many questions, Sidney did.'

'Did he ever mention any remedies in particular?' I asked.

Hanes' face didn't offer much in the way of expression and his closed and ruined eyes made it seem even blanker, but something in his manner changed. 'What did you say 'e died of, again?'

'We don't really know, Mr Hanes. Only that he died in his sleep.'

'What does the quack say?'

'He's not sure,' I admitted. Then, because I didn't wish to be the source of speculation, I added, 'Probably natural causes.'

'Goin' t'be an inquest?'

'Of course.'

Hanes took his pipe and tobacco out of his pocket. 'You'll oblige me by stayin' a few more minutes, Mr Rice, so that I can 'ave a pipe before my Susie fills the place up with wet laundry and I'm not allowed.'

He filled his pipe then leaned forward and, with minimal fumbling, located the spills and rested one on the coals, leaving it for a few seconds before applying it to his pipe.

'I don' think Sid was what you'd call a well man,' he said, unexpectedly, drawing on his pipe until the tobacco glowed red. 'Sometimes, 'e'd read one of those remedy things where it'd say like: "Fatigue? No energy? Lacking zest for life? Buy our powders and you'll be a new man," or that type of thing. He'd never say anythin' – and it wa'n't my place to ask – but it always sounded to me as if he was thinkin' "that's me, that is. I've got no zest for life". Which,' he wet his thumb and forefinger and expertly pinched off the burned end of the spill, 'is odd in a young man walking out with a girl. Especially one like Florrie Spellman. A lively young woman by all accounts.'

I watched him lean forward and place the used spill on the hearth next to the jar. The fact that Parker had a sweetheart was a surprise to me, though perhaps it shouldn't have been. Churches were full of young women and St Barnabas was likely to be fuller than most, given the regular attendance of an array of undergraduates.

However, the existence of a romantic aspect to Parker's life might explain the spermatorrhoea ring. A man regularly in the company of a young woman might well fall prey to erotic dreams.

'Do you think he'd tried any of the remedies in the paper?' I asked. Mr Hanes had failed to answer a similar question, earlier.

'Dunno, Mr Rice. But I hope not. All these modern ailments are just made up by the pill sellers, aren't they? When I was a young man, nobody was asking us "are you tired, lost your vital spark?" We was all just gettin' on with it. I told young Sid, you don' want to take no notice of all them advertisements, they'll do you no good. What's troublin' these folk that are lackin' energy is too much sittin' down all day – like you with your studyin', I told him. You want to be out in the fresh air, doin' somethin', not sittin' lookin' at old books. An' you know what he said to me?'

I shook my head, then realised the futility of the gesture and coughed with embarrassment. 'No, what?'

'That' he'd be layin' off his books soon enough. Soon as 'e come of age and got the money that was in trust for him.' He cocked his head in my direction. 'Goin' to be an inquest you say?'

'Yes.'

'Then I hope the University Coroner isn't such a fool that he believes the quack's "natural causes". 'Cause 'e should ask 'imself one question. Who gets young Sidney's money now he's dead?'

Chapter 23

Non

Hara was opposed to me reading Florrie Spellman's letters to Sidney Parker – '*Those letters are private. Leave them to the coroner!*' – but I read them anyway.

They weren't anything like as shocking as Florrie would've had me believe. She'd only made a few coy references to her intimate encounters with Sidney Parker. In fact, now that I'd read the letters, I was pretty sure that the things Florrie didn't want to come out at the inquest weren't to do with what she and Sidney got up to when they were alone. There were much more awkward secrets in the letters than that.

While Sidney'd supposedly been making plans with Mr Spellman for a new business in Jericho, he and Florence had been planning to emigrate to America as soon as he came of age. Which explained why there was a pamphlet amongst his papers offering advice to would-be emigrants to the United States.

And there was something else, too. Several times in Florrie's letters, she referred to 'the spies'. I remembered her complaining about the proctors' bulldogs following her and Sidney after seeing them together at the theatre. Had the bulldogs been spying on her ever since? Was that why she and Sidney'd been planning to go to America? To escape?

But no. That made no sense. As soon as they were married – and Florrie's letters referred to marriage several times, so she hadn't been making it up – the bulldogs would've had no reason to carry on hounding her.

'*Don't you feel even a little bit guilty, reading these letters?*' Hara wanted to know. '*Don't you think you should've just given what you found under the floorboards to Basil for the coroner?*'

'*No. If I can save Florrie's blushes – and her reputation – by just giving Basil the facts he needs and keeping the rest to myself, shouldn't I do that?*'

'*So you think it's for you to decide what Basil does and doesn't need?*'

I ground my teeth. '*I've got a right to decide! Basil would never have found the stuff under the floorboards in a million years, but Lily and I did. Basil didn't even know Sidney Parker had a sweetheart, never mind that he was engaged to be married. It was me and Lily who went to see Florrie. Me who asked the right questions—*'

'*It wasn't you who made Florrie remember the hiding place. It was Lily, being kind and trying to comfort Florrie when she thought her love letters were lost. Perhaps she should decide what to do with the letters and everything.*'

'*Look, Hara, I may have to keep my mouth shut at lectures to help the AEW, but I'm damned if I'm going to keep it shut when it comes to a suspicious death!*'

'*Oh, very high-minded. So this is nothing to do with wanting to prove Archie Peacock wrong?*'

'*Peacock's a fool. Why would I want to prove anything to him?*'

I could feel my sister giving me a look. One that came straight from my mother's face.

'*This isn't about Peacock.*'

'*Isn't it?*'

No. It wasn't. Hara was wrong. This was about how the world was run. All of it. If men were going to keep telling us that women weren't capable of doing anything important, wouldn't it be stupid not to take any opportunity fate gave us to show that we were?

I'd come to Oxford to learn, to study; above all, to become a Celtic scholar. Professor Rhys's work on Old Welsh philology had inspired me. It challenged the English notion that the Brythonic civilisation of the Welsh, Breton and Cornish Celts was inferior to that of the invading Saxons, and proved that Welsh was *not* a degenerate language, ripe to be superseded by English which – according to English scholars – was a more robust and civilised tongue. I'd come to Oxford to do work like that, to change how people thought.

But now I was here, I'd realised that, even if I was to become a scholar, the likelihood of anybody – any men, I mean – listening to me was remote.

Annie Rogers was a salutary lesson. She'd been the cleverest candidate in her year if the local examinations were any indication. But what was she *doing* with the knowledge that would have earned her a first-class honours degree if she'd been allowed to take one? She was teaching other women. In the academic world of men, she had no influence. None whatsoever. Her success hadn't changed anything. She was just an oddity, like a talking dog.

'*Stop ranting about what's not changing and look at what is. Two years ago, you wouldn't have been allowed into any of these colleges except on the arm of a man for dinner. And now you stride in and sit at lectures.*'

'*Not for the next term!*'

'*No. And whose fault is that?*'

If my sister had been there in the flesh, I would've hit her. *Technically*, she was right. I *had* brought this on myself. But only by doing something which no man would ever have been criticised for. If one of his cronies had asked Peacock if he'd read *Lysistrata*, he wouldn't have gone crying to Dr Harper, would he?

And Dr Harper's reaction to my suggestion that he should consult Dr Reckitt had been ridiculous. If I'd been a man, he'd have shaken me by the hand and thanked me. He'd probably have invited me to dinner, not written to the AEW to complain about me.

They might be letting us in to lectures, but they didn't want us to speak when we were there. All we were allowed to do was listen to their pearls of wisdom.

'*Be patient, Non.*'

On this, Hara, Cranogwen and all the AEW ladies were agreed. We must be patient.

'*No. Patience is getting us nowhere.*'

'*Non—*'

'*No, Hara. I'm going to do whatever I can to find out why Sidney Parker died. They might ignore me, but they can't ignore facts.*'

I pushed Florrie's letters aside and picked up Mr Parker's notebook.

I'd tried to persuade myself that it would be dull. Notes for lectures, or his accounts. But when I opened the first page, there were no figures, just writing. But not notes. There was no cursive script, the words were made up of individually written letters, as if Sidney Parker'd never learned to join them up. But the letters didn't form words. Or not ones I could read, anyway.

Whatever Sidney Parker had recorded in this book, he'd seen fit to write in code.

Chapter 24

Basil

Having concluded my conversation with Mr Hanes, I made my way straight back to college, hurrying down Walton Street, where the Worcester College clock told me it wanted five minutes to midday, and wishing I had access to a machine like Non's as I headed up George Street at a run.

As I dashed into college, I caught a startled, if not disapproving look from the porter who called, 'Messages here for you, Mr Rice!' I ignored him and loped across First Quad to my rooms without breaking stride.

I suspected that one of the messages would be from the Principal, summoning me to a meeting with the headmaster of Cowbridge School, and an explanation of his rather melodramatic exhortation to 'beware Parker's guardian'. However, I had a tutorial to deliver and, having spent an uncomfortable morning trying to acquaint myself with a young man whom I should have known better while he had been alive, I was disinclined to neglect the two undergraduates who would be waiting for me outside my door.

As luck would have it, one of my tutees that morning had come up at the same time as Sidney Parker, and the two had lived on the same staircase before Parker had moved out of college. If anybody but Parker himself knew why he had been desperate to quit Jesus at the same time as he had begun attending St Barnabas, it would be his contemporaries. Once our tutorial business was concluded, therefore, I asked Mr Tobias Jenkyn if I could detain him for a moment.

'Sidney Parker,' I said, as Jenkyn seated himself, once more, at the table.

The young man composed his face into what he obviously regarded as a suitably sombre expression. 'Poor chap. It was a bit of a shock to hear that he'd died, I don't mind admitting.'

'Mr Parker lived on the same staircase as you when you first came up. In fact, I think you came into residence on the same day? You must have known him quite well?'

'At first, I suppose, yes. He and I went about together a good bit when we were first up.'

I nudged the fireplace-mounted trivet over the coals and set the kettle to boil again. It was my habit to offer students a cup of coffee while we were discussing their work and I hoped that busying myself with the preparation of a fresh pot would put Jenkyn more at his ease than if I sat opposite him at the table and fixed him with a gimlet eye.

'You were friends, then?' I asked, knocking stale coffee grounds out of the top of the pot into a bowl I kept for the purpose. 'When you were both first up?'

'Well, no, not friends exactly.' Jenkyn seemed a little uncomfortable. 'It was just that we went about a bit together, with some other chaps.'

I don't suppose Jenkyn had ever referred to a contemporary as a 'chap' while he was at school in Wales, but all our undergraduates soon adopted the Oxford patois.

'When you say, "went about a bit"…?'

'Oh, you know,' Jenkyn said, vaguely, as it dawned on him that half the things he and 'the chaps' had got up to would have him up before the Dean, 'this and that. We all took up rowing,' he offered. 'Parker was cox—'

'Was?' I interrupted. 'Because he's no longer with us, or because he didn't persist with rowing? Would you like another cup of coffee, by the way?'

'Yes, please. Thank you. Um, he stopped rowing with us after a while.'

I raised my eyebrows, encouraging him to go on but this was not a tutorial and I was not drawing him out on some finer point of Greek grammar. 'Did he find others to row with?' I prompted.

'No. He'd go off by himself. Took up single sculling. We saw him out a few times when we took a skiff on to the river.'

This could take all day, I decided, as Jenkyn offered one wholesome pursuit after another, none of which would clarify why Sidney Parker had petitioned to be allowed to move into lodgings. A more direct approach was required.

'Given that Mr Parker's death was both sudden and unexpected,' I said, putting coffee beans into the grinder and turning the handle, 'there will, of course, be an inquest. Some questions have arisen,' I glanced up to see his reaction, 'as to certain aspects of his time here and I would like to have those answered to my satisfaction *before* the inquest.' I paused to shake the grinder. 'If you could provide me with the information I need to settle these questions now, there would probably be no need to call you, or others, as witnesses.'

A look of alarm crossed his unlined young face at the notion of giving evidence at an inquest and I felt like a bully. But, as I knew only too well, a man could only feel guilty if he had something to be guilty about.

'Well,' Jenkyn began, cautiously, watching me for any clues as to how he should reply, 'what are the questions that have arisen, Mr Rice?'

We were clearly training our young men well: first define your parameters.

'Something seems to have happened to bring about a change of heart in Mr Parker towards the end of his second term, here,' I said, opening the grinder's box and tipping ground coffee into the pot's drip chamber. 'Do you know what that might have been?'

'Oh yes!' Jenkyn brightened. 'He got religion.'

-

There had, it seemed, been an evangelical preacher in Oxford as part of a tour of provincial towns and, having seen an announcement in the local press, a group including Parker had decided to attend. They'd had no pious motive, Tobias Jenkyn admitted, but had gone to the lecture to amuse themselves by jeering and heckling.

'I know it seems childish,' Jenkyn said, fiddling with one of his waistcoat buttons, 'but you know we wouldn't have been the only ones, Mr Rice – the town boys are terrors for that kind of thing. And those preachers do take themselves awfully seriously.

'Well, along we toddled, and all went as planned, except that the proctors had had the same idea. They arrived just as things started to get lively. The rest of us managed to escape with the townies but Parker was nabbed.'

'Only Parker? The rest of you weren't suspected because you were with him?'

If Jenkyn had been six, he would have squirmed; as he was twenty, he simply looked highly uncomfortable. 'Actually, we weren't all together. We'd got separated, somehow and...'

'You abandoned Sidney to his fate.'

'It was every man for himself,' Jenkyn mumbled. 'You know what the proctors are like, Mr Rice.'

I did. But I also knew a story of ostracism when I heard one. Sidney hadn't really been Jenkyn's friend, he'd just 'gone about' with him and some other chaps. For reasons unspecified, he'd stopped rowing with them but then found nobody else to go out on the water with. I formed the picture of an unhappy young man who'd clung, desperately, to the fringes of a group that hadn't much wanted him.

Parker's punishment from the proctors, Jenkyn told me, had been to face up to the preacher and make an abject apology. 'I don't know what was said, but Parker was a different man after that. Stopped coming with us to—' he pulled up short with an embarrassed cough before he could incriminate himself. 'He was all for the church after that. He even tried to palm some tracts the preacher had given him off on us. I mean, going to church on a Sunday's one thing, but preaching to another chap is going too far, isn't it?'

I wondered how often Jenkyn cut morning chapel and attended roll-call instead. As often as he could get away with it, I suspected.

'Do you know how Parker occupied his free time after he'd moved into lodgings?' I asked. 'If he wasn't going about with you and your friends, do you know who he did associate with?'

Jenkyn shook his head. 'It was all church for Parker, then. St Barnabas. We didn't see him much, only around the quads when he was in college.'

And those, I suspected, would not have been cordial meetings. Not if Parker was in the habit of proselytising. The dead boy's thin, pinched face came to mind, and I thought of his apparent altruism in reading to Corporal Hanes. Had Parker been friendless apart from the old soldier? No, Hanes had referred to a young woman, hadn't he? A sweetheart would surely have compensated Parker for any lack of male friends.

'His other fascination was the gym, of course,' Jenkyn said, as if he'd only just remembered. 'He was there quite a bit. Often hob-nobbing with townies.' He gave a little grin, presumably to lessen the judgement he'd heard in his own words. 'Took up fencing, of all things.'

Such a combative sport seemed an odd choice for a young man with a possible priestly vocation. Father Noel's quotation from the Old Testament sprang to mind with its talk of battling enemies and not being faint hearted.

'Did you consider Parker a coward?' I asked.

Jenkyn seemed at a loss as to how he should answer. 'A coward?' he asked, after a few moments. 'No. Not really. I mean, he wasn't very good at standing up for himself but…' he tailed off uncomfortably.

'Does the phrase "Do not be faint hearted" mean anything to you?'

He shook his head. 'No. I'm afraid not.'

But it had meant something to Sidney Parker. And it had been at his side as he died.

Chapter 25

Non

The longer I worked on Sidney Parker's notebook, the higher he went up in my estimation. From what Basil had said about his academic struggles, I'd expected this code to be easy to crack. But it wasn't. Evidently there'd been more to Sidney Parker than people had realised.

I'd tried all the obvious tricks and I'd got nowhere. The trouble was, I didn't think it was that complicated a code. It wasn't written in blocks of letters that would have to be decoded back into words, I was clearly looking at individual words because there were strings of letters of different lengths with spaces between them.

I was pretty sure Parker wasn't using the Vigenère cipher, the constantly changing alphabetical code that Rev Dodgson had written about in the children's magazine. Not just because the usual way of using a Vigenère doesn't allow for word breaks but because identical strings of letters cropped up here and there, which a Vigenère doesn't produce.

If Parker had made up the code just to make sure that nobody coming across his notebook would be able to read it, he'd still want to be able to write entries and read them back without too much fuss. So, it stood to reason that he must've used a consistent substitution cipher which would be easy to memorise. But simple or not, I hadn't been able to work it out yet.

The text was obviously some kind of journal because each entry started beneath a date. But Parker had been either been cunning or lazy and he'd recorded dates as simple numerals, so there were no clues from repeated substitutions used in the days of the week.

Beneath the date, each entry started with a repetitious string of letters and numbers. For example: *SS – 2*, *SN – 3*, *FCHY – 2*. Over time, some of the letters and numbers varied, and in the last couple of days before he died, FCHY had disappeared and SFG had started cropping up.

Looking at the dates, which started at 5.9.80 and ended on 17.1.81, Parker seemed to have started his journal on the fifth of September last year and written the final entry on the day of his death.

But what had he been writing about? And was it in any way related to the locked box?

Most of the entries weren't long. The first ran to more than a page, but no other entry was much more than half that, and the shortest was only two lines. There were obvious repeated phrases where the same encoded words occurred again and again. So, obviously, Parker was recording consistent things.

Should I ask Florrie?

No. If he'd anticipated keeping his journal after they'd got married, he might well have designed the code as much to keep her in the dark as anybody else.

Perhaps a more careful read through the rest of Mr Parker's papers and cuttings might shed some light on whatever he'd been recording. I closed the journal and pulled the pile of papers towards me but, clumsily, I managed to knock the journal off the desk. When I reached down for it, I noticed a sheet of paper that had been dislodged by the fall.

It was a single sheet, folded in three and must have been slipped in between some of the blank pages.

> *My darling Florrie*
>
> *This is for you. If the worst should happen, I want you to know what I did for you. My friend Davies will decode it for you.*

He'd written an address in Cowbridge, Glamorganshire, and beneath it, an affectionate farewell.

Well, if all else failed, at least now we knew somebody who had the answer.

Chapter 26

Basil

Having seen Mr Jenkyn out, I finished my coffee and made my way back to the lodge. In the quad, windows glowed softly as students and dons found the grey afternoon light insufficient to work by. Their bright warmth made the quad seem more crepuscular than the hour would suggest, but it was barely four weeks since the solstice. We were still in the depths of winter.

As I apologised to the porter, Mr Allen, for ignoring his earlier call to me, he smiled. 'Quite understandable if you were late, Mr Rice. I know you wouldn't want to inconvenience the young men.'

Did he mean to imply that I was too obliging to my undergraduates? That I should have entered college at a more sedate pace and tended to my own correspondence before going to my rooms? His expression was professionally bland, as always.

Muttering my thanks, I took the letters he handed me and stepped outside. If one should happen to be from Teddy, I didn't want my face to betray anything.

One letter was in an envelope and bore Non's unmistakeably bold handwriting. I broke the seal and learned that Mr Parker's personal effects had appeared. *They're very enlightening*, Non had written, without supplying any helpful details as to what light they provided. *Come as soon as possible. (You're invited to supper.)*

The second missive was simply folded and sealed and was, as I had anticipated, from the Principal requiring my presence in his rooms at one o'clock to hear what Morris Williams of Cowbridge School had to tell us. I consulted my watch: twenty minutes before two. Could I get away with claiming that I'd been detained on my errands in Jericho and had only just seen the note? I feared not: the lodgings commanded an excellent view over First Quad and Harper might well have seen me hurrying to my rooms earlier. I would just have to tell the truth and hope that the Principal's disapproval would be tempered by the presence of Mr Williams.

-

I found Dr Harper in a tetchy mood and Morris Williams in a state of some agitation. Once we had been introduced, the headmaster seemed ready to embark on a recapitulation of his news for my benefit, but Harper cut in before he could do more than offer, 'The reason I felt I had to come to Oxford, personally—'

'To cut a long story short,' the Principal said, 'Parker informed his guardian of frequent mistreatment at the hands of one of the older pupils at school. Though the boy was too young to know the term, Reardon inferred that his ward had been the victim of repeated indecent assaults.' Dr Harper glanced at me, then away again. My palms began to sweat. 'The boy asked Reardon to remove him from the school, but Reardon did nothing of the sort. Instead, he started a campaign of extortion. Threatened to write to the papers and—'

'Unmask us,' Morris Williams interrupted, looking up at me. Though Dr Harper had remained standing in front of the drawing room's quietly glowing fire after I had been announced, his guest was seated. 'That was what he said – that he'd "unmask" us as a school where that kind of thing went on.'

'Did you pay?' I asked, wondering whether I had not been invited to sit as punishment for my late arrival.

Morris Williams nodded unhappily. 'I tried to call his bluff. I didn't think Reardon would want news like that made public, given the effect it was bound to have on the boy. But he just showed me the letter he'd already written to the editor of *The Welshman* – he had it there, in a stamped envelope – and said he'd put it in the post box in Cowbridge as soon as he left me if I didn't agree.'

'So you agreed to his terms?'

'It seemed the lesser of two evils. And it wasn't beyond our means. He wanted the boy's fees waived and for the school to guarantee him board and lodging during the holidays.'

'The lesser of two evils or not, it didn't stop there.' The Principal took control of the conversation once more. 'Reardon subsequently threatened the same consequences if Mr Williams failed to recommend Parker for a scholarship here.'

I felt a wave of sadness for Sidney at the thought that his being put forward for a scholarship had not, after all, arisen from a fondness for him. Morris Williams seemed to infer something of my thoughts.

'I didn't like to bow down to threats,' he said, brushing an imaginary speck from his MA gown, 'but it did seem to me that Sidney deserved some kind of compensation for what he'd suffered. Don't misunderstand,' he added, hastily, 'the offending pupil was asked to leave the school, so I hope Sidney didn't suffer any further assaults. But we couldn't undo what had already been done and I felt he deserved something from us.'

'This clearly demonstrates Reardon's readiness to resort to unprincipled behaviour,' Harper said. 'Therefore, we must treat his threat to write to the papers with the utmost seriousness, however spurious his claims of neglect are.'

Were they spurious? I thought of Parker's hollow cheeks, his thin, almost emaciated frame. He had come to us in that state, but was that any excuse for not having recommended that he consult a doctor? Corporal Hanes was blind, yet he had guessed that Parker was 'not a well man'.

'Morrell has written to Dr Pritchard,' I said, 'so he will examine the body as soon as he's able. Meanwhile, I've just received intelligence that some personal papers of Parker's have been found, hidden in his room.' I kept Non's name to myself. How Sidney's effects had come into her possession was a conversation for later.

Dr Harper rose up on the balls of his feet as if he was trying to look down on me; a futile effort as I was several inches taller than he was. 'What sort of personal papers? Do they have any relevance to his death?'

'I can't say, Principal. But, given that he felt the need to hide them, perhaps they have something to tell us. In fact, unless there's anything further, it might be prudent for me to go and bring Mr Parker's property back to college sooner rather than later?'

Dr Harper appeared to be on the brink of agreeing and dismissing me when Mr Williams spoke up. 'Before you go, may I just say a few words about young Sidney?'

I nodded, glancing at Harper who made no objection.

'I don't know what your opinion of him was,' Williams said, 'but to us he seemed an impressionable boy who easily fell under the influence of others. His guardian seldom came to visit him and, though Reardon spoke of his long relationship with Sidney's father, it was obvious that he and the boy didn't know each other at all. It must have taken a great deal of courage – or desperation – for the boy to ask for help. To think of Reardon leaving him there… It seems so cold, doesn't it? Because, although we expelled the offending pupil, Mr Reardon hadn't *asked* us to do so. I don't believe he had any care for Sidney or his suffering, he simply saw an opportunity to make money.'

Williams paused, looking up at me. 'I just hope that Sidney's malleable nature did not take the wrong lessons from what happened to him. I wouldn't like to think of him following his guardian's example.'

Chapter 27

Non

When Basil turned up at Lily's later that evening, he looked tired and preoccupied.

I thought it'd cheer him up to see Sidney Parker's papers, but when he started looking through the things we'd found under the floorboards at Kingston Road, he seemed more depressed than ever. Especially when he came to M. Deslandes' *MANHOOD*.

'Poor chap,' he muttered as he flicked through it.

Sidney Parker deserved his pity. I'd skimmed all the way through the book and, if M. Deslandes was to be believed, manhood was a pretty dismal prospect; or at least, it was if you indulged in 'solitary habits'. According to the Frenchman, 'onanism' brought men to a pretty pitiful state and made them liable to every kind of medical condition known to man: apoplexy, heart disease, pulmonary consumption, scrofula, rickets, 'caries of the vertebrae', spontaneous subluxations of the thigh bone – that's a dislocated hip to you and me – impotence, melancholy and, ultimately, death.

Which was absolute nonsense because, if 'solitary habits' did lead to all that, no sailor would ever have the health to climb on board a ship, still less sail it for months on end then get up to what they did in every port.

After M. Deslandes had spent half the book going into minute detail on the ills of 'self abuse', he spent the next half bending his readers' ears about the infirmity they'd inevitably fall prey to because of it: spermatorrhoea. I took the book from Basil and flicked to a page I'd marked to quote in my next letter to Dr Reckitt.

'Listen to this for the perfect illness for quacks wanting to sell you a cure. *The nocturnal emissions now become conjoined with diurnal pollutions, which latter likewise escape without any sensation, passing off with the urine or when the patient is at stool without either his knowledge or observation.* So, a man doesn't even necessarily know he's got the disease but, if he practises "onanism" then he's bound to, so he'd better buy whatever the quack is peddling!

'Which,' I said, throwing down Deslandes' book and picking up the pile of cuttings and leaflets, 'is what these collected works are all about. Advertisements for spermatorrhoea remedies.'

'*Please!*' Basil was beetroot with embarrassment. 'I beg of you, stop.'

'Why?'

'Because young ladies shouldn't talk about things like this.'

'Why?'

My mother used to hate it when I just kept asking that, and Basil's reaction was no different. 'Don't be obtuse, Non. You may despise social conventions, but they're what keep society civilised.'

'No. *Social conventions* aren't there to keep *society civilised*, they're there to keep society as *men* want it. And I refuse to abide by them in my own home.'

'Has it occurred to you that what men favour isn't always wrong? What would happen if we all said exactly what we thought all the time?'

'That's not what I'm suggesting. I'm not a barbarian. I just want to be able to discuss topics with the same frankness as a man would.'

'Non, I wouldn't happily discuss that book,' Basil nodded at *MANHOOD*, 'with another man, either. Just thinking about it causes me acute embarrassment.'

'Well, more fool you. Anyway, this isn't about social niceties. These papers are important. Why else would Sidney Parker have kept them so carefully hidden?'

'Because he was *embarrassed*—'

We both turned like guilty schoolchildren when the door opened.

'What's the row in here?' Lily asked, looking accusingly at me.

'Basil's cross because I've been reading Mr Parker's papers.'

'So he should be. I told you – those papers are nothing to do with you. This isn't your business.'

'Florrie Spellman's *made* it my business.' I turned to Basil. 'Did you even know he had a sweetheart?'

Embarrassment was written all over his face. Oxford! Full of men who knew everything, except the things that were really important.

'And this might be the answer to what was in those little bottles.' I waved Parker's notebook at Basil. 'It's his journal.'

Basil held out a hand, but I snatched the book out of his way. 'It's in code.'

'Then I should take it to Charles Dodgson.'

Anger flared up. How dare Basil, of all men, assume that Rev Dodgson would be better able to break Sidney Parker's code than me?

'You don't have to be a mathematician to break codes, Basil. A knowledge of how languages work is actually just as useful.'

'Non, I'm very grateful to you and Lily for bringing these papers to my attention, but really, that needs to be the end of your involvement. Sidney Parker's death is Jesus College business.'

Jesus College business. Men's business. Keep out, Non.

'*Stop it, Non. You're working yourself up.*'

'*I'm not working myself up, Hara. I'm seeing things for what they are.*'

I stared at Basil, trying to see him as if I'd never clapped eyes on him before, as if I hadn't come to think of him as a friend. Tall, slim, hair slightly longer than fashionable, thin face clean shaven when most men of his age were wearing beards or bushy sideburns, kind grey eyes. At least, I'd always thought of them as kind. Just now their expression was... what? Hard to read.

'Any man's death diminishes me,' I said, deliberately, 'because I am involved in mankind. Don't tell me I'm not involved, Basil. *That* diminishes *you*.'

'You can quote Donne at me all you like,' Basil said, 'but you know it's not that simple. How is involving yourself in this going to serve your cause? What do you think Dr Harper would say if he knew we were having this conversation? He nearly had an apoplexy yesterday when I tried to suggest that we ask your forensic doctor to do a post-mortem examination of Parker's body. Accused me of having my head turned by you.'

I was pleased that he'd tried to involve Dr Reckitt, but I couldn't help laughing. 'As if *you'd* have your head turned by *me*!'

Basil looked taken aback and I felt a prickle of discomfort. The last thing I wanted was for him to have those sorts of feelings for me. 'Look,' I hurried on, 'Dr Harper doesn't need to know, does he? And anyway, I've already started analysing the code. Rev Dodgson wouldn't get it done any quicker, because he'd be hours behind by the time you got it to him. Especially if I go at it again this evening after supper.'

I watched him weighing up the pros and cons of letting me keep Sidney Parker's journal. Mind, how he thought he was going to take it away from me if I wasn't going to give it up willingly, I had no idea.

'You don't know what's in here,' I said, holding the journal to my breast and wrapping both arms around it. 'It might be very embarrassing to Jesus College. Best not to involve dons from other colleges, don't you think?'

Sidney Parker's romantic attachment to the daughter of a soot merchant, and the 'anomalies' on his naked body would be embarrassing enough to the college, never mind what else might come to light.

Basil gave in. 'Very well then. But please, promise me you won't involve yourself in any other way.'

I hadn't told him that I'd been to the gymnasium and spoken to Sidney Parker's fencing master. 'Sit down, Basil. You too, Lily. The pair of you are making me feel nervous, standing there.'

'No thank you.' Lily was going to let Basil fight his own battle. 'I only came to tell you supper's going to be a bit delayed. The coalman was late coming, and the range went out.'

I put the journal on top of M. Deslandes' book and shuffled all Sidney Parker's papers back into a neat pile on top of the locked box while Lily closed the door behind her.

Avoiding Basil's eye by watching the velvet nap of the dining room tablecloth shine and grow dull in the candlelight as I stroked it this way and that, I explained how we'd happened to be at the Rhys's house when Elspeth Rhys set off to the gymnasium with her little girls. 'Mr Henry the fencing master was very helpful,' I finished.

Mrs Green and all the ladies of the AEW combined couldn't have been less pleased than Basil was. I think it was all he could do not to leap to his feet and start banging the table. 'What were you *thinking of*, Non? You can't just go around asking questions about a man's death!'

'I didn't *just go round asking questions*. I went to tell Mr Henry that Sidney'd died and wouldn't be coming to the gym any more. I thought he might like to know before he read it in the papers.'

Yes, all right, I was trying to make him feel guilty. It wouldn't have occurred to Basil to tell the people whose livelihood depended on young men like Sidney Parker that they wouldn't be seeing him, or his money, again.

'But you *did* ask questions, didn't you?'

'One or two. Entirely appropriate ones.'

From the way Basil looked at me, I could see the phrase 'feminine wiles' flitting through his mind, and I remembered Mr Henry's blushes. 'Look, Basil, do you *want* to know what happened to Sidney Parker or not? Because if you do, you need all the help you can get. As far as I can see, so far, I've done more than half your work for you.'

After that, I couldn't honestly say he was pleased about me getting involved, but at least he stopped grumbling. So, I told him about the Bear Lane loiterer, Bowler Hat.

He was sceptical. 'A flash of brown that might have been a bottle? It's probably got nothing to do with Parker,' he said.

I got up to clear all the papers away before Edie came to lay the table for supper.

'But you don't know that. It needs checking.'

'Don't you dare speak to that man.'

It hadn't occurred to me to speak to Bowler Hat, but I wasn't going to be dictated to. 'Last time I checked, Mr Rice, you weren't my father. Nor my brother. Nor *actually* any relative of mine. So, I'd be grateful if you didn't presume to tell me what I can and can't do.'

But he wasn't going to back down this time. 'I'm *trying* to protect you. You clearly have no notion whatsoever of protecting yourself.'

One day I'd have to show him how wrong he was, although, I must admit, it would be more difficult in a dress than the way I'd learned, in trousers. 'There'd be no point *me* speaking to Bowler Hat, would there?' I pointed out. 'He's outside the men's part of the gym, waiting for *male* customers.' I saw him drawing breath and I knew what he was going to say. 'But *you* couldn't do it either. You'd never pass for an undergraduate. And, anyway, I've got somebody in mind for the task.'

'*What?*' I don't know what bothered him more, the fact that I had a plan about how to get information out of Bowler Hat, or the fact that I had a specific young man in mind. 'Who? Not Albie?'

'No. He's too young. And too Jericho.'

'If you don't tell me, I'll send somebody of my own to do it.'

'Oh, and how are you going to do that without admitting that you might have a suspicious death on your hands?'

'I might ask you the same question.'

'The young man in question already knows about Sidney Parker's death. And about his toothy little ring and breasts.'

Basil gaped at me as if I'd slapped his face. Honestly! How could he not know how quickly gossip spread in Oxford?

I told him about the Popinjay and Mr Askew appearing at the Cipher Club, full of what they'd heard from Gordon Trent in the public bar. Basil tried hard not to show it, but I could tell it was a blow to him. Now, it wasn't just college servants who'd be talking about Parker's death, the undergraduates would, too. But that gave me a good lever to use.

'So, you see, we'd better get the *real* circumstances of Mr Parker's death sorted out so we can keep anything irrelevant from coming out at the inquest.' By 'irrelevant' I meant 'scandalous', obviously.

Basil knew I had him over a barrel. 'I'd like to speak to this young man, whoever he is, before you send him on this errand.'

'Why?'

He heaved a huge sigh. I thought, again, how strained he looked, the rings under his eyes darker and puffier than usual. 'I'd like to impress upon him the serious nature of what we're asking him to do. Parker's guardian, Mr Reardon, wants to drag the good name of the college through the mud. He blames us for Parker's death and for loss of a future business partner.'

'What do you mean, loss of a business partner?'

'Reardon told me that Sidney was going to join him in his advertising agency as soon as he'd graduated.'

'*He* might have thought that,' I said, 'but Sidney had other ideas.'

'So I gather. I thought he was keen on the civil service, but Father Noel at St Barnabas told me he might've been thinking of going into the church.'

'He wasn't going to do either of those things. The two of them – he and Florrie – were going to emigrate to America.' I flipped through the pile of papers and gave him the advice pamphlet for would-be emigrants. The words on its cover couldn't have been clearer.

PRACTICAL ADVICE
for those intending to
EMIGRATE

to the
UNITED STATES OF AMERICA.

'It looks as if Sidney was just stringing Reardon along to keep the peace,' I said. 'Mind you, it wasn't just him. Florrie's dad was under the impression that, as soon as Sidney came of age, he'd marry Florrie and put all his money into a new enterprise with him.'

I watched Basil flicking through the pamphlet and wondered what he was thinking.

Sidney Parker'd obviously been one of those people who tell everybody exactly what they want to hear. To his guardian he'd be the perfect junior partner. To Basil, the struggling but determined scholar. To Florrie's dad, the ideal prospective son-in-law. And to Florrie, he'd been the rescuer, the man who was going to whisk her away from Soot Hall to a new life in America. But perhaps there'd been another Sidney: the one the proctors and their bulldogs knew.

'Florrie Spellman told me that, on the day he died – Monday – he was going to the Proctors' Office to get them to call their dogs off.'

Basil looked up from the leaflet. 'The Proctors' Office?'

I explained about how Sid and Florrie had been stopped after coming out of the theatre and followed home. 'You know what the bulldogs are like,' I said. 'Once the proctors have set them on, they follow people – well, women – until they find out something they don't like. Sidney wasn't going to have them doing that to Florrie. Or so he said.'

Of course, now we knew that Sidney was very free with promises he had no intention of keeping. Maybe he hadn't gone to the Proctors' Office at all.

'You say Sidney wasn't wearing his cap and gown when the proctor's officers stopped him?' Basil said.

'No. Florrie was pretty cross about him being stopped when there was nothing to say he was a member of the University.' I watched Basil. 'But they wouldn't have stopped him unless they knew he was an undergraduate, would they? They must've recognised him from somewhere.'

'It wasn't his first brush with the proctors. He'd been arrested at a religious meeting sometime last year. He and some friends had gone there to make trouble. But the odd thing was, he was the only one that *was* arrested. All his friends got away.'

'Which makes you think that the proctors already knew him before the meeting?'

Basil nodded, still thinking. 'If he was recognised as somebody'd who'd already been in trouble, it would explain why he was caught and the others weren't.'

'But?'

'*But*,' he said, 'no disciplinary action was ever taken against him, that I know of. Even when he was arrested at the religious meeting, nothing came back to college. It was all resolved by the proctors.'

'Is that unusual?'

'Very.'

'So what will you do?'

He seemed troubled, as if he knew exactly what he had to do but didn't like it. 'I'll have to go to the Proctors' Office myself and speak to them.' He looked me squarely in the eye. 'But *now*, I want you to agree to me being present at your meeting with the young man you're going to send to Bear Lane.'

It was on the tip of my tongue to refuse, but then I thought better of it. Tarley Askew might be reassured by Basil being there.

'All right then, be there if you must. In fact, I'll write a note to him, now, and you can deliver it to Corpus Christi for me.'

THE TRUE CAUSES OF MENTAL AND PHYSICAL DECLINE

ADVICE GRATIS. An eminent Specialist whose whole life has been spent in London practice, now issues a pamphlet showing the true cause of Nervous Mental and Physical Debility, lowness of spirits, indigestion, want of energy, premature decline, &c. with the means of cure; whereby the following maladies are speedily and permanently removed and vigorous health restored. Every form and variety of debility, spermatorrhoea, lassitude, depression of spirits, loss of energy and appetite, pains in the back and limbs, timidity, self-distrust, dizziness, love of solitude, groundless fears, palpitation of the heart, noises in the head and ears, indecision, impaired sight and memory, indigestion, and bodily prostration of the whole system.

The most important fact that these alarming complaints may be easily removed is clearly demonstrated, and the entirely new and uniformly successful treatment as followed out by the author fully explained, by which all sufferers are enabled to cure themselves perfectly, and at the least possible cost, without taking quack medicines, or running a doctor's bill.

The publisher will send the book to any part of the world, properly enveloped, on receipt of two penny stamps, by Mr RUSSEL, 17, Crown Terrace, Haverstock Hill, London.

The careful reading of this work will save many from falling a prey to the extortions of advertising sham doctors and their nostrums, and will point out to them a natural and effective mode of curing the above ailments, which has been successful in many thousands of cases, that can be positively proved by grateful testimonials.

The "Glasgow Times" says, "This wonderful tractate by an accomplished medical man will bring comfort to many who have suffered from ignorant treatment."

(Contemporary newspaper advertisement.)

Chapter 28

Basil

Non had asked the young man whom she'd nominated as her cat's paw to come to Shene Road on Saturday morning, so, as I had several things I needed to do before joining them, I had risen before dawn.

Knowing I wouldn't be able to rely on my own internal clock, I'd asked Hollins to wake me. I had been exhausted on Friday evening after spending the whole day walking from Summertown to New Hinksey, Headington to Osney Island, and I knew I would sleep like the dead.

Dismayed by how much Non had managed to discover about Sidney Parker and his life outside college by simply seizing opportunities offered, I had decided that I must match her ad hocery with a degree of considered investigation. I had, therefore, fetched one of the brown Dr Aurum's Tonic bottles and the solitary, anonymous blue bottle from the coach house where Parker's things were being stored, and spent the day visiting every pharmacist, druggist and chemist in the Post Office's Oxford Directory, asking whether they recognised the bottles.

None had, or at least, none had admitted doing so. One more forthcoming assistant had volunteered that Dr Aurum's Tonic was rumoured to be available from McLaren's gymnasium, but he had nothing to say about the blue bottle from Parker's nightstand.

But, though fruitless, at least my enquiries had kept me from fretting about the Principal's decision to ignore George Reardon's ultimatum. Given Reardon's bullish response to Morris Williams's attempt to call his bluff, I couldn't help feeling that Dr Harper was being unwisely cavalier. Surely it would have been more sensible to contact Reardon and seek further negotiations as a stalling tactic?

My anxiety had been exacerbated when, on a visit to the lodgings before dinner on Friday, the Principal had told me that there had been no response from Reardon to the college's silence.

'Then we must hope that tomorrow's papers don't make grim reading for us,' I said.

Those papers represented one of two trials I had to face before meeting with Non and her Corpus undergraduate; the other was my visit to the Proctors' Office.

Having shaved, dressed carefully, and breakfasted on milky coffee in my rooms, I donned cap and gown and left college.

After days of murk and fog, the weather had changed. As I turned from the Turl onto the Broad, sunlight poured down the wide street, causing the tea-drinking cabbies at the cab station in the middle of the road to turn their faces towards its warmth. The early light made the verdigris roof of the Sheldonian's cupola seem almost luminous, and the shadows it threw sharply delineated the imposing, pillared façade of my destination: the Clarendon Building.

The new editions of the local papers were being sold on the street and, having parted with a few coppers, I opened the *Journal* where I stood, turning swiftly to page five, where letters to the editor were printed. Common sense told me that, as weekly newspapers, the final contents of both *Journal* and *Chronicle* had probably been decided well before any letter from Reardon could reach their editors. But I had to be sure.

My heart pounded as I identified three letters. Much to my relief, none of them was from Reardon, though one caught my eye – a rebuttal of a charge, made in a previous letter, that a local official had taken a bribe. I devoutly hoped that Dr Harper would not find himself issuing a rebuttal on behalf of Jesus College in weeks to come.

I folded the paper and put it under my arm while I turned to the correspondence section on the back page of the *Chronicle*.

No letter from Reardon.

We now faced a week of nervous anticipation before the new editions came out, a week during which the inquest into Sidney Parker's death would take place. My stomach contracted painfully at the thought of Reardon standing up and denouncing us, the pencils of the attending journalists flying over their notebooks, recording his every accusation verbatim.

It couldn't be allowed to happen. If Jesus – and by implication, I – was blamed for Parker's premature death, I would not be able to remain in Oxford. Reardon must be given no ammunition to fire. The cause of Parker's death must be determined beyond all doubt.

Folding both newspapers into my jacket pocket beneath my gown, I walked quickly past the Sheldonian, determined not to let my steps falter as I mounted the steps and passed through the Clarendon Building's portico.

I told myself that it was ridiculous to feel so intimidated, that I was a college fellow, here on official business, not an undergraduate facing discipline. But my fear of the Proctors' Office had not diminished with the acquisition of an MA gown and a set of rooms in college. If anything, it had grown as my tenure in Oxford had lengthened. As things stood, the bulldogs touched their hats to me and called me 'sir', but I never lost sight of the fact that one unforeseen encounter could end my career.

Teddy had always laughed at my anxieties. 'Why should they suspect you? Or me, for that matter? We're not stupid, we don't go anywhere near the barracks. We're discreet. And anyway, we confine most of our activities to London.'

But the smallest hint of a rumour took on a life of its own in Oxford, and I had always been acutely aware that discretion might not be enough.

A cold and leaden feeling lodged in my chest at the thought that Teddy and I would no longer lounge comfortably together amongst like-minded men. Certainly not in Oxford and, if his determination to become a respectable family man prevailed, not in London either.

Would I still make trips to the London theatres and clubs with the other chaps? For me, those trips had always, and only, been about Teddy. Even when I was taking my turn in the small rooms set aside for intimate encounters, it was Teddy's hands and mouth I imagined on me, Teddy's face I saw in my mind's eye.

I shook the thoughts off. I had to learn to stop hoping that, one day, he would feel for me as I felt for him. Teddy simply enjoyed sex with men. He didn't want to devote his life to one.

-

The Proctors' Office was small and meanly furnished as befitted a room used simply for procedural matters. Its shelves were stacked with ledgers and files full of the names of undergraduate miscreants, and the solitary small desk sat beneath the light of a north-facing window. There was no chair besides that at the desk; undergraduate visitors were not invited to sit.

I had deliberately timed my visit so that the first undergraduates 'nabbed' by the bulldogs the previous night would not yet have arrived to face whatever music awaited them. The proctorial officer presiding stood before the window, reading through the previous evening's notes, and all I could see of him was the back of his academic cap. Unlike mine, its corners were not battered, nor was it shiny with use. Perhaps, I thought, he had acquired a new one, along with his velvet-sleeved proctorial robe, when he had begun his term of office.

I cleared my throat and the man turned around. A broad smile appeared on his face. 'Rice! How the devil are you?'

I grinned in response. 'Well, thank you, Campbell.'

I remembered the sense of vicarious pride I had felt when I sat in the Sheldonian Theatre, along with hundreds of other University members, to watch Norton Campbell give his speech when he was installed as a junior proctor. It had been a pride not untinged by concern for him. The higher we ascend, the more precipitous and public is any fall from grace.

'And our mutual surgical friend?' Campbell asked.

I schooled my face into a studied neutrality. 'On the move. London and advancement beckon. Marriage too, it seems.'

'Inevitable, I suppose.'

I forced a small smile. 'How does the proctorial robe suit you?'

'A great deal better than hiding in corners. At least with my seat on the Heb, I know what's being said, and by whom. And, obviously, I'm in a position to influence the pro-procs and bulldogs if the need arises.'

Would I have the courage to do what he was doing? I feared not and felt a surge of admiration for one of our own.

He treated me to his endearingly lopsided grin. 'What brings you to our dreaded lair?'

'One Sidney Parker. A Jesus man, now deceased.'

He fixed me with an odd look, his grin quite gone. 'Dead?'

'Sadly, yes.'

Campbell turned to hook the only chair and push it in my direction. 'Take a pew.' He hitched himself up on to the desk, and I couldn't help thinking how un-proctorial he looked sitting there like a schoolboy. 'You may be sad, but I'm afraid I can't quite summon up the same feeling.'

'You knew him, then?'

Campbell grimaced. 'We had an encounter when I was a pro-proctor.'

I waited.

'In his first term, the bulldogs caught Parker with a girl late in the evening. A girl known to us, and not for her outstanding virtue.'

The feeling – present since the discovery of his body – that I had failed to understand the first thing about Sidney Parker ratchetted up a notch.

'The bullers followed him back to Jesus, asked for his name – which, interestingly, was given, so no love lost between him and the porter, I suspect – then sent for him to come in and explain himself. So far, so commonplace. But, when he came to report, things took a turn very much out of the common run.'

Campbell looked away for a moment and the sounds filtering in from Broad Street seemed suddenly magnified, as if all my senses had become more alert. Barrowmen called to each other, hackneys clopped by at the trot, birds sang to the early sun. But in the little office, daily life held its breath.

'To strip the thing to its bones, he told me he knew what I was. Threatened to expose me if I breathed a word of the previous evening's activities to Jesus College.'

I felt a chill go down my spine, as if an eavesdropper had accidentally pushed the door ajar and let in an icy draught. 'How?' I swallowed. 'I mean, how did he know?'

Campbell shook his head, his mouth clamped shut. How Parker knew, or whether he had any actual evidence as to Campbell's sexual proclivities didn't much signify; the mere suggestion of deviance would be enough to blight my friend's career, if not to end it.

'I almost lost my breakfast when I came in on Monday morning and saw his name in the book,' Campbell went on. 'Did you know he'd had another run-in a couple of terms ago?'

'The religious meeting?'

'Yes. One of the bulldogs who'd nabbed him the first time recognised him in the crowd of hecklers. I was waiting outside on that occasion, and I made the best of it. Told the bullers I'd deal with him and marched him off to the padre to apologise.' He grinned, ruefully. 'It was all very "let the punishment fit the crime" which the bulldogs liked.'

I had to admire Campbell's quickness of thought. It was well known that the proctors' officers felt that misbehaving undergraduates got away with murder. A dose of summary justice would have appealed to them.

'The odd thing was, I was all ready to let him go once we were out of sight of the bullers, but he said he'd like to speak to the preacher. I went in with him to make sure he didn't start abusing the man again, but when it was obvious that he was genuinely contrite, I left them to their little tête-à-tête.'

All of which corresponded with what Mr Jenkyn had told me about Sidney's change of heart from that evening onwards. 'And last Monday?' I asked.

'The same bulldog, Staithe, had seen him with a girl on Saturday evening and written him up. Never forgets a name, Staithe. Or a face for that matter. But Parker wasn't contrite on this occasion. According to the pro-proctor who was with them, he professed himself to be outraged that he and the girl – who he claimed was his fiancée – should be stopped in the street when they were going about their lawful business. Lawful bar the fact that, again, he wasn't wearing his cap and gown.' Campbell blinked. 'When I spoke to the pro-proc, he told me Parker'd said that he'd be here first thing on Monday morning to make a complaint.'

I could see why Campbell's stomach had threatened to rebel at the sight of Parker's name. Though he hadn't been one of the party that caught Parker with his girl, he'd been the one who would have to deal with him.

'What happened?' I asked.

'Nothing. Saw neither hide nor hair of him.' Campbell met my eye, and I saw a shameful truth in his face: he was relieved that Parker could make no more threats against him.

After a little more conversation, I left, pondering Sidney Parker's failure to turn up. The most likely explanation was that he had made his threat to complain simply to impress his sweetheart. But there was always the possibility that he had not been well enough on Monday morning to leave his lodgings.

A visit to Mrs Trent was indicated, and I had enough time to visit the house in Kingston Road before meeting with Non and her young man at ten.

Chapter 29

Non

When I came downstairs just before ten on Saturday morning, to wait for Tarley Askew and Basil, my head was still full of Sidney Parker's journal. I'd spent all of Friday on it, then I'd been up half the night wrestling with the damn thing. I would have worked longer, but both the candle I'd taken up to bed with me and the spare one I kept in my room for late nights had been at least two hours the worse for wear before I started. Even using them consecutively, the second one had sputtered out just after three o'clock.

Still, to be honest, it hadn't only been a lack of light to read by that'd made me give up and get into bed. The fire in my bedroom grate had burned out by midnight and the room had gradually got intolerably cold. Even wrapping myself in my bedcover and sitting on my pillow hadn't been enough to stop me shivering and I'd had to warm my fingers at the candle flame every few minutes to keep them working.

If I'd had more candles and extra coal, I could have carried on working but I couldn't go downstairs. Lily would have heard me and known I was working, and she'd already had quite a lot to say on the subject of me getting involved with 'all this' after Basil had left on Thursday evening.

'I don't know what you're thinking of,' she'd ranted. 'This is the last thing you should be doing if you want to be allowed back into lectures.'

'But if I can help Basil make sure there's no scandal—'

'If you think that's going to make Dr Harper *grateful*, my girl, you can think again!' She shook her head. 'You really don't know these men at all, do you? If Dr Harper hears that you've been helping Basil, he'll have even more to hold against you than he's got now. Men like him can't accept help from women. Especially not when they've told them they don't need it.' She glared at me. 'You should've let Basil take that code book to Rev Dodgson.'

Et tu, Lily. 'Speaking of Rev Dodgson,' I said. 'You haven't forgotten that we're having lunch with him today, have you?' All right, I was getting my own back, but I was sick of being told what I could and couldn't do.

Lily looked at me darkly. 'No, I haven't forgotten. Maybe *I'll* tell him about the code book.'

I stared at her. She wouldn't. Would she?

-

Basil arrived in a rush a few minutes before ten, his clothes smelling of coal smoke and cold air.

'I've just been to see Mrs Trent,' he said after he'd hung his things on the hallstand. 'It seems that Sidney Parker was a little more "under the weather" than she'd previously admitted.'

Edie'd come up from the basement when she heard the door, so I asked her to bring the tea tray up, then Basil and I joined Lily in the sitting room. She'd long ago stopped chaperoning me where Basil was concerned, but she didn't know Tarley Askew from Adam, so she was taking no chances.

Basil folded his long limbs on to the sofa. However often he came to our house, he never seemed able to make himself quite at home. Always looked as if he was ready to leap up and justify himself to somebody.

'Why did you go back to the Trents' house?' I asked.

'Because of what Florence Spellman told you about her and Sidney having a run-in with the proctors on Saturday evening. I checked and there was no record of Sidney having gone to the Proctors' Office on Monday. So, just to dot all the i's and cross all the t's, I thought I'd just have another word with Mrs Trent, find out how Sidney had seemed to her that morning.'

'And what exactly did she say?'

'She admitted that he hadn't stirred from his room all day bar visits to the lavatory. Said she thought his bowels had been plaguing him again.'

Lily turned to me. 'Florrie said he had bouts with his stomach, didn't he?'

I nodded. 'That's probably why he was drinking bottles of paregoric,' I said. Lily was a great believer in dosing the family with all sorts and paregoric always came out if anybody had diarrhoea.

'Whatever he was taking,' Basil said, 'the point is, we now know that Sidney hadn't been well since Sunday night, which means that he didn't just die in his sleep without warning, he was suffering from something. I hope we'll find out more when Dr Pritchard carries out the post-mortem this morning.'

'I'm surprised Betty Trent didn't tell you straight away how poorly Sidney had been,' Lily said. 'It's not like her to hold back.'

'I think she felt a little guilty, Lily,' Basil said. 'That she hadn't done more for him.'

More likely, Betty Trent hadn't wanted to talk about bowels in front of Dr Harper.

'But she wasn't to know, was she?' Lily protested. 'Especially if he often had trouble with his digestion.'

I turned to Basil. 'Do you think she might have given him a bit more Godfrey's Cordial than she admitted? That's probably got opium in it as well – most of those patent remedies have.'

Lily looked as if she was about to defend Betty Trent but, just then, the wooden bird popped out of the clock on the wall to give us the first of its annoyingly fatuous 'cuckoos', and there was a knock at the door.

'That'll be Mr Askew,' I said, getting up.

With her usual uncanny timing, Edie was coming up from the basement with the tea tray as I went to the front door, so I sent her into the sitting room with it then made sure she saw me watching her go back along the passage and down the steps to the basement while I waited for Tarley Askew to take his cap, gown and scarf off.

I hadn't taken much notice of him when he'd turned up at the Cipher Club. He'd just been quieter and less annoying than Peacock. Now, standing in our hall, he seemed to take up more space than he had in the back room at the Jericho. He wasn't as tall as Basil, but he was taller than average, and his broad shoulders made me wonder whether he was a rower. After he'd put his cap on the hallstand, he pushed the fingers of one hand through his dark, curly hair but I could have told him there was no point trying to keep hair like that tidy. Unless he was going to slather it with macassar oil it would always do exactly what it wanted. My own hair was the same and I'd given up trying to tame it.

'Your note was very mysterious,' he said.

'Yes, I apologise for being a bit obscure. As I said, I need a favour. But it's not just for me. And you might not want to get involved.'

He frowned a tiny little frown. 'Involved?'

'Come into the sitting room and I'll explain.'

-

Tarley Askew turned out to be quick on the uptake and, by the time Basil and I had finished explaining, he'd already guessed what we wanted him to do.

'I take it you'd like me to track down this character in Bear Lane and see if I can obtain a bottle of Dr Aurum's Tonic and whatever he's selling in blue bottles, for analysis?'

Lily'd been looking more and more unhappy the longer Basil and I had gone on and now she decided that enough was enough. 'Mr Rice, I don't think you should be getting Mr Askew mixed up in all this. Non thinks she's got a right to push her way in because Mr Parker happened to come here for supper once and I know Betty Trent. But this is nothing to do with Mr Askew and, if you don't mind me saying, I don't think it's fair to him.'

'Mrs Maddox, I don't mind, really.'

'No, I'm sure you don't. But that's because you've had your head turned by this one.' Lily glared at me. 'But it'll do you no good. You won't win her round by helping—'

'Excuse me!' This might be Lily's house but that didn't give her the right to talk about me as if I wasn't there. 'It's very insulting to imply that Mr Askew's only here to curry favour with me.'

'And why else would he be here? Not to help Sidney Parker, I'm sure.' She turned to Tarley Askew. 'Did she mention any of this when she invited you here?'

'What I did or didn't say to Mr Askew isn't any of your business, Lily Maddox.'

She ignored me. 'Mr Askew, what would your parents say if they knew you were sitting here? This isn't why they sent you to Oxford, is it?'

Tarley Askew leaned forward, earnestly. 'Mrs Maddox, I'm very grateful to you for having my best interests at heart. Truly. And I know my mother would thank you, too. Sadly, my father's dead so he can't have an opinion either way, but he was an officer in the Indian Army and I'm sure he never shrank from a challenge. I know my mother would think less of me if I didn't help when it's within my power to do so.'

Lily looked at him as if he didn't know what he was talking about. 'This should be a matter for the police.'

'And how near do you think a man in uniform would get to the character we want to talk to?' I asked. 'Not within a hundred yards.'

Lily stood up. 'I see you're all determined, so I'll leave you to it. But you need to ask yourself, Rhiannon Vaughan… what would Miss Rees say?'

I knew the answer to that without a breath of doubt. In advice Cranogwen had given in the 'questions from readers' column of her periodical, *Y Frythones*, she'd made it very clear that she thought tasks should be done by those most suited to them, irrespective of gender. She'd be on my side.

I could see that Lily's opposition to Mr Askew being involved had rattled Basil, so, once she'd left, it wasn't a surprise when he asked, 'Are you quite sure that you wish to act on our behalf in this matter, Mr Askew? As Mrs Maddox has indicated, we are proceeding quite without official sanction.'

Tarley Askew leaned towards us. 'I'm sure. Parker was a member of the University. That gives us all some degree of responsibility, doesn't it? Besides, I don't believe I'll open myself to anything worse than a charge of credulousness if I approach this peddler.'

Basil reached over the arm of the sofa to put his cup and saucer down on the floor where he wouldn't kick them over when he got up. 'Actually, your very kind offer to help notwithstanding, approaching the peddler may turn out not to be necessary. The coroner, Mr Morrell, has asked one of the surgeons at the Infirmary to carry out a post-mortem.'

'Who?' Even though I hadn't been optimistic that Dr Harper would relent and call for Dr Reckitt, I was still disappointed. 'The surgeon who acts for Dr Hussey's inquests?'

Basil shifted as if the sofa'd suddenly developed uncomfortable lumps. 'No, actually. A Jesus graduate. It was felt that perhaps it might be prudent to ask a doctor who would be sympathetic to the college and its reputation.'

I glanced at Tarley Askew and found him looking at me, probably to gauge my reaction to this blatant closing of ranks.

'I hope you're not trying to suppress evidence?' I tried to sound flippant but, really, I was appalled. These college men!

'We're not trying to keep anything from the jury,' Basil said. 'Only from the public gaze. And the press, of course.'

Oh, dear me. It wouldn't do to have people reading about what Oxford undergraduates were really like, would it?

'When will we know the doctor's findings?' Tarley Askew asked.

'With luck,' Basil said, shifting on the non-existent lumps again, 'he may be at Jesus now. Our best course might be to make our way to college before you take any action. See what he has to say.'

I knew there was no point in asking if I could go with them. If Dr Harper saw me on Jesus premises there'd be no end of a row. 'Right, off you go then, the pair of you,' I said. 'Meanwhile, I'll get back to Mr Parker's journal. Shall we compare notes later on?'

Chapter 30

Basil

As it was possible that the post-mortem examination might already be underway, Non suggested that Tarley Askew and I borrow her tandem. Cycling, we'd reach Jesus more quickly and give ourselves the opportunity to hear Teddy's conclusions before he left. If Parker had died of natural causes, Mr Askew would not need to brave an encounter with the man in the bowler hat.

I must confess, I was intrigued by the tandem and had always wanted to try my hand at it. Given that it was a tricycle, there was no danger that I would lose my balance as I might on an ordinary, and if Non and Lily could propel the thing about, surely it would not be beyond Mr Askew and me?

Five minutes later I wished we'd walked. Either the tricycle was intended for much shorter people or there was a design flaw that meant that one had to pedal the cranks with one's knees bent at an uncomfortable angle. Added to which, there was the matter of directing the thing accurately. The steering handles, one on either side at thigh-height, proved unexpectedly difficult to master and I regretted taking the helm. I suspected Mr Askew would have proved more adept.

By the time we reached the northern end of Turl Street, however, I had become more proficient, and I managed to direct us down towards college and to turn along Ship Street and the back gate without incident.

'I wouldn't willingly acquire one of those in preference to an ordinary,' Mr Askew said, swinging himself off the machine to allow me to get down. 'The riding position's much less comfortable. On an ordinary, I felt I could cycle all day if I needed to. Still,' he added, 'I can see that for ladies it's the only practical kind of machine. What with their skirts and so on.'

'Don't let Non hear you say that. She's always threatening to acquire a bicycle and don trousers to ride it.'

Most young men would have been aghast at the thought of a young woman in trousers, particularly one they found attractive, but Askew merely raised an eyebrow slightly. Was he actually impressed by the idea?

I had known Non for some time now, and, to a certain extent, had stopped noticing her oddness. Being Welsh set her apart of course, as did her constant questioning of social conventions. But it was, perhaps, the freedom with which she moved through the world which most marked her as different; not simply the physical freedom allowed by her refusal to wear constraining clothing, but the freedom to go wherever she liked, which she laid as determined a claim to in Oxford as she had in Cardiganshire. The AEW might try to hedge her about with chaperones and respectability, but Rhiannon Vaughan was, at heart, a wild thing determined not to be domesticated.

I brushed myself down, trying to arrange my gown in a respectable fashion, but it had been creased by my sitting on it to stop it catching in the drive wheel and it hung rather forlornly; I would have preferred Teddy not to see me looking so dishevelled but there was nothing to be done about it.

But perhaps he had already finished the examination and would no longer be here? My hand shook as I raised it to unlatch the door to the service range. As always, I wanted to see Teddy, but I was afraid that I would be unable to hide my continuing distress at his decision to leave. I could not bear to be pitied, still less despised as effeminate.

We wheeled the tandem awkwardly into the stable yard and as we passed between the old stables and the ball court into the main part of the yard it became apparent that the post-mortem examination was well advanced. The trestle table bearing Parker's body had been moved out of the stygian gloom of the coach house, and the cadaver – for that was what Parker's body very obviously now was – lay opened and bloody beneath the smoky blue of the January sky.

I found myself considerably less repulsed by the sight of Sidney Parker's internal organs than I'd anticipated. Perhaps it was because I hadn't been obliged to watch the scalpel cutting through skin and muscle, the folding back of tissues that now hung over the sides of the largely empty torso. With the sheet that had previously covered the boy's nakedness folded carefully over his head, his corpse seemed hardly human.

I was surprised to see Dr Fielding; I'd quite forgotten Morrell's stipulation that he be present at the examination. As we approached, he was shrugging into his overcoat as if his part in the proceedings was now over.

Teddy looked up as we approached. 'Good morning,' he said, his normal exuberance slightly subdued. By his task or my appearance?

'Good morning.' I looked from Teddy to Fielding, including the latter in my greeting and introducing Mr Askew, to polite mutual nods.

'Dr Fielding was the physician initially asked to certify Mr Parker's death,' I said, 'and the fellow currently unable to shake your hand for obvious reasons is Dr Edmund Pritchard.' I heard my attempt at a light-hearted introduction of a good friend and was dismayed at how far short I fell.

'I'm afraid I must take my leave,' Dr Fielding said. 'I've observed the post-mortem, as requested, and can be called on at the inquest to confirm Dr Pritchard's evidence if necessary.'

'Thank you, doctor.' I felt uncomfortable. The University was highly unlikely to pay him for his time and Fielding would know perfectly well why he had been asked to attend.

'I'll see you out,' I said.

'No need. Good day, gentlemen.' He swept past me, medical bag in hand. I wondered whether his brusqueness arose from something Teddy had said. I knew he wouldn't have appreciated Morrell's insistence on another doctor being present and he might have been less than entirely gracious in declining any offer of assistance.

I cleared my throat and moved a little closer to the dissecting table. 'You've made good progress.'

A second table had been erected at right angles to the one on which the body lay and on it stood a selection of bowls and platters, each containing an organ. Or, in the case of the intestine Teddy was currently dissecting, largely failing to contain.

'As per Mr Morrell's request,' Teddy did not look up, but continued to wield his scalpel, 'I called on Fielding and came over first thing.'

'We're lucky it's such a bright day.'

Teddy kept his eyes on his work. 'Any kind of daylight would've done. It's what the human eye has evolved to see in.'

He was a great evolutionist. Charles Darwin's books had the status of holy writ as far as Teddy Pritchard was concerned.

Askew approached the table and watched with apparent fascination. After half a minute or so, Teddy looked up. 'What's your interest, here, Mr Askew?'

'He's helping the college gather evidence for the inquest,' I said. 'Including the identification of some patent remedies Mr Parker was apparently dosing himself with.'

'I see.' Teddy turned back to his work. 'Well, I can understand this poor chap wanting to take something. He was quite unwell.'

As he spoke, I noticed the bucket on the ground behind him and detected the unmistakeable smell of faeces. Why had I not noticed it before? Had my attention been so taken up with mastering my emotions?

'See this?' Teddy used his scalpel to point at a thickened, misshapen part of the bowel. 'It's part of a colovesical fistula – an opening between the lower intestine and the bladder.'

'What would cause that?' Askew asked.

'This,' Teddy responded and opened out part of the dissected – and obviously rinsed out – bowel. 'The colon is badly ulcerated and inflamed. He would often have been in considerable pain.'

I thought of Parker's constant visits to the lavatory on the day before he died. 'Would it have caused diarrhoea?'

Teddy looked up and, as our eyes met, I felt the familiar physical jolt. After all these years, it still shook me. 'Undoubtedly. And some of it would have entered the bladder, resulting in chronic urinary tract inflammation and infection.'

I looked away, unable to bear the exposure of eye contact.

'He'd obviously been suffering from this condition for some time,' Teddy continued. 'His kidneys are badly affected.' He turned ninety degrees and addressed himself to the cadaver. 'Not only that, but he's made things worse by self-diagnosing and using patent cures—'

'He believed he had spermatorrhoea,' I interrupted as Teddy's hand went to Parker's penis which had been bisected down the midline.

'I can tell you categorically that he didn't,' Teddy said.

'How?' Askew asked.

'Because nobody does. Spermatorrhoea doesn't exist. It's an entirely fabricated disease dreamed up by doctors who use medicine in the cause of morality. It's a bogey-man, designed to frighten young men out of certain habits and into fresh air and exercise. How we've allowed it to persist I don't know, but its existence – not to mention various quack remedies which are supposed to cure it – have been pushed by a certain sort of doctor for donkey's years.'

'How is that possible, if it doesn't exist?' Tarley asked.

'Because it's difficult to prove a negative, and because all young men demonstrate the alleged symptoms occasionally: spontaneous erections and involuntary emissions. And also because pretty well every malady known to man is laid at spermatorrhoea's door. Which means that any man can believe he's got it if he's credulous.'

'But are *doctors* so credulous?'

Teddy snorted humourlessly. 'Believe it or not, Mr Askew, doctors are just like everybody else. Some are credulous fools and some are very keen on making money for very little effort. *I'm afraid you have spermatorrhoea, my dear fellow,*' he said, adopting the plummy tones of an upper-class physician of a previous generation; he was an excellent, and sometimes cruel, mimic. '*What have you been up to? Har har har! Here, take these pills, only ten shillings for three dozen.*' He gazed at Askew for a moment or two. 'Spermatorrhoea is like Hans Christian Anderson's emperor and his new clothes. Chattered about incessantly by men afraid to speak up against orthodoxy, and *entirely non-existent*.'

The anxiety gripping my stomach and speeding my pulse suddenly turned, on a sixpence, to anger. How dare he denigrate men who were afraid to speak up against orthodoxy when he was no better? What was his flight to London and the prospect of married life but a blatant failure to withstand orthodoxy?

'And see this?' Teddy motioned to the bisected penis. 'He's been sold some unspeakable quack remedy which he's been pushing up his urethra. The whole thing is scarred, inflamed and infected and it's affected his prostate too.'

'He sounds a mess,' Askew said. 'Is all this what killed him?'

'Difficult to say. His bowel condition is of long standing, which will have imposed an enormous strain on his system.'

'He was taking several proprietary medicines,' I said, getting a grip on my unruly emotions. 'Including paregoric and Chlorodyne. We found laudanum in his nightstand too. Could he have died of opium poisoning?'

'I doubt it,' Teddy said, his eyes on the cadaver, 'but individual tolerance to opium does vary enormously.' He glanced at me, then immediately away again. 'Given the state of his kidneys, it's possible that it wouldn't have taken a particularly large dose to have killed him.'

'Normal doses of paregoric and Chlorodyne, together with a conventional dose of laudanum?'

He shook his head. 'No. Not that little.'

In which case, there was a chance that the contents of either Dr Aurum's Tonic or the nameless blue bottle had contributed to his death.

'Do you know what caused the gynaecomastia?' I asked.

'That's a very technical medical term for a layman,' Teddy mocked, grinning.

'Dr Fielding used it at the initial examination,' I said, managing to keep my voice steady.

Teddy turned his attention to Tarley Askew. 'Gynaecomastia is the development of breast tissue in men,' he said, in anatomical demonstrator mode. 'Some boys and young men develop the condition, which then disappears as they approach manhood. It's embarrassing but not pathological.' His eyes flicked back to me. 'How old was this boy?'

'Mr Parker was almost twenty-one,' I said, recalling Florence Spellman's claim that she and Sidney were to be married as soon as he had come of age.

'It's unusual for immature tissue to persist that long,' Teddy said, 'but for every rule there's an exception, obviously.'

Tarley Asked frowned slightly. 'I know I have no medical training,' he began, carefully, 'but is it possible that he developed gynaecomastia in the normal course of development, as you say, but instead of seeking medical attention and being assured that it would go away, leapt to the conclusion that it was all of a piece with wet dreams and inconvenient erections, diagnosed himself with spermatorrhoea and began looking for cures, one of which may, inadvertently, have made the condition persist?'

Teddy gave his question some consideration. 'I believe there are herbs that predispose to gynaecomastia. Agrimony springs to mind for some reason. Must've read it somewhere. And hops, of course. Beer is always blamed when a man develops mammary tissue,' he said, 'and hops do seem to cause a certain degree of impotence – what they call "brewer's droop" – so tincture of hops might've been included in a so-called remedy for spermatorrhoea. If the number or hardness of erections fell, then a boy might imagine that the remedy was working.'

'And perhaps this remedy might also have contained substances which led to the ulceration of his bowel?' Mr Askew suggested.

Teddy nodded, eyes on Tarley Askew. 'It's a very elegant theory. Have you thought of medicine as a career, Mr Askew?'

I cleared my throat before Askew could reply to this blatant bit of flattery. 'So, your conclusion as to cause of death, when the coroner asks?'

'I'll tell him what I've told you. That the deceased had an ulcerated lower bowel, a colovesical fistula, an acutely inflamed penis and prostate, and damaged kidneys. These things, by themselves, may have been enough to kill him if he developed a sufficiently severe infection.'

'But you don't think he died of opium poisoning?' I asked.

'Unlikely, despite his paregoric and laudanum habit.'

Tarley Askew shook his head. 'Why are these medicines freely available if they're so potentially dangerous? Why doesn't the government do something?'

Teddy smiled cynically. 'Because they're mostly relied on by people who can't afford a doctor, Mr Askew. And, as they don't have the vote, the government isn't much disposed to care.'

Chapter 31

Non

Lily and I left the house not long after Tarley and Basil. It was a good twenty minutes' walk to Christ Church College with Lily in her going-out stays, and she always added on fifteen minutes to the time we needed to get to any appointment, in case we were held up talking to people we knew. Well, people *she* knew. I never minded telling people I couldn't stop but Lily seemed to think her acquaintances would be mortally offended if she didn't exchange a few words with them.

Lily was still in a mood with me for getting Tarley Askew involved with the Sidney Parker investigations, so she just marched along by my side as we went down Walton Street. Suited me, I'd heard enough about my shortcomings.

As we walked past the University Press, I could hear the steam presses and wondered how loud it must be inside. I'd noticed that people in the city got cross about noise in a way that just didn't happen back home. Just now, the iron rails had started being laid for the new horse trams, and to try and dampen the noise of the wheels on the rails, some sections of the tramway were going to be paved with wooden blocks. Sounded like a mad idea to me – how long would wooden bricks last with horses tramping up and down them all day? But that was the way the local board thought. Maybe they'd come under pressure from the colleges not to disturb the undergraduates' labour.

Lily glanced at me, and I gave her my most innocent smile. She frowned. 'Don't you give me that butter-wouldn't-melt look, my girl. You haven't redeemed yourself yet.' Then, after stomping on for another half a minute or so she looked at me out of the corner of her eye. 'Are you going to tell Rev Dodgson what you've got his protégé doing?'

Lily'd recently learned the word protégé, when Elspeth Rhys had used it to describe my relationship to her husband, and she liked to use it whenever she could.

'You know I'm not. And I'd ask you not to either,' I said, speaking more calmly than I felt.

'Oh, you would, would you?'

'Yes. You can't speak for Mr Askew,' I said. 'What he does or doesn't get involved with is his business, not yours or Charles Dodgson's. But I *will* talk to him about the code Sidney Parker used.' To be honest, I still thought I could break it, left to myself, but I didn't have unlimited time. The inquest was in four days.

If anybody could cut through the Gordian knot of Sidney Parker's odd cipher it would be Charles Dodgson.

-

'Mrs Maddox, might I take the liberty of asking you to cut the pie?' Rev Dodgson asked when a college servant had brought our lunch to his dining room. 'I'm afraid I'm the most awful duffer with a sharp knife.'

He watched her cutting the raised pie with quick, decisive strokes and, as she served it to us without a crumb falling on to the crisp, white napery, he told us how he'd once cut into the lace doily underneath a rather hard pastry and served it up to his guests with their tart.

Charles Dodgson was the sort of man who would quite happily tell stories which made him look duffer-ish himself, but he was very sensitive to criticism from other people. Maybe that's why he'd never left Christ Church after coming here as an undergraduate; he wouldn't have survived in the real world.

Mind, it wasn't a bad place to have ended up. His first-floor rooms overlooking Tom Quad were bigger than Lily's house, and he had access to the flat roof above. When he'd taken Lily and me up there on our first visit to show us the view, he'd been like a proud Satan showing Jesus how all the kingdoms of the world lay within his gift. He'd had a photographic studio installed up there but, recently, he'd given up taking photographs. Said it was too time-consuming for him these days, that he had too much else to do. Presumably he was busy with things like learning how to use the new type-writing machine he'd had sent over from America. He was very taken with it. Personally, I couldn't see the advantage of thing, unless you had really awful handwriting. And it was so noisy you couldn't hear yourself think.

As we ate our pie and Rev Dodgson started on another amusing anecdote, I looked around the dining room. We hadn't been in there before. On our previous visit we'd taken tea in one of his sitting rooms. The dining room was smaller but beautifully furnished and, like every inch of Rev Dodgson's rooms, it was as neat as a chemist's shop. The walls were hung with paintings, and objects he'd collected – or invented – were carefully displayed on the mantelpiece.

I'd never been to Basil's rooms in Jesus College, but I was fairly sure they wouldn't be the equal of Rev Dodgson's. For one thing, Basil wasn't so senior. For another, he didn't have the income which Dodgson's literary work gave him. Still, at least Basil had a degree and his fellowship; Annie Rogers, who was undoubtedly his intellectual superior, had neither and was forced to live with her parents in Beaumont Street.

There was a sudden silence and I realised that Rev Dodgson had been watching me while I looked around his room. I felt myself blush, but he was far too courteous to comment on my nosiness. Instead, he offered an apology of his own.

'I'm sorry we weren't a better company on Wednesday night, Miss Vaughan. The proceedings were so derailed by Mr Peacock's gossip that I quite forgot to give you a rather interesting little cipher puzzle I'd invented. But perhaps you've been working on something of your own?'

I looked quickly over at Lily. Had she written to him, telling him about my struggles with Sidney Parker's cipher? No, I could see from her face that she hadn't. And she obviously wasn't going to mention it now, either. She was casting rapid glances at a painting of fairies on the wall as if she couldn't quite believe it was really there.

'As it happens,' I said, 'something rather interesting has come my way.' Then, without mentioning Sidney Parker or letting Rev Dodgson know that I'd become involved with the subject of Mr Peacock's gossip, I told him about the cipher and what I'd done so far to try and break it.

He speared a portion of hard-boiled egg then added a chunk of pork with pastry attached, before chewing methodically, while his eyes moved between me, Lily and the fairies on the wall. Evidently he'd noticed her fascination with it. 'You have, of course, taken all the steps any competent cryptographer would have done,' he said. 'But have you considered the context?'

I put my cutlery down and concentrated. 'What kind of context?'

'Who created the cipher? How old were they? What level of education had they?' He sipped his wine. 'And above all, my dear Miss Vaughan, who was the intended recipient?'

I thought of Florence Spellman and the disparity between her education and Sidney's. But then, Florrie hadn't *been* the intended recipient, had she? Not of the encoded version, at any rate. Sidney had meant her to send the book to this Mr Davies in Cowbridge so that he could decode it.

And then I had it.

Cowbridge.

In Glamorgan.

Where they spoke the Welsh dialect called Gwenhwyseg.

I nodded. 'Thank you. I believe you've just given me a new avenue to explore.'

Rev Dodgson smiled. 'Excellent. I'm sure you'll have it in no time. And, as for the Cipher Club, I must give some consideration to who I might invite next time. Mr Peacock is, perhaps, a little too excitable.'

So, the Popinjay wouldn't be back. Good. 'Perhaps Mr Askew might be worth inviting again?' I suggested. 'He seemed more level-headed?'

Dodgson's eyes crinkled up in a delighted beam. 'Did you take to Mr Askew? I'm so pleased. He's very appropriate.'

I stared at him. 'I beg your pardon? Appropriate in what way?'

At my side, Lily's attention had snapped from the fairies to me. I ignored her and waited for Charles Dodgson to say something.

'Oh, don't be cross, my dear. You have no Oxford mama to introduce you to suitable young men—' He cut himself short. Perhaps he was afraid I was about to shout at him.

Lily was obviously afraid of that, too, because she put a warning hand on my arm. 'Rev Dodgson,' she said, with a conciliatory little smile, 'have you been introducing Non to potential suitors all this time? Is that what the Cipher Club has been for?'

'No, no, my dear Mrs Maddox! You quite misunderstand me. Such introductions as I've been able to make have merely been a happy consequence of bringing lively minded young people together. I'm a mathematician, not a matchmaker.' His smile was a bit less sure of itself now, but I could see he was pleased with his bit of alliteration. 'My intention with the Cipher Club has always been to lead young minds beyond the dry mathematical text books and into the sunlit fields of what some are pleased to dismiss as *recreational* mathematics.'

'But nevertheless, you thought it would be a good idea to use the club to introduce me to potential husbands?' I was barely able to contain my fury.

'My dear Miss Vaughan, here in Oxford you are amongst the finest minds of your generation. If you do not find a husband here, where will you?'

'Is it not a little presumptuous to assume that I *want* a husband? After all, you've never felt the need to marry, yourself.'

The question visibly flustered him. 'I am a m-man, Miss Vaughan. Men may remain bachelors and yet lead full and fulfilling lives. Especially here in Oxford. N-no such solitary avenue exists for women. Unless they are women of fortune, of course.'

'So, given my lowly birth, I must make the most of Oxford and catch a husband while I'm here, so that I can be somebody's wife?'

'*Non, calm down. Don't take your anger with the world out on him.*'

I ignored my sister. Dodgson thought that being a wife was all I was good for. That my mathematical abilities were incidental. A party trick that might entertain my husband and nothing more. Humiliation boiled the blood in my veins and the acid in my stomach.

Dodgson shook his head, as if he hadn't understood my question. 'Is that not what all women aspire to? Their own household, husband, children?'

'No. Some women – far more of us than you might imagine – would prefer to see a world where women can also live *full and fulfilling lives* while remaining unmarried. Where women could, for instance, be fellows at Oxford. Or lawyers, doctors. Or even, God forbid, a world where we might – like men – have both! A career *and* a family.' I could hear my outrage getting the better of me. I took a breath. 'Perhaps you know of Dr Elizabeth Garrett-Anderson who, with the help of other women, has established the School of Medicine for Women in London? Dr Garrett-Anderson is both a doctor *and* a wife and mother.'

Lily's hand was back on my arm, gripping hard. I knew what that hand was saying. *Stop. Now.*

'I—' Charles Dodgson found his capacity for speech blocked by my own fluent fury. But I was damned if I was going to wait for him to find his voice.

'I can assure you that I have *not* come to Oxford to find a husband, Rev Dodgson. A husband would be nothing but an encumbrance to me.'

'But h-how would you support yourself?' Dodgson seemed genuinely concerned. 'You cannot rely on your sponsor for ever.'

'My sponsor, Miss Rees, is a first-class example of how I will support myself! She isn't married. She has no fortune to fall back on. She makes her own way in the world as a writer and public speaker.'

He stared at me. 'I find your p-passion and ambition truly admirable, Miss Vaughan. B-but I fear that it may also be naïve.'

I forced a smile. 'Times are changing, Rev Dodgson. There are women at Oxford, now. And we're not going away.'

'I beg your pardon, Miss Vaughan. You may be *in* Oxford, but you are not *at* Oxford. And, loath as I am to sound brutal, I feel I must warn you that there are many people who will exert themselves to the utmost to ensure that that situation does not change. You may not go away but I fear that your presence may not change things as you wish.'

Chapter 32

Basil

'Morrell's instructions were to be as thorough as possible.' Teddy scrubbed his hands free of blood in the basin of clean water that stood to one side. 'So I've collected the stomach contents, such as they were, and I'll take them over to Chemistry to see if they find anything.'

'What will you ask them to look for?' Tarley Askew asked.

'There's not much we can test for definitively. Arsenic might fit the symptoms. Apart from that I don't hold out much hope. But they know what they're doing and I'm sure there are things they'll look for that wouldn't occur to me.'

He finished packing his bags. 'Right,' he said, with a cheery smile, 'I'll be off. See you at the inquest, Bas, if not before.'

Much as I wanted to stop him, to beg him to come to dinner in college tonight, for things to be as they used to between us, I restrained myself and let him go with a weak, 'Absolutely!'

I asked Tarley Askew to wait while I made provision for the disposal of Parker's dissected organs, and the placing of what remained of his body in the coffin which had already been delivered.

When I returned to the coachyard, I found Askew experimenting with the tandem. He had taken up the rear position and stood as upright as he could while still holding the steering handles.

'It's far easier to get the thing in motion if one stands and bears vertically down on the cranks instead of sitting and pushing forward,' he said.

I smiled, remembering Non's tale of how she had surprised the tandem's previous owner by coming to exactly the same conclusion and executing a timed dash down Walton Street from Jericho House to the University Press to win a bet.

'You should tell Non that,' I told him. 'She'd be impressed that you'd worked it out so quickly.'

'But it's obvious.' Askew dismounted from the machine and stood, looking at it.

'Only if you have a particular facility for mechanics, I suspect. What are you hoping to take your degree in?'

'Mathematics.'

'Hence your membership of the Cipher Club.'

He smiled wryly. 'I'm hardly a member, Mr Rice. I was invited once.'

'Play your cards right and you may find that Non sees to it that you're invited again.'

He cocked his head on one side, questioning her influence over Charles Dodgson.

'You do know that Dodgson set up the club for her?' I asked. 'They'd been writing to each other for years before Non came to Oxford.'

'I see.'

Evidently Askew hadn't known. Why on earth had Non seen fit to involve him in Parker's death on an acquaintance so slight?

'She's quite out of the ordinary, don't you think?' A man with a different colouring might have blushed, but Tarley Askew's complexion would never betray him in that way.

'She is,' I agreed. 'She's also infuriating, opinionated, intellectually vain and impetuous.'

The boy looked affronted on Non's behalf. He was smitten.

'And I say those things,' I said, 'as I would of anybody, man or woman, of whom I was inordinately fond.'

'I beg your pardon, are you...?' He floundered. 'I mean, is there an understanding between you and Miss Vaughan?'

Dr Harper had accused me of having my head turned by Non and now, here was Tarley Askew assuming something even more binding. Could Non herself be under a similar impression? I recalled her odd little comment as to the unlikelihood of my having my head turned by her; had she been inviting me to make a declaration of some kind? The thought made me extremely uncomfortable.

'No, Mr Askew,' I managed, 'there is no understanding between Non and myself, nor is there likely to be.' He nodded, his expression easing a fraction. 'Now, then, without wishing to prejudge the chemistry department's conclusions, there are clearly questions to answer as to what substances Mr Parker had been ingesting before his unfortunate demise. So, would this afternoon be a convenient time for you to attempt a rendezvous with the fellow in Bear Lane? If so, I suggest that we leave the tandem here and reconvene, later, to return it to Shene Road. Shall we say six o'clock?'

Chapter 33

Non

Back in front of Sidney Parker's journal, as soon as I stopped assuming that he'd written his code in English and looked for Welsh patterns instead, it only took an hour or so for his notebook journal to start giving up its secrets.

How had it not even crossed my mind that a man at Oxford's Welsh college would have written in Welsh?

'*Because it's Oxford!*' Hara said. '*More English than the rest of England put together. I don't suppose there's a word of Welsh spoken at Jesus from one week's end to the next. Not* educated, *is it?*'

She was being ironic, but that's what people – including a lot of our own countrymen – believed. They saw Welsh as *iaith y werin*, a folk language, not suitable for anything but hearth, farm and chapel; a *tafodiaith*, a spoken language that wasn't elevated enough for education. It was that attitude that made parents send children to schools where they used the Welsh Not, a plaque on a string that was hung around the neck of any child heard speaking Welsh. Children fell over themselves to accuse each other because the last person wearing the Welsh Not at the end of the day got a beating.

It was that attitude towards our own language that Cranogwen was trying to change with her magazine, *Y Frythones*; and that Professor Rhys was trying to challenge with his studies into our language and our history.

'*You've let Oxford prejudices affect you. English is the language that first comes to your mind these days.*'

I wanted to argue with Hara, but I didn't have the heart. She was right.

But I was damned if I was going to let Oxford prejudices take a hold. If I went down that road, I might as well let Charles Dodgson find me a husband now.

I'd still been boiling with rage when we left his rooms in Christ Church. And, with only Lily to hear me, I could give full vent to my anger as soon as we were out of the gates.

Lily said nothing, just marched me across St Aldate's Street and down Brewer's Lane. 'We'll go this way. I don't want your nonsense to attract a crowd.'

I pulled up in the middle of the lane and faced her. '*Nonsense?* You think he's right, do you?'

Lily looked up furtively at the windows on either side of us – Pembroke College on the right, Christ Church Cathedral School on the left – as if she expected to see heads poking out, asking what all the row was about. Then she took my arm and pulled me onwards. 'He was only trying to be kind. He's fond of you. It's not his fault you're contrary.'

'I'm not *contrary*,' I said, throwing off her hand. 'I just don't want a *husband*. I want my own life.'

'Yes… in Cloud Cuckoo Land. You want to think about Mr Askew or somebody like him. A man who'd let you carry on with your studying—'

'*Let* me?'

'Oh, there's no talking to you, Non Vaughan!'

'No, there isn't. Not when you're telling me that I'm wasting my time.'

I'd stalked on ahead then. I didn't need a chaperone to walk home.

I hadn't even bothered taking my coat off in the hall. Just walked straight upstairs to look at Sidney Parker's journal again.

Now, I was making progress. And it seemed that, even while my brain had been focused for all those hours on breaking the code, some part of my mind had been thinking about the collections of letters and numbers at the beginning of every journal entry. What if they were lists of the remedies Sidney Parker had been taking, and their dosages? We knew he'd been taking Chlorodyne, paregoric, laudanum, and whatever Dr Aurum's Tonic was. Dr Aurum's Tonic had three initials which might explain one of the groups of letters but what about the others?

Think, Non.

Paregoric was always just paregoric, like laudanum was just laudanum. But Chlorodyne was patented – it was *Dr J. Collis Brown's* Chlorodyne, with Dr Brown's signature on every label. If that was shortened to Collis Brown's Chlorodyne, then with a simple, three-letter shift, CBC translated, in the Welsh alphabet, to DDDDD which appeared on many of the entry-opening lists. (In Welsh, 'dd' – pronounced 'th' as in 'this' and 'the' – is a digraph: two letters but one sound, and it's treated as one alphabetical symbol.) The same goes for 'ch' (the sound made at the back of the mouth that English people find impossible in Welsh but manage when it occurs in the Scottish 'loch') 'ff' (English 'f' – Welsh uses 'f' for 'v') 'll', the 'lateral l' sound in so many Welsh placenames beginning with 'Llan', and 'rh', a voiceless version of 'r' which English doesn't have and which is the first sound in my name. Rhiannon.

Using the three-letter shift, SS became PP in the Welsh alphabet which doesn't use the letter 'q'. Something and paregoric? But what?

SN would be PL. Did the P in both those sets of initials stand for the same thing? Laudanum and paregoric weren't patented under a person's name, they were free for anybody to produce.

No, not just anybody… any *pharmacist*!

PP: pharmacist's paregoric. PL: pharmacist's laudanum.

I consulted the Welsh alphabet which I'd written out with a four-letter shift beneath:

A	B	C	CH	D	DD	E	F	FF	G	H	I	J	L	LL
CH	D	DD	E	F	FF	G	H	I	J	L	LL	M	N	O

M	N	O	P	R	RH	S	T	U	W	Y
P	R	RH	S	T	U	W	Y	A	B	C

Reading off the shifted alphabet chart, FCHY, which I'd seen in many lists, became DAT. Dr Aurum's Tonic.

I looked at the letters and numbers Sidney Parker had recorded on the last day of his life. This time, unusually, there were times, too:

9 am – SFG – 3
6 pm – SFG – 5

I flicked to the previous day and saw:

> *6 pm – SFG – 2*

SFG: PDE. I had no idea what those letters might represent. And did the numbers refer to pills, spoonsful, grains, or something else? I hoped the journal would tell me.

It would be a simple, if time-consuming, job to translate each page so, instead of just starting at the beginning and ploughing through, I decided to pick off the repeated strings of letters I'd noticed in the text to see if those gave me any clues. After some wrangling, I'd decoded several words which recurred over and over again.

'INRHTLL' decoded to 'FFLORI' or, in English spelling, Florrie – Florence Spellman.

'HTRRHGN' – 'FRNOEL' – Father Noel from St Barnabas.

'LLGWA' – 'IESU' – Jesus. Presumably the college rather than the Son of God but Sidney Parker had been a churchgoer, so I'd have to decode more to find out.

'CHSYBP' – 'APTWM'. That made me pause for a second until I separated it into two words 'ap Twm' – Tom's son. Somebody called Thompson?

I wondered why Mr Parker had translated the name into Welsh. To give himself some power over this person? Maybe he'd translated people's names into Welsh for the same reason our chapel minister had advised me to imagine people in shops or on farms at home. To make them less strange, less threatening.

Had this Thompson been a threat to Sidney?

His name appeared in an entry three days before Sidney died.

> *Received PDE from Thompson. I'm doing this for you, Florrie. If it works, I'll be cured. If it doesn't, you'll only have half a man for a husband.*

What if there'd been a third option? What if PDE had killed Sidney Parker?

I turned to the first entry in the journal. It was one of the longest at more than a page.

Tea would be needed.

Chapter 34

Basil

Once Tarley Askew had set off for Bear Lane, I returned to the coach house and the old tea-chest in which Mrs Trent had placed everything she hadn't been able to find room for in Parker's trunk: his pictures, books and writing things.

These were the items Sidney Parker had displayed to the world as the possessions of a gownsman; a rather impecunious one but a gownsman nonetheless. But the real Sidney had been hidden, under the floorboards, between the covers of an encoded notebook, in a locked box.

While Non worked to discover the secrets contained in the notebook, might I be able to find the key that opened the box? The box was now in my possession, Non having given it up to me whilst insisting on retaining Parker's papers in case they helped decrypt his journal.

Parker's trunk was full of his clothes, so I began by putting aside the cap and gown that had been placed on the top of the pile and looking through the pockets of the jackets and trousers folded neatly beneath. But I came across nothing more than a handkerchief, and a button which had obviously come from the front of the waistcoat whose pocket I found it in. Sighing, I placed the suits on top of Parker's gown and continued my search.

Neither his sporting gear, his footwear, nor his spare shirts revealed a hidden key. Had it been in the nightstand? It might easily have been shoved into a corner, after all. But no, Parker had been careful to protect the things he had kept under the floorboards, and a key without an obvious lock would have excited interest in anybody who had ventured into his room with less than noble intentions; it would have invited a search.

I replaced everything I'd removed from the trunk and took up Parker's gown. Perhaps I'd put it aside too soon. Gowns didn't have pockets, but the deep hems and facings might easily be unpicked, and a small item stowed inside.

Holding the gown up by the gathers at the neck, I ran my fingers down the facings on one side, then the other. Finding nothing, I tried the hem with the same result.

I sat back on my haunches and applied logic. Parker wouldn't have left the key where it might have been found by Mrs Trent when she was cleaning his room, nor where it might have been discovered by accident. It was unlikely, therefore, that it had been slipped inside a drawer or cupboard. I looked at the trunk. Though I'd searched its contents, I'd not searched the trunk itself.

Once more I removed Parker's clothes and put them aside.

Now, the trunk stood empty in front of me, battered canvas and leather straps on the outside, striped calico within.

I loosened the straps and felt beneath them, but no key had been slipped between leather and canvas. The calico lining had seen better days and its seams had parted here and there, revealing the wicker beneath. Sliding a hand through the broken seam at the back, I investigated the bottom of the trunk, moving my fingers carefully this way and that beneath the calico, then tipping the trunk up, lest a small item like a key had slipped from its hiding place. As I did so, there was a definite metallic sound. I tore a wider hole in the seam and pulled out a brass key about an inch long.

Parker's box sat on the floor next to the trunk. It was obviously intended as a cashbox: black-painted metal with bronze-coloured reinforcements to the corners and bronze edging to the lid and around the keyhole.

I hesitated before putting the key in the lock. Having been shocked to discover that Non had read Florence Spellman's letters to Parker, was I not committing an equally egregious invasion of privacy in opening this box? Possibly more to the point, should we not have simply handed all Parker's possessions over to the coroner straight away? But Non, having been the one to discover the existence of Sidney Parker's hiding place, had assumed the right to investigate its contents, which had somewhat pulled that particular rug from under my feet.

Should I take the box and its key to Morrell? That would be the correct thing to do. But I had a duty to protect both Parker's reputation, and that of the college. If this box contained anything scandalous, was it not better to be forewarned?

I supressed my reservations and inserted the key.

The box was full of folded bank notes. I picked one up and unfolded it. It was for five pounds. If all the notes were for a similar sum, there was a small fortune here.

I unfolded each of the notes in turn. Not all were for as much as five pounds, some were for one pound, but a smaller number were for ten. When I had smoothed the creases from the last note in the box, I totted up the sum represented and came to one hundred and seventy-five pounds.

How had the apparently impoverished Sidney Parker come to possess a sum that, for the average man, would be the fruits of three or four years' labour?

Chapter 35

Non

I'm writing this for you, Florrie my love, in case this disease kills me, and this record is all you have left of me. I'm sorry I had to take the precaution of writing in code, but there's nowhere completely safe and I don't want anybody else reading this. The spies have been hanging about here and I can't be sure they haven't persuaded Mrs Trent to let them in. But, if I can't overcome what ails me, I want you to know how I tried to make myself well. Maybe by the time you read this I'll have worked up the courage to tell you that I've been taking Reardon's tonic myself, but I don't know if I can be that brave. But I want to be well for you, Florrie. I want to be the man you deserve.

The first page of Mr Parker's journal raised a lot of questions.

'This disease.' Was that a reference to spermatorrhoea or something else?

And what was 'Reardon's tonic'?

Basil had wanted to take all Sidney's things to the coroner, but the coroner wouldn't need much more than a minute's glance at the pile of papers Mr Parker had hidden beneath his loose floorboard to see that they were all evidence of his obsession with spermatorrhoea, and his attempts to cure himself. Mr Morrell could cast his eye over them before the inquest. And anyway, I had a feeling that Sidney Parker's papers might tell me something.

For instance, his reference to ApTwm – Thomson – had jogged my memory. I pulled the stack of leaflets out of Parker's hoard.

The one on top of the pile was addressed to '**YOUNG MEN!**' in huge, eye-catching letters and I could easily imagine Bowler Hat in Bear Lane waving about a sheaf of leaflets like this. Underneath the large letters, on the left of the handbill, was the sketch of a young man, his head in his hands, in apparent despair. On the right, there was a question:

HAS OVERINDULGENCE
in
Secret Vices
or
Imprudent relations
RESULTED IN
Nervous debility
Nocturnal disturbances
Lowness of manly spirits
A diminution of vital energy?

If so, **DR AURUM'S TONIC** was the guaranteed cure.

Dr Aurum claimed to have prepared '**a unique formulation of herbs and minerals recently discovered to have been employed by the warriors of ancient Greece and Sparta**' and offered to supply '**warranties as to efficacy on request**'.

There was a London address to which customers could apply and the assurance that local stockists would also have supplies on hand. And, as proof of that, handwritten on the line beneath was the name that had jogged my memory:

Local stockist: Carmichael Thompson, Bear Lane.

-

The address 'Bear Lane' implied a pharmacist's shop. But there was no pharmacy on Bear Lane. So, if the little brown bottle I'd seen changing hands had contained Dr Aurum's Tonic, Carmichael Thompson was nothing more than a street hawker. Thompson must be Bowler Hat.

It seemed likely that he had supplied Sidney with Dr Aurum's Tonic – had he also supplied him with whatever PDE was?

I stood up and started walking around my room to try and encourage my brain to work a bit faster. If the Welsh 'ApTwm' did represent the English name 'Thompson', then Mr Parker obviously knew 'local stockist' Carmichael Thompson. Presumably he had bought Dr Aurum's Tonic from him on a regular basis. Basil had said there were at least four little brown bottles in Parker's nightstand drawer.

But what about 'PDE'?

I reached back to the pile and shuffled through it. There were several of the Doctor Aurum's leaflets, all more or less the same, though one had an additional box of text declaring that the tonic was now a '**New, even more potent formulation!**'

Was the new formulation PDE? And, if so, had it been sold by Carmichael Thompson or somebody else? Thompson's name was on the first two Dr Aurum's handbills I looked at, but I had a shock when I looked at the last and oldest-looking leaflet.

Local stockist: *Sidney Parker, McLaren's Gymnasium.*

Chapter 36

Basil

Consideration of the matter over coffee in my rooms led me to the conclusion that there were two potential sources of information as to Sidney Parker's unexpected wealth: his sweetheart, Florence Spellman, and his erstwhile friends in college.

As I was loath to speak to Miss Spellman alone, I decided to capitalise on the fact that I was in college and see if I could locate Mr Tobias Jenkyn. Though he'd said he and Parker hadn't 'gone about together' much after Parker's sudden access of religion, our previous conversation had left me with the impression that Jenkyn wasn't telling me everything he knew.

-

Standing on the small landing outside Jenkyn's rooms, I found his outer, oak door closed, indicating either that he was out, or that he didn't want to be disturbed by his friends. Falling well outside that category, I knocked loudly.

'Oh! Mr Rice!' Jenkyn's face hastily rearranged itself from frowning annoyance to amiably obliging.

'I wonder if I might have a few moments of your time?' I asked.

'Of course.' Jenkyn glanced back uneasily into his sitting room as he held the door open for me.

'I'm not here to inspect your rooms, Jenkyn. I just want to ask you a few more questions about Sidney Parker.'

'Oh. Right-ho.'

I followed him into the sitting room. It was, presumably, as tidy as his bedmaker could keep it, but the man was obviously fighting a battle he had no hope of winning and succeeding only in keeping squalor at bay. Jenkyn's desk was covered, not with evidence of studiousness but with the detritus of a life lived to the full. A theatre token lay amongst a collection of change, a litter of notes and letters, a necktie, two pencils, several pens with dried-up nibs and a watch whose back lay open as if I had interrupted him in the act of winding it. Invitation cards and bills vied for space on his mantelpiece, and a cabinet – which, I suspected, was not as expensive as it was designed to look – stood in one corner pretending not to contain a store of bottles.

Unlike the undergraduates at colleges associated with the great public schools of England, the young men of Jesus tended to be of moderate means. Nevertheless, at one time or another, most of them found themselves living beyond those means in pursuit of pleasure.

Jenkyn noticed my swift assessment of his room and glanced around as if wondering what he could do to make it look more like the sanctum of a scholar. 'Do sit down, Mr Rice,' he said, indicating a small sofa and, simultaneously, pulling an aged-looking ladderback chair from under his desk. The chair clearly had not had a great deal of recent use as it was piled with clean linen which still bore its laundry tags.

Giving me an embarrassed glance, Jenkyn whipped the pile away, opened the door to his bedroom and flung the linen on to his bed.

I sat down, feeling ill at ease in my role of inquisitor. It had been one thing asking a few questions after a tutorial, it was quite another making a deliberate visit to a man in his own rooms. I cleared my throat.

'An examination of Mr Parker's effects has revealed a rather startling sum of money,' I said. 'The kind of sum which should have been sitting in a bank account.'

Jenkyn sat gingerly on the ladderback chair as if he was afraid it might disintegrate and I had a sudden, vivid recollection of using just such a chair as an impromptu stage when, quite drunk, I had sung some ditty for the entertainment of my equally inebriated undergraduate friends. 'I think a savings bank would've been rather beneath him,' Jenkyn said. 'And, of course, if he'd tried to open an account somewhere like the Old Bank, they'd have wanted his guardian involved.'

He was right. As a minor, any account Parker might have held at a bank which had the facility to lend money, rather than simply provide interest on savings, would have required a guarantor.

'I don't know much about Parker's background,' Jenkyn added, 'but I do know his guardian was a bit of a tartar. Kept the purse strings very tight. Parker resented it bitterly.'

I thought of Parker's unhappy time at school and asked, carefully, 'Was his allowance the only cause of animosity between them?'

Jenkyn sighed and shifted uneasily on the hard chair. 'I don't think so, no. He said his guardian – I don't remember his name?'

'Reardon.'

'Yes, of course. He said Reardon had sent him here as a business venture.' He looked at me unhappily, reluctant to go on. I made an encouraging gesture.

'Mr Reardon runs an advertising agency. Some of his clients were keen to sell their wares to Oxford men.'

'What kind of wares?'

The boy swallowed, glancing away from me then back again. 'Patent remedies. Not the snake-oil, cure-all type. Ones aimed at a specific market. And not a shilling a bottle either. Much higher class.'

A sudden suspicion bloomed. 'When you say they were aimed at a specific market, were they also to treat a specific condition?'

Jenkyn's demeanour turned from unhappy to profoundly uncomfortable. 'Yes.'

'Spermatorrhoea?'

He sighed with relief at not having to explain. Did he think I'd never heard the word? Probably. Undergraduates tended to think of anybody over the age of thirty as sadly aged.

'Yes. That. Exactly.'

'And what was Mr Parker's role in bringing these wares to market?'

Jenkyn leapt to his feet. 'Mr Rice, I'm so sorry, I'm a very poor host. May I offer you a cup of tea?'

I almost smiled at the domesticity of the suggestion, but he clearly wanted to remove himself to a position where his discomfort would be easier to hide.

'Thank you. That would be very welcome.'

'The chaps laugh at me, but I like tea while I'm working.'

Silently, I applauded his ability to stand up for what he liked, despite the fact that tea, with all its connotations of ladies sitting about gossiping the afternoon away, was seen as a less masculine drink than coffee.

The fire in the grate was quiescent under a blanket of small coal. Jenkyn poked it into vivid vermillion life before pouring water into his kettle from a rather tasteless frog-shaped jug and setting it on the trivet.

'We were discussing how Mr Reardon expected Mr Parker to be able to bring these remedies to people's attention,' I said. 'What did he ask him to do?' There had been a thin bundle of handbills amongst the possessions Non and Lily had found hidden in Parker's room in Kingston Road; I had assumed that the boy had collected them with a view to ordering the remedy concerned but perhaps he had been distributing them himself.

'When he first came up,' Jenkyn said, his eyes fixed firmly on the fire, 'he'd invite chaps back to his rooms for a drink after hall. And he'd just happen to have a particular advertisement lying about for all to see. Somebody always eventually commented on it and that was his cue, as it were.'

'Let me be quite clear,' I said to the back of Jenkyn's head. 'This was an advertisement for a spermatorrhoea remedy?'

'Yes. Dr Aurum's Tonic.'

'Some handbills advertising a tonic were found in Parker's effects. I'd assumed he'd picked them up somewhere.'

'No, he was the one dropping them. Sometimes literally. I remember coming across one in Second Quad once, just blowing about. And there were nearly always a few in the library.' He hesitated. 'But that wasn't till later. At first, he just used to leave one on the table in his room and, when anybody new commented on it, he'd start talking about how different things had been for him since he started taking the tonic.'

'He said he was taking it himself?'

'Yes. But later – after he'd got religion – he told me that'd just been a ploy to encourage people to buy.'

'Where from? Where did they buy it?'

He looked at me in surprise. 'From him. That was the point. He was both advertiser and supplier.'

I thought of the pale, shy boy I had known and felt a profound sorrow on his behalf. How could he have hoped to make friends when Reardon had required him to be a salesman to his peers? No wonder he had been desperate to move into the safe anonymity of the Trents' lodging house.

Once again I wondered why Reardon had made no fuss about the move. Had Sidney persuaded him that, somehow, it would be good for business were he not confined within the walls of Jesus?

'Did many buy from him?' I asked, hoping that the answer would be no, that the young men of Jesus did not, as a body, consider themselves to be suffering from a potentially debilitating affliction brought on by excessive indulgence in masturbation.

He turned away to look at the fire. 'I couldn't say,' he mumbled.

'But you think that might be the source of the money?'

Jenkyn nudged the kettle a little further over the fire. It was now perilously close to toppling over the edge of the trivet, but it sang more convincingly. 'Possibly.'

Discomfort was coming off the boy like heat off the fire and he staunchly kept his eyes on the burning coals.

'I understand that this wasn't a run-of-the-mill remedy he was offering,' I said. 'But, unless he was selling it for an astonishing sum, I don't think it can account for the money in his possession.' I waited. 'Is there something else you can think of…?'

This time I waited longer. Much longer. In the end, Jenkyn couldn't bear the interrogative silence.

'The price didn't remain the same,' he said. 'Once a chap had started using the remedy… I gather,' he added, quickly, 'Parker soon started asking for more than the "introductory price" and each time a new supply was required, the price went up again. I did hear that some chaps tried to stop buying when the price got to a guinea, but Sidney had some rather subtle tricks up his sleeve.'

Now that Jenkyn had started, he spoke rapidly, as if he needed to get the whole thing off his chest before he lost his nerve. 'He'd let you have credit – as a friend, he'd say – and let you build up a bit of a debt as he kept supplying you with the stuff. Kept saying that soon you wouldn't need it because it would've done its work. I think a lot of the chaps thought that he was marking it up terrifically and that they'd be able to get away with paying him a lot less, in the end. He was a friend, of sorts, after all. And a Jesus man. But, when the debt got to a certain point, there was no more credit. He was very regretful. Told me – I mean, he told chaps that he couldn't supply any more to anybody until he'd paid his own supplier. Then, if you said he'd have to wait, he'd intimate that it'd be a pity if he was forced to write to your father and ask for the money.'

Credit. The young man's downfall. 'Leaving the men he'd entrapped,' I said, choosing my words carefully, 'no choice but to apply to their fathers themselves to cover their debt. Without saying what it was for, of course. That must have been difficult. There'd have been no bills to produce.'

Jenkyn nodded miserably. His father would have assumed that he had been drinking in public houses and possibly visiting prostitutes; both of which might also be true, of course.

'If it makes any difference,' Jenkyn said, 'I don't think Parker wanted to do it. He was terribly upset on one occasion, told me that his guardian would cut off his allowance if he didn't make so much money every term.' He looked at me earnestly. 'The man was a tyrant, Mr Rice.'

Chapter 37

Non

Now that I knew Bowler Hat's name, it seemed to me that the best thing I could do was find Tarley Askew and tell him. He'd be far more likely to get the information we needed if he could ask for the man by name.

I took my watch out of my pocket. It had been my father's best watch – his 'land' watch – and with no son to pass it on to, I'd inherited it. I thought of him every time I looked at it. Ten to four. Would Tarley Askew still be in Bear Lane or would he have given up now and gone back to his college? Then again, Corpus Christi was literally a minute's walk from Bear Lane, perhaps his strategy was to pop back and forth?

If I was going to leave the house, I'd have to do it without arousing Lily's suspicions. She'd come in from our visit to Christ Church two or three minutes after me and I hadn't seen her since. Normally she'd have brought a cup of tea up for me when she had one, so I was obviously still in the dog house. The last thing she needed to know was that I was going down to Bear Lane.

Hara spoke up. '*Are you sure this is wise? What if Thompson sees you talking to Tarley?*'

'*So much the better. He'll think I'm his sweetheart. What could be less suspicious?*'

I put my copy of *Lysistrata* and a notebook in my satchel to back up the story I was going to tell Lily if she caught me creeping out, then slipped quietly downstairs. I'd managed to lace up my boots and half-button my coat before Lily caught wind of me.

'What are you up to?' she wanted to know, coming towards me at full steam.

'I'm going to the library to check something. If Basil and Mr Askew bring the tandem back before I'm home, make them wait, will you? I need to speak to them, urgently.' I hoped that would throw her off the scent, but she was too astute to be sidetracked.

'What about the code book? You're not telling me you've finished that already?'

'No, that's why I'm going out. There's something I need to look up.' I finished buttoning my coat and looked Lily right in the eye.

Her eyes narrowed. 'What are you up to, my girl?'

'I'm not up to anything! I just want to get enough of the code book done to be useful before Basil comes back with the tandem.' She still didn't look convinced. 'It's important, Lily.'

'When will you be back?'

I hesitated. I should be quick if I found Tarley Askew straight away, but what If I didn't? 'No more than a couple of hours,' I said.

'That's too long. I don't want you walking around after dark.'

'Lily, it's the Bodleian, right in the middle of town,' I said. 'Gaslights nearly all the way home. And all the shops will still be open, I'll come to no harm.'

'I'll come with you, then.'

I could see her heart wasn't in it, so I called her bluff. 'If you must.'

She let me go.

-

As I hurried down Walton Street, I devoutly wished that I hadn't lent The Contraption to Tarley and Basil. Whatever I'd said to Lily, I'd have felt safer riding. Running in skirts wasn't easy whereas standing up and cranking the tandem along got up a fair head of steam really quickly.

Nipping through the crowds on Beaumont Street, I stepped out of the way of a nanny with her two little charges held firmly by the hand and almost collided with a man carrying luggage into the Randolph hotel. That was another disadvantage of going on foot. Other pedestrians. Were people getting in Tarley's way too? If members of the gym saw him loitering, they might get funny with him.

Three minutes later, after dodging the cabs on Broad Street, I was on Turl Street. If I happened to see Basil coming out of Jesus College, so much the better, though I doubted I would. The likelihood of bumping into somebody you actually needed to see seemed to work on some kind of inverse law: the more useful a chance meeting would be, the less likely it was and vice versa.

Turl Street was almost all college: Exeter and Jesus on opposite sides at the top and Lincoln at the southern end. Shops sprang up opposite Lincoln after the junction with Market Street and I felt myself breathing more easily. It was ridiculous, this stupid ban from attending college lectures was making me feel as if fellows were watching me from college windows, waiting for me to put a foot inside so that they could complain about me to the AEW.

I passed Lily's friend's hairdressing room and The Mitre, crossed the High Street and jinked down narrow little Alfred Street towards Bear Lane. My heart speeded up as I got closer to McLaren's gymnasium, and I slowed down a bit. The setts Alfred Street was paved with would've made coming down here on The Contraption a bit uncomfortable, but I still missed it. Even if I was pushing it rather than riding, I felt as if the tandem gave me a reason for being somewhere.

The big, round-headed windows of McLaren's came up on my left, and I glanced in at the young men at their exercises. Was Tarley Askew in there? I didn't want to stop and stare, but as I passed by each of the windows in turn, I did scan the big room, looking for him. If he was there amongst the apparatus and sweating youths, I couldn't see him.

At the corner, I stopped and peered around, first to my right into Blue Boar Street and then left, into Bear Lane. There was nobody to be seen in the growing dusk and I realised that I'd imagined Tarley Askew walking up and down, waiting for Thompson, which was stupid of me.

I strolled along Bear Lane to the women's and children's part of the gymnasium. When I'd been there with Elspeth Rhys and her girls, I'd noticed piles of leaflets on the counter, advertising various classes. If I picked one up, I could stand about outside pretending to read it. I wasn't sure what I'd do after that, but something would occur to me.

The young woman who acted as gatekeeper and purveyor of information smiled and said, 'Hello again.'

I was taken aback. I wasn't used to being recognised in Oxford. People were a lot more anonymous, here, than back home.

'You came in with Mrs Rhys earlier in the week, didn't you?'

I admitted that I had and asked her if she'd mind telling me all the different classes that the gymnasium put on for women. I was only half listening as she reeled off times and days, callisthenics and gymnastics.

But when she said 'fencing', I took notice. 'You offer classes in fencing for women?'

'We've just started, yes.'

'When do those classes take place?'

She told me and underlined the relevant day and hour on a printed schedule which she handed to me. I felt pretty confident in my ability to defend myself but another string to my bow – so to speak – might come in handy.

'Thank you,' I said. 'May I just watch the class taking place at the moment?' There were sounds of instruction coming from the adjacent room and watching what was going on would take up a few minutes, during which time Tarley Askew might appear.

The young woman smiled and left her desk to open the door. Inside the exercise room, six women were wielding small dumbbell weights in rhythmic patterns, guided by their instructor's voice. It wasn't quite hauling up sails, but it was better than embroidery.

I watched for as long as I thought I could get away with then thanked the young woman and slipped back out into Bear Lane with the schedule of classes in my hand.

There was still nobody about. Nobody I wanted to see, that is: only a couple of undergraduates heading for The Bear, stuffing their caps and gowns into a bag as they went.

I stood there, pretending to read the brochure, for as long as I could, then looked up and down the street. Twilight was darkening fast, but there was enough light to see that nobody was there.

I weighed up my options: I could give up and go home, or I could wander about for a while, hoping that either Tarley Askew or Bowler Hat – Thompson – might appear. I wasn't entirely sure what I'd do if I saw Thompson on his own, but I'd cross that bridge when I came to it.

To my right, Blue Boar Lane ran along the back wall of Christ Church College down to St Aldate's Street. To my left, Bear Lane led to Oriel Square and the back entrance to Christ Church, then on to Merton Street where Tarley Askew's college, Corpus Christi, stood between Christ Church and Merton.

I decided to wander towards St Aldate's first, then, if I saw no sign of anybody, I'd go back towards Merton Street. There was always a chance I might see Mr Askew coming or going from his college.

I hadn't gone very far past The Bear when I heard footsteps hurrying up behind me. I turned quickly, ready to defend myself, and breathed a sigh of relief when I saw Tarley Askew coming towards me. 'Non! Is everything all right?'

'Everything's fine. I've got some information that might be useful to you, that's all.'

Quickly, I told him what I'd learned from the leaflets and the notebook. He nodded. 'Excellent. Even if Bowler Hat turns out not to be this Thompson, then the name will be useful to ask around for. So far, I've dawdled about a bit outside and gone into the pub. That's where I was when I saw you go past the window. I was about to start making enquiries – having a name will make things far easier.'

'You're going to ask around in The Bear rather than the gymnasium?'

'That was the initial plan, yes. Seems to me that chaps who are happy to break rules are more likely to buy remedies from a man on the street than the ones in the gym.'

'Except Sidney Parker seems to have spent most of his time in the gym,' I pointed out.

'But that might've been for his own benefit rather than to drum up custom.'

'Fair point.' Tarley Askew didn't mind arguing with me. I liked that.

'How did the post-mortem examination go?' I asked. I knew that, really, now I'd delivered the message about Thompson, I should leave Mr Askew to it, but I was desperate to know whether the dissection had shown anything.

'Dr Pritchard seemed to think it was all a bit inconclusive, to be honest. But he did discover that Parker wasn't a well man. He had an ulcerated bowel, kidney disease and all sorts of other things wrong with him, partly due to patent remedies for his supposed spermatorrhoea.'

'You don't think it's a real disease either?'

'I'd never given it much thought one way or the other until now. But Dr Pritchard was quite definitive. It doesn't exist. It's just a ploy to sell remedies to the unwary.'

'So, could he determine cause of death or not?'

'He thought it was most likely that some sudden infection had carried Parker off, because he was in such a weakened state. But he's taken the stomach contents to the chaps at Chemistry to see if they can find anything.'

I knew, from Dr Reckitt, that there weren't all that many poisons you could test for, so I wished the chemists luck with their stomach contents.

'What he *was* able to say,' Tarley Askew went on, 'was that Parker would've been liable to die of even quite a moderate overdose of opium.'

'Which he could have got from all the remedies he was taking?'

'Apparently not. At least not from the ones we know about – the paregoric and laudanum and Chlorodyne. Not if he was taking the usual doses.'

'But possibly from whatever the others were?'

'Possible. Which is why I'm here, isn't it? If I can get a sample of whatever it was Parker was taking, and it includes opium, then the most likely verdict would be that he accidentally poisoned himself. Hopefully, then, the criticism would fall on the makers of patent remedies, not on Jesus College.'

I nodded, but I wasn't sure that the college would – or should – be able to avoid all responsibility.

Because, if Sidney Parker had been as unwell as this Dr Pritchard said, why hadn't anybody noticed?

Chapter 38

Basil

Tarley Askew let himself in through the Ship Street gate to the Jesus coachyard promptly at six o'clock.

'Success?' I asked.

'Some, though in a rather unexpected direction.'

I waited for him to elaborate but, instead, he sighed. 'Look, Mr Rice, I know this is a Jesus College death and so forth, but all the information I've been working on has come from Miss Vaughan.'

Though he seemed slightly embarrassed, I could see that he was determined that Non should be present when he recounted what he'd learned. 'Very well. Let's brave this rather uncomfortable machine again, then.'

-

As we waited on the Shene Road doorstep for my knock to be answered, I was aware of a degree of barely-concealed anticipation on Tarley Askew's part. And, when Non opened the door and greeted us both with the same degree of warmth, my heart went out to him as I watched him muster up a brave smile. Poor boy, I suspected that Non's love would be hard to win.

Lily met us in the hall and, instead of following Tarley Askew and Non into the sitting room, she indicated that I should remain in the hallway with her. Fixing me with a look that was part sympathy, part annoyance she said, 'Look, Basil, I know she's wormed her way in to this whole Sidney Parker business, and I don't suppose you can stop her when she's set her mind to something, any more than I can. But please, don't let her do anything that's going to damage her future. She's here to study and I don't know what she'll do if she can't do that. It's what she lives for.'

I sighed. Lily was right: I had very little confidence in my ability to stop Rhiannon Vaughan doing anything. But I reassured her that I would do my best and, having obviously decided that Non was safe with Tarley and me, Lily patted my arm and went off to the kitchen.

Askew was speaking as I opened the living room door.

'After you'd left, I asked around in The Bear—' He looked up at my entry and fell silent, but I made the obvious inference.

'You went down to Bear Lane? After I *specifically* asked you not to speak to that man?'

'I didn't go there to speak to *him*,' Non said in a carefully reasonable tone. 'I went to give Mr Askew some information.' She gazed at me steadily, daring me to make something of it. 'I broke the code and discovered Bowler Hat's real name. I thought it would be easier for Mr Askew to ask for a Mr Thompson than for a man who wears a bowler hat.'

Logic was on her side but the thought of her potentially putting herself in harm's way filled me with protective feelings that I knew she would despise.

'Why don't you tell Mr Rice what you've managed to decode so far?' Tarley Askew said. 'Then we can get on to what I discovered.'

Non explained that, from the portions of the notebook she'd so far managed to decipher, it was clear that Sidney Parker had written it for Florence Spellman.

'He knew he was ill,' Non concluded, 'but I don't think he'd been to a doctor. He was convinced that all the different symptoms he was suffering from were caused by spermatorrhoea because that's what that ridiculous book had told him. So, he was dosing himself with various remedies to try and make himself well again. For Florence. So that they could get married.'

She proffered the notebook. 'Look – at the beginning of every entry he records doses of the drugs he was taking. PP: pharmacist's paregoric. CBC: Collis Brown's Chlorodyne. PL: pharmacist's laudanum and DAT: Doctor Aurum's Tonic. That's the brown bottle I saw Thompson passing to the young man in Bear Lane.'

'*Thought* you saw,' I said. 'We don't know that Bowler Hat is definitely this Thompson character, and whoever Bowler Hat is, we have only minimal evidence that he was selling Doctor Aurum's Tonic.'

'The evidence of my own eyes that money and a bottle changed hands,' Non flared, 'is not *minimal*.'

'Circumstantial then.'

She glared at my refusal to see her leap of imagination as solid proof.

'However,' she said, emphasising the word as if now, she was about to present incontrovertible evidence, 'I don't think it's Dr Aurum's Tonic that we need to be concerned with. I think it's whatever Sidney Parker started taking just before he died. Something with the initials PDE.'

She turned to the final entries in Parker's journal and showed me the three letters, SFG. 'Using a three-letter shift in the Welsh alphabet, these become PDE.'

I looked at the entries. 16. 1. 81: 6pm *SFG – 1*, 17.1.81 9 am: *SFG – 3*, 17.1.81 6 pm: *SFG – 5* + 7pm, *3*.

On the seventeenth of January, the day he died, Sidney Parker had taken eleven doses of PDE. I remembered the teaspoon that I'd seen on the floor between his bed and his nightstand.

'And we have no idea what SFG, or rather PDE, is?'

'No. But what are the odds that it comes in a blue bottle like the one you saw in his drawer?' Non opened the back cover of the notebook and removed something. 'Then there's this.'

I took the sheet she held out and scrutinised it. It was a small, printed handbill of the kind that you saw being handed out on the streets every day, advertising anything from shop sales to theatre productions. This one, advertising Dr Aurum's Tonic was relatively well produced and caught the eye, as it was meant to.

'See here?' Non said, pointing to the handwritten line at the bottom. 'Local stockist: Sidney Parker—'

'—McLaren's gymnasium,' I finished. 'Yes, I found out this afternoon that Mr Parker had been selling this remedy.' I explained about my visit to Mr Jenkyn, and, slightly against my better judgement, did not omit either details of Parker's extortionary selling methods or the large sum of money I'd found in his cashbox. I knew that, if Parker's stomach contents revealed poison, these things would be made public at the inquest: Non and Mr Askew were entitled to know. But I dreaded such an eventuality: the boy's conduct would, as Dr Harper feared, drag the name of Jesus College into the mud.

'I'm not sure he was selling the tonic at the time of his death,' Non said. 'The other, later advertising leaflets – ones with "new improved formulation" on them – have Carmichael Thompson at the bottom instead of Sidney Parker.'

'Indicating that Thompson took over from Parker?'

Non wasn't given to shrugging but the face she made conveyed the same message. 'That's the most obvious interpretation, isn't it?'

'Are we inferring that Parker stopped being a local stockist after his religious experience?' Mr Askew said.

'He certainly seems to have lived a reformed life thereafter.' I hoped it was true, that Parker genuinely had changed when he found God and Florence Spellman.

'What isn't clear,' I said, 'is why Mr Parker retained the money rather than passing it on to whoever he was selling for.'

'Perhaps, when Thompson took over,' Non suggested, 'Sidney was supposed to pass the money on to him, but didn't?'

'That would fit with something I discovered today,' Mr Askew replied, removing something from his pocket. 'Certainly, there seems to have been no love lost between Parker and Thompson. Always assuming that Thompson's responsible for this, of course.' He unfolded the sheet of paper, revealing it to be another handbill. 'I found it on the floor at The Bear.'

The typeface looked identical to the one used on the advertisement Non had shown us. But its message was very different.

Instead of the sketch of a young man with his head in his hands, the left-hand side of the bill was occupied by a black-cloaked grim reaper, poised in the act of swinging his scythe, death's head grinning horribly.

And, underneath, were the words:

GENTLEMEN!
Don't wait another day
to remedy
what ails you.
SPERMATORRHOEA KILLS

And then, beneath a small but perfectly rendered picture of a headstone, the words:

Sidney Parker, late of Jesus College
R.I.P.

CIVIALE'S PRE-MARITAL TONIC COURSE.

This is the course we have already adverted to under the head of marriage, and we believe that enough was there said to make plain both its object and application. This, unlike the preceding courses, is, so to speak, a mixed one, consisting of a combination of (1) Tonics and Sexual Nervines to be taken by the mouth; (2) A Specially Prepared Course of Crayons (tonic, anti-spasmodic and detergent), to be used in the urethra, and (3) a lotion or application which, by being gently applied to the parts once a day with a sponge, soft cloth or the hand, adds greatly to the strength and erectile power, as well as the tone, development and vigor of the testicles.

Our Treatment is Pleasant, Quick and Lasting.

These are put up under the strict personal supervision of our head chemist, Mr. Du Bell, and are exactly in accordance with the formulæ and instructions of the late Prof. Civiale.

(Advertisement included in some editions of L. Deslandes' *Manhood*)

Chapter 39

Non

I spent the whole of Sunday on Sidney Parker's journal. He'd only started writing it in September, which was presumably when things had started to get serious between him and Florence, so there wasn't much about him selling Dr Aurum's Tonic, only the odd reference here and there.

In mid-October, he confessed:

> *I did as you said and tried to befriend Jenkyn, invited him along to church, but he's wary of me. Thinks I'm still trying to sell him something, only now it's church.*

Then, the next month he was worrying that:

> *I saved what I could when I was selling, but I worry that if Reardon makes things difficult over the will and my money, we won't be well off when we emigrate.*

But Sidney was a lot more forthcoming than you might've expected about what he called his 'condition'. Evidently, it'd been easier for him to write about it when he thought Florence would only be reading the words if he wasn't there any more to be embarrassed. He didn't exactly give what Dr Reckitt would have called a case history, but there were enough details and references to his past for me to get a pretty clear idea about how his disease had developed. Interestingly, he never referred to it as spermatorrhoea. Perhaps he'd thought even naming it would be shameful.

15th September

I know I'm shunned at Jesus but it's nothing to my time at school. I was treated vilely there in ways I cannot describe. Dreams and nightmares left me covered in my own pollution.

1st October

When I remember happier times during school holidays (times when my symptoms seemed to ease, somewhat, though they never went away) I realise that, until I met you, I did not know what happiness was.

7th October

Meeting you seemed like a miracle. I felt well again. My symptoms were gone. Even the pain in my bowels went away for a time. I hope that DAT will restore me to the man I was then. After three weeks on the tonic, I feel improved, less weak. But I am still not sleeping well.

14th October

No pain for a whole week! I feel full of energy, a real man again!

1st December

The recurrence of my weakness and loss of appetite dismays me.

14th December

Pain has crept up on me again, and there are bubbles in my urine, like before. My relapse overshadows my times with you. Forgive me, Florence – I hope I've not been too bad tempered.

7th January

Thompson has told me, privately, that there is to be a new remedy. Reardon seems to have become more ambitious since Blain has been involved. The new remedy isn't to be another formulation of Reardon's tonic but something completely new. Thompson says it'll be much stronger than DAT and more curative. And quick. Only three doses. He says that if I agree to start selling again, he'll supply me with the new remedy. I have no choice, Florrie. I must get well again before we marry.

Reardon's tonic. I flicked back to the beginning of the journal. Yes, Sidney Parker had referred to 'taking Reardon's tonic myself' in the very first entry. I'd thought nothing of it then. But perhaps Reardon wasn't just advertising the tonic, but producing it as well? If so, was he also responsible for the new remedy? And who was Blain – a new advertising client?

16th January

I have the new remedy. Professor Deneuve's Elixir. I have taken my last dose of DAT.

I put the journal to one side and flipped through the pile of papers on my desk until I found what I was looking for.

GENTLEMEN!
Don't Wait Another Day
To Remedy
What Ails you
SPERMATORRHOEA KILLS
Sidney Parker, late of Jesus College
R.I.P.

It was obviously designed to drive young men into the arms of patent medicine sellers. But there was no mention of any particular remedy. Was that because there was only one remedy being sold in Oxford – Dr Aurum's Tonic? Or was this a more subtle form of advertising, one designed to send customers back to Carmichael Thompson, looking for reassurance that Dr Aurum's Tonic would cure them? If it was, that would give Thompson the perfect opportunity to tell them – just as he'd told Sidney – about this new drug. Professor Deneuve's Elixir. Which, I'd be prepared to bet, would be a lot more expensive.

A horrible thought crept up on me then, and I felt its icy breath down the back of my neck. What if this wasn't just Thompson using Sidney's death in a cold-blooded way to advertise his wares? What if his death was actually *part of the advertising plan*?

No. Surely, nobody would commit murder just to scare young men into buying something?

I turned back to the notebook. It was getting late, but I wanted to finish it before I went to bed.

> *16th January*
>
> *My first dose of PDE. The instructions Thompson gave me are highly specific. Firstly, as to timings and dosage: first dose this evening, second tomorrow morning, last tomorrow evening. Secondly, as to some potentially distressing symptoms I'll have to withstand. This remedy isn't like others. It doesn't work gradually but swiftly and completely purges the overstimulated generative system. Treatment is brief, but powerful and the body doesn't tolerate it well. Thompson told me it was 'Not for the faint hearted'. Florrie, there's a danger that, if my system is too weakened, I may not be able to withstand it. It may be kill or cure. But if it cures me, I'm prepared to endure anything! I cannot be less than a whole man for you. I WILL NOT be faint hearted.*

I read the words again. *I will not be faint hearted.* The previous evening, Basil had asked me whether I'd come across the words 'Do not be faint hearted' in the journal. He'd shown Tarley and me a note he'd found at Sidney Parker's bedside. If Thompson had told Parker that Professor Deneuve's Elixir wasn't for the faint hearted, had he given Sidney the note, too? Or had Sidney written it himself? Basil hadn't been sure it was his handwriting.

I started decoding the next entry.

> *17th January, 9am – PDE: 3*
>
> *Last evening, my body's reaction to the remedy was not pleasant but neither was it intolerable. Though nauseous, I did not vomit but needed to use the chamber pot several times – my insides cramped too much to allow me to risk going downstairs.*

Not pleasant but not intolerable. Had he written the note to himself after the second dose, anticipating things getting worse?

17th January, 6pm – PDE: 5

The second dose, this morning, was even less pleasant and, as Thompson had warned, it has left me very weak. The instructions he gave me indicate that I must be prepared for a still worse reaction with this last dose. If my body tries to expel the remedy by vomiting, I must try to keep it down so that it can do its work. My heart will beat more slowly – which I believe it did yesterday – depriving the generative organs of blood. If it slows down to the point where I feel faint, I should lie down and try to sleep. That is the body's own way of counteracting the nausea and the stomach cramps. But I may know if it is working by changes to my vision. If things start to appear greenish and my vision blurs, I will know that the drug is having the desired effect.

No. That was the point when he would have written himself the note. Now that he knew how bad things might get.

Later, he'd written more, his hand less steady.

I have not been able to keep down all that I took earlier so I have taken another 3 spoons, and drained the bottle, in compensation, as advised. I feel weak and faint and am sweating and shaking so I will lie on the bed now. Tomorrow, God willing, I shall be well and soon the two of us we will be far away from Reardon, Thompson and Blain. The day cannot come soon enough, Florrie!

I looked at his last words: he hadn't been made well, and they hadn't been destined to be together, either in America or anywhere else. But it wasn't that tragedy that was uppermost in my mind but the names. Reardon and Thompson we knew. But who was Blain? And why did Sidney want to escape him, too?

HOP BITTERS. If you are a man of business or labourer, weakened by the strain of your duties, avoid stimulants and take

HOP BITTERS.

If you are a man of letters, toiling over your midnight work, to restore brain and nerve waste, take

HOP BITTERS.

If you are suffering from over-eating or drinking, any indiscretion or dissipation, take

HOP BITTERS.

If you are married or single, old or young, rich or poor, suffering from poor health or languishing on a bed of sickness, take

HOP BITTERS.

Whoever you are, wherever you are, whenever you feel that your system needs cleaning, toning or stimulating, without *intoxicating*, one bottle of

HOP BITTERS.

will do more good than £5 in all other medicines or doctors' visits!

Have you *dyspepsia, kidney* or *urinary complaint*, disease of the *stomach, bowels, blood, liver* or *nerves*?
You will be cured if you take

HOP BITTERS.

If you have flatulency, rheumatism, or gout, or are simply ailing, are weak and low-spirited, try it!
Ask your chemist and druggist for

HOP BITTERS.

It may save your life. It has saved hundreds.
FOR SALE BY ALL CHEMISTS AND DRUGGISTS.

(Contemporary newspaper advertisement)

Chapter 40

Basil

On Monday morning, I made my way down the High Street and over Magdalen Bridge to the Plain, the flat expanse where old St Clement's church had once stood and where the roads to Headington, Cowley and Iffley meet. In other circumstances, the walk would have been a pleasant one as the low sun was bright and almost warm, but I was too preoccupied to be grateful for such quotidian blessings. Despite the respite of a Sunday spent variously in worship and in companionable society at the home of John and Elspeth Rhys, I was now oppressed, once more, by the burden of trying to get to the bottom of Sidney Parker's relationship with the producers and peddlers of Dr Aurum's Tonic.

A little way up St Clement's Street, I found what I was looking for: a shop whose front bore the legend 'G. J. Alder, Printer'. This was the name and address that appeared, in tiny type, along the bottom of the handbills found in Sidney Parker's room.

As I walked in, I thought how scornful Billy Nicholson would be of this little business. Of course, there was nothing in the city that could compare with the might of the University Press, but still, this tiny shop must surely rank near the bottom on any directory of printworks.

Having said that, not all businesses could be judged on size alone, and the pasteboard-mounted examples of Alder's work on the walls suggested a skill that belied their surroundings. Either Alder employed a talented engraver, or he was something of an artist himself; the illustrations on some of the bills were rather fine.

The sound of the sprung bell over the door summoned a small figure in a blackened apron.

'Help you, sir?' he asked. My heart sank. This man did not look bribeable. His cheeks were shaved to a shine and his dark hair was parted as if with a sharp knife. He looked like a stickler. Still, I had to try.

I had left off my cap and gown for this visit. Though the prosperity of Oxford depended on college business, many tradesmen resented the University's influence over the city's governance, and I suspected that I would be more successful in my quest if I simply presented myself as a gentleman.

'Mr Alder?' I enquired.

'Yes?' The neat little man regarded me slightly warily; obviously I wasn't the sort of person who usually sought his services.

'I'm in need of information,' I said. I didn't have to pretend embarrassment; I was acutely uncomfortable. But I hoped it would be to my advantage if Alder saw that. 'And you, I believe, are the only gentleman in a position to help me.'

Alder dipped his head slightly, his sharp eyes never leaving my face: I had been given leave to proceed.

I produced the handbill bearing Carmichael Thompson's handwritten name. 'I believe you printed this,' I said, laying it on the counter.

A glance was enough. 'I did.'

'And this.' I placed a second handbill in front of him: the warning that 'Spermatorrhoea Kills', with its perfectly depicted headstone, and Sidney Parker's name.

'Yes. That one too.' He looked up, a slight frown on his face.

I took a breath. 'I should like to know whether they were produced for the same person.'

Disconcertingly, his expression didn't change. 'Should you indeed?'

I took this as a rhetorical question.

'And why would you like to know that, Mr...?'

'I don't think my name is relevant.'

'You expect me to give you the name of a customer without knowing who I'm giving it to? That's a rather inequitable transaction, wouldn't you say?'

Inequitable. Alder's shop might not advertise him as the most successful printer in Oxford, but he was an articulate man whom it would not be easy to browbeat.

'Rice,' I acquiesced. 'My name is Rice. And I'm making inquiries in anticipation of an inquest this week.'

'Are you telling me that you're here on behalf of the coroner, Mr Rice?'

'Not exactly, though I have consulted with Mr Morrell—'

'Morrell? This is a University matter then?'

I felt sweat prickling in my armpits and on my scalp. I was handling this badly.

'Mr Alder, you may very well be in a position to help clarify whether a recent death was suspicious or not.'

'If it's suspicious, why are you here instead of the police?'

I tried to project a calm confidence. 'As I said, it isn't yet clear that the death was suspicious. I'm trying to gather evidence to present to the coroner and the inquest jury.'

Alder pushed the two handbills back across the counter to me and my heart sank. 'Let me see if I understand you, Mr Rice. You think that whoever commissioned these leaflets – or one of them at least – might be responsible for somebody's death?'

'No! Not exactly. That is to say, not directly. I'm just trying to get a picture of those involved.'

'And what if my customers are entirely blameless in this matter? They'd be within their rights to traduce me and my lack of discretion from one end of the city to the other.'

'So, they were commissioned by different people?'

Alder hesitated, though I was certain he'd been quite deliberate in appearing to let the information slip.

'They were.'

'Mr Alder, it's imperative that I know who commissioned these. Particularly this one.' I laid my hand on the 'Spermatorrhoea Kills' handbill. 'I can assure you, nobody would know that you had given me their names.'

'But, if it came to court, I could be called to testify. To say, yes, it was Mr So-and-so.'

'*If* it comes to court,' I said, carefully, 'there will already be evidence against those responsible. You would be called only to give confirmation as to your customer's identity. And only because your name appears on the bills. No one would know that you had supplied any names.'

Alder didn't take his eyes from me. What was most visible in my face, my trustworthiness, or the fact that I was completely out of my depth?

'Unfortunately, without this information, the inquest jury may decide that this was an accidental death. I wish to discover evidence – if evidence exists – that might suggest otherwise.'

Finding it difficult to bear his unblinking scrutiny, I glanced down at the handbills. 'I know you must be very busy,' I said, though all indications were to the contrary, 'and I would, of course, compensate you for your time.'

'Are you offering to pay me for this information, Mr Rice?'

His tone gave no indication as to whether payment would be welcome, and I had no idea how to respond.

Alder sighed as if my ineptitude wearied him. 'I'm caught on the horns of a dilemma, Mr Rice. I want to do what's right, but I'm finding it hard to know which is the more moral course. To give you your information and potentially facilitate a criminal prosecution, or to maintain my customers' privacy. As a tradesman I have a reputation to maintain.'

'The customers will never know that you named them, I give you my word.'

Alder said nothing, simply continued to stare at me.

I moved a hand toward my jacket pocket; before coming to St Clements, I had withdrawn a sum of money from my bank.

'Don't demean yourself or me, Mr Rice,' Alder said, sharply. 'If I give you this information I'll do so because it's the right thing to do, not because you cross my palm with silver.'

I let my hand drop to my side. 'I beg your pardon.'

The jaded suggestion of a smile tweaked at Alder's features. 'I don't suppose a gentleman like you has much to do with tradesmen, but we're not all money-grubbing rogues.' He drummed his fingers on the counter. 'Wait there.'

As he disappeared into the back room, I took the first decent breath I'd managed since I walked into the shop. Seeking information from undergraduates like Tobias Jenkyn, or from Norton Campbell in the Proctors' Office, was one thing, but I was as uncomfortable here as Alder would be at high table with the Principal.

I wiped my sweaty palms with my handkerchief and looked around the little shop. A more detailed perusal of the mounted handbills displayed on the wall behind the counter further increased my respect for Mr Alder and I wondered at his lack of prosperity. I would have expected to find a man of his talents in more prestigious premises.

The printer returned and handed me a slip of paper. 'The first leaflet you showed me was printed for this gentleman.' He indicated the first name he'd written: Geo. Reardon Esq. 'And the second was commissioned by this one.'

Again, he indicated a name, this time one I did not recognise, as if speaking the men's identities out loud might somehow implicate him in a way that handwriting did not.

'The invoice address was the same for both,' he said. 'And I'm breaking no confidences there. You already have it. It's the one advertised on the first leaflet.' He hesitated. 'Though, in fact, the second order was marked to be collected from the shop and the invoice settled in person, rather than either being put in the post.'

Was this collection in person significant? And if so, what exactly did it mean?

Alder looked at me steadily. 'I hope you're as good as your word, Mr Rice, and this doesn't come back to bite me.'

I assured him that I would not divulge the source of my information to anybody but the proper authorities. Then I pocketed the slip of paper and left.

Chapter 41

Non

When I'd won The Contraption – from a preening idiot Albie and I had seen boasting to a crowd one day outside the Jericho – I'd wondered whether I should sell it and buy a normal tricycle which would be easier to ride by myself. But I soon realised that, complain as she might about it, Lily enjoyed riding the tandem with me.

So, I kept it. And every time I rode it, I laughed in the sneering face of the stripy-jacketed fool who'd told me I wouldn't be able to ride it faster than he had over the hundred-yard dash down to the press and back. '*I don't think so, miss. It's not built for a lady to ride by herself.*' But I'd watched him do it when the crowd had asked for a demonstration, and I'd seen that he had no idea how to get the best out of the machine.

The tandem's one drawback was that I had to do something with it when I got to wherever I was going. So, when I reached the main post office on St Aldate's first thing on Monday, to send a telegram to Dr Reckitt, I looked about for somebody to watch if for me. A small boy was loitering on the pavement, making the most of the last few minutes before he had to be in school. He was trying to pretend he wasn't interested in me and The Contraption, but I'd seen him watching. I beckoned him over.

'You can have a penny if you make sure nobody steals my machine while I'm inside.'

'What if *I* steal it?'

Cheeky little scrap! 'Then I'll hunt you down and pull your teeth out one by one.'

Eyes like saucers, he nodded, and I went in to the post office. I had my telegram already composed in the cheapest number of words:

> Symptoms: vomiting, diarrhoea, abdominal cramp, bradycardia, syncope, sweating, greenish-tinged vision. Cause? Regards, Non.

If anybody could tell me what Sidney Parker had taken it was Dr Reckitt.

When I came out, boy and tandem were still there. The urchin gave me a bit of a look when I held his penny out to him. I think he'd been afraid he'd get a clip round the ear instead.

-

When I steered the tandem into the soot merchant's yard, I was surprised to find Florrie Spellman at the scullery door, giving orders to a girl of about fourteen; I'd expected her to be getting her washing done like most people did on a Monday, while there were Sunday leftovers to eat. Florrie must send her washing out. Which was sensible, with soot everywhere.

'Make sure the brisket's fresh, this time,' she said. 'And don't just take Noah Jeffers's word for it, give it a sniff, use your common sense.'

She sent the girl off and turned to me. 'Good morning, Non,' she said. 'Have you brought my letters?'

I parked the tandem in the corner of the yard. 'No, I'm afraid not. Have you got time for a quick word?'

'Monday morning's usually when I do the accounts.'

'It won't take long. And it's important.'

When we went inside, I could see she hadn't been trying to fob me off with talk of accounts. There was a ledger on the table, along with a pile of bills and the kind of hefty leather money bag that market traders wear on a belt.

Florrie didn't offer me tea this time, so I just pulled a chair out and sat down. 'I won't keep you long. It's just that I need to talk to you about a diary – well, no, more of a record really, that Sidney Parker had been keeping—'

'A diary? Can I see it?'

'It'd do you no good if you did. It's in code.'

She stared at me as if I'd said it was in Swahili. '*Code?* Why?'

'Same reason he hid things under the floorboards, I expect. To keep it away from prying eyes.' I pulled my decoded version of the journal's text out of my bag. 'I decoded it.'

'What was it about? Him and me?' She looked a bit uncomfortable. It wasn't hard to guess why, I knew from what she'd already told me that theirs hadn't been the kind of courtship the young ladies of Somerville and Lady Margaret Hall would expect.

'No. But he did write it *for* you.'

'Can I see?'

'It'll be no more use to you than the original. It's in Welsh.'

At least she didn't seem surprised at that. In fact, she gave a sad little smile. 'He'd speak Welsh to me sometimes. Used to call it "the language of my heart". I think it was because it was his mother's language.' She blinked back the tears that'd started gathering in her eyes.

'Let me read you the beginning,' I said.

Florrie sucked in her bottom lip and nodded.

'*I'm writing this for you, Florrie my love,*' I translated, freely, '*in case this disease kills me, and this record is all you have left. I'm sorry to write in code, but there's nowhere completely safe and I don't want anybody else reading this. The spies have been about, and I can't be sure Mrs Trent hasn't let them in. But, if I can't overcome my illness, I want you to know I tried. Maybe by the time you read this I'll have had the courage to tell you I've been taking Reardon's tonic myself, but I don't know if I can be that brave. But I want to be well for you, Florrie. I want to be the man you deserve.*'

She'd been fighting off tears all the way through, but that last sentence made her sob. I waited while she pulled her apron up and hid her face for a little while. When she took it away again, she was calm.

'I've decoded the whole thing,' I told her. 'I can write a translation for you, if you'd like?'

'Yes, please. What does he say in it?'

'It's a record of his health, mostly. And the medicines he was taking to try and cure himself. He thought he had a condition. And he did as it happens – the post-mortem examination showed that – but it wasn't the condition he thought he had.'

I explained that Sidney Parker had diagnosed himself with spermatorrhoea, a disease that didn't actually exist. 'That stopped him getting proper medical help for the real condition he had,' I said. 'A condition that had eaten a hole from his bowel through to his bladder.' Florrie looked at me, aghast. 'He was very unwell,' I said. 'He must have been in pain a lot of the time.'

She covered her face and started crying again. I wondered if she'd been impatient with him sometimes.

'He wanted you to know how hard he'd been trying to get well, in case he didn't live long enough to marry you,' I said.

'And the poor lamb didn't, didn't he?' Florrie stared at me with watery, red eyes. 'Did he die of the trouble with his bowels, then?'

'The doctor who did the post-mortem examination wasn't sure. But then he didn't know what Sidney'd written in his last couple of entries.'

'Read them to me.'

'They might upset you again.'

'I'll manage. He wrote it for me, didn't he?'

I turned to the last entries in the exercise book I'd used to decode the journal. Florrie listened as I translated, biting her lip.

'*The second dose was even less pleasant*,' I read, '*and, like Thompson said, it's left me very weak. From the instructions he gave me, I know I must be prepared for an even worse reaction with this last dose. If my body tries to vomit it up, I must try to keep it down so that it can do its work. My heart will beat more slowly – I believe it did yesterday – depriving my manhood of blood.*' (I was translating into more easily understood language than Sidney'd actually used because I didn't think she'd understand terms like 'generative organs'). '*If it slows down so much that I feel faint, I must lie down and try to sleep. That's the body's way of fighting the nausea and stomach cramps. But I'll know if it's working if things start to have a tinge of green. I'll know the drug is working.*'

Florrie was concentrating hard, her eyes on my face.

'Then this is the last paragraph,' I said. '*I haven't been able to keep all the last dose down, so I've taken another 3 spoons to make up for it and the bottle's empty. I feel weak and faint. I'm sweating and shaking. I'll lie on the bed now. Tomorrow, I'll be well. We'll be together and far away from Reardon, Thompson, Blain and everyone who wants to control us, Florrie.* That's where it finishes.' I looked at her stricken face. 'I'm sure he'd have written more if he'd known he was dying. I believe he just went to sleep then, fully expecting to wake up cured and well.'

I waited for tears, but no more came. 'I think whatever was in that so-called remedy – Professor Deneuve's Elixir – killed him,' I said. 'I've sent a telegram to an expert I know. He'll know, if anybody does, what produces the symptoms this man Thompson told Sidney to expect.'

Florrie got up and pushed the kettle from the cool end of the range on to the plate directly over the firebox. It started singing straight away.

'Are you saying you think Thompson poisoned Sid? Deliberately?'

'No. It's just that it's nobody's job to check what goes into these patent medicines and sometimes they contain something dangerous. This was a brand new remedy. Sidney may have been the very first person to take it. And, if his constitution was weakened… In the journal, when he'd started taking the remedy, Sidney used the words "kill or cure" – as if that's what this Thompson had told him.' Florrie said nothing. 'Do you know a Carmichael Thompson?' I asked. 'He's the man whose name is on these handbills. I found them in Sidney's hiding place.'

She came back to the table and took the leaflet out of my hand. I pointed to the handwriting at the bottom. 'This name here.'

'Yes, Sid talked about Carmichael Thompson.' She handed the leaflet back to me. 'He works for Reardon.'

I waited.

'Let me make the tea,' Florrie said. 'It's a long story.'

-

In actual fact, the story wasn't that long, Florrie just took a long time telling it because she kept breaking off to talk about Sidney. It was as if his journal, and the things he'd written in it, had given her permission to tell me everything.

The bones of the story were these: George Reardon had originally worked for a London advertising agency but decided to leave – 'Sidney reckoned he'd probably been sacked for swindling the company' – and set up his own company in the same line. The maker of Dr Aurum's Tonic was one of his first customers, and whoever was behind the name evidently had ambitions for his spermatorrhoea remedy. Didn't want it to be seen as just another poor man's substitute for a doctor. Wanted it to be exclusive. Expensive. And he claimed that, unlike other remedies, this was proper medicine based on ancient wisdom from the East. Medicine that worked. And, for that reason, according to Florrie, he saw Dr Aurum's Tonic being bought by high society, even the nobility.

'And George Reardon was perfect for that, wasn't he?' Florrie said, bitterly. 'Because he had Sidney coming up to Oxford where he'd meet all the rich boys.'

I didn't say so, but if George Reardon had wanted Sidney Parker to meet rich boys, he'd sent him to the wrong college. The boys at Jesus were firmly middle class. Not a lot of money there, and certainly no nobility. But the likes of George Reardon probably didn't understand that Oxford's colleges all had different characters, different reputations, and their own associations with specific parts of the country or even individual schools. Prestigious colleges like New College were associated with Eton and Winchester, just the kind of customers that Dr Aurum was after. Except he'd probably call them patrons. Jesus College was associated with schools like Cowbridge Grammar. Not the same kind of families at all.

'Reardon pushed Sid to go further,' Florrie told me. 'Wanted him to force young men into buying. Find out their little secrets and then threaten to make them public if they didn't buy *and* recommend the tonic to their friends.'

'Blackmail?'

'Good as, I suppose. But Sidney refused. He wasn't like that.' She put my cup of tea on the table in front of me. She obviously didn't know about the techniques her fiancé'd used to lure his friends into spending more than they could afford on Dr Aurum's Tonic.

'I thought Sidney hated Reardon,' I said. 'Why didn't he just refuse?'

'Reardon was his guardian. He controlled Sid's money. Said he wasn't just going to shell money out, Sid had to earn it.'

Florrie told me that, after Sidney's first term, George Reardon had pushed him to look outside Jesus College for customers. That's why he'd joined MacLaren's gym.

'But it wasn't long after he started going there that he came to St Barneys and we met,' Florrie said. 'After that, he didn't want to sell any more.'

'But could he stop? If Reardon controlled the purse strings?'

'I think Sid was a bit wiser to him by then. He'd saved some money for himself by that point.'

'Saved? Kept some back from the money he'd got from selling?'

Florrie clasped her hands together on the table as if she was afraid one of them might reach out and slap me of its own accord. 'He had a right to it! It was him doing all the work. And he needed to pay his rent so he didn't have to live in college where everybody hated him. Reardon would never've paid. Not when he had rooms with his scholarship.'

But Reardon had disliked Sidney's sudden show of independence. 'He said Sid was ruining his campaign,' Florrie told me. 'That's what he called it, a campaign, like he was going into battle for Dr Aurum. Said Sid was *crucial*, that he had to keep going. Get a few lords and politicians' sons to buy.' Florrie's eyes were unfocused. She was seeing things in the past, remembering Sidney telling her what Reardon had said. 'He said Sid didn't have to do so much of the selling any more if he didn't want to, but he needed to talk it up – the tonic. Say that it was such a success, Dr Aurum had other people selling it now. Agents, he called them.'

And that's when Thompson had arrived on the scene.

'This Thompson was the new *selling agent* and Sid was supposed to persuade people to buy from him.'

'How did that work?' I asked. 'I mean, how would Reardon know that Sidney was persuading people?'

'Simple. When they came to him to buy, Thompson asked them where they'd heard about the tonic.'

So, Sidney's job had been to spread the word, and Thompson had been checking up on him each time a new customer came his way. 'Sidney mentioned spies in his journal, and you said something about a spy in your letters to him. Who were they?'

Florrie looked very uncomfortable. 'There were people watching us. Me and Sidney. And just me sometimes, as well. I'd see one in particular, coming out of The Jericho, hanging about. He was stood outside, opposite the yard, one day, bold as brass. Gave me the proper creeps.'

'Was this Blain one of them?'

A quick look of something like dislike crossed her face. 'No, he was just another one in Thompson's line.'

'Sidney obviously felt that his life was being controlled by Reardon and the others. Was that why the pair of you were planning to run away to America?'

Florrie's face was a picture. You'd have thought I'd just reached into her mind and plucked a memory out. 'When were you going to tell your father?' I asked.

She recovered quickly. 'Dad? It was his idea. We were all going together. Make a new start. Set up a new business in America.'

That put a different complexion on things. 'Does your father drink in The Jericho?' I asked.

'Sometimes.' The way she said it, I knew the real answer was 'more often than not'. Did Mr Spellman let his tongue run away with him when he was in his cups? If this spy had overheard him boasting about their move across the Atlantic, the news would've gone straight back to George Reardon.

The same George Reardon who was expecting Sidney to bring his inheritance into the advertising business.

I looked at my watch. Coming up for eleven. If a telegraph boy had taken my telegram to Dr Reckitt as soon as it arrived at the Cardigan office, and if the doctor had been at home to answer it by return, I'd know whether Sidney'd been poisoned within the next hour.

Chapter 42

Basil

Back on St Clements, I took the slip of paper out and looked, again, at the two names Mr Alder had written. 'Geo. Reardon, Esq. Wm. Blain Esq.'

Who was William Blain?

In going to the printer's, I had assumed that Alder would confirm George Reardon as the person who'd commissioned the earlier leaflet – he was the advertising agent for Dr Aurum's Tonic, after all – and I had suspected, or perhaps simply hoped, that a different hand would prove to be behind the 'Sidney Parker R.I.P' handbill. But William Blain had given the same London invoice address as George Reardon. What did it mean? If Reardon was still involved, why had he not commissioned the leaflet? And why had this Blain specified that he would pay cash on delivery rather than invoicing the address given?

Was Blain an employee of Reardon's, or did he work for the company which produced Dr Aurum's Tonic? And, if he was Reardon's employee, did that mean that Parker's guardian had sanctioned the use of the poor boy's death as advertising fodder?

With this new conundrum, it was clear that we could not rely on Mr Askew's efforts alone. Though it was essential that we obtain a sample of whatever Carmichael Thompson was peddling, it was also now clear that we needed to know who produced the two remedies, and whether Mr William Blain had commissioned the gruesome Spermatorrhoea Kills handbill at their request.

I saw no choice but to go to London and present myself at the address quoted on the leaflet. Perhaps Mr Alder would have argued that this was the responsibility of the police but, unless and until the inquest jury was in a position to bring in the necessary verdict, I feared that the police response would be lacklustre at best.

The thought that I might find myself interrogating George Reardon was disconcerting. I knew he was in London as he had asked Morrell to delay the inquest until he had completed urgent business there and could return to Oxford. What would his reaction be if he realised that I was investigating his business dealings?

But perhaps I was prejudging the man too harshly. Just because he was prepared to extort 'compensation' from Dr Harper and the college, did it automatically follow that he would knowingly advertise a remedy that contained potentially fatal ingredients? Wasn't it possible that he would willingly co-operate in facilitating an analysis of Dr Aurum's Tonic? Or, indeed, the mysterious PDE of Mr Parker's journal.

Of course, it was possible that Reardon had nothing to do with PDE, that William Blain was responsible for it. But if Blain was behind whatever had been in Mr Parker's little bottle, what might the relationship between him and George Reardon be, beyond a shared London invoice address?

-

I detoured, briefly, to college intending to write a note to Dr Harper explaining my absence. The Principal and I had spoken the previous day, after Sunday service in chapel, and I had told him everything we'd learned about Sidney Parker. I had expected him to be outraged at Parker's having used his place at Jesus to sell patent remedies to our undergraduates, but, in fact, he'd been more pragmatic and had simply asked, 'Will all that need to come out at the inquest, do you think?'

Stepping through the wicket gate into college, I wondered whether perhaps I was being hasty. Perhaps I should await the chemists' analysis of Parker's stomach contents before going barrelling off to London?

But as I passed the lodge, the porter called out to me. 'Letter here for you, sir. Dropped in no more than a minute ago.'

As I took the letter from him and recognised Teddy's writing, I had to curb the urge to run out into the Turl to see if he was still there. Teddy would never have welcomed such importunity and would be even less likely to do so now.

I tore open the envelope.

Bas

Just received word from the chemistry department. Stomach contents contained unidentifiable plant alkaloid. Not definitive re foul play but suggestive. Have informed coroner.

TP.

TP. Two initials that drove home the truth of his determination to forge a new life. Teddy had always been 'T' to me in correspondence. 'TP' not only held me at arm's length, it pushed me firmly away.

He was removing himself to London. If he had his way, he'd soon be married.

He would never be 'T' to me again.

Glancing up at the porter, I stuffed the note into my coat pocket and made my way to my rooms.

-

The brightness of the day should have promised untold possibilities, but, as I walked down to the GWR station on the Botley Road, I felt a growing sense of grey desolation. Journeys to London would never be the same again. Not without Teddy.

TP.

As undergraduates, we'd made the trip to London theatres at least once a term, staying overnight in hotels we could ill afford and pretending to be men of the world. We'd always chosen a carriage which offered lively conversation so that the conviviality of a trip began before we even arrived in London, and I had come to associate rail travel with laughter and light-heartedness.

Now, I walked the length of the train, peering in through the windows to find an empty carriage. To further discourage any spontaneous interaction, and to ensure that I had time enough to rehearse what I would say when I arrived at my destination, I'd bought a newspaper which I proceeded to use as a defence against the one person I was forced to share with, a fellow whose rather large suitcase and much-worn suit suggested a commercial traveller.

By the time we reached Paddington, my hands were filthy with newsprint, so I visited the gentlemen's lavatories to wash them. I kept my eyes down as I entered and fixed them firmly on the basin. Catching another man's eye might be misconstrued and I didn't want to risk any trouble.

Teddy would have laughed at me. He had always been far more adventurous, often risking casual encounters with guardsmen and working-class lads. 'I know they're only in it for the money,' he'd say if I challenged him. 'But I'm only in it for the sex! Not like you, Bas, with your ideals of perfect Hellenistic affection.'

He'd always been dismissive of Oxford's idealisation of male camaraderie. When I'd arrived in Oxford after the barely civilised physicality of school, I'd been delighted by the intellectual collegiality fostered by dons who'd chosen to remain celibate in pursuit of learning, and I'd settled into it with the anticipation of spending the rest of my life in congenial company. However, the recent concession that dons might marry had swiftly begun to change both expectations and behaviour. With dismaying speed, the belief in the sequestered male ideal with its intimate and abiding friendships was coming to be regarded as something of an anachronism; the new aspirant status was marriage and family life in North Oxford's modern villas.

Perhaps I had simply been slow to adapt, but the prospect of a wife held no allure for me. My mother, faced with a son who espoused scholarly bachelordom, had waged a constant campaign over the last three years to introduce me to appropriate young women, all the while assuring me that, when I met 'the right girl', I wouldn't feel I was giving anything up. On the contrary, she maintained, I would rejoice in conjugal felicity.

Perhaps she was right. I seemed, by nature, to be disinclined towards promiscuity, so perhaps it was inevitable that I did not find myself attracted to young women simply on the basis of their appearance. It was possible, I supposed, that were a young woman to lay hold of my heart, my body would respond in the expected way.

And yet… Only yesterday I had assured Tarley Askew that he need not fear competition from me for Non's affections. And if an increasingly intimate acquaintance with a young woman like Rhiannon Vaughan did not stir me, then what kind of woman would?

Some of the crowd Teddy and I had racketed around with as younger men – whom we had, on many an occasion, come to London with – found the mollies who tricked themselves out in women's clothes highly alluring. There was something about the concealment of raw male desire beneath the feminine decorousness of skirts and petticoats that aroused them in a way I neither shared nor understood. Though I'd found many of the female personators highly entertaining, I had never been tempted to venture beneath their rustling silks. In fact, until my desire for Teddy had shocked me with its carnal intensity, I had thought myself the epitome of a natural celibate.

Might a woman truly catch me equally unawares?

-

Outside Paddington, I found a hansom and clambered in, calling up the address to the cabby. I didn't ask if it was far: that would tell him I didn't know the area and give him licence to take me all round the houses to attract a bigger fare.

Despite the clog of trams, omnibuses and commercial traffic in the fashionable area south of the station, we made good time, passing the busy and seemingly endless departments of William Whiteley's stores on Westbourne Grove, before turning off into the residential streets behind. The cab eventually stopped opposite a row of buildings under construction, and I climbed out on to the pavement outside a modest terrace of three-storey houses whose flights of steps to their front doors bridged a drop down to the area in front of the basement.

Confident that I could find my way back to the station, I paid the cabby and told him not to wait.

From the pavement, I surveyed the house to which potential customers were invited to apply to for samples of Dr Aurum's Tonic. It seemed entirely respectable: its stucco had obviously been painted recently, and the slightly unusual, twelve-light windows which were a common feature of all the houses in the terrace, were as clean as London air allowed. It seemed, like all its neighbours, to be the home of a modestly well-to-do family.

I looked around. Above the occasional tree, and the gables of the houses on an adjoining street, I could see a verdigris-covered church tower. This whole area was comfortable, expanding, prosperous, when I'd expected something more down-at-heel and mercantile.

Bracing myself, I mounted the steps to number fifteen and applied the knocker smartly. Footsteps soon approached within, and the door was opened by a young maid.

I raised my hat, my heart beating uncomfortably fast. 'Good day, I wonder if I might have a word with Mr Blain.'

'William Blain?'

'The very same.'

She shook her head. 'He don't live here.'

'Mr Reardon, then?'

'Same goes for him. You can leave a message, if you like.' She had a weary air, as if she'd repeated a similar offer many times. I wondered how many men had applied here in person, rather than have a package which might give rise to a difficult conversation delivered to their home.

'If you write it down,' she added, with a continued lack of enthusiasm, 'I'll see he gets it. Either of them.'

'How will you do that it if neither of them lives here?'

She looked at me appraisingly. Perhaps I was proving less easily deterred than other callers. 'After the tonic, are you?'

I felt uncomfortable at the very suggestion. 'No. I simply wish to speak to Mr Blain. Or Mr Reardon.' Then, in the face of her refusal to waste her breath reiterating their unavailability, I found myself saying, 'I'm afraid I don't understand. I was given this address—'

She grunted. 'You and a lot of other people, going by the letters. Not to mention them as come to the door.' She gazed at me and something in her weakened. 'Look, all I know is, we take their mail in and every week it gets parcelled up and sent on.'

'So, there's a forwarding address?'

A blink but no confirmation.

'Might you be able to provide me with it?'

'Joking, aren't you? I'd be out on me ear!'

I drew out of my pocket a few of the half-crowns with which I'd intended to bribe George Alder and counted them out into my left palm. 'Ten shillings would give you a while to find a new job if your employers find out.'

She tore her eyes from the money and cast a quick glance over her shoulder.

'Hard to find a new job without a character. Make it a guinea and you're on.'

I nodded and looked expectant.

She held her hand out. 'Five shillings for the town.'

I handed over two half-crowns.

'Reardon or Blain?'

I hesitated, thinking quickly. It had been Blain who commissioned the handbill bearing the coffin and Sidney Parker's name, besides, the college already had Reardon's address. 'Blain.'

'Oxford,' she said, holding out her hand.

I paid her five more shillings to know the district.

'Jericho.'

The final eleven shillings, delivered all at once, revealed an address in Laud Street.

The maid took a handkerchief from her pocket and tied the coins up tightly before stowing the silent knot.

'Anything else?' she asked.

I shook my head.

'Well, you've been fair with me, so I'll tell you one last thing for free,' she said. 'Don't know if it's any use to you but you can be the judge of that.' I waited. 'Used to be we sent Mr Reardon's letters on to a different address. In Reading. Then, four days ago, a letter come saying it had to be changed. To the one I just give you.'

'Who was the letter from?'

'Couldn't tell you. Just got my instructions from the missus, didn't I? From now on, any letters for Mr Reardon or Mr Blain go to that address in Oxford.' She looked me squarely in the eye. 'Worth anything to you?'

I gave her another half a crown.

Chapter 43

Non

The clock in the hall had just struck midday when there was a knock on the door.

'Miss Non!' Edie called. 'Telegram for you.'

She'd never have shouted if Lily hadn't been out with Ivy and the baby. Lily didn't tolerate shouting in the house.

I ran downstairs. 'Thank you, Edie.'

'Boy's waiting in case,' she said, nodding at the front door which stood slightly ajar. She knew I wouldn't open the telegram with her standing there, so she moved away, but I heard her footsteps stop halfway along the hallway, just in case.

The telegram was from Dr Reckitt. And he was as straight to the point as ever.

> Digitalis. Lethal poison extracted from fermented foxglove leaves. Reckitt.

He wouldn't expect a reply, so I sent the telegraph boy away with a small tip instead. What Dr Reckitt would really appreciate was a full account of Sidney Parker's illness and death, which I'd write up for him in due course.

Lethal poison.

Even though I'd had my suspicions, it was still a shock to discover that Sidney Parker had been murdered. And to know that I'd seen the person who'd given him the poison, along with reassurance about what were supposed to be its 'side effects'. He'd been standing there in Bear Lane like a normal person. Carmichael Thompson. The very same Carmichael Thompson whom Tarley Askew had gone in search of again today. He was going to tell Thompson that Sidney'd told him there was a new preparation called Professor Deneuve's Elixir, and that Thompson could supply it.

A sudden, terrifying thought sent a chill down my back. What if there was no such thing Professor Deneuve's Elixir? What if it had only ever been a ploy to poison Sidney? I'd assumed that the Spermatorrhoea Kills handbill must be the beginning of a campaign for the new remedy, but that was because Sidney'd talked about something new and better in his journal. We had no real proof that Professor Deneuve's Elixir actually existed. All we had was one blue bottle.

If Professor Deneuve's Elixir was just the name Thompson had made up for the poison he was going to give Sidney, then Tarley Askew asking for it would be disastrous.

He'd said he was due to go out with his rowing crew this morning, but he'd promised to go down to The Bear again this afternoon before his tutorial at three o'clock. If I was lucky, I might still be able to stop him.

-

I rode faster than I'd ever done across the city – faster even than when I'd won The Contraption – and steered into Merton Street just in time to see a pack of young men in sweaters and rowing tights spilling out of Corpus Christi. This must be Tarley Askew's rowing crew. But they should be coming back from the river now, not going down. Perhaps the college had more than one crew?

I pedalled alongside as they ran, but I could see that Tarley Askew wasn't with them.

'Excuse me!'

Heads turned in my direction and they all pulled up, jostling and pretending to run into each other in astonishment. Apparently, they'd never seen a woman riding a tandem on her own before.

'Is Mr Tarley Askew one of your crew?' I asked.

A tall, burly young man who was probably the captain of the boat, if they had such a thing, turned to me, hands on his hips. 'And what business might that be of yours, Miss?'

I didn't have time for an argument about what was and wasn't my business. 'I need to speak to him urgently.'

'We've been trying to speak to him for the last half an hour,' one of the rowers said. 'To no avail.'

This *was* his crew, then. So where was he?

Tall and Burly had had enough. 'If you need to speak to him, leave a note at the lodge,' he said. 'We're late getting on to the water as it is.' He turned and set off and, after a few backward glances at me his crew followed. But then, as they turned down the lane between Corpus Christi and Merton College, the man at the back hesitated and looked back at me. I pushed the tandem towards him.

'What's so urgent?' he asked.

'Mr Askew may be in danger.'

The boy – probably the boat's cox from his slight stature – looked worried. 'It's not like Askew to miss an outing. We *were* supposed to be going out at nine, but arrangements had to be changed to midday which we all agreed at breakfast.'

'Including Mr Askew?'

'Yes. But then he didn't appear. We've been waiting for him for the last twenty minutes.'

'He's not in his room?'

'Not unless he's locked himself in and isn't answering.'

'Look, it's probably not wise for me to go into the lodge,' I said. He looked as if he was about to ask why but I cut him off. 'I'm sorry, I haven't got time to explain. If I write a note, will you just take it in and leave it for him?'

He glanced over his shoulder. Probably worried that one of the others would come back and see him talking to me.

'Yes, all right, but you need to be quick. Barnes is cross enough about the delay as it is.'

Barnes must be Tall and Burly. I swung my satchel round from my back and took out my notebook and pencil.

Tarley, I wrote, *Imperative you DO NOT go to The Bear. DO NOT approach Thompson. Come and see me as soon as you can.*

Non.

I gave him the note. 'Thank you, Mr…?'

'Chigley,' he said. 'And you're welcome.'

Thinking hard, I cycled back round into Oriel Square and up the wide thoroughfare of King Edward Street with its impressive new shops and houses. But the break from college buildings was short. When I got to the High Street, Brasenose College stood on the other side of the road and, beyond that, Turl Street and Jesus College.

And Basil.

Basil was better placed than me to make enquiries. And, anyway, I needed to tell him that Sidney Parker had been poisoned.

But, at Jesus College, I faced the same problem as I had at Corpus Christi. I couldn't go in. I didn't like to think of the number of letters that'd go flying around Oxford if I came face to face with Dr Harper, so I pedalled slowly past the college and peered in through the wicket gate. What I could see of the area in front of the lodge was deserted. Where were all the gownsmen of Jesus when you needed one? I'd just have to loiter out here and wait for one.

Fortunately for me, the tandem made loitering a lot easier. To start with, I cycled up and down the street a bit, as if I was practising riding the thing. But it was difficult to look incompetent on a tricycle because there was no danger of wobbling or falling off. Still, I tried my best.

After four times up and down the top end of Turl Street, it seemed like a good idea to do something else, so I dismounted just up from the Jesus College gate and started fiddling with the tandem's chain.

Out of the corner of my eye I could see people and carts and barrows, going in and out of Ship Street on one side, and cutting through from Radcliffe Square on the other. But here, between Jesus and Exeter colleges, the street was deserted.

So why did I feel as if I was being watched?

That sixth sense we've all got made me look up at the three storeys of Exeter College windows on the other side of Turl Street. There was somebody standing in a window on the first floor, looking down at me. As soon as he realised I'd seen him, he moved away.

Seeing him had given me a bit of a shock, but I was relieved to know why the hackles on the back of my neck had been prickling.

I went back to fiddling with the tandem's chain. I was using my handkerchief to do the dirty end of the work, so my fingers were still pretty clean, but the handkerchief would never be the same again.

'What do you think you're doing, lurking there? You're not supposed to be hanging round our colleges.'

I knew who it was before I even looked up. The bray was the clue.

I kept my eyes on the chain. 'I think you'll find, Mr Peacock, that the actual stipulation was that I shouldn't attend *lectures* for the rest of this term. As long as I don't do that, I have the same freedom to walk Oxford's streets as you. Or to cycle them if I see fit.'

'But why would you cycle up and down endlessly? You're clearly trying to waylay somebody. Some fool of a Welshie, no doubt.'

Now I looked up. Right into his mean little eyes. 'I don't see what business it is of yours, Mr Peacock.'

'Even Welshies are University men. They need protecting from women like you.'

I straightened up and took a step towards him. But, before I could say anything, Peacock was braying again.

'If you don't get on your machine and be on your way within the minute, I shall write another letter to the committee in charge of this ridiculous fiasco of admitting women to lectures and make a further complaint. I'm fairly certain that you wouldn't be welcome in lectures ever again if they heard that you were loitering outside colleges trying to waylay undergraduates.' His nasty little eyes narrowed. 'Or is it Rice you're waiting for? He seemed very keen to defend you at the lecture last week. Quite the knight in shining armour.'

I drew breath to call him all the vile names under the sun, but Hara stopped me.

'*That's exactly what he wants you to do. So that he can quote what you've called him in his letter.*'

Quietly, I let my breath out again and stared at Peacock until he looked away. Then I balled the oily handkerchief up, shoved it into my pocket and wheeled the tricycle back down Turl Street.

I'd have to send Basil a telegram instead and hope for the best.

Chapter 44

Basil

I made my way back to Jesus from the station just after six, wearily aware that I had a lecture to prepare for the following day. Had it really only been a week since Dr Harper had swooped into my lecture to tell me of Sidney Parker's death? I seemed to have lived several months since he broke the news.

As I passed the lodge, Mr Allen called out to me. 'Telegram here for you, Mr Rice.'

I ducked into the lodge and asked him to bring his lamp over with the telegram so that I could read it straight away.

It was from Non.

> Please bring TA to Shene Rd. Left note at CCC, midday.
> EXTREMELY urgent we speak.

Non wasn't given to hyperbole, so those capital letters were disturbing. And the rest of the rather cryptic note suggested that she'd tried to speak with Tarley Askew, failed, and left him a note at Corpus. Of course, hours had passed since midday; there was every possibility that Mr Askew was now ensconced in Lily Maddox's house, preparing to eat dinner with the family.

I was cold and hungry and wanted nothing so much as a decent cup of coffee, followed by dinner in hall. Instead, I thanked Allen and made my way to my rooms to fetch my cap and gown.

-

Less than an hour later, Non flung the front door open to me. Her face fell abruptly when she saw I was alone.

'You didn't find him?'

I shook my head. 'And he hadn't picked your note up. It was clever of you to include that in the telegram.'

I made to take my gown off, but she stopped me. 'No. We need to go to the police. Now.' As she took her coat and scarf from the hallstand, Lily appeared.

'He's not back,' Non told her.

'You're going to the police, then?'

'Yes.'

'To tell them what, exactly?' I asked.

'I'll explain on the way,' Non said. 'Shall we take the tandem?'

'No.' I was too weary to face the tricycle. 'I saw a cab outside Jericho House. Let's see if he's still there.'

We secured the cab and, on our way to the police station, Non outlined what she'd learned from Parker's journal and her medical friend. I, in my turn, told her what I had discovered from Mr Alder and the corruptible maid in London.

'Blain gets a mention in Parker's journal,' she said. 'And I asked Florrie Spellman about him. She said he was "another one in Thompson's line". But you think he might be behind the whole Dr Aurum enterprise?'

'I don't know,' I admitted. 'His name at the forwarding address may be hiding somebody else. But whoever's behind it all, Blain's certainly involved, and as the Jericho address is the only one we have, I think that's where we must start looking for Mr Askew.'

The cab pulled up on the High next to the blue police lamp. After I'd paid the cabbie, we made our way down Alfred Street to the station's entrance. I'd never had any previous occasion to visit what I still thought of as the new police station. The former station, home of the 'watch and ward' force that had predated the Oxford City Police, had lurked untidily on the corner of Queen's Street and St Aldate's throughout my undergraduate days. Looking back, the arrangement under which a rather shabby body of men had policed the city's streets by day while ceding nocturnal patrols to the University force, now seemed positively medieval. The city Corporation had obviously felt the same and, shortly after I'd graduated, had petitioned parliament for powers to establish a more modern force, based on the Metropolitan model.

Relying on the proctors as we did for undergraduate discipline, college men had little to do with the police force. I hoped that wouldn't affect the officers' reaction to Mr Askew's disappearance.

-

'Let me see if I've understood what you're telling me, sir,' the sergeant behind the desk said when I'd explained our concerns. 'You want my constables to go to a certain man's house in Jericho to look for this undergraduate, because he may or may not have spoken to *another* man, who may or may not know the first man, and who may or may not have been involved in the death of a *different* undergraduate. Except we don't actually know whether that death was suspicious, because there's been no inquest yet. And this man, the one *your* young man *might* have met with, may or may not think that he – the undergraduate – knows something about this other undergraduate's death that he shouldn't.' He took a breath as if the summoning up of such a synopsis had taxed him. He obviously thought we were making a fuss about a very elaborated degree of nothing. 'Have I got that right?'

'More or less.'

'If you don't mind me saying so, sir, it all seems a bit far-fetched. This young man was seen this morning. So, as it stands, all he's failed to do is turn up for some rowing.'

'He didn't turn up for dinner, either.' When the porter had failed to find Mr Askew in his room, I'd stationed myself outside the hall at Corpus while the undergraduates filed in for their evening meal.

'I believe it's not unknown for an undergraduate to eat his dinner in a public house.'

I was about to respond when Non's patience expired. 'What about what Mr Rice has told you about this man Thompson?'

'You mean that he's selling patent remedies to young gentlemen, miss? I'm afraid there's no law against that.'

'But if one of the remedies *killed* Sidney Parker—'

'Begging your pardon, miss, but there's no evidence. Cause of death will be for the University Coroner to decide.' The sergeant turned back to me. 'If this young man has gone absent without leave, sir, I suggest you involve the proctors.'

'This isn't a matter of college discipline, sergeant. It's a matter of life and death.'

'So you say, sir, but I'm afraid I see no evidence of that.'

I didn't want Non to say anything she, or I, might regret, so I made a last ditch attempt. 'This is a member of the University we are talking about, sergeant. I hope I don't have to remind you that the University contributes almost half the cost of policing the city and this young man may be in mortal danger.'

The sergeant fixed me with the dead eye of officialdom. 'Mr Rice, I've heard no substantive evidence from you that this young man is in danger. He's probably just given everybody the slip and is off enjoying himself. He'll be back in college before morning I have no doubt. Now, if you'll excuse me, I have proper police work to attend to.'

-

'He's right,' Non said, as we regrouped beneath the blue lantern on the High. 'We should go to the proctors. They can demand entry if they think there's an undergraduate on the premises, can't they?'

I'd been thinking this over since the sergeant had suggested it. 'It's one thing for the proctors to demand entry to brothels and drinking dens, it's quite another when we're talking about a private house. If it turns out Mr Askew isn't there, there'd be outrage. You know what people think about the University's powers.'

'Fine.' Non was already walking away from me. 'Go home then. I'll go and see the proctors myself.'

'You can't.'

'Oh no. I forgot, I'm not a member of this ridiculous boys' club of yours so they won't even be able to see I'm there. This is Tarley's *life*, Basil.'

Her outrage made her seem three inches taller. She positively levitated with fury.

'Yes. Of course. I'm sorry. You're right.'

Non didn't reply, just glared at me and stomped off towards St Mary's Passage, leaving me to hurry in her wake.

-

By the time we went through the gates into the precincts of the Clarendon Building, I'd managed to persuade Non to let me speak to the proctors while she waited outside. Her presence could only muddy the waters.

However, our visit was in vain. I found the Proctors' Office locked and silent.

'What now?' I asked.

Non looked at me and, even in the light of the gas lamps, I could see the determined set of her face. 'We've got no choice. We'll have to go to Blain's house ourselves.'

Chapter 45

Non

On the way back to Shene Road, we came up with a plan. A plan that involved Basil posing as a proctor with suspicions about one of the University's undergraduates being in Blain's house.

Basil hadn't said as much – yet – but I knew perfectly well that he wasn't going to let me go with him, so while he was explaining the plan to Billy Nicholson and Albie, I took a candle and excused myself. 'Won't be a minute,' I said, over my shoulder. 'As soon as I'm back we can go.'

As I went along the passage to the WC at the back of the house, I wondered what Lily would think when she and Ivy came back from their church ladies' meeting and found only Edie and the baby at home. But then, if everything went well, we might be back before her.

If you were clumsy about it, the sound of the bolt on the WC's door was so loud you could hear it three rooms away, but, with a bit of care, you could pull it back without making a sound. So, about five seconds after I'd locked myself in, I slipped quietly out again, then went through the scullery and into the garden. Luckily for me, Edie was upstairs with the baby.

I lifted the shed door on its hinges as I opened it, so that it didn't squeak where the bottom caught the frame, then I lifted it closed again behind me. I didn't want anybody to see the light from my candle.

There was a quick scurrying as I pulled the door to – Albie'd need to put down more rat poison. I stood the candlestick on the workbench and took the lid off the barrel in the corner. My boy's clothes were carefully hidden from Lily under a tarpaulin we'd had on the shed when its roof had sprung a leak.

I changed as quickly as I could, which was slower than I would've liked, seeing as the dress I was wearing was fastened with about three dozen buttons. Shivering, I pulled the cold shirt on over my head then, still with my boots on, I managed to slip my feet down the legs of the trousers. My breasts splayed the braces out sideways, but I was used to just buttoning the waistcoat tight and bundling myself up in the jacket. I shoved my hair up under the cap I'd got from the same second-hand shop as the clothes.

With my dress and petticoat folded quickly and stuffed back inside the barrel with my coat, I blew the candle out, closed the shed door behind me and waited till my eyes could see again. Then, I made my way as best I could to the bottom of the garden. As I stumbled up to the wall and climbed over into the garden behind ours, I blinked hard, trying to force my eyes to see better while I waited to see if anybody'd spotted me. But nobody came out of our neighbours' house.

Crouched over, I picked my way as quietly as I could to the side gate, let myself out and cut back round to the junction with Shene Road.

On the corner, I strained my eyes into the dark towards Lily's house. As hard as I looked, I couldn't see any sign of Basil and the boys. Either they were still inside, waiting for me, or they'd done what I expected and left the house as soon as I'd gone to the WC. With any luck, they'd have gone the long way round via Walton Street, to make the most of the better lighting there. I was going a darker, but quicker, way.

Luckily for me, the moon was full so, even without gas lamps, there was enough light to see where I was going. I trotted along with my head down, trying to look like a boy who's late home and expecting a hiding.

Even though I might be heading into danger, I couldn't help enjoying the freedom to run. My walking dress allowed me to stride out pretty quickly, but if I tried to run in it, the skirts tangled themselves around my legs and slowed me down or threatened to trip me up. Being able to run without feeling held back was exhilarating, even if I couldn't run as fast as I wanted to for fear of missing my footing in the dark.

'*What would the ladies of the AEW say if they could see you now?*'

I ignored my sister. I wasn't going to get into an argument, now. And anyway, I knew exactly what the AEW ladies' reaction would be. They'd have a collective fit.

But I'd had a totally different life from the women of the AEW. A life of work and argument and learning and sailing, not to mention hardship when Dada's ship had gone down. How could they expect me to behave like the middle-class girls who'd come to Oxford to attend lectures and live respectably at Somerville and Lady Margaret Hall? Those girls had been brought up to be quiet and polite, not to run or fight or argue. And definitely not to think about how unfair it was that men did as they liked and expected us to do as they liked, too.

Could I learn to think like them, to have their expectations? The truth was, I didn't want to and had no intention of trying.

The rarity of my night-time excursions on to the meadow meant that I wasn't used to running much any more, and my heart was thumping. But perhaps it wasn't just the running that was making it beat so hard. My stomach was in knots, and I had to admit that I was afraid. Not for myself. For Tarley Askew.

The 'remedy' Thompson had given to Sidney Parker had contained digitalis. And it had killed him. If Thompson and this Blain character suspected that Tarley knew anything about that, I dreaded to think what they might do.

At Cranham Street I jinked right then left and soon found myself on the corner of Laud Street where Blain's house was. I peered along the road, trying to pant silently, and I could feel my breath chilling on my face.

People had their curtains closed, so the only light in the street came from the moon. But that was enough to see that Laud Street was deserted. What it wasn't enough to see was the numbers on the doors.

The houses I'd just passed all had their doors right on the pavement. You could reach out and touch them if you wanted to. But the houses on Laud Street were set back behind tiny front gardens with low walls and railings around them. In the dark, the doors were too far away to be able to see the numbers.

I heard a voice behind me and crouched down. A door slammed and I heard a shout from inside the house that sounded like 'Good riddance!'. The figure striding away muttered something, but he was already too far away from me to make out the words. Off to the pub to drink away more money the family couldn't afford, probably. I was glad he hadn't come my way. A man in that mood might well cuff a boy around the ear just for being there.

I put my head around the corner again. Nobody about. Then, just as I was considering going up the nearest garden path to get a closer look at the house number, I saw Basil and the boys coming along Laud

Street from the Walton Street end. Weak as the light was, you couldn't mistake a man in a cap and gown. I watched as they looked for the right house. When they found Blain's front door, the plan was for Albie and Billy to leave Basil there and wait on the corner for him to be let in. Then, as soon as he was inside, they'd nip around to the back of the house and get in through the garden, in case somebody tried to take Tarley out the back way.

There were footsteps coming up behind me, along Laud Street from the other end. I pulled back and crouched down, as if I was re-tying a bootlace, until whoever it was went by.

As the owner of the footsteps walked past, I saw his outline.

He was wearing a bowler hat.

Thompson.

'*Lots of men wear bowlers*,' Hara pointed out.

'*Yes, but not men of just the right size and shape. And not just where I'd expect Thompson to be.*'

It was too much of a coincidence not to be him.

Almost as if he was confirming my thoughts, Bowler Hat turned down a narrow alleyway between two houses.

I looked quickly up the road. The boys were just leaving Basil.

Quick as a mouse across a barn floor, I was out on to Laud Street and following Thompson down the alley. I wasn't going to have Billy Nicholson trying to send me home. Not at this point in proceedings.

I flattened myself against a garden wall and watched which gate Thompson went in.

Then I counted to five, my heart hammering at three times the speed of my measured count, and followed him.

Chapter 46

Basil

I watched Billy and Albie walk to the corner where they were going to wait for me to gain admittance to Blain's house, then knocked smartly on the door. There was no knocker and the rap of my knuckles seemed peremptory, almost threatening, in the dark street.

To my left, the curtains were drawn across the little bay window, but if the room was lit, there was no sign of it. Perhaps the curtains were of superior quality, but I suspected that the room was unoccupied.

I knocked again and, receiving no answer for a second time, stepped back to the front gate and looked up at the first-floor window. It, too, was dark, though I couldn't tell whether the curtains were drawn.

'And who might you be?'

The sudden voice spun me around. A man was standing with his hand on the garden gate, staring at me.

'Mr Blain? Mr William Blain?'

'Who wants to know?'

'Norton Campbell, University proctor.' There was no more than a minimal chance that Blain knew the names of the University's proctors, but their elections were announced in the papers, so it seemed rash to use an invented name. 'I have reason to believe that one of our undergraduates may have paid you a visit. May indeed, for reasons that are unclear to me, still be in your house. I'm sure it's all a misunderstanding...' Non and I had decided that no accusations should be levelled until Tarley Askew was safe.

Blain took a step towards me. 'Misunderstanding or not, I can tell you, your boy's not here.' He was definitive, his voice the equivalent of a rebuffing hand on my chest. 'I don't know why he'd have *paid me a visit*, as you say, but I've not been here all day so, if he did, he'd've been disappointed.'

He wore a hat, but beneath it, his head seemed completely bald which gave him a menacing aspect. I lowered the lantern lest he see it as a threat. Lit from beneath, his face was a thing of shadows, teeth and eyes, and I found it difficult to read his expression. Nevertheless, his displeasure at finding me here was obvious.

'I see,' I forged on, my stomach tight with the fear of violence. 'Yes, of course. I'm so sorry to have to trouble you but I do have reliable information that—'

'That what? That he's been here? I couldn't tell you. As you see, I'm only now getting home. All I *can* tell you is that he's not here now.'

'Nevertheless—'

Blain closed the small gap between us, and apprehension crawled across my scalp. Though I had a slight height advantage, I had no doubt that he would fell me with a single blow.

'I'd like to get into my house now, Mr Norton Campbell. Without you, if you don't mind.'

I was unable to prevent myself glancing along the road to where Albie and Billy were standing. Blain caught the gesture.

'Waiting for your bulldogs, are you? Going to try and force your way in, like you do at the brothels?' He shook his head slowly, eyes on me. 'I wouldn't advise it.'

And, with that, he turned the key in the lock, stepped into his dark house, and closed the door in my face.

Chapter 47

Non

I stood outside the gate that Thompson had disappeared through, my ears out on stalks to try and hear anything from the garden side. But there was nothing. No voices, no door opening and closing.

Then I heard the quiet but definite sound of a stream of liquid hitting earth. Thompson was pissing in the garden. I had to tamp down a sudden urge to laugh.

Nerves. I was shaking like a newborn lamb.

There was a silence when the pissing stopped as Thompson fastened his flies then I waited until I heard his footsteps on the cinder path. A door opened and closed.

As quietly as I could, I raised the latch on the tall gate and pushed gently. It opened. Thompson hadn't thought to bolt it, more fool him.

At the other end of the garden, I could see a weak light in the scullery window as if there was a lamp lit in the kitchen. I knew that if anybody looked out into the garden now, they'd most likely be able to see me. My shirt was covered up by a grey muffler, but my pale face and hands would stand out every time the moon came out from behind the clouds.

I moved over to the side of the garden opposite where I'd heard the pissing coming from and kicked at the thin, ashy soil where somebody'd been growing vegetables. I bent down and scraped up a handful, then I spat on it and rubbed it between my palms and smeared it over my face and the backs of my hands. Soot would've been better, but beggars can't be choosers.

The little stones in the soil gave me an idea so I scrabbled about until I found a couple of bigger ones and put them in my pockets. Then I wiped my palms as well as I could on bare sprout-stalks and bits of dead weed, before drying them on my trousers.

'*Wearing trousers makes you behave just like a boy*,' Hara said.

'*It's only earth, it'll brush off when it's dry.*'

Just hearing Hara's voice in my head made me feel as if I wasn't completely alone. And anyway, Basil would be at the front door before long. Then, if they stuck to the plan, Albie and Billy'd come in through the gate. To make things easier for them, I'd left it wide open.

As quietly as I could, I crept down the garden. Then, as the cinder path turned to back-yard flagstones under my feet, I crouched down, slipped past the door to the outside WC and up to the scullery, trying to keep myself out of sight of anybody in the kitchen. Stupid really, I could see the curtains were closed, but still.

Light from the kitchen picked out things in the scullery. Through the grimy window, I could see a sink with a tap, a copper, and shelves on the wall. In the corner, a tin bath stood on its end. Good job it was out of the way, I wouldn't want that to go clattering to the floor if I knocked into it.

Slowly, I turned the knob on the scullery door.

'*Aren't you going to wait for Albie and Billy?*'

I listened as hard as I could, but I couldn't hear footsteps outside the garden gate. So, I waited another minute, counting slowly in my head, hoping the numbers'd keep Hara quiet. It worked until I stopped.

'*You've got to wait for them, Non.*'

'*What if something's happened to hold them up?*' I objected.

'*Like what?*'

'*I don't know. But we need to know what's going on in there.*'

'*No. We need to wait.*'

My hand was still on the doorknob, turning it as slowly as I could so as not to make any noise. I felt the moment when the catch slid free. With great care, I opened the door an inch and, *very* slowly, let the handle's mechanism turn back again.

Luckily for me, the scullery door fitted well. There were no squeaks as I pushed it open another inch.

'*Don't, Non!*'

'*I'm not going in, I'm just going to see what I can hear.*' My heart was punching at my ribs from fear of being heard, I wasn't sure my legs would hold me up if I went in.

Just then, I heard a sound inside the house and a voice called, 'Bill? That you?'

The voice had come from the kitchen. From where I was standing, whoever had spoken was probably no more than two or three paces away.

Bill. William Blain.

I heard a door opening, and a voice which sounded as if it had long ago lost patience with the first speaker asked, 'Who else is it going to fuckin' be?'

Still crouching, I pushed the door a little further open. I could see the doorway to the kitchen but couldn't see anything through it because of the angle. Fortunately for me, that meant that whoever was in there wouldn't be able to see me either. Not unless they stood right in the kitchen doorway. I moved forward until I was crouching inside the scullery.

'Thought it might be the boss. Where is he anyway?'

'Reardon? Still in the Smoke most likely. Doesn't need to be back till Wednesday, does he? And he may be your boss, Thompson, but he's not mine. Anyway, you should be glad he's not here. Cocked up, haven't you?' Blain's voice sounded hard and taut, like a halyard when the mainsail's stretched. 'I've just had to deal with a bloody University proctor on my doorstep looking for an undergraduate. What've you done?'

Basil! He'd found the right house, but obviously hadn't been able to persuade Blain to let him in.

Where were Basil and the boys now? Standing somewhere on the street, more than likely, trying to work out what to do next.

'Shit!' Carmichael Thompson sounded panicked. 'How did the proctor know he was here?'

'Know *who's* here?'

'A student came up to me in The Bear. He knew about Parker. Knew I'd given him the new stuff. Professor Deneuve's. Knew it *by name*. Wanted some himself.'

'Didn't he know Parker's dead?'

'Yeah. That's why he wanted the remedy.' Thompson was falling over himself to explain. The way Sidney'd referred to Blain and Thompson in his journal had made them seem like equals, but Blain was obviously in charge, here, and didn't think he answered to Reardon. 'He had one of your bills,' Thompson gabbled, 'the Spermattyreea Kills one. He said Parker must've died because he left it too late to take the remedy, should've taken it sooner—'

Oh clever, clever Tarley!

'—but what if he's told other people and they think he died *because* he took it?'

'Hold on… Parker *told* him he had the new remedy?'

'Yes! And that's what *he* wanted. Said he knew Parker'd got it off me!' Carmichael Thompson was getting more and more wound up. 'If Parker told *him*, who else did he tell? How long before everybody's saying it was the new remedy that killed him?'

'Shut up,' Blain said. 'Lemme think.' But he didn't think for long. 'Where is he?'

'Coal cellar.'

'Alive?'

'Yes! Fuck! Course he's alive.'

'Why the hell did you bring him back here? Why didn't you just tell him you'd never heard of any Professor Deneuve?'

'I dunno. Thought you'd know what to say to him.'

'Christ.' Blain hit something. The table, probably. 'You were supposed to tell the little shit not to mention that he was taking it to anybody.'

'I did. Told him to keep mum till we got the bills out.'

'Well, he took no fuckin' notice, did he?' I could hear that Blain was holding on to whatever was left of his temper by a whisker. 'Didn't you tell him to stay inside and rest while he was taking the stuff, like I told you?'

'Yes, I did! Told him exactly what you said – stay indoors, rest, and that'll give it the best chance to work.'

So that was why Sidney Parker had kept to his room on Monday. Not just because he was dealing with bowel cramps and sitting on his chamber pot, but because he thought that was the way to give the 'remedy' the best chance to cure him.

'So how come whoever you've got down there knows about Professor Deneuve's?'

'I don't know, do I? Maybe Parker didn't go out – maybe this one came to see him?'

There was a pause then Blain said, 'You'll have to get rid of him.'

'*What?* No!'

'Yes.' Blain's voice was like a fist in the face. 'Weigh him down and chuck him in the canal. Nobody'll ever find him.'

'But they'll come here looking for him, won't they? That proctor knew he was here. What if he goes to the police?'

'If they come, I'll let 'em in. Let 'em look round. You'll just have to make sure he's gone by then. Doesn't matter if he's dead or not when you throw him in the canal, just make sure he doesn't make any noise on the way there. Hammer to the head'll see to that.'

My legs were beginning to tremble from crouching down and from the cold. I put one knee to the ground.

'Fuck off!' Thompson sounded as if he'd grown a backbone. 'I'm not hanging for nobody. You want him dead, *you* put an 'ammer to his head.'

'I'll put one to yours if you don't fuckin' do as you're told,' Blain threatened. 'Think I wouldn't *kill you where you sit*?' I felt fear run down my spine like a trickle of icy rain. He sounded as if the thought appealed to him. 'Don't try me.'

My heart was racing, and I was suddenly trembling all over. Tarley'd be able to hear all this from the coal cellar. If he was conscious.

I had to do something.

Most of the kitchen was hidden from me by the angle of the open doorway, but I could see what must be the cellar door, right there in the corner in front of me.

'What about the stuff?' Thompson whined. 'There's four bloody crates of it down there. If the police come, they'll see it.'

'Let 'em. That stuff's fine. You just need to get rid of Sidney's pal down there.'

I turned my head towards the garden. Were Basil and the boys out there, arguing about what to do? Blain had fobbed Basil off so perhaps they'd given the plan up and gone home with their tails between their legs. They'd be back when they saw I wasn't at home, but they might be too late, then.

Thompson was still talking. 'But what if they test it? What if they find out it *was* that that killed the boy?'

A sound came from Blain that was probably his version of a laugh. 'Just how stupid are you, you cretinous fucker? Let me spell it out. The stuff you gave him *did* kill him. It was *supposed* to kill him. But it wasn't what's in those crates downstairs.'

There was a silence then. In my mind's eye, I saw Thompson gaping at him. 'What?' Blain sounded amused. 'Did you think the instructions you gave him were going to go out with every bottle of Professor Deneuve's? Why d'you think they weren't written down?'

'Because the leaflets weren't back from the printers yet. You told me!'

'Jesus. You really are as stupid as you look, aren't you? Diarrhoea, vomiting, sweating, fainting – who the fuck'd take something that caused all that, apart from a cretin like Parker?'

There was a silence while Thompson took in what he'd said. Then he started shouting. 'No! He'd just left it too long. It's like you said – it was dicey in his condition. Kill or cure. *That's what you said.*'

'Yeah, and you believed it. You stupid fucker, what you gave him wasn't Professor Deneuve's.' I didn't know what Blain's face looked like, but I knew he was sneering.

'What was it, then?'

'Doesn't matter. Did its job, that's all you need to know.'

'*Why* though?' Thompson sounded panicked.

'Why d'you think? Little sod was going to run off to America. He'd've wanted his money. And it was all gone, wasn't it? Reardon'd sunk it all into the business.'

Just then, a sound came from the direction of the back gate. Panic shot through me. I moved backwards as silently as I could, still crouching, and peered into the dark. My heart was going nineteen to the dozen and I was shaking so much I could barely keep myself from falling flat on my back. I put a hand to the ground to steady myself and squinted into the darkness at the end of the garden. But the moon had gone behind a cloud so I couldn't see a thing. Was somebody there? I held my breath and listened. A shout from a nearby street made me jump so hard I could've sworn I left the ground.

I stared and stared in the direction of the gate. Was it still open? The dark seemed to have a different shade where it should be, but I couldn't be sure.

Were Basil and the boys here? God, I hoped they were. Without help, I had no chance of getting Tarley out of Blain's cellar.

But what if it was another one of Blain and Thompson's lot? What if they'd seen me and were just standing there, watching, waiting? A man standing in the corner behind the privy would be out of sight.

I strained my ears, but all I could hear were shouts coming from outside one of the beer houses on Cranham Street. My eyes were sore from straining into the dark.

Blain wanted Thompson to kill Tarley. Immediately. By the time Basil came back with reinforcements, Tarley could be dead.

Whether I was being watched or not, I had to do something *now*.

Chapter 48

Basil

Billy and Albie were hiding just out of sight around the corner.

'He wasn't having it, then.' Albie was subdued, and I wondered if he felt as foolish and humiliated as I did. Our plan now seemed hopelessly naïve.

'I think he believed I was a proctor,' I said, 'but he refused to let me in.'

'What now?' Billy asked, his breath visible in the lamplight.

I hesitated. 'We'll have to try and get in through the back.'

A look passed between Billy and Albie. They obviously didn't think I had it in me to storm the house.

'We might get more than we bargain for if we do that,' Albie said. 'Somebody's just gone down between the houses. Could be they were going into Blain's.'

Billy rolled his shoulders uncertainly. He'd been full of bravado when I'd outlined Non's plan but, within sight of Blain's house, his swaggering confidence had turned to apprehension.

I tried to bolster my own flagging resolve by chivvying them. 'Do you want to go back and tell Non – or Lily for that matter – that we've left him here?'

Albie chewed his lip. 'Don't really *know* he's here though, do we? It's only a guess.'

He was right, of course. But if there was the smallest chance that Tarley Askew was in William Blain's house, we couldn't simply allow ourselves to be turned away like worn-down door-to-door salesmen. If he was in there, the boy was unlikely to be released without harm unless we intervened.

'I quite understand if you'd rather not get involved,' I said, stiffly, 'but Mr Askew's in this position because of me, and I can't simply walk away.'

'He's *here* because Non stuck her nose in where it's not wanted, as usual,' Billy said.

'That's not fair,' I countered. 'Without Non, we'd know next to nothing about how Sidney Parker died and nothing at all about Blain's involvement. So I, for one, am glad she put her nose in.'

Billy grunted.

'I'm going to go in via the back door,' I said, trying to sound decisive. 'I have to know whether he's there. But please don't feel you have to.'

'No, we'll come with you,' Albie said. 'We'd never hear the end of it if we let you go by yourself.'

Billy sucked his teeth but didn't argue.

'Thank you,' I said, shamefully relieved. 'Right then. Let's proceed, shall we?'

Blain's house was the first in a row of six and, at each end of the short terrace, there was a passage through to the back gardens. Finding the gate that gave on to the appropriate garden was a simple matter. It was open.

'Looks like the bloke I saw did come in here,' Albie murmured.

I wondered whether his stomach was as knotted as my own, whether his hands were shaking and frozen with fear. I raised the lantern and stepped forward.

'Leave that here,' Billy whispered, nodding at the lantern, 'or they'll see us coming.'

He was right, but nevertheless, I felt as if I was relinquishing a weapon as I set the lantern down by the wall.

We filed through into the garden, each of us treading with immense care so as to make as little noise as possible. Huddled together, almost touching, in the confined space of the little garden, our dark forms seemed grotesquely large. I couldn't believe that we wouldn't be instantly visible to anybody inside the house.

Habit made me turn to close the gate, but Billy put a hand out to stop me and shook his head. He was right, of course. We might need a quick escape.

Then, without warning, Albie grabbed my arm and pulled me into the corner of the garden that was hidden from the scullery door.

'There's somebody there,' he whispered as Billy darted after us. 'Just in the scullery doorway.'

'Askew?' I asked, barely able to hear myself.

'Don't know.'

'What could you see exactly?' I asked, my lips almost touching his ear.

'He's crouching in the doorway. Difficult to tell, but I don't think it's Mr Askew. Not big enough.'

Had Mr Askew recruited somebody else in his desperate venture? I felt emboldened by the thought that we were not alone, but Billy Nicholson brought me to my senses.

'It's probably one of them. A lookout,' he said, his voice so quiet that I had to strain to catch the words. 'You raised the alarm, didn't you, going to the door like that?'

Non's antipathy towards Billy Nicholson wasn't hard to understand. He contrived to make everything he said sound like a criticism.

'If it's one of them, then it's not just Blain we're dealing with,' I said. 'And we may need to do more than talk our way in.' The odds weren't in our favour. I couldn't speak for Billy, but Albie wasn't a pugilist – his mother would have had his guts for garters if he'd got into fights – and, though I'd boxed at school, the gentlemanly bouts I'd engaged in probably wouldn't stand me in much stead in a real fight.

'I think we should revert to the original pincer movement,' I said, 'otherwise we run the risk of losing Tarley. I'll go back to the front. Wait until you hear me shouting and knocking, then get in through that door,' I indicated the scullery, 'if you can.'

The plan had failed once. Were we clutching at straws to think it would succeed now?

There was only one way to find out.

Chapter 49

Non

I considered my options. Now I knew that Tarley was in the coal hole, I could see that it wasn't going to be easy to get him out. It wasn't a case of flinging the cellar door open and shouting 'run Tarley!'

If he was free down there, he'd have escaped by now because all he'd have had to do was unbolt the coal hatch from below and climb out. Which meant he had to be tied up. Or unconscious.

Was there any way I could get into the house without being seen? If I could get into the cellar, as long as Tarley could move under his own steam, I might be able to get him out. At the very least, I'd be able to open the hatch and come back with help.

I peered around the dark scullery, looking for something I could use to defend myself, but the floor and shelves were almost bare. You could tell that these men didn't cook, clean or wash clothes in this house. There was no handy skillet to crown them with. Nor a washing dolly to swing at their heads. There'd be a poker in the kitchen to stir the fire, no doubt, but that was no help to me.

The entrance to the cellar was right next to the kitchen door. Two strides and I'd be there. Trouble was, anybody whose back wasn't turned to the door would see me straight away.

I wished I had my sailor's knife on me. It would've made me feel a lot better. Not that I wanted to go on the attack, but it would've been useful to wave around in my own defence.

'*You don't need a knife for that. Don't you remember Dada's lessons?*'

My father had been under no illusions about the dangers I'd face around sailors, and he'd taught me well. How to break a choke hold. How to disable a man if he came right at me.

'*Of course,*' I told Hara. '*But I still wish I had my knife.*'

Then I remembered the stones I'd picked up when I came into the garden. I could throw one of the stones at their lamp or candle. The light coming into the scullery wasn't very bright, so they probably only had one lamp lit. There was a chance that I'd set the house on fire but it might be worth it if it got me into the cellar. At the very least, I could get down there, open the hatch and scream blue murder. Hopefully that might bring the odd neighbour in.

The stones in my pocket weren't as smooth as the beach pebbles I was used to throwing. They were lumpy and dusty. It was possible that one of them was actually a chunk of coal. But they'd do the job. I had a good arm, and I was pretty confident that I'd be able to knock the light out with the second one if not the first. Then, while Blain and Thompson were thrashing about in the dark, I could let myself down into the cellar. If I was clever, perhaps I could wedge something behind the door to stop them following me. I looked around the scullery again, but nothing useful had turned up since I last looked, so I'd just have to manage.

With my heart going like a steam train, I stepped into the kitchen doorway, a stone in each hand. The room was almost bare. A table pushed up against the scullery wall. A rocker by the range. At the table, a big, entirely bald man with a beard that made it look as if his head was on upside down. The man I'd seen in Bear Lane was hunched in the chair. The bald one – Blain – saw me first.

'Who the hell—?'

I wasn't there to play twenty questions. And I didn't need my stones. I stepped forward, swept the lamp off the table and, in the same movement, turned back to face the cellar door as the room went dark. Hand out in front of me, I reached for the door's bolt. I'd fixed in my mind where it was just before the lamp went out, and I quickly pulled it back and pushed the door open. The cellar steps were pitch black and I had to put both hands on the walls either side of me to stop myself falling as I went down.

'Tarley!' I called. 'Are you there?'

Just then, a thunderous banging started on the front door overhead.

'Open this door, Blain. Open it now.' It sounded like Basil's voice, but I couldn't be sure. I'd never heard him yell at the top of his voice before.

Behind me there was a thudding sound that seemed to come from the scullery and the sound of somebody crying out. I didn't turn back.

I knew I'd reached the bottom of the steps when I stumbled onto the beaten earth floor of the coal cellar.

'Tarley?' I called into the darkness as the battering on the front door continued. For some reason, the noise made the blackness less stifling. As if noise was doing duty for light.

A muffled voice came from somewhere to my left. Crouching down, I began to search for him, creeping forward, reaching out blindly. Complete darkness confuses your senses. You can't tell where your body ends and the rest of the world begins. I couldn't see my fingers reaching out, and I had the sudden sensation that I was falling. I went down on one knee and took a breath to steady myself. It smelled as if a rat had died down here.

'Tarley?'

The sound of the muffled voice came again. This time, it was obviously trying to say, 'here'. Tarley Askew sounded close. Still on one knee, I reached out around me. First my fingers connected with something hard, wooden. Thompson's crates. I pushed my hands further into the darkness. Felt cloth. And warm human.

Tarley cried out at my touch, and I moved my hands carefully in case of injuries. He was sitting up, thank goodness, so he couldn't be too badly hurt. Once I'd found his head, I pulled his gag off and he spat something out.

After coughing for a bit, he said, 'Knife. Right jacket pocket.'

I ran my hands down his jacket and found the pocket and his tiny penknife. Small it might be, but it was sharp and when I'd found the rope binding his hands behind his back, very little sawing was required. My father would've been impressed; he always said that the most dangerous kind of knife was a blunt one.

Tarley groaned. His arms'd been held in one position for hours, moving them would be agony. 'How did you find me?'

I folded the penknife's blade back into the handle. 'Basil's been busy. That's him up there now.'

Above our heads, in the street, Basil was still battering at the door, and I could hear other voices, shouting at him to stop, asking what on earth he thought he was doing.

'Basil!' I shouted.

The battering stopped.

'Can you see the coal hole cover?' I shouted up.

After a few seconds, he must've grasped what I meant and looked about him. 'Yes,' he called.

'Start banging on it so I can find it. Better still, if you've got a light, put it by the edge so I can see it.'

The other voices I'd heard had shut up now. Blain's neighbours must have heard me.

I imagined Basil moving away from the door and I stared into the darkness where his voice had come from. But no light appeared. The hatch must be well fitted. I waited a few seconds in case he hadn't moved the lantern into position yet. I was beginning to see sparks in the darkness now, as if my eyes were trying to create their own light.

'Can't see anything!' I shouted. 'Start banging.'

Thumps started landing on the wooden cover and I stood and moved cautiously towards the sound, hands outstretched at knee height lest I walk into something. One shuffling pace, two. My feet bumped up against the heap of coal that'd been tipped down through the hatch. Carefully, I put I one foot onto the coal, then the other, and raised my hands above my head, searching. Another small, cautious step up the unstable coal heap and I could feel the front room's floorboards, then the top of the cellar wall. My fingers soon found what they were looking for: the underside of the hatch. Several splinters later, I found the big bolt that locked it and drew it back. 'Pull the cover up now!' I called to Basil and, a few seconds later, Basil's face appeared.

'Are you all right?'

'Yes, both of us. We'll manage now. Get round the back. See what's happening.'

Basil disappeared. And so did the light from his lamp. Still, there was enough dim sky light for Tarley to see where the hatch was and join me.

'Are we going out this way or up the steps?' he asked.

This way meant certain escape. Going up the steps meant we might just deliver ourselves into the hands of Thompson and Blain. 'This way.'

I scrambled up the heap of coal, stopping each time to let it settle under my feet, until hands reached down to pull me out. Tarley followed and, less than three minutes after I'd gone down the cellar steps, we were standing in Laud Street, surrounded by people who were very keen to know exactly what was going on, and why 'a university type' had been making 'all that racket and disturbing the peace'.

I was hoping, in the gloom, that they'd assume I was a boy so the less I spoke, the better. 'A man brought me here earlier today,' Tarley said. 'He knocked me down, tied me up and locked me in the coal cellar. Mr Rice, the University gentleman, suspected where I was and bravely came to my rescue. And now, if you don't mind, I think we'd better go to his.'

Chapter 50

Basil

Once I'd seen that Non and Tarley were unharmed, I hared around to the back of the house and clattered in via the scullery door. Billy Nicholson was standing over a prone form, his boot between the shoulder blades of a man who wasn't William Blain.

'The other one got away,' he said, as I stepped into the poorly furnished back room. 'Albie's gone after him.'

That was not good news. Albie would be no match for Blain.

'Didn't stop to ask who we were or what we wanted.' Billy was keen to add detail. 'Head down, shoulder forward,' he adopted a crouched, aggressive stance in illustration, 'and he was gone.

'This one thought he was going too,' he said. 'But it's hard to go anywhere when you've got no wind in your lungs.' He rubbed his right knuckles against his left palm, and I imagined a swift and unexpected blow to the solar plexus.

I set the lantern down on the table and looked down as my boot crunched on broken glass.

'That was Non,' Billy said, nodding at the broken lamp at my feet. 'Heard her shouting at you from the cellar. Must've been her Albie saw watching by the door.'

'Apparently so.'

'In boy's clothes.' Apparently, Billy was more concerned about Non's choice of attire than her presence in a house full of dangerous men.

'Surely only sensible?' I demurred.

'Sensible would've been her staying at home.'

'Would you have thought to knock the lamp over to sow confusion, Mr Nicholson?'

I turned to the sound of footsteps in the yard outside the scullery and saw Non, Tarley Askew at her side. An unexpected retinue had formed behind them. Blain's neighbours were determined to see what was going on.

Tarley extended both his hands to shake mine. 'Mr Rice. Thank you so much for finding me.'

I didn't want to say too much in front of witnesses so, having had my hand shaken fervently, I stepped past him into the scullery and addressed the people who had followed him and Non.

'Ladies and gentlemen, many thanks for your concern but, as you can see, we're all well and the culprit is subdued. Might I trouble you to fetch a constable?'

As our audience dispersed, casting uncertain glances at us as they went, I turned to Tarley Askew. 'Are you all right?'

He looked down at himself. 'These clothes will never be the same again,' he said, knocking coal dust from the front of his jacket, 'but there's no lasting damage to me.' He did, however, put up an exploratory hand to his left eye – visibly blackened and half shut in the light of the lantern – and winced as he touched the swelling.

'You'll be fending off questions about that for a fortnight,' Non smirked.

'Unfortunately, I can't claim that the other fellow came off worse,' Askew said, flicking a glance at the man pinned to the floor by Billy's boot. 'As soon as we were through there,' he nodded at the door connecting the house's two principal rooms, 'he dotted me in the eye, hit me with a left hook and laid me out cold. When I came to, he was trussing me up. Then he all but threw me down the stairs. It all happened so quickly I didn't have time to grasp what was happening, still less defend myself.'

'But why on earth did you come here with him in the first place?' I asked.

'He said this was where the new remedy was being stored before it went into public distribution. I thought you'd want a sample.'

'We would have,' Non said. 'But, since we last saw you, we've found out that it wasn't Professor Deneuve's Elixir that Sidney Parker was given.' She stared at the man on the floor. 'It was a poison. Digitalis.'

'I didn't know that!' Thompson protested into the square of oilcloth that occupied the central part of the floor. 'That bastard, Blain, told me it was the new remedy. Reckoned Sid was in a bad way and Professor Deneuve's was his only hope. Kill or cure, he said.'

'I heard him saying the same to Blain,' Non said. 'I think he really believed it.'

'I did!' Despite Billy Nicholson's heavy foot on his back, Thompson twisted his head and upper body, trying to make eye contact with me.

'Save it for the police, Mr Thompson.' I turned back to Non. 'While we're waiting for the constable, we should see if there's anything here that needs to be taken in as evidence. There'll be a murder investigation now. Or, at least, there will after the inquest. There can't be any other verdict.'

'I heard him say that there are crates of something in the coal hole,' Non volunteered, indicating Thompson. 'Shall we start there?'

'You and Mr Askew go and have a look. I'll stay here with Billy.'

Chapter 51

Non

I'd never been in a proper cellar before. We didn't really have them at home. People in Cardiganshire had outhouses for the things that city folk needed cellars for. Lily's house had a basement, but that still had windows in. Under this house it'd be pitch dark even in broad daylight.

In the light of the candle I'd found upstairs, I could see what my fingers had found when I was searching for Tarley: four wooden crates, shoved against the back wall of the cellar, out of the way of the heap of coal under the hatch. On top of one crate was a paper-wrapped parcel tied with string. I put the candle down and started on the string's knots while Tarley took the top off one of the crates. It wasn't difficult – the lid had been levered off already and was just sitting on top of the box, nails pointing upwards.

He lifted a bottle out and moved closer to me and the light. The bottle was blue, though most of it was covered by a label with the words **Professor Deneuve's Elixir** above a picture of a runner, naked from the waist up, leaping over a river. He had a bow in his hand, a quiver of arrows on his back, and three little banners waving over his head. I took the bottle from Tarley and held it closer to the candle. There was a single word on each of the banners: Swift, Strong, Sure.

I handed the bottle back. 'Can I borrow your penknife again?'

Tarley slipped his hand into his pocket and gave me the knife. Now I could see that it was a small, ivory-handled object such as you might cut up an apple with, but it parted the string on the first touch, and I pulled the paper wrappings open.

Inside the parcel there were two stacks of handbills, three inches deep. I took one and held it up to the light.

The picture from the handbill advertising Doctor Aurum's Tonic – the dejected, hollow-cheeked young man – was here again but, this time, alongside him were the words:

YOUNG MEN!
In the light of a recent tragic death,
Do not depend on
Doctor Aurum's Tonic.

Then, moving to the middle of the handbill, the text continued:

Turn to the best:
the SWIFTEST, STRONGEST, SUREST
Remedy available
PROFESSOR DENEUVE'S ELIXIR
an ENTIRELY NEW FORMULATION
from The East
combining SCIENCE and ANCIENT WISDOM.
POWERFUL HERBS used for centuries
to promote strength & stamina,
SCIENTIFICALLY TESTED animal ingredients.

Take only THREE
medically proven doses
and you will be CURED!
PROFESSOR DENEUVE'S ELIXIR
will make you
A NEW MAN!

To the right of those two ringing promises, the warrior from the bottle leapt over the river, bow in hand, his body honed for action.

'Do not depend on Doctor Aurum's Tonic,' Tarley read. 'If Reardon was behind this stuff *and* Doctor Aurum's Tonic, why would he run down his own product?'

I moved my face closer to the leaflet and peered at the small print at the bottom. 'That's certainly the same London address as on the Dr Aurum's handbills,' I said, pointing to the little block of text which invited buyers to apply by post. 'But Basil went to London today, and he discovered that Blain was diverting post from there to here. I heard Blain tell Thompson that Reardon wasn't his boss. What if it was Blain, not Reardon, who was behind this new remedy? It'd be in his interests to run Dr Aurum's down then, wouldn't it?'

But, whoever was behind Professor Deneuve's Elixir, the crates had nothing more to tell us. I gathered up a handful of the leaflets and tucked them into my pocket. Tarley did the same with two bottles of the elixir. Then, as I swung the lantern round to light our way back up the steps, something caught my eye.

I moved back towards the coal heap and held the lantern out towards it. Tarley followed me. 'Is that—'

'Yes.'

I heard the sound of voices at the top of the steps behind us and turned to listen. 'Albie?' I called up.

'I'm back!' came Albie's voice. 'But I didn't catch him.'

I was just glad he was safe. 'Basil? Can you come down here for a minute?'

I turned back to the coal heap and looked at the hand that was sticking out. Where there was a hand, there had to be a body.

I put the lantern down and started to move coal. It would have been quicker with a shovel, but my hands were all I had. Tarley joined in but his eyes were on me more than his work, I could feel them.

'Who d'you think it is?' he asked. From the subdued tone of his voice, he knew he was lucky it wasn't him.

'Unless Blain and Thompson make a habit of killing customers who ask too many questions, there's only one likely candidate,' I said. 'Basil should be able to say one way or the other.'

'Basil should be able to say what?' the man himself asked as he came cautiously down the steps, a candle lighting his way.

'Whether this dead man here is George Reardon.'

Chapter 52

Basil

Once both Carmichael Thompson and the body of George Reardon had been removed from Laud Street by the police, we all made our way back to Lily's house in a mood that combined triumph with a degree of manic over-excitement at our brush with violence.

Fortunately, Lily and Ivy hadn't yet returned from their ladies' meeting at St Barnabas, so Non retrieved her normal clothes from the shed then hurried upstairs with some hot water to wash and change. We both felt it would be prudent to allow Lily to see that everybody was safe and well before Non's part in the proceedings was acknowledged.

Fortunately, I would not be forced to tell Lily that her only son had pursued a violent criminal on his own, in the dark. 'It was a stupid thing to do, running after him like that,' Albie said. 'Best not tell Mum, eh?'

The police, however, would have to be informed, because Albie's pursuit of Blain had not been entirely fruitless. At one point, the boy had seen Blain duck into a public house and, expecting him to emerge from the back, had doubled back and run into the street behind, only to see his quarry disappearing around the corner, carpet bag in hand. Blain had obviously planned his escape in advance.

Had Reardon's murder been similarly planned? Or had Blain acted on the spur of the moment – during an argument, perhaps? The cause of his death, a blow or blows to the head which had left what Non referred to as a 'depressed fracture', did not suggest premeditation. But, premeditated or not, Reardon's demise explained the change of forwarding address for Doctor Aurum's correspondence.

The nature of the working relationship between Reardon, Blain and Thompson was not yet clear, but I was sure the police would persuade Carmichael Thompson to cast some light upon the matter. His life would literally depend on how much faith he could persuade both the police and a trial jury to place in his version of events.

While Non restored herself to respectability, I persuaded Edie to make tea and butter some bread. Neither Tarley nor I had eaten since breakfast, and it was all I could do not to devour the food like a savage.

'When I discovered Sidney'd been poisoned, I immediately thought Thompson must've just made Professor Deneuve's Elixir up to convince Sidney that he was being offered a new remedy,' Non said, her eyes on Tarley. 'I was afraid that you asking for it would set off all sorts of alarm bells. So, we had to come and find you and rescue you.' She grinned and the boy grinned back, grimacing as he did so. Thompson's left hook had produced a large and swollen bruise on his jaw.

'But then, when I heard Blain and Thompson talking, I realised it was more complicated than that. Professor Deneuve's does exist. Thompson was panicking because he thought it was the elixir that'd killed Sidney Parker. But Blain laughed at him. Told him what he'd actually given Sidney was poison. But even if Thompson *delivered* the poison to Sidney, Blain's the murderer.'

Tarley Askew nodded, gulping down the last of his bread and butter. 'Yes. And he'd have murdered me, too. I heard him talking about hitting me over the head with a hammer and throwing me into the canal.'

A silence fell and I suspected I was not alone in picturing George Reardon, lying dead under the coal less than eight feet from where Askew had sat, tied up and gagged. If we had not found Askew when we did, he would have suffered the same fate.

'If we can believe what I heard Thompson saying,' Non continued, 'Blain had convinced him that Sidney's condition had weakened him so much that this remedy was kill or cure. Which meant that Thompson wasn't too shocked when Sidney died.'

'Still, shocked or not, I wonder what he thought when Blain told him to hand out those Spermatorrhoea Kills handbills,' I said. 'He must've realised that they'd been ordered – if not printed – before Sidney died.'

'I don't think Carmichael Thompson's the brightest button in the box,' Non said.

'D'you think Blain was behind Professor Deneuve's from the beginning?' Mr Askew asked. 'Or did he just steal it all, lock stock and barrel, when he killed Reardon? And what about Dr Aurum's Tonic? Was

Reardon just the advertising agent for that or was it his product all along?'

Non drew in a long, deliberate breath. 'Reading between the lines of Sidney Parker's journal, Reardon *was* Dr Aurum. He referred to it as "Reardon's tonic". I think Reardon must've done some advertising for other remedies and come up with the idea of cutting out the middle man. Then, at some point, he started working with Blain. Sidney disliked Blain from the beginning. It's all in the journal.'

Non raised her teacup to her lips but I could see that she was still thinking, sorting out the sequence of events. 'Blain didn't strike me as just a hired thug when I overheard him talking to Thompson,' she said. 'He's vicious, but he's got a brain. I think he decided Reardon had outlived his usefulness. And Sidney Parker, too. Sidney would've wanted his inheritance, but Blain knew that Reardon'd used the money to start his business. He couldn't risk Reardon being forced to sell. And he would've been. Sidney was an educated boy. He'd know enough to go to law.'

'You think Blain alone was responsible for Parker's death?' Mr Askew asked. 'You don't think Reardon had an equally good motive to see him dead?'

'George Reardon was a man with no scruples,' I interjected, before Non could answer. 'He was a blackmailer and he used Mr Parker for his own ends, but I don't think he'd have risked committing murder. He struck me very much as an opportunist, not a cold-blooded plotter.'

Mr Askew seemed happy to take my assessment of Reardon at face value. 'But isn't it odd that Blain killed Parker with poison, and Reardon with a blunt instrument?'

'I suspect Reardon turning up at Laud Street after Sidney's death took Blain by surprise,' Non said. 'Perhaps Reardon even accused him of being responsible. Blain's the sort of man who'd deal with a problem as soon as it presented itself. He was probably going to do what he told Thompson to do with you – weigh Reardon's body down and throw it in the canal. But something stopped him and he had to improvise so he buried him in the coal.'

I stared at her. Even a man might balk at finding a dead body, uncovering it and watching as it was removed, but Non could sit here discussing the course of events with what appeared to be total equanimity. I had never met a woman like her.

She looked at me over the teacup she'd just refilled from the pot. 'I assume you're going to see the coroner in the morning?'

'Of course,' I said. 'This is all germane to the inquest on Wednesday.'

'All?'

It was as if she could see into my mind. I had already been mentally parsing what information it would be necessary to share with Mr Morrell and what could be omitted.

'Will you tell him I was wearing trousers?'

The sight of Non in boy's clothes had been very confusing. To all intents and purposes, the young person before me had been a boy, and yet the face was still Non's though, admittedly blackened with mud. Was it the mud that had turned a young woman into a boy, or just the clothes and everybody's expectations of the person wearing them?

'Are the trousers relevant to the inquest?' I asked.

'They were very relevant to me.'

'Yes, quite. But I worry that they might make the jury doubt your judgement.'

'They won't be asked to consider my *judgement*, will they? Only my hearing. The rest of you could have rescued Tarley, but you wouldn't have known he was there, if I hadn't heard the conversation between Thompson and Blain.'

I held her gaze. Even in the lamplight, I was aware of an uncomfortable degree of simmering rage behind those hazel eyes. 'True. But nevertheless.'

She huffed out a sigh. 'Very well, leave my sartorial choices out of it if you think it'll help.'

Neither she nor I foresaw that it was not her sartorial choices that would prove to be the problem.

To Nervous Sufferers—The Great European Remedy—Dr J. B. Simpson's Specific Medicine

is a positive cure for Spermatorrhoea, Seminal Weakness, Impotency, and all diseases resulting from Self-abuse, As Mental anxiety, Pains in Back or Side, Loss of Memory, and diseases that lead to Consumption, Insanity and early grave.

The Specific Medicine is being used with wonderful success.

Pamphlets sent free to all. Write for them and get full particulars.

Price, Specific $1.00 per package or six packages for $5.00.

Address all orders to

J. B. SIMPSON MEDICINE CO.,

Nos. 104 and 106 Main St., Buffalo, NY

(Contemporary US advertisement.)

Chapter 53

Non

You'd have thought I'd have slept well, what with the relief of getting Tarley Askew back, but I didn't. I was awake half the night arguing with Hara.

'*You should've waited till you heard back from Dr Reckitt before sending Tarley Askew off to talk to Thompson.*'

'*I didn't know Reckitt was going to reply by return. You know what he's like – he can go weeks without answering.*'

'*A letter, yes. But not a telegram. Even Benton Reckitt can't ignore the urgency of a telegram.*'

I knew she was right. But with the inquest looming, it had felt as if everything needed to be done without delay.

'*It's like Mam's always said – you can't just wait and see, can you? You have a thought, and straight away you want to act on it. And woe betide anybody who tries to stop you.*'

'*All right then, what about last night? If I hadn't told Basil that Tarley was missing, if we hadn't done something – straight away – when the police wouldn't, he'd most likely be dead by now. Thompson might not have had the stomach for it but I'm pretty sure Blain would.*'

'*But Tarley wouldn't have been in that situation in the first place if you hadn't sent him off to find Thompson!*'

'*Oh, shut up, Hara. He's fine.*'

But she was right, I had nearly got Tarley Askew killed.

–

I started translating Sidney Parker's journal into English at first light, but it was after midday by the time I'd finished, written a note to the coroner, and parcelled up the journal and the English translation for him, along with all the papers Sidney Parker'd hidden under his floorboards. All, that is, except for Florrie's letters. I'd decided that Mr Morrell didn't need to see them. The only relevant bit of information they contained – Sid and Florrie's intention to marry and emigrate to America – was clear from the journal.

Then, with the parcel in my satchel, I cycled down to Mr Morrell's office on St Giles.

It was a dreary day. The mist that had greeted me when I opened my curtains first thing still hadn't cleared and Oxford was hushed and half-concealed. We often had days like that in the city, days where the river mist from the Thames seemed to hang in the air on every street and Matthew Arnold's 'dreaming spires' were lost in muffled grey dampness.

The air was cold and wet on my face as I cycled and, by the time I reached Mr Morrell's office, the drops that'd formed on my eyelashes were so big it was as if I'd been crying.

I knew I'd have trouble settling to anything when I got back to Lily's so, after I'd left the package with a clerk who looked at me as if I had two heads when I told him it was material for the Parker inquest, I took the long route home. Down to Broad Street, then back up the long, wraith-wrapped drag of Parks Road past one of my favourite places in Oxford, the University's Museum of Natural History. I almost stopped and went in for twenty minutes to look at the specimens but decided against. If I wasn't welcome in colleges this term, the authorities might decide that I wasn't welcome on any University premises. A few minutes in the Museum wasn't worth the risk. Not if it meant they decided to keep me out of the Bodleian as well.

When I got back to Lily's there was a surprise waiting for me.

'Your friend Miss Rogers is here.' Edie'd come dashing up from the basement when she heard me come in. 'She's in there with Lily.' She nodded at the front room.

I went to open the sitting room door, only for it to swing open in front of me.

'Don't take your coat off,' Annie Rogers said. 'I'm here to take you to headquarters.'

'What have I done now?'

Annie glanced over at Edie. *Not in front of the servants.* 'Mrs Green would just like a word, that's all.'

–

She told me what it was all about on the way. Evidently, Basil had told the Jesus College principal everything that had happened last night, and Dr Harper had taken exception to my involvement.

'I gather he visited the Greens first thing,' Annie said. 'Disturbed them at their breakfast.'

He must've been there early if he'd found Professor Green at home. Thomas Green was a busy man. As well as lecturing and all his other University responsibilities, he also sat on the local board – and not as a representative of the University either. As an Oxford citizen. He believed in doing good, did Thomas Green.

My heart began to race faster than it had done in the alley behind Blain's house last night. I wasn't going to be able to run or fight my way out of this.

When Annie led me in to the smaller of the AEW's rooms, I saw that, this time, Charlotte Green had reinforcements. Arthur and Bertha Johnson were AEW bigwigs. He was chaplain at All Souls College and a lecturer in history. (And quite a passable one, as it happened.) Like Mrs Green, the Johnsons were in their early thirties. Unlike Mrs Green, who was pleasant looking without being one to turn heads, the Johnsons were striking, particularly him. His wife looked at him constantly, her eyes soft, as if she couldn't believe her luck. Which was fair enough; if rumour was to be believed, marrying him had rescued Bertha Johnson from a life of looking after her eight brothers.

'Miss Vaughan,' Mrs Green began, 'I trust you're well?'

'Yes, thank you,' I said, trying to work out what she knew. If Dr Harper had told her what'd gone on at Laud Street last night, wouldn't she expect me to be prostrate on a sofa, needing constant application of smelling salts?

'*Stop it,*' Hara said. '*She's paying you a compliment. Taking you seriously. Telling you she knows you're not like the rest of them.*'

'Are you acquainted with Rev and Mrs Johnson?' Mrs Green asked.

'We've not been introduced, but obviously, I know you by repute,' I said to the lovebirds, my stomach in knots.

'Rev and Mrs Johnson have joined us at my request. I found it necessary to consult with them, as members of the board, on the matter of your conduct last evening.

'As I'm sure Miss Rogers has already told you, Dr Harper of Jesus College paid my husband and me a visit this morning to inform us that, despite our last conversation, you had involved yourself in Jesus College's investigations into the death which was the subject of our discussions on your last visit here.'

'As it happens, circumstances arose that *forced* me to become involved,' I said, trying to sound dignified.

There was a silence while Mrs Green and I locked eyes. If we'd been cats, we'd have been growling, our ears flat to our heads. Mrs Green believed that I'd let her and the AEW down, that I'd behaved without due decorum; I thought her ideas of decorum were senseless.

Rev Johnson broke the tension. 'Perhaps you could outline those circumstances for us.'

So, I told them. All about poor Sidney's death and the pitiable state his body'd been in. About realising that I'd known him, that he'd eaten at our house. (All right, I may not have mentioned how many times.) That Lily knew Betty Trent well and had helped her clear Sidney's room, and that Florence Spellman – 'Sidney's fiancée,' I said, pointedly – was also somebody we knew from church. How it'd been Lily and me who found Parker's effects, I who'd made the connection between Carmichael Thompson – whom I'd just happened to see when I'd been on a visit to McLaren's gymnasium with the wife of the Jesus Professor of Celtic – and the patent remedies Sidney Parker had been taking. I, with my knowledge of Welsh, who'd decoded the journal we'd found beneath his floorboards. I who'd got in touch with Dr Reckitt to identify the toxin that had killed Sidney Parker, and I who had – inadvertently – sent Tarley Askew into mortal danger. I had to tell them that to explain why I'd had to be part of the rescue party the previous evening.

But I left out the trousers.

Fair play to the four of them, they listened without interrupting. There were some sharp intakes of breath when I mentioned Sidney Parker's spermatorrhoea ring and gynaecomastia, and a few shocked glances flew around the room. But how else was I supposed to make them understand how embarrassing this could have been for Jesus College, how much gossip I'd saved the college from?

'As you can see, far from *involving myself*,' I finished, 'I *became* involved because of the consideration of my landlady, Mrs Maddox, in thinking to take the news of Sidney Parker's death to his fiancée. Everything else flowed from that. Not from me putting myself forward.'

'Perhaps I wasn't paying sufficient attention,' Mrs Johnson suggested, 'but I don't think you explained exactly how this young man from Corpus became involved.'

I looked at her, all aristocratic cheekbones and kind eyes. But it wouldn't do to rely on that kindness. We both knew perfectly well that I'd skated over the issue of how Tarley had come to offer his services. I was going to have to be very careful here. 'Mr Askew was already aware of the circumstances of Sidney Parker's death—'

'I beg your pardon,' Rev Johnson interrupted, 'but how, exactly, did he know?'

Dammit. I was going to have to tell them about the Cipher Club. 'It's a slightly convoluted story,' I warned.

'Please, Miss Vaughan, you have the floor.'

'When I was twelve years old, I read an article in a children's' magazine,' I began. Well, they needed to know the context. My association with Charles Dodgson went back before Lectures for Ladies were even thought of.

'It's a purely private arrangement,' I said when I'd explained about the letters Rev Dodgson and I had exchanged over the years, his invitation to the Cipher Club when I arrived in Oxford and the most recent meeting which had included Tarley Askew. 'It has nothing to do with the University. The Cipher Club meet as private citizens. The young men don't wear their academic dress, and neither does Rev Dodgson.'

'And you, Miss Vaughan?' Charlotte Green asked. My mouth opened to tell her that of course I didn't wear academic dress, but she saved me from that piece of fatuous cheek by pressing on. 'Are you chaperoned?'

Dear God. Last night I'd saved Tarley Askew from being murdered and discovered George Reardon's corpse. Now, here I was, perfectly calm and collected, and all they could think to ask me was whether, in meetings with gentlemen including a revered Oxford don, I had a chaperone!

'Yes.' I hoped I didn't sound as impatient as I felt. 'Mr Higgins, the landlord of Jericho House insists on it.' I knew people like her probably thought the morals of the lower classes meant that we were all constantly consorting with the opposite sex, so I thought I'd get that in. Mind, I wasn't going to mention that the chaperone was an unmarried Jericho girl. Eva Simkins wouldn't be respectable enough or old enough to satisfy the AEW folk, but then they wouldn't understand that her main role was to shout for John Higgins if she thought any of the young men were getting a bit fresh.

'We don't encourage young women who are here under the aegis of the AEW to fraternise with the undergraduates,' Mrs Johnson said. 'It's not really appropriate. You're here to study. Besides, there are enough voices raised in objection to women in lectures on the grounds that the young men will be distracted. If the sexes start mingling at clubs too—'

'As I said, it's not a University club. Just as Professor Green sits on the local board as a resident of Oxford, so the undergraduates and I join Rev Dodgson as private citizens.'

The same Rev Dodgson who thinks we're here to catch husbands, I thought, a taste like lemons in my mouth.

'I don't think you can compare your situation with Professor Green's, Non,' Annie said. Her tone told me me I was sailing dangerously close to the wind.

I glanced over at Arthur Johnson. He gave me a slightly embarrassed half-smile as if he knew I was right but had to toe the AEW's line.

Mrs Green was more forthright. 'Though my husband may sit in a private capacity at local board meetings, Miss Vaughan, he's a member of the University and cannot but be seen as its representative, at least in part. As yet, young women are not members of the University and, if we don't play our cards very carefully, it's unlikely that they ever will be.'

She stopped, then, and let silence fill the room. She probably hoped I'd reflect on my conduct; I just watched her and waited.

'To return to the subject at hand,' she said, eventually, 'you became acquainted with Mr Askew through the auspices of Rev Dodgson's club and asked him to become involved?'

I wasn't going tell them about Tarley's letter. That would only make them think I'd set my cap at him, and he'd succumbed to my charms.

'I introduced him to Mr Rice,' I said. 'Obviously, Mr Rice wouldn't pass for an undergraduate in search of a spermatorrhoea remedy.'

I saw them all flinch at the word. I knew it was petty, but their discomfort felt like a point to me.

'And is Mr Askew a man to be depended on?' Arthur Johnson asked. What he meant was: *will he blab?*

I looked Mr Johnson in the eye. 'I'd put my life in his hands.' Seemed only fair. His had ended up more or less in mine.

'Good,' Mrs Green said, crisply. 'Because he will need to convince the jury that it was he who overheard the two malefactors discussing Mr Parker's death and not you.'

I felt as if the air had chilled on my skin, the way you do if you walk out of the sun and into the damp of a sea-cave. 'I beg your pardon?'

Mrs Green's expression didn't change. She didn't so much as blink. 'The Principal of Jesus College,' she said, carefully, as if she had to pay a pound for every word she used, 'has made it very clear that you are not to give evidence at the inquest.'

Can rage be roused in a second? Or had it been building in me all the time I'd been sitting there, being made to explain myself? 'May I ask why?' I asked, every muscle trembling. 'Might it be because Dr Harper doesn't want everybody to know that, without women's help, Sidney Parker's murder would never have come to light?'

Charlotte Green didn't move a muscle, but I felt the tension in the air increase as if somebody'd turned a screw. 'Whatever Dr Harper's reasons, we, as members of the AEW, are inclined to agree with him. It could do our cause untold harm if your involvement were to become known—'

'How?' It came out less as a question and more as a demand, so I tried to row back a bit. 'I don't understand how it can be deleterious to the cause of women's education if a woman shows that she's as competent as the men she's working with?'

Mrs Green glanced at Annie and the Johnsons. Was there some kind of signalling going on between them? Either way, Rev Johnson took the tiller and steered onto a different tack.

'Miss Vaughan, speaking as a member of the University, I'm sure the Corpus fellows would wish to thank you for your part in rescuing Mr Askew.'

My *part*? My part had been to come up with the whole plan. And to adapt it when Basil failed to do his bit.

'No young man could have done better and I'm sure many would not have had the courage to act as you did. However, we're asking you to show a different kind of courage now. The courage to remain silent when everything in you wishes to speak.'

I felt tears pricking at the back of my eyes. Haughtiness was easy to defy but humility always kicked the legs from under me. Still, I wasn't giving up that easily.

'Nobody asked Annie not to speak out when she came top in the local exam,' I pointed out.

'Wrong,' Annie said, wielding the word like a dagger. 'I was absolutely forbidden to boast. But my father couldn't resist. It was he who was responsible for making my marks public, not me.'

'And what you won't be aware of,' Charlotte Green took over, 'are reactions to the news at the time. Though some – those who are of our mind, obviously – were jubilant and maintained there must be no more talk of women's brains not being as capable as men's, others simply shifted their ground and said that those brains might be *capable* but that such academic work wasn't *suitable* for young women. That it would warp them, distort the unique beauty of their feminine virtues.' She was obviously quoting somebody. I wondered who.

'I've been keeping quiet about it ever since,' Annie said. 'Nevertheless, I'm an object lesson as far as they're concerned. Look at me, almost twenty-five years old and not a husband in sight. Education has made me unmarriageable.' She held up a hand to stop the complaint I was going to make. 'I'm not saying *I* believe that, Non. I'm just telling you what our opponents choose to see.'

'Because, God forbid a woman should *decide for herself* not to marry,' I muttered.

The three other AEW board members – all happily married – looked as if they wished they could hide their discomfort behind handy teacups but, despite the cold, there was no fire in the grate, still less a kettle singing on it. Did these straight-backed, pearl-wearing women even know how to make tea? Probably not. Had servants for that, didn't they?

'I fear that we are diverging from the point,' Mrs Green said. 'Miss Vaughan, I won't flatter you by reiterating Rev Johnson's thanks, but I will say this: nobody here doubts your courage for a moment. You risked your life for this young man which is extraordinarily commendable. But Rev Johnson is right. To step back, out of the limelight, sometimes requires more courage. Moral courage rather than physical.'

'Is that what you think I want?' I demanded. 'My moment in the limelight? You're wrong. I just want them to know what women are capable of.'

'Unfortunately, Miss Vaughan, if the men of England see your exploits in the newspapers – and there is no doubt that every newspaper in the land would take you up, either as a cause célèbre or a cautionary tale – the whole question of education for women would be set back decades. *This*, our opponents would say, *this* is what will come of female education. Women thinking they can do everything men can do.'

'So, I must withdraw, and other people – Mr Rice, Mr Askew – must lie on behalf of all women who aspire to be educated?'

Mrs Johnson hadn't said much up to this point, but she grabbed the baton now. 'Sometimes something may be *true* but not *helpful*, Miss Vaughan. Think of the girls you've met at our lectures – the girls who've come to Somerville and to Lady Margaret Hall. Their parents have entrusted those young women to our care, and they would be horrified if they thought their daughters might be encouraged to grub around in the seamier aspects of life. The mere notion that their girls might be exposed to the existence of facts that you discuss with such *sang froid* would have every right-thinking mama and papa removing their daughter from our halls forthwith.'

Because, God knows, nobody'd marry a girl who knew that a man might use a toothed ring to quell his nocturnal emissions. Or one who could discover a dead body beneath a coal heap and not have a fit of the vapours.

'*Stop thinking of yourself for once!*'

Hara sounded exasperated and I felt a tinge of shame. But it didn't stop me challenging them. 'And if, knowing these consequences, I refuse to allow Mr Askew to speak for me? If I insist on giving my own evidence?'

Rev Johnson sighed. 'To give evidence you must be called. Dr Harper sought Mr Morrell's counsel before meeting with Mr and Mrs Green this morning and has received an assurance that, as long as all the relevant evidence is heard, the inquest jury does not need to hear it from your own lips.'

I stared at them in disbelief. These people had fought for years for women's education, yet here they were, telling me to lie and keep silent, as if I was a scullery maid who'd seen something the grand family she worked for would find embarrassing.

'And you're happy to stand by and let all this happen? My being silenced? My friends asked to lie?'

'If we are seen to fight your corner, Miss Vaughan,' Mrs Green said, 'then the situation of every woman who attends lectures in a college or reads in the Bodleian is potentially compromised. Are *you* happy to let *that* happen?'

Chapter 54

Basil

At midday on Tuesday, after delivering the previous week's postponed lecture on Greek drama, I met Tarley Askew in Merton Street. We had agreed to go to the police station together to give our statements, but events had overtaken me, and I needed to speak to him before we could put on record what had taken place at Blain's house.

'There have been developments,' I told him. 'Let's take a stroll in the meadows and I'll explain.'

The mist that had filled the quads at Jesus first thing was still refusing to clear as we walked down the narrow lane between Corpus and Merton, past Dead Man's Walk and Merton Fields and on to Christ Church Meadow.

'I met with the Principal first thing this morning to inform him of recent events,' I said. 'Following which, he went into conclave with the AEW. It seems they've found common ground when it comes to Non's testimony at the inquest tomorrow. She's going to be asked not to testify.'

The news stopped Askew in his tracks. 'Why ever shouldn't she?' The eye that Thompson had blacked was swollen and looked painful, but that didn't stop him from staring at me in astonishment.

I sighed and indicated that we should resume our walk.

'The AEW board members apparently believe that it will frighten the horses if Miss Vaughan's exploits are made public. And, however unpalatable we find it, they do have a point.'

'That's not—'

'Mr Askew,' I interrupted, 'imagine Non as a witness. She doesn't turn a hair when discussing spermatorrhoea, dead bodies, penile rings or the existence and potential causes of gynaecomastia. And that's without even touching on the subject of the way she was dressed last evening.'

'I think she's magnificent.'

I sighed and felt old. And unequal to the task Harper had set me.

'Surely her evidence is crucial to getting at the truth?' he asked.

I sighed. 'Her *evidence* is. Sadly, *she* isn't.' I hesitated, but there was no way round it. 'Dr Harper and the AEW have decided that her evidence can be given by you.'

He pulled up again. 'No. Absolutely not. I won't connive at her exclusion.'

I listened to the birds calling to each other in the bare branches of the new avenue on either side of the walk and tried not to feel resentful at being expected to win Mr Askew over.

'I know it seems unfair,' I said, 'but there are procedural issues at stake which you and I must talk about.' I took a fortifying breath and, as the cold, damp air rushed into my lungs, I shivered despite my heavy gown. 'Now that we know Mr Parker was deliberately poisoned, criminal proceedings are inevitable. Whoever stands trial for his murder and that of George Reardon, it's essential that evidence given at the inquest tomorrow, and at the subsequent trial, coincide.'

'Oh, no!' Askew said, realising what I meant. 'No, Mr Rice. Absolutely not. Even if I *was* prepared to deny Non's part in all of this and claim her actions as my own before the University Coroner – which I'm not – how can you expect me to lie under oath to a judge and jury?'

I forbore to point out that he'd be under oath at the inquest, too, and he moved off once more, his pace that of a man to whom vigorous activity is suddenly essential. I sighed and adjusted my stride accordingly. Perhaps I would do better to make this less of a personal dilemma and more of a philosophical one.

I drew alongside his outrage. 'Mr Askew, I assume you're familiar with the work of John Stuart Mill?'

He made an inarticulate sound of frustration. 'Please tell me you're not going to use the greatest good for the greatest number argument. Presumably that's the AEW's line?'

'No, I had in mind an axiom of Mill's on freedom. That an individual shouldn't be prevented from following a certain course of action just because that course might lead him – or her – into harm's way; that he must be allowed to make his own choices, even if they are poor ones. But Mill also says that those same individuals *should* be prevented from following a course of action if it will lead to harm to *others*. And Miss Vaughan's being allowed to give evidence at either inquest or trial would, the AEW believe, do significant harm to the prospects of women at Oxford.'

Askew made a dismissive sound. 'The greatest good, the least harm – it's the same argument, in different words.'

Two rowers in tights and sweaters jogged past, casting sidelong looks in our direction, and we walked in silence for a minute until we reached the riverbank. At this time of the day, the meadow was all but deserted, save for rowers going to and fro to the river and the odd abstracted academic stimulating his brain by perambulation.

'I'm sorry, Mr Rice. I can't do what you ask. I'm Non's friend.'

Wretchedness filled me like cold bathwater as I recalled the countless occasions on which I'd stepped in to prevent Teddy from harming his own prospects and had been called a timid conformist for my pains.

'Sometimes,' I managed, 'it's a friend's *duty* to prevent us making decisions that might have consequences we can never row back from. Even at the expense of that friendship.'

'Perhaps that's true if the friends find themselves on equal terms. But the whole point here is that Miss Vaughan and I *aren't* on equal terms. Not in the eyes of the world, anyway.'

Mrs Askew had brought her boy up splendidly if she had intended to nurture a champion for other women. But, just at that moment, that wasn't what was required.

'What, then, will you do about your statement to the police?'

Askew heaved in a breath as if he were about to lift an unprecedented weight. 'I must speak to Miss Vaughan before I do anything. Please tell the sergeant that I'll be unable to give my statement until after the inquest tomorrow.'

And with that, he inclined his head courteously, turned on his heel and left me standing next to the cold, turbid waters of the Isis.

Chapter 55

Non

Lily heard me come in from my meeting with the AEW.

'Not good news, I expect?' she asked, halfway between sympathy and exasperation.

'We're being written out of the story,' I said as I hung my coat up. 'You, me and Florrie.' Including them lessened the loneliness that the AEW people had made me feel.

When I'd finished explaining what Mrs Green and the others wanted me to do, Lily stared at me. Was she surprised? I think so. This was playing fast and loose with the law, wasn't it?

'If you believe them, it's all for the good of women studying at Oxford,' I said. 'But if you ask me, it's because the men who run the University can't abide the thought of crediting a woman with anything.'

'Can they really stop you?' Lily asked.

'No. Well. Maybe. An inquest's a public hearing. The coroner wouldn't be able to stop me if I got up. If I said I had evidence, he'd have to hear it.'

'Would he, though? Wouldn't he just tell you to sit down and not interrupt his inquest?'

'The press'll be there.' That seemed important. The newspapers loved a story and surely everything I'd done *would* be a story?

Suddenly, all the fight that had been boiling up in me on the way home curdled and became a cold, solid lump in my throat. I didn't want to talk about it any more. Didn't want to hear Lily being sensible and telling me that I was a fool if I thought I could go against these men. Didn't want her sympathy, either.

'I'm going for a walk.'

It was a mark of how upset Lily could see I was that she didn't even try to stop me wearing my walking dress.

-

Port Meadow lay flat and colourless under the mist, and I couldn't see the trees that usually told me where the horizon was. That was something I'd had to get used to in Oxford: the horizon being so close because of the land being so much flatter than at home.

I kicked through the dead winter grass. Maybe that was why everybody here was so insular and close-minded – the geography around them just hemmed them in. They couldn't see for miles and miles to hills in the far distance, so they weren't encouraged to wonder what lay beyond. There was just flat land, then trees.

But with the horizon invisible, there wasn't even much of that. Just dead grass and mud under my feet and mist greying out any bits of colour. In the sun, the haws and rosehips would've been bright as jewels in the hedges, but now you couldn't see them unless you went right up close.

Even the sounds were grey. The train on the line behind me sounded subdued, and when I looked around, instead of rising into the sky, the steam from its chimney was just swallowed up into the low-hanging mist.

'*Oh, stop feeling so sorry for yourself.*'

I tried to ignore Hara, but she always annoyed me when she was right. And she was right now: I'd gone from boiling rage to feeling hard done by.

Rage suited me better.

'*Rage gets you nowhere,*' Hara said. '*You know what Miss Rees says: being angry isn't a sin but stoking your anger is.*'

'*That's because she's a good Christian woman and it says that in the Bible. Doesn't mean I have to agree.*'

'*Instead of being angry with everybody, just think about what you've done. You decoded Parker's journal. You worked out what it was that killed Sidney Parker.*'

'*Dr Reckitt did that.*'

'*Who gave him all the information?*'

'*Pah! Nobody cares, do they? It's all impersonal to them. This was done. That was found out. This person was overheard. Those papers were found. Not Non did this, Non found that out, Non saw Carmichael Thompson, Non decoded the journal.*'

Sometimes, Hara just went quiet in the middle of a conversation; usually when she was making a point. I knew the point she was making now. My own words had spelled it out. It was all Non, Non, Non, Non, Non.

Think you're important, don't you? Not Hara this time. An accusation that used to get flung at me in our parish school whenever the teacher gave me a job to do, because I always finished my work long before anybody else. *Just because your father's Captain Vaughan. Well, your Dada's a drunk!*

I'd blacked many an eye in retaliation for taunts about my father, but they'd still called him a drunk.

Because he was. Hara'd never seen Dada drunk any more than I had. He never drank at home. But we'd heard the stories. And seen him come home with a sore head, soaked to the skin after sleeping the drink off under a hedge.

But accepting that something's true and being forced to see it for yourself are two different things.

'*Is that what's put you in a mood?*' Hara asked. '*Them forcing you to see the truth? Did you really think that you were going to be able to win them all over by your brilliance, be lifted up onto admiring shoulders and carried through the streets?*'

Yes. I had thought that. And now I felt stupid. '*The AEW are supposed to be on our side.*'

'*Well, like it or not, they're all you've got, here. Are you really going to go against them just to make a point?*'

'*Giving evidence isn't about making a point. It's about telling the truth.*'

'The truth *is that Sidney Parker was poisoned so that he couldn't ask for his money when he came of age. The truth is, he was very ill, but not with the made-up disease he was treating himself for. The truth is, he died of digitalis poisoning. The* point *you want to make is that* you *found out those truths.*'

'*Well, I did!*'

'*But is that the truth that matters?*'

'Miss Vaughan!'

I spun round, embarrassed that somebody'd seen me talking to my dead twin, until I remembered that the whole conversation had been happening in my head.

'Mr Askew.'

He pulled up no more than a pace away from me. 'I've just spoken to Mr Rice, and I had to see you. He wants – well, to be fair to him, Dr *Harper* wants me to take credit for things you've done.'

'I know. I've just come from a meeting with the AEW.'

'Yes, Mrs Maddox said. So, it's true? They agree with this?'

I nodded.

'It's outrageous.'

Fair play to him, he seemed genuinely angry on my behalf. I grinned. Hara was wrong. The AEW wasn't all I had here.

'Yes, it is. But I'm not sure there's much I can do about it. They have all the power in this situation. I have no choice.'

He looked at me. 'That's not true. You have the power to show everybody that they're prepared to distort the truth for their own ends.'

'Which, to be fair, are my ends too: smuggling women into the University.' I said. 'If it was just the AEW asking nicely – because they did, in their way – I'd do it without question.' All right, not exactly without question, but I would have done it. Because I did understand their position. They couldn't have everybody knowing that they'd failed to rein in one of their young women. We weren't members of the University, nor even of a college, so if the AEW wasn't in charge of us, nobody was. And that couldn't be allowed, could it – young women in charge of themselves?

'It's obliging Harper that sticks in my throat.' I couldn't forget the look he'd given me when I'd tried to tell him about Dr Reckitt: the look of a man to a dog barking for attention. 'He thinks his position gives him the right to tell me what to do,' I said. 'And that makes me want to stand up and defy him.'

'But that's not a bad thing, is it? To stand up for yourself?'

'I don't know. It's just what I've always done. For me and my twin.'

'You have a twin?'

'I did. She died when she was six. She was deaf,' I added. It wasn't relevant, but there was something about Tarley Askew's fierceness on my behalf that made me want to give him something.

'And that made some people think she was unintelligent?'

I turned to look at him. He'd understood. Just like that.

'Yes. But she wasn't. She was as clever as me. We found a way of communicating with each other. Invented a sign language. It used to drive the boys mad when one of us said something with our hands and the other laughed.'

'No wonder you're so determined. You grew up fighting for two.'

He was right. I'd learned to fight, and I was good at it. The thing I wasn't very good at was knowing when to back down.

'It is a pretence in everybody, men and women alike, to try to be what they are not; and it is a loss for anybody not to be what they are.'

(Ymhongarwch yn mhawb, meibion a merched yn ogystal a'u gilydd, ydwy ceision bod yr hyn nad ydynt; a cholled ydyw i un beido bod yr hyn ydyw.)

—Cranogwen (Sarah Jane Rees), *Y Frythones*

Chapter 56

Basil

When Frederick Morrell walked into the Jesus College hall on Wednesday morning, flanked by Dr Harper, I breathed a sigh of relief. Now, the inquest could begin, and I could stand down. Dr Harper had made me responsible for policing all the comings and goings in the hall and had tried to insist that only those with a legitimate interest in attending the hearing into Sidney Parker's death were admitted.

However, given that an inquest is, by definition, a *public* inquiry, I felt I had no right to bar anybody from entry, so I'd given Mr Allen instructions that as long as those wishing to attend seemed respectable, they should be admitted to college. With luck, frivolous attendees to our hallowed portals would be few or absent.

The whole college had been informed that the hearing into Sidney Parker's death was taking place that morning and, out of a respect few had shown the young man when he walked amongst them, most of our undergraduate body and all resident fellows were present. Much to their obvious disgruntlement, the dons sat at refectory tables which they had not put their feet under since their own undergraduate days: this morning, high table was reserved for the coroner and his jury.

Non and Lily had been the first to arrive, reminding me of the lecture Non had attended here on the day of Sidney Parker's death. On that occasion, she and Lily had been early so as not to have to run the undergraduate gauntlet; today, I suspected that their earliness was intended to make a point. They would not be excluded.

I gazed across the hall at Non. Despite repeated entreaties, she'd given me no assurance that she would not attempt to speak. Worse, Tarley Askew had stated that, if she stood up when he was called, he would cede the floor to her. Members of the AEW board had, I knew, instructed Non to ensure that Tarley Askew was made privy to everything she'd heard from the scullery in Blain's house, and I hoped that her rehearsing him with me yesterday evening at Shene Road meant that she had resigned herself to remaining silent. But, where Rhiannon Vaughan was concerned, one could never be sure.

I chose to see it as a good thing that Non had not seated herself in the coroner's direct line of sight. She was sitting at one of the side tables, in the company of Lily and a young woman who was, presumably, Parker's fiancée. Albie Maddox and Billy Nicholson had not been asked to give evidence as it was felt that their testimony could add nothing to my own, so they were not here. And, though it felt a little unjust to deny them their moment in the limelight, I was glad that Billy wouldn't be given the opportunity to inflate his part in proceedings by taking credit for Non's actions. Watching him puff up his chest and claim her quick-thinking as his own might well have been enough to bring Non to her feet in protest.

As Dr Harper and the coroner marched down the aisle in full academic dress at the head of the jury, I peered through the ranks of young men who had risen to their feet, searching for the gentlemen of the press. I finally spotted them sitting on an otherwise empty bench at the back of the hall, where they were ideally situated to see not only coroner, jury and witnesses but also the reactions of the spectators. University inquests were a relative rarity and both the *Journal* and the *Chronicle* always reported proceedings in deferential detail.

Watching the journalists scribble made me apprehensive. George Reardon might no longer be able to traduce the college, but if Non chose to insist on speaking, the papers would have a field day. Even worse, such a titillating story might well be taken up by other newspapers, making both college and University a national laughing stock.

Tarley Askew had agreed not to sit with Non and Lily but, as he had arrived at the same time as the Jericho contingent, he'd been able to choose a seat from which he could easily see Non and any move she made to stand. Mr Askew's loyalties were clear and, as he belonged to another college, I had little or no influence over him. However, that did not stop me obliging one of our own undergraduates to give up his place so that I could sit next to Askew once the coroner and jury had been seated.

As Frederick Morrell opened proceedings, my gaze slid across the table to Teddy. He was sitting slightly ahead of me, alongside Dr Fielding.

It was the first time I'd seen him since the post-mortem, and though we might previously have gone several days without seeing each other, it now felt as if a great gulf had opened up between the present and the years during which we had been… What exactly had we been?

Friends, certainly; intimate friends. But Teddy had been far more than that to me; yet there was no apposite term I might use. What word could exist for a man who harboured feelings for a friend that might, if the thought were not so unnatural, be equated with romantic love?

Teddy felt my gaze on him and looked around to see who might be staring. As our eyes met, his expression flitted from smiling recognition to something else, something more complex that I couldn't identify. He held my gaze for a few seconds then gave the smallest of smiles and looked away.

When Morrell called Mrs Trent to give evidence, she seemed so overawed that her testimony had to be teased painstakingly from her. But, in the end, the coroner and the jury – twelve men drawn largely from the Jesus fellowship but including some tradesmen who had been matriculated as University members in order to do business with the colleges – understood that Sidney Parker had been sufficiently unwell to keep to his room on Sunday evening and all through Monday, had apparently 'suffered mightily with his bowels' during the day on Monday, and had been quite dead when she tried to wake him on Tuesday morning.

Mrs Trent further testified that, on Monday, Parker had taken soup but little else, and she had administered Godfrey's Cordial. 'But only what I would give one of my own. Like family to us, our young men are.'

Delivered of her evidence, Parker's landlady resumed her seat next to Lily Maddox with every evidence of relief, and the coroner's clerk called Dr Fielding to come forward.

I knew that the Principal had visited Fielding to discuss the necessity or otherwise of revealing details of Sidney Parker's penile ring and gynaecomastia, and the doctor's testimony proved so uncontroversial that the watching undergraduates began to get restless and to whisper amongst themselves. I wondered whether they'd heard rumours of Sidney Parker's 'anomalies' from their bedmakers and had come to hear salacious details. Of slightly more concern was the thought that the press might have heard those same rumours. If they had, what might they make of the doctor's omissions?

'Mr Parker was evidently an habitual user of patent medicines,' Fielding finished. 'Many bottles were discovered in his nightstand.'

'Thank you doctor,' Morrell watched as his clerk noted the detail, 'I believe that will become relevant later.'

The undergraduates perked up. Finally, something they didn't already know.

Irrationally, my heart thumped at my ribs as Teddy stood to take the stand; I knew he would cause the college no embarrassment. He'd sent me a note telling me that Dr Harper had appealed to him as a Jesus man. 'And, as you know only too well Bas,' he'd said in his usual provocative way, 'it's in my interest as much as Harper's that people aren't encouraged to speculate too much about what Jesus men get up to with their trousers off.'

I watched as he strode to the front and stood to give his evidence. Teddy wasn't a tall man, but he had the kind of presence that seemed to add inches to his height. Always well-turned out, his gown looked particularly splendid today: perhaps he had acquired a new one in anticipation of his forthcoming move to King's College hospital.

Unlike Fielding, Teddy presented his evidence as if he were giving a performance, making asides to the jurymen on the function of the various organs whose diseased state he described, providing them with vivid descriptions of the likely effect on Sidney Parker of his disease, offering the occasional complicit smile to the spectators.

'Though spermatorrhoea is not a real disease, if any man will be persuaded that it is, it's the man who suffers a colovesical fistula,' he told the jury. 'The lurid literature produced on the subject of spermatorrhoea makes great play of "cloudy urine" and "bubbles in the stream", and as the jury will readily imagine, the contamination of the bladder by the contents of the colon – both gaseous and solid – would most definitely induce cloudiness and bubbles.'

His words induced much shaking of heads and some murmured conversation between the jurors.

'We've heard from Dr Fielding,' Teddy went on, 'that the deceased was apt to rely on patent remedies rather than consulting a qualified physician and I found evidence to corroborate that assertion. His urethra – the urinary tract running down the male member – was scarred and inflamed from the insertion of what I believe are called urethral crayons in an attempt to cure himself. I believe some quack may also have attempted to cauterise his prostate.'

Every male in the room winced at the thought, and I saw some legs crossed protectively. The pressmen's pencils quirked and squiggled busily over their notebooks and Dr Harper looked thunderous. Sidney Parker's insertion of urethral crayons into his penis was almost as embarrassingly indecent as his use of a spermatorrhoea ring. Teddy was obviously determined to use the inquest to drive home the message that spermatorrhoea didn't exist.

'So, Dr Pritchard,' Morrell asked, when Teddy's testimony eventually drew to a close, 'can you tell us what the cause of Mr Parker's death was?'

On the other side of the hall, Non's eyes were trained intently on Teddy.

'Initially, it seemed entirely plausible that Mr Parker's diseased colon, kidneys and urinary tract had given rise to an overwhelming infection, leading to death from acute sepsis. However, this was by no means certain, so I took samples of Mr Parker's stomach contents. These were analysed and found to contain a vegetable alkaloid. Later, when a description of Mr Parker's ante-mortem symptoms became available – in a manner which I believe we'll hear from another witness – it was possible to consult an expert who identified the alkaloid as digitalis, the toxic substance present in the leaves of the common foxglove.'

I could almost feel Non's fury. At any moment, I expected her to leap to her feet and accuse him of implying that it was he who was acquainted with, and had consulted, this expert in toxins, when in fact, had it not been for *her* decoding of Parker's journal and *her* subsequent telegram to Dr Reckitt in Cardiganshire – yes, *Cardiganshire* – nobody would have been any the wiser. The fixity with which she was staring at Teddy might almost have made one believe the ancient Greek philosophers' notion that the act of vision entailed the emission of beams from the eye. Had that been true, Non's eye-beams would have been fatally corrosive.

But, despite her fury, she did not challenge Teddy's evidence. She remained seated and silent.

How long she would continue to do so, however, remained to be seen.

Chapter 57

Non

The doctor – Pritchard – was a show-off, but he wasn't a fool, so that was something. But I fumed over him not giving credit to Reckitt. He just let everybody believe that some Oxford man had diagnosed digitalis poisoning. Typical.

Not that Dr Reckitt would've cared, to be honest. Or not much, anyway. 'Facts, my dear Miss Vaughan,' he'd have said. 'They're what matter.'

I watched Dr Pritchard take his seat again. Basil obviously knew him, his eyes were on the doctor as he sat down, and he nodded. *Thank you.*

The coroner was no fool either as his next comment showed.

'Gentlemen of the jury, you've now heard the means by which Mr Parker came by his death. Digitalis poisoning. But in order to establish how he came to ingest this poison, in other words, in order that you may determine whether this was self-destruction, accidental death, manslaughter or murder, we must hear from other witnesses.'

A Mr Tobias Jenkyn – 'commoner of Jesus College' as he'd be referred to in the press reports – was called to give evidence. This was the undergraduate Basil had persuaded to part with information about Parker selling Doctor Aurum's Tonic to the other students. And very nervous he was, too.

Mr Jenkyn offered no more and no less than exactly what the coroner asked for and kept looking anxiously at Basil. So… it wasn't only Tarley Askew who'd been rehearsed before this inquest. I could almost hear Basil appealing to the boy.

Let's not mention the less savoury aspects of Mr Parker's dealings with his customers at Jesus, shall we, Jenkyn? The little credit-and-threat scheme he was running doesn't reflect well on him, nor, sadly, on the college. The fellowship saw fit to give him a scholarship, after all.

The way these men stuck together to protect the reputation of their college and, by extension, the University, made me sick. Did I really want to let an institution like this rule my life, tell me I had to be chaperoned everywhere, that I couldn't go to their lectures, couldn't tell the truth in a legally constituted public hearing?

'*When in Rome…*' Hara murmured, not for the first time and probably not for the last.

But did I *want* to be in Rome if I had to do as the Romans did?

If women weren't allowed to show what we could do, why would things ever change?

'*If you show them what you can do, they'll call you unnatural,*' Hara said. '*You know they will. And they'd tar the rest of the women with the same brush, even though they're nothing like you.*'

'*Nobody calls Cranogwen unnatural.*'

'*Oxford people would. All that putting herself forward, public speaking, not marrying—*'

'*And what about Elspeth Rhys? She speaks in public, addresses meetings.*'

'*But she does those things in North Wales. When have you ever heard her addressing crowds about women's education here? Never.*'

I tried to focus on Tobias Jenkyn who was still feeling his way cautiously through his evidence. He wasn't a very impressive-looking young man. Looked like the kind of boy who always tries to keep everybody happy. Which, as we all know, can't be done. His gown was so creased he might have slept in it. Probably because it was always getting crammed into a bag with his cap when he followed his friends into one of the pubs the undergraduates liked to drink in.

Yes, he answered the latest question, Mr Parker had definitely said he was taking Doctor Aurum's Tonic to try and cure his spermatorrhoea. He looked around, then, to see if saying the word was allowed. Basil nodded encouragement.

Yes, he said, Sidney Parker had persuaded other undergraduates to buy the tonic.

Yes, he, Jenkyn, had known that the advertising agency Parker's guardian ran was employed by the makers of Doctor Aurum's Tonic. Parker had told him so himself.

Jenkyn hesitated when the coroner asked what means Parker had used to induce his fellow students to purchase the tonic and mumbled something about handbills in his room and around college.

Florrie stirred at my side. She hadn't made a sound since gasping when she heard that Sidney'd been poisoned. 'Are you sure he won't make me give evidence?' she asked.

'You didn't get a letter asking you to be here, so I don't think they'll call you,' I told her. But I couldn't be absolutely sure.

At home, if there was an inquest happening, everybody who could manage it turned up. Partly for the entertainment value, and partly because you'd be bound to know the person who'd died, even if only by sight. Here, things were different.

I knew Florrie'd been relieved that she wouldn't have to get up in front of this audience of gowns and talk about her and Sidney, but it made me furious. What gave these men the right to decide that Sidney's life outside college was irrelevant?

I wondered if his parish priest might be called. I assumed that the person in the odd hat and cassock was him. Apart from the journalists, he was the only man here not wearing a gown. Presumably he thought clerical dress trumped academic. Much as I was no great supporter of the Anglican Church, his attitude cheered me up. At that moment, I was on the side of anybody who didn't fall into line with the University.

'What if he wants to know about the letters I sent to Sid?' Florrie still wasn't convinced.

I shook my head. 'I didn't give them to him.'

'But you said you had to.'

I looked her in the eye. 'D'you think *they* follow the rules?'

She gave a snort of a laugh which was answer enough.

Since my meeting with Mrs Green and the Johnsons yesterday, I was glad I'd let Florrie keep her letters private. Keeping them secret was nothing compared to what they were prepared to do, was it?

I glanced over at Tarley Askew. He was watching Tobias Jenkyn stumble and sweat his way to the end of his testimony. Probably worrying that he'd make it just as obvious that there were things he was hiding. But I didn't think he would. Tarley was a man of a different stripe to Tobias Jenkyn.

'We learn two things from Mr Jenkyn's testimony,' Frederick Morrell said, once the boy had gone back to sit with his friends. 'Firstly, that as Dr Fielding has already testified, Mr Parker habitually resorted to patent medicines. Secondly, that he was engaged in their sale on behalf of his guardian, Mr George Reardon, who acted as advertising agent to one particular remedy. To wit, Doctor Aurum's Tonic. Both these facts become very relevant as we hear the testimony of our next witness.'

The coroner's clerk called Basil's name. He went up, swore the oath, and told the hearing how, as Sidney Parker's tutor, he'd gone to his lodgings to make a search of his room for anything that might be relevant to how he'd come by his death. He gave Mr Morrell details of the little bottles – labelled and unlabelled, clear, blue and brown – that he'd found in Parker's nightstand.

Nothing controversial there. Basil had done all of those things without any help from me.

But then it began.

'There was also a bundle of papers, concealed in Mr Parker's room,' Basil said. And nobody'd know, from his careful choice of words, that those papers weren't discovered that day, or that they'd have stayed exactly where they were but for Lily and me.

'The papers included an encoded journal which a subsequent witness was able to decode.' It was lucky for Basil that his back was to me, or he'd never have been able to tell that lie, not with me glaring at him.

At my side, Florrie nudged me. 'That's you, isn't it?' she whispered. 'You did the decoding.'

I turned and put my fingers on my lips. 'Sssh.' I hadn't decided, yet, whether I was going to stand up and tell the truth, and I didn't want the decision taken out of my hands by loose lips.

'Those papers indicated that, as well as Sidney Parker, a certain Mr Thompson was employed to sell the patent remedies that were advertised by Mr Parker's guardian, George Reardon. Furthermore, Parker's journal revealed that Mr Thompson had supplied Mr Parker with an entirely new patent medicine which was referred to as Professor Deneuve's Elixir. Prior to our learning that Mr Parker had been poisoned with digitalis, news that was only received on Monday—'

From Dr Benton Reckitt! I wanted to shout.

'—it seemed entirely possible that some ingredient in this new preparation might, when combined with the other remedies Mr Parker was taking, have caused his death. It therefore became imperative that we find Mr Thompson, or the person responsible for manufacturing these remedies, and investigate further.'

Thompson. Bowler Hat. A man Basil would never have connected with the name on the handbills if I hadn't gone to Maclaren's gym with Elspeth Rhys.

'I took responsibility for visiting an address in London which appeared on the handbills advertising Doctor Aurum's Tonic, and I enlisted the help of an undergraduate to pose as a customer in order to try and locate Mr Thompson.'

Oh, so you enlisted him did you, Basil Rice?

Even though I'd known he was going to bend the truth, I hadn't realised just how much twisting it was going to need to leave me out. How did Basil square all this ducking and diving with his conscience? He was a churchgoer. Did he really believe God would agree that the end justified the means?

'We will hear from that undergraduate in due course,' the coroner said. 'Meanwhile, will you tell the hearing the result of your enquiries in London?'

The address proved to be a species of *poste restante* which simply forwarded all mail to an address in Oxford. By the time I returned to the city, the undergraduate I had deputed to make contact with Carmichael Thompson – Mr Tarley Askew of Corpus Christi College – had not been seen for several hours and had missed both a rowing outing and dinner in hall.

I remembered the sick feeling that had come over me when I realised that Tarley Askew'd gone missing.

'*So keeping quiet about it can be your penance,*' Hara warned. She knew I was losing my temper.

'I went to the police station to report Mr Askew missing,' Basil went on. 'But, when I informed the sergeant that I thought Mr Askew might be being held at the address I'd been given, I was not taken seriously. So, I sought the help of two young men of Mr Parker's acquaintance. Members, like him, of the St Barnabas congregation—'

Young men that everybody listening would assume were undergraduates, like Sidney, not a junior printer from the Press and an apprentice engineer from Lucy's ironworks. Because this was all about protecting the University. I could feel my heart thumping in my chest and rage fizzing in my blood.

'—and went to the address I had been given in Jericho. The home of a Mr William Blain. When Mr Blain would not admit me, the other members of the party were forced to effect an entry at the back of the property.'

I remembered Basil battering on the door, shouting at Blain to let him in, while I went down those cellar steps in pitch darkness to look for Tarley. I'd been so afraid I'd find him badly injured, maybe even dead.

'And you were able to rescue Mr Askew, who was being held there against his will, and to apprehend Carmichael Thompson?'

Hooray for Basil Rice, MA. Single-handed saviour of the day.

'With the help of the two young men, yes. But Blain escaped in the confusion.'

'Thank you, Mr Rice. I think, now, we should hear from Mr Askew himself. I believe he overheard a conversation between the two criminals which sheds light on the fate of the unfortunate Mr Parker?'

'Indeed.'

Basil stepped down, the clerk called Tarley to come forward, and he stood up. But, before he moved any further, his eyes fixed on me.

His question was clear. *Are you sure you want me to do this?*

Chapter 58

Basil

The time between Tarley Askew rising to his feet and going forward to give evidence seemed to last an eternity. What must Frederick Morell and the Principal be thinking as they watched him stand there, looking across the hall at the tiny group of women in a sea of gown-clad men?

My heart pounded. If Non shook her head and Tarley invited her to give evidence in his stead, I'd be a laughing stock, and the college with me. A young woman running around in trousers with one of its fellows? Such a thing would entirely eclipse even Sidney Parker's spermatorrhoea as a talking point. I might as well resign now, follow Teddy, and try my luck at King's.

The thought made me quake. Oxford had been my home all my adult life. London had always been somewhere to escape to, the occasional focus for thrill and pleasure; but it was also a dangerous place for men like me. The Metropolitan Police made sure of that.

However, when Non finally gave one definitive nod of her head, releasing Tarley to come forward, I realised that no one else in the hall – with the possible exception of the Principal and Lily Maddox – had been aware of any delay. Everybody had taken the opportunity offered by a lull between witnesses to engage in chatter with their neighbour or attempt to find a more comfortable position on the unyielding refectory benches.

Like the other witnesses, Mr Askew stood at right angles to the high table so that he might be heard equally well by the coroner and the spectators. To my dismay, however, he took up his position on the coroner's right-hand side, facing Non, rather than on Mr Morrell's left where all the other witnesses had stood.

However, as Askew began giving his testimony, his calm, clear voice carrying easily to the back of the hall, I relaxed and allowed my gaze to sweep around the spectators. My eye snagged on a figure sitting next to the two journalists near the hall's doorway. Like them, the young man was gownless which marked him out in this company even before I recognised him.

Billy Nicholson.

When had he slipped in? More to the point what was he doing here? He attended St Barnabas with Lily and Ivy, did that mean he'd been better acquainted with Sidney Parker than I'd realised? It seemed unlikely. Despite his employment at the Press, Billy despised the University and everything about it; I couldn't imagine his ever having formed a friendship with an undergraduate, even one as *déclassé* as Sidney Parker.

But the mystery of Billy's presence failed to hold my attention as I heard Morrell ask how Mr Askew had come to be involved in the events consequent upon Sidney Parker's death. Had he, perhaps, bought Doctor Aurum's Tonic from Mr Parker?

I watched as Tarley explained – without going into any details about where he had been at the time (much grinning from the undergraduate contingent as all the young men present realised that he had been in a public house) – that he had overheard a man who claimed to be Sidney Parker's landlord gossiping about the young man's death. Concerned that the college might not know what was being bruited abroad and being slightly acquainted with me from attending my lectures, he had sought me out.

'It all seemed most unfortunate,' his voice held every indication of sincerity, 'and I promised that I'd do what I could to quell any unhelpful rumours. That made me the obvious chap to call on when a tame undergrad was required.'

'Perhaps you might now tell us what transpired when you sought out this Mr Thompson?' Morrell suggested.

'I went incognito – that is to say, without my cap and gown – to Bear Lane and asked a few people where I might find a Mr Carmichael Thompson. Thompson was named on Parker's handbills as the local stockist of Doctor Aurum's Tonic, and we assumed that he might be able to provide me with the new preparation Mr Parker had mentioned in his journal: Professor Deneuve's Elixir. But that proved my downfall. I didn't know it at the time, but only Sidney Parker had ever heard the name Professor Deneuve, and only in the context of the bottle he had been given which, we now know, contained the poison that killed him. Thompson therefore became worried that Parker had spoken to me *after* he started taking what he thought was a new remedy, and that I must suspect the remedy of being responsible for his death.'

'What evidence do you have for that?' Morrell asked.

'When I was being held captive in Blain's house, I heard Thompson and Blain talking about it. Thompson appeared not to have known that the remedy Blain had given him for Parker contained poison. He was simply concerned that the new remedy would be seen as dangerous if other people discovered that Mr Parker had been taking it at the time of his death.'

Morrell shuffled amongst the papers in front of him and selected one of the handbills which he passed to the juryman seated next to him. 'Having examined the documents found in Mr Parker's lodgings, it seems that the manufacturers – or advertisers – of Professor Deneuve's Elixir had intended to capitalise on Mr Parker's death by stating, as the advertisement the jury are now reading does, that "spermatorrhoea kills". I believe that you found evidence that they intended to follow this rather alarmist statement with advertisements for new remedies?'

'Yes, I found a printer's parcel with hundreds of exactly that kind of advertisement in Blain's cellar after he'd fled.' Mr Askew reached into his pocket and produced one of the handbills he and Non had found. 'Young men,' he read, glancing up at both jury and spectators, 'in the light of a recent tragic death, do not depend on Dr Aurum's Tonic. Turn to the best: the strongest, swiftest, surest remedy available. Professor Deneuve's Elixir.'

He stepped forward and placed the handbill on the table in front of Morrell who stared at it in fascination. 'Take only three, scientifically tested doses,' he read, 'and you will be cured.'

Tarley Askew nodded. 'I believe it was that advertisement that created Thompson's panic. Mr Parker's journal indicates that Thompson had given him instructions to take the so-called remedy in three increasingly large doses. Thompson had also listed its likely unpleasant side effects and told Mr Parker to disregard them, that they were just evidence that the remedy was doing its job. Mr Rice and I believe that the poison was given to Parker in a blue bottle, just like the ones I found in crates in Blain's house.' He reached into his pocket and produced a small blue bottle which he placed in front of Mr Morrell.

'One of the side effects was a tendency for one's entire view of the world to appear green-tinged. That's how the expert we consulted, Dr Benton Reckitt, was able to diagnose digitalis poisoning.'

Mr Askew paused and looked around at the spectators, his eyes finally coming to rest on Non.

'When you approached Thompson,' Morrell said, 'did he persuade you to accompany him to the home of William Blain, in Jericho?'

'He did. He told me that was where the new preparation, Professor Deneuve's Elixir, was stored.'

'But, in fact, you now believe he meant you harm?'

I watched Mr Askew very carefully. His eyes were on Non, asking her for permission, once more, to take credit for her bravery, for the things she had learned.

And, once again, she nodded, though this time the movement was far less definite than before.

'In fact, Mr Coroner,' Askew said, 'it wasn't Carmichael Thompson who threatened me with harm – though he did knock me down and tie me up – it was William Blain. I heard them talking to each other when Blain came back to the house. Blain told Thompson that as it was he who'd given the poison to Sidney Parker, and he who'd brought me to his house, it must be he who "got rid of me".'

'Let me be clear, here,' Morrell said, sharply. 'William Blain accused Carmichael Thompson of poisoning the deceased, Mr Parker?'

'He did. But Thompson denied that he'd done it knowingly. He claimed to believe that what he'd given Parker was the new remedy: Professor Deneuve's Elixir. Blain laughed and told him he was stupid if he believed that.'

'Do you think Blain had used Thompson as his dupe?'

'I do.'

Morrell turned his attention to the jury, looking from right to left as he said, 'As you are aware, gentlemen, if this hearing finds that Mr Parker was the victim of deliberate homicide, it is not your responsibility to decide who the guilty party is. That is the role of the police who have Carmichael Thompson in custody and who are currently searching the city and beyond for William Blain.'

Then he turned his attention back to Tarley Askew. 'I believe that's all these proceedings require of you, Mr Askew. You may sit down.'

But before Tarley Askew could descend from the dais, a voice came from the back of the hall. 'Oy, what about us? Don't we even get a mention?'

Chapter 59

Non

I turned around. My ears told me I knew the voice, but I refused to believe that I'd heard it here, where it didn't belong.

But there he was. Billy Nicholson. Standing at the back of the hall, next to the newspapermen. This would give them something to write about. *Unseemly outburst at University Inquest.*

He came marching down the hall like a bantam cock. Every eye was on him. A few undergraduates got to their feet. But Mr Morrell stopped them before they could lay hands on him.

'This is a public hearing, gentlemen. If interested members of the public wish to question witnesses or make observations pertinent to the proceedings, they may do so. Young man, would you care to introduce yourself?'

Billy drew himself up to his full height. Which was about five and a half feet in his socks. 'William Nicholson. I'm one of the two young gentlemen referred to earlier. The ones who rescued Mr Askew, here. The other's my brother-in-law, Albert Maddox.'

Morrell gazed at Billy. You couldn't tell what the coroner was thinking but I don't suppose he was pleased to have his inquest interrupted. 'Do you have anything pertinent to say, Mr Nicholson? That is to say, anything pertinent to the inquest into the cause of Mr Sidney Parker's death.'

Tarley stepped down from the dais and motioned for Billy to get up.

At my side Florrie stirred. 'One of Reardon's spies is here,' she said.

'Where?'

'End of the middle table nearest the door. Light brown hair and dark green tie.'

He'd probably come in just as proceedings started, so as to avoid having to explain who he was to the Jesus boys. He blended in well, I'll give him that. But then, I suppose spies had to. He didn't look much different to any other young man in the hall, though once you knew, perhaps his hair wasn't quite as neatly cut, and his gown looked to be on the elderly side. But he wouldn't be the only student in a second-hand gown.

'You're sure?'

'Course I am. Seen him hanging about enough times, watching me.'

I knew he must be there to report back to Blain. Which meant Blain was still in Oxford. But I couldn't think about him now. I needed to know what Billy Nicholson was up to.

He stood on the dais, back to the jury, hands in his pockets. If he was trying to show he wasn't impressed with the proceedings, or with the grandeur of the hall, he missed it by a mile. He just looked ignorant.

'What I've got to *say* is this,' he said. 'You can see if it's *pertinent* or not. And the people who read the newspapers can see what they think. This inquest is a pack of lies and dodging the truth. Sidney Parker's journal was in code, and the person who cracked it wasn't one of your men, it was a woman. *Her*.' He spun and pointed at me. 'Rhiannon Vaughan. And *she* was the one who found Thompson and sent Mr Askew off to find him. Then, on Monday evening, she dressed in trousers and followed us when we went to rescue him, and pretty near started a fire when she went into Blain's house looking for him. She's the one who solved this whole thing, not your University types. Isn't that right, Miss Vaughan?'

I stared at him. He stood there, furious. But it wasn't the hearing he was angry with, it was me. He wasn't *crediting* me with having done those things, he was *accusing* me of them. Because he knew that, if the University men realised the part I'd played in all this, they'd never let me near a college again.

And that's what he wanted.

Billy Nicholson wanted me gone.

Chapter 60

Basil

Non rose, apparently unwillingly, to her feet. She gazed coolly at Billy Nicholson for a few seconds before addressing herself to Frederick Morrell.

'Mr Coroner, my name is Rhiannon Vaughan. I'm from Cardiganshire, and I've come to Oxford to study under the auspices of the AEW – the Association for Promoting the Higher Education of Women in Oxford – and to attend lectures in the colleges that, like Jesus College, kindly permit that.'

Morrell inclined his head and indicated to his clerk that he should make a note of Non's identity.

'Mr Morrell, members of the jury, Principal Harper, I very much regret that Mr Nicholson is attempting to use this hearing to pursue a grievance against me. It's my belief that he is trying to blacken my name so that I will be denied entry to lectures and so that the AEW will withdraw its support from me.'

'Hold on a minute—' Billy began. But Morrell ignored him and addressed himself to Non.

'And why would he do that, Miss Vaughan?'

'Because I lodge with his mother-in-law. He lives in the same house, with his wife and child, and he dislikes the conversations that take place at the dinner table. He lacks the kind of education that allows a man to feel secure in his own opinions, so intellectual conversations make him uncomfortable. As a consequence, he'd like me to be removed.'

My eyes were drawn from Non to Lily, sitting at her side; it was hard to gauge Lily's feelings, but she could be nothing other than highly uncomfortable, despite not having been identified as the mother-in-law in question.

'So, there is no truth in what he says?' Morrell asked.

The coroner knew nothing of the part Non had played in my investigation into Sidney Parker's death. We had asked him only for permission to refrain from mentioning Mr Parker's spermatorrhoea ring and gynaecomastia. The decision to put Non's testimony in Mr Askew's mouth had resided entirely with Dr Harper and me.

Non did not hesitate. Evidently Billy Nicholson's intervention had made up her mind for her. She would rather oblige the AEW and Dr Harper than prove Nicholson right. 'No, Mr Coroner, no truth at all.'

'Yet, as this young man says, the journal *was*, I believe, encoded?' Morrell had both the original and Non's deciphered version in front of him.

'Indeed. And I'm sure Mr Askew was more than capable of decrypting it.'

'You're acquainted with Mr Askew?'

'We are both members of a small group that meets to discuss recreational mathematics.'

The journalists' pencils were flickering over their notebooks, and I wondered how much of what was being said would eventually make its way into the *Journal* or the *Chronicle*.

'I see.'

'Mr Parker was known to our household as he attended the church at which we all worship,' Non included the other women with a gesture, 'and we have come here today with Mr Parker's fiancée, Miss Spellman, to hear the truth of his sad demise. We are all shocked beyond measure to hear that he was murdered.'

She paused briefly, as if the reference to murder had upset her, while the susurrus caused by news of Parker's having had a fiancée hissed around the hall. 'I can only beg your pardon, Mr Coroner, that Mr Nicholson's urge to be rid of me has intruded into your proceedings.'

'Please, Miss Vaughan, it's not for you to apologise. But your sentiments do you great credit. Thank you. Mr Nicholson, would you return to your seat, please?'

'It's all lies, everything she just said—'

This time, the young men of Jesus were not going to be prevented from frog-marching Billy Nicholson out of the hall. And, having done that, I don't doubt that they threw him out of college.

Chapter 61

Non

I seethed for the rest of the proceedings. How *dare* Billy Nicholson try a trick like that? How dare he take away any choice I had about giving my own evidence? Lily could see how it'd affected me. She took my hand and leaned in. 'We'll talk about this later. He had no right to do that.' Talk was all very well, but if I had any say in the matter, he'd be gone from Lily's house before the week was up. Either that or I'd pack my bags. I was sorry for Ivy and little Tommy who'd have to go with him, but I couldn't live under the same roof as Billy Nicholson now.

But seething rage didn't stop me keeping an eye on Florrie's spy, and as soon as the coroner'd wound up the proceedings, I told Lily I'd see her back at home and pushed through the undergraduates towards Tarley and Basil. By the time I got there, Basil had been drawn away by Dr Harper, but Tarley looked pleased to see me.

I grabbed his arm. 'One of Reardon's spies is here. We need to follow him, see if he'll take us to Blain.'

I looked towards the end of the hall, but I couldn't see the spy, now. He'd probably left as soon as everybody stood up. I started pushing my way through gowned bodies until Tarley took my elbow and moved me out of the way. He dropped a shoulder and started ploughing through the undergrads with a 'Coming through, gentlemen!' I stepped into the space he'd created and followed him out.

Nobody else was in the hurry we were, and the quad was virtually deserted when we left the hall, so it was easy to spot the spy heading quickly for the main gates.

We followed, more slowly, so that he didn't take fright.

The Contraption was standing to one side of the wicket gate. Tarley and I and hauled it out into Turl Street.

'If he leads us to Blain,' Tarley said, as he lifted his end of the tandem over the threshold. 'What then?'

'I don't know. But we can't just let him go. We've got to do *something*.'

The spy was heading down Turl Street towards the High Street, shrugging his way out of his gown as he went.

'If he looks like turning round,' I said, as we climbed on to The Contraption, 'just start laughing and say something sweet to me. That'll throw him off.'

'Oh, yes? Followed people before, have you?'

'No. Just stands to reason. Men get embarrassed around courting couples.'

'Fair enough.'

As his long legs pushed at the cranks, I felt the tandem moving forward without much effort from me. It was a novel experience, riding on the front seat. I always sat at the back, steering, but Tarley'd been at that end of The Contraption, and we'd been in too much of a hurry for me to bother arguing about who sat where.

'I have to tell you,' Tarley said, 'that the geometry of this thing doesn't suit me at all.'

'Easier if you stand on the cranks.'

'I know, but crouching over to reach the steering handles isn't very comfortable either.'

'I can just about steer from here. Put your hands on my shoulders.' If it meant we could go faster, I was prepared to be used as a prop.

I felt a lurch and a heavy hand on my shoulder as he found his balance. 'Oh,' he said, once he had both his hands lightly steadying him, 'that's better.'

We followed the spy down Turl Street, pedalling steadily.

'Blain got on a train when he escaped from Albie,' Tarley said, voice low to stop his words carrying in the quiet street. 'Will we follow this chap if he does the same?'

'Have you got enough money for tickets?'

'Possibly.' He didn't sound very sure. Because he didn't know how much money he had with him, or because he didn't really want to follow the spy on to a train?

The spy reached the junction with the High Street, and turned right, past the Mitre. I pushed harder at the cranks and the tandem smoothly picked up speed.

At the junction, I back-pedalled to brake which almost made Tarley fall over my shoulder, because his cranks stopped going round, too.

I looked round. 'Sorry, should have warned you.' I looked up and down the street. Luckily for us, there wasn't an omnibus in sight, and with me awkwardly reaching back for the steering handles, we managed to cross in front of a cab which was trotting down from Carfax.

We pedalled along slowly, the warmth of Tarley's hands on my shoulders coming through my coat. I kept my eyes on the road so that the spy wouldn't feel me watching him, but I could see him well enough out of the corner of my eye.

I kept looking round at Tarley to maintain the illusion of us as a courting couple and, each time I did, he'd grin down at me. It was probably pointless because the spy couldn't really see us, not unless he was watching our reflection in the shop windows. But you never knew.

As he came to the corner with Cornmarket Street, instead of turning right, he crossed the road towards the huge frontage of St Martin's church.

'Stopping,' I warned, then back-pedalled.

Tarley adjusted his balance, and I felt more of his weight on my shoulders. 'Sit down again and pretend to talk to me,' I said, not looking round.

'Shall I pretend to talk or really talk?' He grinned as I turned around.

'What's he doing?' I asked.

A young woman holding the hands of two small children passed by on the pavement and gave us an odd look. I suppose it was unusual to see people cycling on a weekday.

'He's talking to someone. A man.'

'Is he bald with a beard?'

'He's got a hat on, but I can't see any hair. No beard though.'

If Blain had any sense, he'd have shaved his beard off by now, wouldn't he? To make himself less recognisable to anybody who was looking for him.

I adjusted my position on the tandem as if I was just trying to make myself more comfortable and looked around. I'd had only a fleeting glimpse of William Blain before I knocked the lamp out. All I could say was that the man the spy was talking to could easily be him.

'What now?' Tarley asked.

'We can't just let him go.' I looked around for a policeman. There was usually a constable strolling up and down the four streets that met at Carfax, making sure that order was kept. I could see him halfway up Cornmarket Street, speaking to somebody.

'There's the Carfax copper,' I said, eye-pointing up the road.

'I'll go and talk to him,' Tarley said.

'Let's both go—'

'No. *I'll* go,' Tarley was firm. 'He'll know about what happened on Monday night and if you're there it'll just confuse things. You weren't there, remember? Stay here and watch in case they move.'

He extracted himself from the tandem and strode off.

I watched the man who might be Blain. He looked as if he was listening hard to what the spy had to say. Which was obviously a lot more than 'run away, they know what you did.'

I flicked my eyes up the road to Tarley. He'd reached the constable now and was speaking to him. What would the policeman do, wait until the spy had moved away, then get Tarley to help him make the arrest, or go down the High Street to the police station for reinforcements?

Blain reached into an inner pocket and handed something to the spy. Payment for services rendered?

The spy touched his forehead with one finger and went off up Cornmarket Street.

Tarley and the policeman were still talking, and Blain was already in motion.

I climbed on to the back seat of the tandem and pushed off. But as I weaved in and out of people and carts crossing the road to Queen Street, I lost sight of him. Had he gone into a shop? If he had, was he planning to go out through the back like he had done when he'd given Albie the slip? I cycled slowly, scanning the crowd. Then, suddenly, I saw him up ahead, opening the door into a pub. I steered over to the other side of the road, where I could watch the door more easily, and pulled up outside an ironmonger's.

I sat beneath buckets and pans hanging on the wall outside the shop and ignored the stares of passers-by while I watched the pub door.

Footsteps came thudding up behind me and Tarley arrived, with the policeman puffing a few yards behind.

'He's gone in there,' I nodded at the door Blain had disappeared into.

'Well done for following him.'

That made me smile. Tarley was probably the only man in Oxford who wouldn't tell me off for following a murderer.

'Right,' the puffing bobby said to Tarley, 'if you'll just come in with me, sir, and point him out, I'll do the rest.'

He was all flab and self-importance. I gave him about as much chance of subduing Blain as he had of winning a sprint. But the two of them together might manage.

The door closed behind them. If Blain'd already nipped out through the back of the pub into the yards and lanes behind, we'd never find him.

While I was picturing him walking away, the pub's double doors crashed open and Blain barrelled out into the street, almost falling as he turned sharply and started running down Queen Street.

I was crouched over and bearing down on the cranks before I could ask myself what I was doing. Behind me I heard the door thud again and glanced back. 'Here!' I shouted.

I'd barely got the tandem moving so Tarley managed to get himself on and started pushing at the revolving cranks as hard as he could. Trouble was, he was now on the front. So, I stood up and leaned on him, working the cranks as hard as I could.

Within seconds, people were dodging out of our way as we picked up speed and started gaining on Blain. As long as he didn't jink into a side street, we'd soon overtake him.

At the bottom of Queen Street, Blain kept left, along Castle Street. I didn't know this part of town very well, but I knew that Castle Street turned into Paradise Street which led to the warren of lanes between St Thomas's church and the breweries. If there was a place to hide in Oxford, that was it.

'Push harder,' I shouted to Tarley. It didn't matter if Blain heard me, now, it was a straight race.

'You'll have to steer then.' Tarley stopped reaching back for the steering handles and crouched over the passenger's handles to steady himself as he bore down on the cranks.

We were going twice as fast as Blain, now, and gaining on him rapidly.

I sat on the saddle and steered hard across the road. I could hear Blain panting as we drew alongside him. He must've caught our movement in the corner of his eye because he glanced over. His eyes widened and he stumbled. That small turn of his head had been enough to throw him off balance and he was half-falling, half-running, arms flung out to try and get his balance back.

It was a simple matter to angle the front wheel of the tandem into his path. His foot caught the tyre and he measured his length on the street.

I opened my mouth to shout 'brake,' but Tarley was ahead of me. The wheels locked and we came skidding to a halt with me just about managing not to run Blain over.

Tarley jumped off and bent over him. He was already trying to get up.

'No, you don't!' Tarley twisted Blain's arm up behind his back and put a boot between his shoulder blades to force him back down on to the road. 'You can stay there till the police catch up.'

Chapter 62

Basil

Having been summoned to the police station by a constable in order to confirm Blain's identity, I was very surprised to find Non and Tarley Askew there. They explained briefly what had happened.

'Just as well I managed to persuade Florrie to come to the inquest,' Non said, pointedly. 'Without her, Blain would have got away and never been seen again.'

'Now you're here, Mr Rice,' the sergeant at the desk said, 'you might be interested to know that the constable guarding Blain's house in Laud Street overnight came in this morning with a story about a carrier having come, wanting to take away a consignment of crates that were still in the house. Said Professor Deneuve' – he pronounced the name Dinuve – 'had been informed that his advertising agent was dead and wanted his goods back. 'Course, the constable sent him away with a flea in his ear. Should have brought him in, by rights, but if he'd done that he'd've left the house unguarded and somebody else could've got in and had the lot away.'

Had it been those crates of little blue bottles that had induced Blain to show his face in the city again, even though he must know he'd be a wanted man?

Subsequent conversation suggested that this was the moment when Tarley might most usefully give his statement about events on Monday so, once Non had accounted for her part in Blain's apprehension, I suggested that I should walk her home. Slightly to my surprise, she agreed.

'There's something I'd like to talk to you about,' she said as we crossed the High to go back up the Turl.

'Billy Nicholson?' I said.

I detected a slight hesitation at my side. 'No. As a matter of fact, in all the excitement, I'd forgotten about that.'

All the excitement. How many other young women would describe her pursuit of a murderer with such *sang froid*? 'What did Lily say about Billy's little performance?' I asked.

Non sighed as she lifted the tandem's front wheel on to the pavement. 'That we'd discuss it this evening. But, as far as I'm concerned there's nothing to discuss. I can't live under the same roof as him now – it was bad enough before with him always finding fault and sniping. Either he goes or I do.'

'Where would you go?'

'Plenty of other landladies in Oxford. Bertha Trent's got a vacancy now.'

'You can't live in a house full of undergraduates!'

'Can't I indeed?'

Belatedly, I realised that she was baiting me. 'You're incorrigible.'

We walked up the Turl in silence for a minute or so, Non biding her time before she raised whatever it was she wished to speak to me about. 'By the way,' I said, as we passed the gates to Jesus, 'Dr Harper wished me to convey his thanks for all your efforts on our behalf. And to assure you that you're welcome to recommence attending lectures at Jesus.'

Non frowned. 'That's not for him to say. This term's ban was the AEW's sanction, not Harper's.'

'But I'm sure that, in the circumstances…'

'D'you know what, Basil? I don't really feel like accepting a reward for lying. But if he's grateful, then somebody else can benefit.'

I waited, suspecting that we'd arrived at the subject she wanted to discuss.

'Now that Reardon's dead, who's Sidney Parker's next of kin?'

The question took me by surprise. 'I have no idea.'

'Then what will happen to his belongings?'

I had given no consideration to what might happen to the trunk and other effects that were still in the old stables at Jesus. 'I imagine they'll be sold.'

'And the college will get the money?'

'Mr Parker was a member of the college, so yes, I suppose so. Unless there are unanticipated cousins lurking, obviously.'

'But if he'd lived another few weeks, the banns would've been read and he'd have married Florrie Spellman,' Non pointed out. 'Then *she'd* be his next of kin. It should all go to her.' She paused slightly. 'Including the money in the strongbox.'

The thought of the cashbox sitting in my rooms made me feel slightly queasy when I recalled my conversation with young Jenkyn. 'You do remember me telling you where that money came from?'

'Selling Dr Aurum's Tonic for a fortune and getting people into debt, yes. But that was before he met Florrie. He'd given all that up by then, hadn't he?'

I wasn't entirely clear on the moral chronology, but it seemed best to agree.

'From what I overheard Blain telling Thompson,' Non went on, 'George Reardon had control of the money left in trust for Sidney and he'd sunk it all into his business. That money would've been Florrie's if they'd married. She and her father had plans to emigrate, with Sidney. They could still go without him.'

'I don't suppose the sum in the cashbox would be anything like as much as the money left in trust.'

'Maybe not. But it's a lot more than they've got now.'

Had some part of me anticipated this request? I had told nobody about the cash Sidney Parker had hidden beneath the floorboards. Not even the coroner. Non and I were the only people aware of its existence. Its disposal was, if we so chose, up to us. And, as Non kept reminding everybody, had she and Lily not visited Florrie Spellman to tell her of Sidney's death, the money and everything else that he'd hidden beneath the floorboards would have stayed there. And the truth would have been buried with his body.

'Very well.'

'…take care then to form a correct and mature opinion on everything… Amongst pioneers, some succeed, and some run to destruction.'

'…cymerwch ofal gan hyny i ffurfio barn gywir ac aeddfed ar bobpeth… O blith pioneers, y mae rhai yn llwyddo, a rhai yn rhedeg i ddinystr.'

—Cranogwen (Sarah Jane Rees), *Y Frythones*

Chapter 63

Non

As I walked over to the Spellmans' soot yard first thing on Thursday morning, the cashbox in my satchel, I wondered whether I should explain to Florrie why Edie hadn't let her in when she'd paid an unannounced visit the previous evening.

We'd all heard the knock. The dining room wasn't far from the front door and the knocker had made the whole family jump as if a gun had gone off outside. But then, the atmosphere over supper had been tense.

Edie must have answered the door within three seconds of Florrie's knock. She'd been in the passageway, of course, listening outside the dining room door. Earlier, she'd heard Lily and me talking about what Billy'd said at the inquest and she'd known the reckoning would happen as soon as we were all home. But she must've been surprised when Lily started on Billy as soon as we'd sat down for dinner. I knew I had been.

'I want you to apologise to Non for what you did today.' Lily'd sounded as if she was talking to a naughty child. One who'd be getting a hiding if they didn't do what they were told.

Billy started cutting up his chop and wouldn't meet her eye. 'What am I supposed to apologise for? I just told the truth. That's what we're supposed to do, isn't it?'

'Don't you come the clever one with me, William Nicholson.'

'She's always going on about how they don't take any notice of women,' he said. 'Then, when she has the *chance* to be noticed, she keeps her lips sewn up.'

I couldn't leave it all to Lily. 'If I'd *wanted* to speak,' I said, 'I would have. But I'd agreed with the AEW committee that I'd keep quiet. For the good of all the other women students.'

All right, I hadn't *actually* agreed, not strictly speaking, but he wasn't to know that.

The argument'd gone on, back and forth, Billy digging his heels in like a mule and saying that he'd just told the truth, me accusing him of knowing exactly what he was doing and Lily battering at him for an apology. I didn't want an apology. It'd only be empty words. I just wanted him gone.

In the end, it'd been Ivy who settled it. 'I think it's time we moved out, Mum,' she said, quietly. 'To our own place, where Billy can be the head of the family, like he's supposed to be.'

As a way of saving face and avoiding being thrown out, it was brilliant. It meant that they could still be on speaking terms with Lily – which would've been difficult if she'd given Billy his marching orders – and he hadn't had to back down. My respect for Ivy went up quite a bit, I must admit. I'd never had her down as much of a strategist before. But then she was quiet, so there'd never been much to go on, really.

Florrie's knock had come just as Ivy said her piece. What had she thought when Edie'd turned her away? People in Jericho didn't generally decide that they weren't receiving visitors, even after dark.

Halfway up Canal Street I saw the girl I'd seen at Florrie's house the last time I'd been there; the one she'd been sending for meat. I stopped her and asked if Florrie was at home. She looked at me as if she was thinking about asking what it was worth, then decided against it.

'She's in but there's no work today an' she's not worth talking to.' I raised my eyebrows for more information. ''Er dad's done a flit, 'asn't he? Wen' out Monday an' 'an't come back.' She looked me in the eye. 'You doan' want nothin' doin' I s'pose? Shoppin', laundry?'

I felt sorry for her. But I also saw a chance to find something out. 'No, but I'll give you sixpence if you answer me a question.'

She scowled as if she thought I was trying to trick her. 'What question?'

'Do you know a William Blain? Bill Blain?' Something had been nagging at me about Blain since the constable had cuffed him and frogmarched him away up Castle Street. Where had he come from? How had he got involved with Reardon?

'Know who he *is*, if that's what you mean. Don't *know* him, know him. I were only a nipper when 'e wen' away and 'e's not long out is he?'

'Out?'

'From the Castle.'

The Castle. Oxford gaol.

'What was he in for?'

The girl shrugged. 'Dunno. Swindlin' people prob'ly. Like I said, I were only a li'l 'un. You askin' 'cos of the bother round his place the other night?'

'What did you hear about that?'

'Had a toff from one of the colleges there, didn't he? And a dead body!' She gave an odd little whinnying laugh. 'Maybe 'im and Dan've done a flit together.'

'Why would they do that?'

'Brothers aren't they? Long as you're not looking which side of the blanket they was born on. Everybody roun' Jericho knows Dan an' Bill got the same dad.'

I gave her sixpence and walked on, trying to work out what Dan Spellman and Bill Blain being brothers might mean.

On the Spellmans' street, I saw a man limp up from the direction of the coal wharf and walk in through the soot yard's gates. If he was a customer, I'd have to wait. But perhaps he was one of Spellman's sweeps, come late to work?

I followed him in through the gates just in time to see him going in through the open scullery door. Damn. Now I'd definitely have to wait. Unless I knocked on the front door? Florrie might hurry her business up then.

I was about to go back out on to Canal Street when I heard Florrie's voice from inside the house.

'Hah! Back, are you? Thought you'd gone for good.'

I tiptoed back towards the open scullery door and stood to one side. A bass voice was rumbling in the kitchen beyond, and I strained to hear what it was saying.

'…couldn' leave you could I, my little dove?'

'Don't you "little dove" me.' Florrie's voice was far more carrying than the man's and I could hear how angry she was. 'You were gone as soon as you realised Bill'd done for Reardon, and never a thought for me. Run out of money now, I suppose? Drunk it all already?'

The man must be Dan Spellman.

'Don't be shrill, Florrie.'

'Shrill? What should I be when Bill's wrecked all our plans?'

'But *we're* all right.'

'How are we all right? Bill's done for us. No business. No money. We can't even get at those crates in Laud Street to relabel the stuff and sell it on.'

Did she think they should be able to claim the bottles of Professor Deneuve's Elixir because of their relationship with Blain? And what did she mean 'no business'? Had she and Sidney been contemplating joining Reardon after all?

'But we're no worse off than we used to be, are we?' Spellman sounded almost pleading.

'*You* may not be, but you weren't the one courting Sid Parker for six months! I put a lot of work in there, and all Bill had to do was stick to the plan and wait till we were married. But he was never *going* to stick to the plan, was he? Not Bill Blain. Didn't want you and me in business with him, any more than he wanted Reardon. Bastard saw his chance. Did you know about those handbills telling boys not to go the way Sid had gone?'

'What're you talking about?'

'They had one in the inquest. "Don't delay, get the right remedy today, or end up like poor Sidney Parker!"' In the sudden silence, I imagined her glaring at her father. 'Sid was a hell of a lot more use to Bill dead than he was alive, wasn't he? No Sid, no inheritance to pay out, so Reardon and Bill keep their business. Get rid of Reardon and, with me and Sid not yet married, everything belongs to Bill. Bastard! I hope they hang him.'

'Florrie—'

'Thought he was so clever, didn't he? Found some bloody weed to kill Sid with. Bet he learned that inside. All very slick. Except not quite slick enough, as it turned out. Sid was a student, and students take notes. They pay attention.'

'Stop talking in riddles, girl!'

'It's not riddles, it's plain fact! It all came out in the inquest while you were busy getting tanked. Bill gave Car Thompson a potion for Sid – said it was Professor Deneuve's and it'd cure him. But Sid went and *wrote down* what he was taking and when, and what *bloody effect it had*! D'you understand? He wrote down *exactly what happened to him*. Kept an exact record *of his own murder*. That's how some doctor or other knew what Bill'd used. Too bloody clever for his own good, Bill Blain is.'

I waited for Dan Spellman to speak up, but Florrie hadn't finished yet. I could see her in my mind's eye, pacing back and forth in that gleaming kitchen. 'All he had to do was wait for me to marry Sid. I *told* him I'd get it done. Everybody knew Sid wasn't well. Nobody'd have turned a hair. But no. He was never going to wait, was he? He wanted the whole business. And now the stupid sod'll hang for it and none of us any the better off.'

Silence. Dan Spellman had no answer to that.

I knew how he felt. Here I was, ready to hand over Sidney Parker's money to a girl who'd planned to kill him. Poor Sid. He'd been right all along. He was doomed to die – had been from the moment Florrie and her father had realised that his guardian owned a promising business. While he was just another undergraduate with the usual prospects, Florrie might've been content to be Sid's wife. But with Sid a partner in Reardon's business, she'd have had a lot more freedom to spend the money as his widow. Especially if Reardon had always been destined to go the same way as Sidney. *All he had to do was wait for me to marry Sid.*

'Are you goin' to come then?' Dan Spellman asked.

'Come where?'

'Anywhere. Away from here. Before the bobbies come for us.'

'You think Bill'd rat?'

'No, but he's my brother.'

'It's not a crime to be related to a criminal. Even a murderer. And I'm the grieving fiancée, remember? Look at bit fishy if I did a flit, now, wouldn't it? And anyway, I want my money.'

I heard no reply from Spellman, but he'd obviously looked blank because Florrie snapped, 'The money Sid hid under his floorboards. That nosy Welsh cow must have it. She found all Sid's things. I went over last night to see if I could talk her into giving it to me but got turned away. I'll go over later today. Then we can see.'

'Why's she goin' to give it to you when you an' Sid weren't married?'

'Thought of a way round that, haven't I? Came to me the other day.'

'What?'

'Never you mind.'

It was time to leave the yard, before she decided that sooner might be better than later to go over to the nosy Welsh cow's house.

I'd be ready for her when she came. We all would.

Chapter 64

Basil

I was sitting at my desk, innocently preparing a lecture in the belief that the Sidney Parker affair had been satisfactorily concluded and that we could all return to less eventful lives, when Mr Askew paid me a visit.

'I've just seen Non,' he said. 'There have been developments.'

'What sort of developments?'

'Something to do with Parker's fiancée, but she wouldn't tell me any more. She wants us both to be there.'

–

'It's very inconvenient not being able to set foot in Jesus College,' Non said when Askew and I rendezvous'd with her at the coffee cart on Ship Street. 'I had to send Mr Askew to come and fetch you.' Though he tried, manfully, to hide it, Tarley Askew looked a little crestfallen at the thought that he'd been no more than a messenger. However, his chagrin was swiftly dispelled when Non added, 'Not that we wouldn't have needed his assistance anyway.'

I forbore to point out that she was now perfectly at liberty to step over the Jesus College threshold; she'd made her feelings on the primacy of the AEW's role in her exclusion quite plain.

Non and I consumed coffee from the cart while Askew wolfed down four slices of bread and butter with the insatiability of youth, and Non told us what she'd heard at the Spellmans' back door.

'There's no point going to the police,' she said. 'It'd be just my word against hers. But if *you* hear her incriminating herself, it'll be a different matter.'

'You don't imagine she's going to confess to you?' From the account Non had given of Miss Spellman's involvement in the conspiracy to murder Sidney Parker, that seemed very unlikely.

'No. But she wants Sidney Parker's money, and she thinks she's got a way to make me give it to her. I don't suppose for a second that it'll be an honest way, so if we can catch her lying, or even better, committing fraud of some kind, then a jury's more likely to believe me when I tell them what I heard earlier.'

Her plan seemed more or less plausible. 'And Mr Askew's role?'

'He'll bring the police along to wait outside until you signal to them.'

'But how will he know when to come?'

'Before I came into town to get you two, I told Edie that if Florrie Spellman came round, she was to tell her I'd be back this afternoon and that, if Florrie wanted to catch me, two o'clock would be the best time. And Florrie definitely *does* want to catch me.'

-

As agreed, I presented myself at Lily's front door at a quarter to two. Non drew me in, glancing both ways along the street.

'Are you sure she'll come?' I asked.

'She'll come. She wants her money.'

The knock came, punctually, at two. Non let Edie answer the door and admit Miss Spellman, while I hid behind the sitting room's long, thick drapes.

Fortunately, in an attempt to thoroughly exclude draughts and retain the warmth of the fire, Lily's curtains not only reached the floor but spilled generously on to the floorboards, successfully hiding my feet.

As I waited for the two young women to settle themselves, I tried to conjure up Miss Spellman's face from my brief glances at her during the inquest, but the only impression I'd been left with had been of a girl with blonde hair wearing a Jericho milliner's version of a fashionable, large-bowed hat. It was hard to imagine that young woman being a cold-blooded potential murderess but, if Non had not misinterpreted what she had heard at the Spellmans' back door, that's exactly what Florence Spellman was. It was chastening to think that I had, as Dr Harper might have said, been taken in by a pretty face. 'Do you think they always intended to kill Reardon as well?' I'd asked after Non had finished recounting the Spellmans' conversation to Askew and me.

'Who knows? It didn't sound as if Reardon was part of the conspiracy to murder Sidney, so maybe when Sidney died, he suspected that Blain'd had something to do with it. If he was challenged, I can easily see Blain turning violent.'

Beyond the curtains, I could hear Non making Florence Spellman comfortable. 'I hope you've got over all the shocks of the inquest?' she asked. 'It must have been very upsetting hearing that Sidney'd been poisoned.'

'It was, yes.' Miss Spellman sounded subdued. 'I mean, I'd sort of got used to the idea that Sid was going to die. He'd told me often enough that he didn't think he was long for the world. That's why he wanted to get married so quickly. So that I'd inherit his money if he did die, and not his cousin, Reardon. But it's another thing now I know he was murdered.'

Non murmured sympathetically and I heard the door open, followed by the clinking of a tea tray being placed on the little occasional table.

Non waited for Edie to leave the room before she spoke again.

'When I asked you about Bill Blain before, you didn't mention that he was your uncle.' Her tone suggested just a hint of reproach, as if she was hurt that Florrie would keep such a thing from her.

Listening to the silence that greeted this remark, I would have given a good deal to see the effort to which Miss Spellman was put in order to govern her face. Interestingly, she didn't ask how Non knew. Street gossip was a simple fact of life for her, and she would have assumed that, on hearing of Blain's arrest, some Jericho local had made a comment.

'Yes, well,' she said, eventually, 'he's not the kind of relative you talk about, is he? I'd never have *chosen* to introduce him to Sid,' she added, 'but he just came round one day wanting to know who *my new beau* was.'

Non didn't respond and Florrie apparently felt compelled to offer more explanation.

'He'll have heard people talking, you know what they're like. *I see Florrie Spellman's got ideas above her station,*' she said, adopting a spiteful sneer. '*Thinks she's caught an undergrad, doesn't she?* That's the sort of thing they'll have been saying. And he's always had an eye to the main chance, Bill Blain. He'll have made it his business to find out all about Sidney, see if there was anything in it for him.'

I imagined Blain asking Sidney which college he belonged to, what he liked to do when he wasn't studying. Had he followed him to McLaren's gym, seen the flyers with **Local stockist:** *Sidney Parker,*

McLaren's Gymnasium on them and 'applied' to Reardon's Reading address?

'It's my fault Sidney's dead, isn't it?' Florrie asked. 'If Sid hadn't got involved with me, Bill Blain would never have heard of George Reardon.'

There was a pause. Was Miss Spellman shedding crocodile tears?

'Did Blain work for Reardon?' Non asked. 'Or were they partners in the business?'

'Partners.' Miss Spellman sounded composed so perhaps there had been no tears. 'Bill had some money to invest. Not honestly come by, for sure, but Reardon didn't know that. Or, if he did, he didn't care.'

A clink indicated that Miss Spellman had taken a sip of her tea and replaced her cup in the saucer. 'Bill got Carmichael Thompson involved as well,' she said. 'He was a pal of Bill's.'

'And the spies?'

A hesitation. 'I'm not sure. Reardon's doing, I think.'

Given that the spy who'd been present at the inquest had gone straight to Blain once the hearing was over, it seemed clear that Miss Spellman was lying.

Only now did it occur to me to wonder why, if Florrie Spellman had been implicated in Blain's conspiracy, she had pointed out his spy to Non at the inquest. Had she wanted to see Blain arrested as revenge for double crossing her and her father? Or did she imagine that, if Blain was no longer at liberty, she might, somehow, manage take possession of whatever remained of the business?

I listened to a tea-drinking silence for half a minute or so, grateful that Lily kept a clean house. Had the heavy curtains been full of dust, I would surely have given myself away by now with a sneeze or a cough. Still, the linen-lined velvet was very close to my face and standing completely still was proving more difficult than I had anticipated. I hoped Non had been able to seat Miss Spellman with her back to the window as planned.

'Anyway, let's forget about all the unpleasantness of yesterday,' Non said, brightly. 'I assume you've come to ask about Sidney's possessions. The journal and so on? Only I'm afraid they're still with the coroner, at the moment. But I can give you your letters, now, if you like.'

Non had placed the letters strategically on a little cushioned footstool by the side of the fire and I imagined her reaching out for them and offering them to Florence Spellman.

'Thank you,' Florence said. 'Will I get the other things back as well? You know the journal and… so on.'

'Yes, of course. The journal, its translation and all the other bits and pieces that Sidney kept. Most of it was advertising leaflets and bits from the paper. Except for the little book of advice to emigrants to the United States, of course.'

There was no reply and the next voice I heard was Non's. 'Oh, don't cry, Florrie. Here, have my hanky.'

'I'd love to go to America,' Miss Spellman said in a small, strangled voice. 'To move away from all this. From Bill Blain and the way he's ruined my life. And my useless father. And all the memories of Sid, as well – he's everywhere I look and it's making me so sad.' In my mind's eye, I saw Miss Spellman dabbing at her eyes with Non's handkerchief. She was a cunning little thing: had Non been ignorant of the truth, Florence had just offered her the ideal opportunity to hand over the cashbox and its contents.

But Non would make her play her hand, whatever it turned out to be.

'Could you manage that?' she asked. 'Do you have any money?'

'No, not really. Only… well, I was wondering about… the money Sid had hidden under the floorboards…'

'I'm afraid the coroner will have to decide about that.'

Non knew as well as I did that Mr Morrell had no notion that the money even existed, but her regretful tone was so convincing that I almost believed her. 'He'll have to look into who Sidney's legal heir might be.'

'Actually, that won't be necessary.' Florrie sounded quite sure of her ground. '*I'm* Sidney's legal heir. I'm his wife.'

I don't think even Non had expected that.

'I'm sorry, Florrie, I hadn't realised. I thought you told me that the banns would be read in a few weeks, when Sidney'd come of age?'

'Yes, we were going to go through with a church wedding for show. But we'd already got married in secret at Christmas. At Gretna Green.' There was a pause during which neither spoke, then Miss Spellman said. 'Here, this is the certificate.'

Non did not immediately congratulate her so I assumed that she must be using her perusal of whatever Florrie had shown her to formulate her next question.

'With the spies watching, how on earth did the pair of you manage to slip away?'

'I put it about that I was going to see my mum, to bury the hatchet. And Sid just told Betty Trent he was going to a college friend's house for Christmas.'

Did she imagine such things wouldn't be checked? Perhaps she thought that, as another young woman, Non would just take her word.

'It was clever of you to do it over the holidays,' Non said. 'So that Sidney could be away over Christmas and New Year without arousing suspicion.'

'Yes, he went up a couple of days before Christmas and back a few days after—' she stopped abruptly. 'What do the Scots call it? Hogmany?'

'Hogma*nay*, I think.'

'Yes. I wanted to stay and come back with him, but he said it would be too risky. So, I just went up, we got married and I came back. Then he came back a couple of days later.'

'Sidney was only away from Mrs Trent's house for ten days or so, then?'

'Yes, why are you asking?' Did Miss Spellman sound a little less sure of herself all of a sudden?

'Just because, under Scottish law, one of the couple has to actually live in Scotland for *twenty-one* days before they can be married.' Was I fanciful to imagine Non handing back the forged certificate to Florrie as she delivered this coup-de-grâce? Perhaps. But I hoped she had. It would have been theatrically appropriate.

'That's not true,' Florrie blustered, 'you don't know what you're talking about.'

'Sadly for you, Florrie, I do. And now, at the very least, the police can charge you with trying to obtain money fraudulently. That's if they don't charge you with conspiracy to commit murder.'

'we know it is only a matter of time before [women's enfranchisement] becomes a fact… We understand that, to some, it seems like a turning away from the straight path to indelicate terrain, and something opposite to what is purely feminine and elevated, but no doubt people will look back at these ideas with pity in a hundred years' time, marvelling at how childishly reform was viewed before its coming. It is a step which, once taken, will lead womankind closer to its rightful elevation.'

'gwyddom nad yw ond cwestiwn o amser iddo ddyfod yn ffaith… I rai, deallwn yr ymddengys megys yn wyro oddiar y ffordd uniawn i dir afleidneisrwydd, a rhywbeth gwrth-wyneb i'r hyn sydd bur fenywaidd a dyrchafedig, ond yn mhen can' mlynedd, diau genym yr edrychir yn ol ar y syniadau hyn gyda thosturi, gan ryfeddu mor blentynaidd yr edrychid ar ddiwygiad cyn ei ddyfod. Cam ydyw yn ddiau, a fydd, wedi ei gymeryd, yn dwyn y ddynoliaeth fenywaidd yn nes yn mlaen ar raddfa eu dyrchafiad cyfreithlawn.'

—Cranogwen (Sarah Jane Rees), *Y Frythones*

Epilogue

Non

I suppose I'd been expecting to hear from Dr Harper, so when I received an invitation to tea at the Principal's lodgings on Sunday, it wasn't a great surprise.

What *was* a surprise was the other guests. When I was shown in to the Harpers' first-floor drawing room, I found a contingent of AEW women there: Mrs Green, Mrs Johnson – without her husband this time – and Annie Rogers.

Once all the business of bidding each other good afternoon and establishing how we all were was done with, and I'd been asked what I was working on at the moment – *so* Oxford – everybody's eyes turned to Dr Harper.

'Miss Vaughan,' he said as Bertha Johnson handed around tiny sandwiches which'd had their crusts cut off, so we didn't have to do anything as physical as chew vigorously, 'we all owe you a debt of gratitude. Jesus College in particular. Not only were you instrumental in helping Mr Rice discover what had happened to poor Parker, but you were good enough, under severe provocation at the inquest, not to mention your very considerable involvement. We're most grateful.'

'We are *all* most grateful,' Charlotte Green amended. Mrs Johnson and Annie nodded. All most grateful.

'As I believe Mr Rice has already indicated,' Dr Harper said, 'you would be most welcome – with the AEW's agreement, of course – to recommence attending lectures at Jesus. And I hope that our extending this privilege not only to you but to other young women will encourage increasing numbers of other colleges to open their doors too.'

I glanced around the room: ladylike agreement all round. But there was something in the air that told me I wasn't here just to be thanked.

And where was Basil? If thanks were being dished out, he should be here too.

I waited. The AEW ladies and Dr Harper were looking at each other as if they hadn't really decided who was going to say whatever I was there to hear.

In the end, Charlotte Green grabbed the nettle. Or the tip of a leaf, anyway.

'Miss Vaughan, what were your hopes in coming to Oxford? Most of our young women, as you know, aspire to a career in teaching.'

What she meant was, *the only thing we can encourage them to hope for* is a career in teaching.

'As I think I mentioned the last time you asked me that question,' I said, 'my aim in being here is to learn all I can from Professor Rhys, the Chair of Celtic Studies. The Welsh language is generally denigrated,' I kept my eyes well away from Dr Harper, because he was as guilty of that as anybody, 'and it seems to me that Professor Rhys's research will go a long way to counter the charges that it's one of the lower, barbarous languages. If so, perhaps its use won't be so frowned upon, and our people won't feel the need to abandon it on their own hearths in order to allow their children to advance in the world.'

I sipped my tea and watched the glances going round the room. Had they thought I was here on a whim?

'And your ultimate aim would be to…?' Mrs Johnson invited.

'Write, speak, pursue research with other philologists of the Celtic languages.'

'And how would you support yourself?' Mrs Green asked.

An image of Cranogwen appeared in my mind's eye. 'My sponsor, Miss Rees, has indicated that she would provide financial support for five years. After that, I hope I would be able to earn my living by writing.'

'On Celtic subjects?'

'No,' I said, annoyed by her assumption that everything was about Oxford and what went on here, 'as a journalist.'

More looks. Hara would have looked at me too, if she could; it was the first time becoming a journalist had occurred to me. It had literally just popped into my head as something to say to wipe the 'you don't know what you're doing' looks off their faces. But now I'd said it, I liked the idea.

'Women do write for newspapers,' I said.

'True,' Dr Harper said, 'but they are usually ladies of means or influence. Ladies whose name will sell what they write.'

'Then I must get a name for myself, I suppose.' I was getting irritated. Where was all this leading?

'Miss Rees's support of you is very generous,' Mrs Green said, 'but you are, if I'm not mistaken, a young woman who would prefer to be independent?'

'Doesn't every sensible person want to be independent if they can?'

Mrs Green blinked. From her that was the equivalent of scornful laughter.

'We have a proposal,' Annie Rogers announced. 'At the moment, I'm the only female don.' She looked at Dr Harper with a slight smile. 'Don't flinch, Principal. What else would you call somebody who teaches here and who's passed examinations equivalent to those taken by male undergraduates?'

'I know, my dear. And you're right, of course, but your appropriation of the term still strikes my ear as the equivalent of my being called "madam".'

Mrs Green put her teacup down decisively. 'As Miss Rogers says, at the moment, her post is the only one we have that even approximates the position of college lecturer, which means that the vast majority of our lectures must be covered by college men.'

'But that's what we're here for, isn't it,' I asked, 'to hear the men who are foremost in their field?'

'Miss Vaughan, please do me the courtesy of allowing me to finish.'

'I beg your pardon.'

'We believe that, where possible, it's more appropriate – and a better *example* – to have women taught by women. You have come to Oxford well versed in all the necessary subjects and, were you a man, you would already have sat and passed Responsions and, no doubt, Honour Moderations, by now. In another year or so, we believe you will be ready to take the final examinations that Miss Rogers has already passed with such distinction.' She paused for a moment. 'At which point, if you are agreeable, we would offer you a position as lecturer.'

That was unexpected. 'In what subject?' I asked.

'Mathematics, principally. But others as necessary. At the moment, women are not required to sit Responsions but that may change if they are admitted to the same honours examinations as the men, and the AEW would like to be able to ensure that we have the necessary lecturers – in house, as it were – to offer teaching at least to that standard.'

Her face was calm, her eyes didn't move from mine as I answered.

'I hadn't necessarily intended to take the exams,' I said. 'It seems to me that unless we can take the same papers as the men, they'll never accept that we are their intellectual equals.'

'If one takes a step at a time, Miss Vaughan,' Dr Harper said, 'one is far more likely to reach the heights one desires than if one attempts a single leap.'

Annie grabbed the baton from him. 'We can't just say, "We want everything you have, give it to us immediately". We have to prove our worth. And if that means a few years of doing women's papers, isn't that worth it?'

Was it? More to the point, why were they offering me this?

'*You know what Dada would've said,*' Hara piped up, unexpectedly. '*That they'd rather have you inside the tent pissing out than outside pissing in. They can control you if you work for them.*'

She was right. Working for the AEW might give me financial independence, but it wouldn't necessarily give me any other kind. In fact, I might be worse off as a lecturer than I was now. The AEW would probably think they had even more right to tell me how to behave if I actually worked for them.

'That's very flattering,' I said. 'Let me give it some thought, and I'll let you have my decision at the end of the academic year.'

'*Meanwhile,*' I told Hara, silently, '*we'll start approaching newspapers.*'

Historical Note

Readers of historical fiction generally want to know how much of a novel is the product of the author's imagination and how much is historically accurate. As a reader I'm no exception, so I thought it was important to let you know what is based on historical fact in *A Bitter Remedy* and what I've made up.

Firstly, my depiction of the patent remedy industry is, if anything, a massive understatement. You only have to look at the advertising pages of any contemporary newspaper to see how much of this stuff was being peddled. And yes, many remedies which were given to children, including Godfrey's Cordial, contained opium. The Pharmacy Act of 1868 did restrict the sale of opium, but it neglected to restrict its inclusion as an ingredient in patent medicines. Legislation notwithstanding, the sale of opium over the counter by pharmacists continued until the Dangerous Drugs Act was passed in 1920.

Spermatorrhoea was, as described, widely believed to be the root cause of many male illnesses both real and imagined, and M. Deslandes' book, *Manhood*, was widely available. (All quotations Non makes from the book are accurate.) Advertisements for spermatorrhoea remedies, including spermatorrhoea rings, continued to appear in print well into the twentieth century.

The Association for Promoting the Education of Women in Oxford was the body that was responsible for the establishment of Somerville Hall (later Somerville College) and Lady Margaret Hall in 1879 and which continued to promote the cause of women's university education until women were granted the right to take degrees in 1920. Charlotte Green, Arthur and Bertha Johnson and Annie Rogers were all real people and are worth reading up on. The AEW journey has been brilliantly captured by a project called 'Education and Activism: Women at Oxford 1878–1920' which was commissioned to celebrate the centenary of women's formal admission to Oxford University. You can find it on their website: www.firstwomenatoxford.ox.ac.uk

Non's benefactor, Sarah-Jane Rees, otherwise known by her bardic name, Cranogwen, (I think she'd have loved and been exasperated by Non in equal measure) was, as depicted, famous throughout Wales as a speaker, writer and poet, though many people were unaware of her unconventional early life on her father's ship and as a qualified master mariner. Only now is she beginning to regain the fame she deserves in her homeland, and I'm delighted to say that I contributed, in a very small way, to the commissioning of a statue of her which will find its home in Llangranog, the village where she spent much of her life.

Jesus College – which is still known as Oxford's 'Welsh college' – was indeed being steered through a series of measures designed to break its historic and exclusive ties to Wales by Dr H. D. Harper, who was also, as depicted, a supporter of female education. Dr Harper plays a significant part in *A Bitter Remedy*, so I've tried to represent him as faithfully as possible. Many thanks to Robin Darwall-Smith, Jesus College archivist, for the inside track on what the fellowship of the time thought of him. A somewhat eulogistic memoir of Harper by L. V. Lester-Garland is worth a read, though it should be borne in mind that Lester-Garland is predisposed to see his friend through rose-tinted spectacles.

It's hard to overstate the influence of the University in Oxford in the nineteenth century. As depicted in the novel, there were two coroners for the University when the city had to make do with one, and until 1950, the University returned two MPs to parliament. The University was also very influential on the local board, the contemporary equivalent of the city council.

As depicted, Rev Charles Dodgson – better known by his pen name, Lewis Carroll – was a lecturer in mathematics and lived the whole of his adult life at Christ Church College. He did indeed write an article on the Vigenère Cypher for a children's magazine and was a lifelong enthusiast for recreational mathematics. He was also a prolific letter writer and took great pains to respond to letters from his young fans. All the details of his life shown in the book have been lifted from the wonderful *The Life and Letters of Lewis Carroll* compiled and written by his nephew Stuart Dodgson Collingwood. As a portrait of a lively and complicated man, as well as contemporary Oxford, I highly recommend the book which is available free online as part of Project

Gutenberg. You will, however, look in vain for the Cipher Club, which is entirely my invention.

I hope it goes without saying that all the colleges mentioned are real, as is the Jericho Tavern, still serving the people of west Oxford. But you won't find Lily's house or Blain's as neither Shene Road, nor Laud Street exist. However, the houses as described are entirely typical of Jericho in the 1880s. Fortunately, due to the efforts of local residents, the suburb of Jericho has resisted all attempts to clear its old housing stock in favour of new build, so it's possible to get a very good impression of Non and Basil's Jericho by simply visiting Oxford and walking around the area which lies to the west of Walton Street.

# *Acknowledgements*

As always, I'm going to start by acknowledging that neither this book, nor any other book of mine would be written without the support of my other half, Edwina. Every author needs a rock, and she is mine. Thank you, my love, for everything. Thanks too, to Sam and Nancy, and to Rob, Flo and Olivia – your love and support keeps me going when the going gets tough.

But other people contribute so much to the making of a book and, at the outset, I must thank Canelo CEO, Michael Bhaskar, for suggesting that I write a series set in Oxford. Michael's support and encouragement, along with that of everybody else at Canelo, has been so important. Authors always thank their publishers, but I feel very lucky to work with the wonderful, friendly, collaborative team at Canelo. Thank you, Iain, Michael, Francesca, Kit and Hannah – it's such a pleasure to work with you all! Thanks must also go to Sarah Whittaker for the gorgeous cover which I loved the second I saw it, and to Deborah Blake for her eagle-eyed copyediting.

Without booksellers, authors would not reach their audience and I'm undyingly grateful to those booksellers who understand that authors who are yet to achieve bestseller status need hand selling. My most heartfelt thanks, this year, go to Chloe Tilson, manager of the Aberystwyth branch of Waterstones who, as well as championing my Teifi Valley Coroner series, has been a cheerleader for *A Bitter Remedy* since it was nothing but an idea. But other stalwarts in the independent book trade have been beavering away on my behalf this year too, recommending my books to readers and eagerly anticipating Non and Basil's first outing. Huge thanks to Emma and the team at Book-ish, Matt at Chepstow Books, Bethan at Victoria Books and Nikki and Karen at Gwisgo Bookworm as well as new friends at Browsers in Porthmadog and Woodbridge Emporium in Suffolk.

Crime fiction writers are an enormously friendly and supportive bunch and writing would be a lonely business without the support of my fellow writers both on Twitter and in person. Supportive comments and shout-outs for books can make all the difference when the going gets tough and I'm very grateful to my fellow writers who have taken the time to encourage me on social media and when we meet up. Particular thanks go to my long-standing friends in the Macmillan New Writing crew and at Welsh crime writers' collective Crime Cymru – you guys are the best!

Research takes a big chunk of the available time in each book-writing cycle and novelists are always looking for sources of valuable information that they can ruthlessly exploit. In recent years I've discovered that PhD theses, published online, are an amazing resource. I've used different ones in each of my Teifi Valley Coroner novels, but, for *A Bitter Remedy*, particular thanks are due to Dr Malcolm Graham for his work, *The Suburbs of Victorian Oxford: Growth in a Pre-Industrial City*. Without his detailed scholarship, I wouldn't have had a clue about Non and Lily's Jericho, nor the very rapid way in which Oxford was changing in the 1880s. If my Oxford seems a believable place, I owe that in large part to Dr Graham.

Other custodians of primary sources are archivists and librarians and I've been privileged to have the support of library professionals at various Oxford colleges. Dr Robin Darwall-Smith of Jesus College, and Dr Anne Manuel and her team at Somerville College have been enormously helpful. Robin has been very generous with his time and has answered arcane questions like 'when did First Quad switch from gravel to grass?' and 'when did the stables at Jesus go out of use?' He also provided some extremely helpful snippets from college papers, details from which have informed various aspects of this novel. At Somerville I spent a very happy few hours in the John Stuart Mill room, reading letters written by Somerville Hall's very first residents which were tremendously illuminating. Huge thanks to Robin, and to Anne and her team – I hope it goes without saying that any errors that remain amongst these pages are mine and mine alone.

It's an enormous privilege, as an Oxford graduate, to be given lifelong access to the Bodleian Library. I renewed my 'Bod card' forty years, to the week, after I was first admitted as a reader and used the privilege not only to order and read books in the Bodleian itself but in the library of my own college, Corpus Christi, where I was made very welcome. It was quite a thing to be sitting in the library, reading at a desk overlooking the front quad as if the intervening forty years had never happened! Many thanks to assistant librarian Julie Blyth for finding the books I needed and being so kind.

While I was doing the necessary research for *A Bitter Remedy*, much to my frustration, I failed to lay my hands on the two out-of-print Welsh-language biographies of Cranogwen. There is an English-language biography in the works from Professor Jane Aaron, and, while I eagerly await that book, I'm enormously grateful to Professor Aaron for her chapter on Cranogwen's life and work in *Queer Wales: The History, Culture and Politics of Queer Life in Wales*, edited by Huw Osborne. Errors of fact, or biases in emphasis, are all mine and reflect the needs of fiction, rather than any failure in scholarship on Prof Aaron's part.

And finally, many heartfelt thanks to you, my readers. Thank you for buying my books, for borrowing them, for listening to them and for lending and recommending them to your friends and family. Thank you for your kind comments and retweets on Twitter, for your messages via my Facebook page and website, and for coming to see me at libraries and festival events. Your support means the world to me, and, in the most literal sense, I would not be able to write my books without it.

Diolch yn fawr iawn i chi gyd.